EDIBLE

EXQUISITE SERIES #3

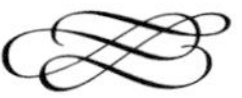

ELLA FRANK

ELLA FRANK, LLC

COPYRIGHT

Cover Design: Jay Aheer, Simply Defined Art

ISBN: 9781635761368

ALSO BY ELLA FRANK

The Exquisite Series

Exquisite

Entice

The Temptation Series

Try

Take

Trust

Tease

Tate

Sunset Cove Series

Finley

Devil's Kiss

Masters Among Monsters Series

Alasdair

Isadora

Thanos

Standalones

Blind Obsession

Veiled Innocence

Co-Authored with Brooke Blaine

Sex Addict

Shiver

PresLocke Series

Co-Authored with Brooke Blaine

Aced

Locked

Wedlocked

DEDICATION

This book is for every person that stepped inside a little place I call Exquisite and asked to know more about a purple-haired pastry chef named Rachel Langley.

You think you know her? So did I...

Xx Ella

CHAPTER 1

Past

"LET GO," RACHEL demanded, trying to free herself from Ben's punishing grip around her upper arm.

"I told you to stop," he shouted as his fingers dug tight into her tender flesh.

That's going to leave a mark, she thought with a grimace.

Spinning around to face him, Rachel glared up into her boyfriend's irate eyes. "And I told you not to touch me when you're angry."

Ben hauled her in close, and Rachel knew whatever was about to happen wouldn't be good.

Twenty minutes earlier, he'd come home in a foul mood. That usually equaled a painful evening in the bedroom for her but not tonight. Tonight, she was done.

"I'll touch you whenever I want to touch you. You got that?" he sneered down at her.

Rachel narrowed her eyes and yanked on her arm again. Instead of letting go, he reached up, gripped the other one, and pushed her back against the living room wall. She hit it so hard that her teeth clattered, and she could have sworn the bookcase beside her shook.

"You're mine, remember? You do what *I* say."

Staring up at him, Rachel knew she was risking his wrath, but she could no longer stay silent.

"Not anymore. You're leaving. Pack up your shit, Ben, and get out of my place. I'm sick of being your punching bag."

What happened after that blurred into slow motion.

Rachel saw him raise his hand, and before she could move her face, his large palm connected with her cheek, the brutal force of it resounding in a loud crack. Her face felt like someone had lit it up with a blowtorch.

As she reached up to grip her cheek, a throbbing ache ricocheted in her skull. When she heard the front door crash open, Rachel turned her head against the wall, squinting because of the light shining in from behind the person now standing in the doorway.

"Take your hands off of her."

Rachel recognized her father's voice, but it was filled with a cold anger that she had never heard before. Ben took one step away from her, and her father was instantly on him.

Sliding back against the wall, she crumpled to the floor. Through a rapidly swelling eye, she watched while her father punched Ben in the face before he repeatedly landed blows to his gut. When her father finally let up, Ben pulled himself up to his feet and ran from the house, yelling about what a bitch she was and how she had to have "her daddy" save her.

Crouching down in front of her, her father reached out to gently cup her cheek. "What are you doing, baby girl? This is not love."

Looking up at him, Rachel saw the grim line of his mouth and noticed his hair falling forward. She absentmindedly thought about how Mason had inherited their father's dark looks. "No man should ever hit you, Rach. Ever."

He reached down and helped her to her feet. Wrapping a solid arm around her waist, he guided her as she staggered to the sink. He wet a paper towel and then dabbed at the cut on her cheek.

With a quivering lip, Rachel blinked up at him as tears pooled in her eyes. "Please don't tell Mase or Mom."

Her father held her in his arms and softly spoke into her ear. "I won't as long as you don't tell them I beat the shit out of him."

Chuckling a little, she kissed his cheek. "I promise," she whispered.

~

Present

January

RACHEL STOOD IN the far corner of Precious Petals, leaning on the handle of the broom she'd been using only minutes before.

Sighing, she reached up to run a hand through her thick black hair—hair that had been tipped electric blue for the moment.

Lately, memories of her father had become harder and more difficult to bear. She knew it had a lot to do with the fact that she and Mason had recently lost their mother, but the pain of losing both parents before she'd even accomplished...*well, anything* was almost too much to take.

Rachel knew that Mason would have killed her if he ever heard her talk that way. He would've been the first to point out the acclaim she now had as a pastry chef, largely due to her famous and good-looking brother and his restaurant. *Oh, sorry,* our *restaurant.*

Not to mention, she had also taken over the flower shop.

During those first few months after their mother had passed, every time Mason had tried to come into Precious Petals, he hadn't been able to do it. Because of her connection with their mom, Lena had been the next person they had all thought of to take over the shop, but that had been impossible since she was a pediatrician down at University Hospital.

So, the task had fallen to Rachel. While she loved the store, she couldn't help but feel the loss of her parents more and more every day.

Glancing up at the clock, she noticed she was running late. *Shit*, she thought, moving over to the bench where Tulip was stretched out on her side. With her paw hanging down lazily like a panther in a tree, the lethargic kitty opened her eyes at the sudden movement.

"Oh, don't you move a single piece of fur, okay? I've got this."

Untying the apron strings from around her waist, she smiled as the cat sat up, dramatically yawning as though she had been working all day. Placing the apron down on the bench, Rachel reached out to scratch the watchful feline's furry head.

After her mother had passed, Rachel would arrive at the shop to find Tulip waiting at the back door. The furball would sit behind the store and meow, almost like a mournful cry, until one day, Rachel had relented and opened the door. From that day on, Rachel had owned a white cat with mottled brown ears—or maybe she should say that they owned each other.

Rushing around the counter, Rachel grabbed the burlap bag she'd thrown under there earlier this morning, and then she made her way to the front door, the bells jingling overhead as she passed through.

Turning to lock up, she reminded herself of how much her mother had loved this place. Lately, it had felt like the memory was becoming too much to handle, and she wasn't sure she could continue burning both ends of the candle—spending days at the shop and nights at Exquisite. She was tired and starting to feel burned-out.

Recently, she'd been running the scenario through her head to hire some help, but she'd yet to mention it to her brother. He was busy enough these days with the restaurant and his recent marriage. He didn't need her whining in his ear.

No, this is something I can work out on my own, she thought as she turned and started a brisk walk to the station to catch the L downtown.

LOOKING out his large office window, Cole leaned back in his leather chair with the phone to his ear.

"No, I don't care about that, Becky. All I asked was for her to have the best. Is that such a difficult thing to deliver? Because if it is, I can go elsewhere."

Raising his left arm, he glanced at his watch. *Shit, I'm running late*, he thought as he stood up from the chair.

Leaning down, he signed the documents he'd read through earlier. He dropped the pen on the desk, straightened, and shook his head.

"You know what? If things don't improve this month, I'm coming up there to get her myself. Now, I have to go. Fix the issue."

He ended the call and stuffed the phone into his pants pocket. He placed both palms on the desk, his head drooping forward. *Damn, I don't need this bullshit in my life right now.*

He took a moment to reflect on everything he needed to do, and then he grabbed the envelopes for Jane to send out and headed toward the door. Taking his long wool coat from the rack, he draped it over his arm and walked out of his office.

Stopping by Jane's desk, he noticed his paralegal was nowhere in sight, so he placed the documents in her tray and made his way to the elevators.

Glancing at his watch again, he took a deep breath and reminded himself that it wouldn't be the end of the world if he were a few minutes late. But as an elevator dinged and metal doors opened, he knew he was lying to himself.

Punctuality was everything, especially in his line of work. After all, the man who turned up first always held the power, and that meant everything to a man like him.

STANDING in the center aisle of the train, Rachel gripped the metal pole that was secured to the roof and floor of the car.

With her earbuds securely placed, she swayed and rocked to the click-clack rhythm she could feel but not hear over her music. Unlike most people, Rachel loved commuting. There was something so peaceful about being on a train. She could zone out and just relax for however long it took to get to a destination. She was also inclined to people watch, and there was always a buffet of the unusual, ranging from the ordinary to the extraordinary, on the L.

Tapping her foot, Rachel glanced up at the Red Line on the map displayed on the side of the train. As the night started to engulf the city, she knew she had one more stop to go.

It was Wednesday, and she was happy that it would be a relatively slow night. *Well, for Exquisite's standards anyway*. For some reason, she just wasn't in the mood tonight. If anything, she'd probably be better off going to the club and spending some time with the bartender, Riley.

As the train heaved to a slow stop, Rachel waited for the heavy metal doors to slide open, and then she, along with around thirty other commuters, piled out of the narrow doorway.

Making her way onto the platform, she stuffed her hands into her blue wool coat, her arm clutching her bag to her side. With her earbuds still firmly in, the hustle and bustle were currently being drowned out by P!nk's latest release.

Eyes down, she watched the pavement as she began exiting the station's tunnel, moving farther away from the train. She was almost free from the main crush of people when her shoulder hit something solid—something in the form of another person.

Stopping, she looked up to apologize, and froze.

Right there in the middle of the chaotic station, she found herself staring up into the eyes of the man she knew only as Cole.

COLE COULDN'T BELIEVE his luck. It seemed as though choosing the subway over the rush hour traffic had paid off.

As he stood there, gazing down at the raven-haired mystery who had a penchant for bright colors, he decided it was almost worth running late. Of all the people he could have run into in the city, running into her seemed somehow fitting, especially since he'd thought about her just the other day.

She was intriguing to him on so many levels.

He'd seen her only a handful of times—twice at Whipped and once again at her brother's Halloween party, which Joshua had invited him to.

Oh, she didn't know this would be their fourth crossing, but he did, and this time, she was not getting away so easily.

The first night he had seen her was when she had walked into the club in a short leather miniskirt. Cole had been convinced that if she were to cough, he would have caught a glimpse of everything she had to offer. She'd paired the skirt with a black leather bra and stiletto heels that could maim. And *that* had been it.

He remembered it perfectly as though it had happened last night and not months before.

He was sitting in one of the side booths, watching her as she stood there, fidgeting. He was contemplating the best way to approach her and persuade her to be his—well, for the night anyway.

However, as he sat there in quiet consideration, sizing up the woman who somehow caught everyone's attention, he was shocked as hell when she walked over to the bar, sat down, and greeted Riley—a man everyone knew was a complete slut. In other words, he would do anything he was told, and he was not picky about who told him to do it.

That was not the shocking part though. What perplexed Cole was how he had misread her. Usually, he was much more astute than that, much more accurate in the people he was drawn to, but it was not that way with her.

He had pegged her as softer and more subdued in nature. She had presented herself that way with her nervousness, which was apparent by her fidgeting. Yet, the minute Riley was in front of her, those bare shoulders straightened as that wickedly tattooed spine stiffened, and Cole was officially intrigued.

"Excuse me," she mumbled, brushing past him.

She was pretending she had no clue who he was. Shaking his head, Cole rounded on his feet to follow her, forgetting all about catching the train.

Hmm, the woman certainly has a love of leather. From under her bright blue coat, he could see tight black leather pants molded to her thighs and calves before they stopped just above her anklebone. Her dark hair was shifting against the blue wool as she walked, and he found himself staring at the tips of her hair that were currently the same shade as her coat.

She seemed to feel his eyes on her—*Hell, that's not surprising since I can't tear them away*—because she stopped when she reached a small clearing. She quickly moved to the side, spinning on her black flats to face him.

Bracing himself, Cole stuffed his hands into his own wool coat and waited. *Oh yeah, here we go. Bring it on.*

RACHEL HIT pause on her music, removed the earbuds and turned to tell Cole yet again, *Thanks, but no thanks.* That was the plan anyway until she looked up and locked eyes with his hazel ones, and then all her thoughts left her brain. *What is it about this guy?*

She'd only seen him a couple of times, and in each of those moments, she had felt such a pull to him that she had tucked tail and run, much like she wanted to do right now.

Maybe it was because he was always so put together, and now was certainly no exception. Dressed in a long black, perfectly tailored wool coat with what she could only assume was an equally expensive suit of some kind underneath, he projected cool, calm sophistication. He exuded confidence.

"Are you stalking me now?" Rachel flippantly asked with a forced smile.

She watched as he lifted his hands and pushed them into his coat pockets, drawing her eyes down his tall body. *Damn, even his shoes are shiny.*

"Not at all," he replied, his voice deep and his words clipped. He was a man who said exactly what he thought. "Stalking would imply premeditation. This was more a spur-of-the-moment decision."

"To follow me?" she clarified.

He nodded once in assent as she noticed his serious mouth tilt at the corner.

"Yes, to follow you."

Rachel finally allowed her eyes to move over him.

Yes, okay, he really is incredibly hot. Most would call him handsome or attractive, but as she stood there, looking up into his eyes, the blazing heat she saw staring back at her screamed one thing: *Hot. Sizzling, scorching, set-you-on-fire hot.*

Determined to end this and forget about the dirty-blond hair, the hot hazel eyes, and the perfectly tailored suit, Rachel ordered herself to relax and move on.

"That's just ridiculous."

"Not really," he pointed out. "Trust me. I've met stalkers, and *this* is not stalking."

Rolling her eyes at the absurdity of the conversation, Rachel internally slapped herself. She knew he wasn't stalking her, but she couldn't make her stupid brain think anything else. He had rendered her mute, which was currently annoying the shit out of her.

When he stepped closer, Rachel also found that he had the superpower to freeze her where she stood because she was suddenly incapable of moving. She stood still, entranced as he removed a hand from his pocket, reached out, and touched a blue strand of hair that was blowing by her cheek.

"You look different outside of work," he observed.

Rachel frowned as she tilted her head to the side. "I've never seen you at Exquisite while I've been working."

He moved, taking one more step toward her, so they were almost touching. As he leaned down slightly, he replied, "No, not there."

Blinking up at him, Rachel shook her head. "Well, you must have me mistaken for someone else because I *know* I have never seen you in the flower shop."

Right there in the middle of the damn train station, she could feel her breathing accelerate, and she was starting to think this guy was weaving spells.

He lowered his face another inch closer to hers. "No, not there either."

For one insane and anticipatory moment, Rachel thought he was going to kiss her. *God help me, I want him to.*

However, at the last moment, he moved his head to the side so when he turned, his mouth intimately brushed her ear, causing a shiver to run straight up Rachel's spine.

"I mean, at the place where you put on a uniform and play a part. I mean, at Whipped."

Rachel slowly turned her head, narrowing her eyes at the man who was now an inch from her face. *How is he making the crowded tunnel feel as though it has emptied out and we are the only two standing here?*

"Excuse me?" were the only words Rachel could seem to find and project.

"You see, Rachel—"

Oh god, the way my name sounds rolling off his tongue and slipping past those seriously lickable lips...

"The coat is a nice touch, but I'm sure if you took it off and threw a few stern words around, then maybe, *just maybe*, Riley would recognize you."

Now *that* coming from his mouth reminded her of exactly who he was and how he knew her. Rachel got her ass in gear and took a step back, squaring her shoulders. "Well, as lovely as this has been, I'm already running late."

She turned, ready to walk away with her dignity still somewhat intact, when his parting line reached her ears and made her blood boil.

"Yes, tardiness is really not something to be proud of. It shows such a lack of dedication to your destination."

Twirling on the ball of her foot, Rachel took a step back toward the arrogant, infuriating wall of a man and tilted up her chin to him in a way that told him she was not running *or* backing down. "As far as I'm aware, I didn't ask you to give an opinion."

Those calculating eyes focused on her as he dipped his head, acknowledging her response. "You're right."

Rachel waited for a moment, sensing another annoying comment was about to come out of his mouth. Instead though, he stuck his hand in his coat pocket and pulled out something wrapped in white wax paper.

Is that candy? she thought as he methodically unwrapped it.

Keeping her eyes on his hands that were so dexterous she felt hypnotized, Rachel felt dazed when he pulled the candy from the wrapper and brought it up to his mouth, pushing it in between those fantasy-inspiring lips. Without a word, he refolded the wrapper. He didn't ball it up or crinkle it; he folded it perfectly before pushing it back into his pocket.

Locking eyes with her, his mouth shifted in a way that let Rachel know he was sucking on the little square he had put in there, and she found she couldn't move or remember what they had been discussing. Rather, all her concentration had zeroed in on his hard jaw that was flexing with each suck of—*What did he put in his mouth?*

"What was that?" she blurted out before she could stop herself.

When he tilted his head to the side, Rachel couldn't help but notice his left cheek bulge slightly as he pushed the candy into it. That was when he began to move, like a wolf on the hunt. As he took two steady steps forward, Rachel found herself retreating faster than she cared to admit. Standing against the side of the tunnel wall, she watched a smooth smile appear on his face, mocking her. He should have looked ridiculous, standing there in the subway walkway with candy shoved in his mouth, but no, he appeared to be the furthest thing from ridiculous that she could think of.

Sinful was what popped into her head—as if she needed the adjective to describe what her body was already screaming. The other thing her body and brain were in agreement on was *run*.

Run far, far away.

"Would you like a taste, Rachel?"

Gripping her bag tightly, she refused to cower. She took a deep breath and lifted up her chin to look him directly in the eye. There was no way she would let him intimidate her, and that was exactly what he was trying to do.

Catch me off-guard? Get me to lower my defenses? I don't think so.

"And if I said yes?"

~

If you say yes, I'm going to have a hard time not pushing my tongue between those brazen fucking lips, was what Cole wanted to say as he looked down at the feisty woman in the tight leather pants.

Cole rolled the sugary confection across his tongue, moving it to the other side of his mouth, as he watched her eyes zero in on his lips. It was hard to believe it was rush hour downtown right now because, as far as he was concerned, the only other person in existence was the enigma who was Rachel.

So, let's test a theory. Cole took the final step he needed. His coat was now brushing hers, and his shiny black Ferragamos were toe-to-toe with her black flats. *Will she be brave? Or will she run?*

He wasn't usually a betting man unless poker counted, and he was pretty fucking good at that now. But if he were to place a bet, he'd bet that she would run.

Bending down just enough so their faces were back on the same level, he wasn't surprised when she kept her blue eyes locked with his.

Let's see if I can rattle that composure.

"If you say yes, I'll give you my tongue to suck on, and you can take a guess at what it is."

Cole had to admit that with the way her eyes automatically moved to his mouth, she provoked the devil in him. So, of course, he moistened his bottom lip with the tip of his tongue, and he took immense delight in seeing the shiver that she couldn't seem control.

"So, Rachel, would you like that taste?"

~

Is he serious? Rachel thought as she stood with her back pressed to the tiled tunnel wall.

This was why she had been deliberately avoiding one-on-one time with him. She knew he was potent, and God help her, as she stood there in the crowded tunnel, she wanted his tongue in her mouth.

"As romantic as that proposition is—" she started before being cut off.

"It wasn't supposed to be romantic."

Swallowing once, Rachel tried to compose herself before continuing. "Then, what was it supposed to be?"

Standing up to his full height, which had to be around six foot four, he placed his hands behind his back. Once again, his cheeks moved, and his damn lips pursed as he sucked on the candy. He then seemed to push it to the right side of his mouth.

Rachel felt like she was being seduced by a piece of candy and a set of smart-ass lips. She needed to escape—*Oh, at least three minutes ago.*

"It was an overtly sexual offer, designed to provide you with the answer to your question."

Shutting her eyes, Rachel tried not to let his voice slide inside her. She tried not to let it tingle all over her body, and she tried not to let that stuffy, I-am-better-than-you attitude stroke her sensitive spots.

I am trying and failing epically.

Knowing she needed to somehow regain the upper hand, Rachel let her eyes roam over his far-too-attractive face to his black wool coat, which was tailored to perfection, and she felt her pulse jump.

Watching his sharp, serious chin tilt down, Rachel inspected the blond stubble shadowing it, and she had to stop herself from reaching out and scraping it lightly with her blue nails.

"Like I was saying before you rudely interrupted me, as romantic as that proposition is, when I want to suck on your tongue or anything else, I'll ask. Until then, no need to offer. It's just embarrassing when I turn you down."

Feeling rather pleased with herself, she lifted her hand and patted the lapel of his coat. It wasn't until she remembered who she was dealing with that she realized, *Bad idea.*

Quicker than she could blink, his large hand was on top of hers, circling her wrist before she could think twice about it. He tugged her forward gently, and Rachel had no choice but to go. Suddenly, she found herself close enough to him that her breasts were pressed firmly against the wool covering his chest.

To anyone passing by, they must have looked like two people—*Oh hell, who am I kidding? With the tension sizzling and cracking around us, we must look like two lovers about to attack each other against the wall.*

But the two involved knew it was a completely different story.

"I don't remember inviting you to touch me," Cole stated in a voice that invited no argument.

But like a fool, she argued. "Well, you actually invited me to suck your tongue. Or have you already forgotten?"

Holding her firmly against him, his hazel eyes heated at the reminder. "An invitation you refused as far as I am aware. So, until I reissue the invite, maybe you should keep your hands to yourself."

Feeling her cheeks flush in the face of the admonishment, Rachel nodded because he was right.

"I'm sorry," she apologized begrudgingly. "Now, can I have my arm back?"

~

I KNEW IT, Cole thought as he released her wrist and took a step back. His instincts hadn't let him down.

"Is this over? I was running late before, and now, I am running *very* late. So, if you are done with...whatever this is, I would like to be on my way," she pointed out in a frustrated and pissy tone.

Stepping aside, Cole removed one hand from his pocket and gestured for her to be on her way. As she tried to move by him, he whispered in a soft and dark tone, "This is so far from over, Rachel. It's barely even begun."

Her spine stiffened, but other than that, she did not look at him, and she did not stop as she marched away.

Oh yes, Cole thought with a tight-lipped grin, *my instincts were spot-on.*

Finally chewing on the sweet treat, he swallowed the sugary remainder and ran a hand up through his hair. Somehow and someway, Rachel was going to be his. It was all just a matter of time.

Time and patience were two things he had an abundance of.

CHAPTER 2

"I'm late, I'm late. I know." Rachel pushed through the back door of Exquisite and attempted to swiftly run by her brother's office.

Unfortunately for her, Mason was quicker, and as she reached his office door, he appeared. Leaning his shoulder against the jamb, he ran a hand through his thick black hair.

"You're not only late; you're very late," he told her, making a show out of looking at his watch.

Tugging on the end of her coat, Rachel arched a brow. "Am I? So, what are you going to do? Dock my pay? Do you know how hard it is to get here on time every night?"

Letting his arm fall back down by his side, Mason pushed off the door. "Okay, cool your jets. What happened? You miss your train?"

If only, Rachel thought as her mind flashed an image of a tall, serious-looking suit who also happened to be one giant pain every time she had seen him.

"No, I missed a stop, and the cab ride was longer than I expected. Did I miss much?"

"Nope. Pretty slow tonight." Mason turned on his heel and moved back into his unorganized office.

Usually, she'd follow him in and see how his day had been. Tonight though, all Rachel could think about was the unsettling run-in she'd had earlier, and she didn't want Mason and his all-knowing ways to figure it out. So, instead of chatting with her brother, she called out, "See ya," and made her way down the back aisles to the humming kitchen.

It might not be a busy night at Exquisite, but that didn't mean there was no activity. Quite the contrary, the kitchen was buzzing. The soft thump of music was playing, and she could see Wendy standing at the pass talking to Ryan, the new head chef Mason had brought in around two months ago.

They had decided to hire him when Mason had told her he wanted to be behind the scenes and only run the restaurant from now on. He no longer wanted to work in the kitchen or on the floor in any capacity.

That's exactly what I need to do—hire someone for the flower shop, Rachel decided as she headed to the small office she shared with Wendy. Dumping her things on her *very* organized desk, she wrote a note on her calendar as a reminder to place a want ad tomorrow.

She tied her hair back, pulled a black ball cap off the peg from the back of the door, and stuffed the low ponytail through the hole in the back of the cap. Removing her blue coat, she put on the bright purple chef's jacket she'd talked Mason into getting her. After fastening the two rows of black buttons, she looked down at her outfit, and she had to grin.

She loved that Mason hadn't been strict when it came to what she wore in the kitchen. She happened to think her black leather pants looked pretty kick-ass with the purple smock. Mason's indulgence didn't surprise her though. He was just like their father had been. They both had always encouraged her to be herself even when it wasn't quite the norm.

~

"I TOLD YOU, I don't want to talk about it."

Mason pushed his hands into his khaki shorts as he walked into her bedroom and took a seat on the bed beside her.

"Come on, Rach. What did Lisa say to you?"

"Nothing." Rachel pouted, crossing her arms under her newest annoyance, her breasts.

"She must have said something. You didn't talk to her the whole way home,

and I noticed you managed to throw her several death stares," he pointed out, tugging on her bright pink braid.

Lisa Jennings, blonde-bimbo extraordinaire, was Josh's latest girlfriend. She was the one girl who represented everything Rachel wanted to be. For a while, Rachel had done anything she could to emulate her idol. But that had all changed today when she'd walked into the girls' restroom and heard Lisa laughing about Mason's stupid pink-haired sister.

So, Rachel had moved Lisa from the really Cool Club to the She-Is-a-Total-Bitch Club. Currently, it only had one member, and Rachel wasn't going to tell Mason it was Lisa. After all, his best friend was dating her.

Tugging her head away from him, Rachel looked up at her brother and wondered how he made everything seem so simple. He was never awkward, and no one considered him to be weird, but then again, he also didn't have pink hair. At that thought, she giggled.

"There you are," he declared, chuckling.

"Seriously, Mase, what does Josh even see in her?"

Stupid question, *Rachel thought with a sigh. She knew he saw tanned legs, blonde hair, and the captain of the cheerleading team.* Guys suck, *and that was Rachel's official sixteen-year-old opinion.*

Mason bumped shoulders with her and grinned. "Maybe she's really good at Scrabble?"

Rachel busted out laughing as she tried to picture Lisa or Josh playing that game.

"You think she can even spell Scrabble?" she asked slyly, arching a brow at her brother.

"Dunno, but you know what she can't do?"

Rachel shook her head as Mason wrapped an arm around her shoulders in a hug.

"She can't pull off bright pink hair and make it look so cool that at least six other girls do it the next day."

Rachel felt tears well in her eyes. That was Mason—always there with the perfect answer. He was about to say something else, but her bedroom door swung open, interrupting their conversation.

Their father stuck his head in. "You two ready for dinner?"

Reaching up, she wiped a tear away.

Almost immediately, their father was through the door, glaring at Mason. "What did you do to her?" he asked as he moved to sit beside Rachel on the bed.

"Nothing," Mason replied with a laugh, holding up his hands. He stood and

walked toward the door. Just as he reached it, Mason turned back, looking at her and their father. "Someone said something about her hair."

Rachel felt her dad pull away from her. He reached over to wipe away a tear from her face, but she turned away, so she could glower at her brother.

"And what could they possibly say about hair that looks so..." He paused as though he was trying to think of the right word. "Sweet?"

"Sweet?" Rachel squeaked.

Mason couldn't help but laugh.

"Yeah." Their father nodded. "Like...like cotton candy."

"Oh, Dad." Rachel finally laughed as she hugged him. "Thank you, but that doesn't really help."

"Well, you're laughing," he pointed out before looking back and forth between the both of them. "Never let someone make you feel like you are not the best version of yourself. You hear me?"

"Yes, Dad," Rachel mumbled.

"And you," he said as he stood and moved over to Mason, "always look after your little sister. Come on now, let's have dinner."

THINKING of that night with her father, Rachel shook her head with a small smile. He had been running through her mind a lot lately, and she couldn't seem to pinpoint why.

Well, I'll have time to think about that later, she thought as she made her way to the walk-in fridge to pull out the pears that had been chilling all day. Tonight's dessert special was cider-poached pears in a puff pastry shell with a warm caramel sauce.

Sarah, Exquisite's other pastry chef, had spent the morning coring the pears and making the puff pastry in preparation for this evening. Rachel returned from the fridge with two large containers of pears and placed them down on the stainless steel prep table.

Smiling at Sarah, Rachel wiped her hands on her apron. "So, did you manage to get the pumpkin spice? I can't believe I forgot to order that the other day. It really does make the difference."

Sarah moved to the other side of the table. "Yeah, it came in this morning, so I made a small sample of the sauce, just to make sure you really want to add it."

Sarah had started working with Rachel around six months ago

when Mason had decided someone needed to come in during the morning hours to help her prepare for the evening. This worked out perfectly since she was down at Precious Petals during the day; before they had hired Sarah, Rachel had come in at four in the morning to do all the prep work herself. Now, when Rachel arrived for the evening, Sarah would go home. It turned out to be a match made in heaven.

"Give me one second. Keep in mind that it's not finished yet," Sarah told her as she stirred the warm dark concoction of cider, brown sugar, pumpkin spice, and Calvados brandy.

Rachel couldn't help but joke with her coworker as she nodded toward the mixture. "Oh good, I was starting to think you forgot to add the butter and vanilla."

Sarah looked over at her from under her blunt brown bangs and sighed dramatically. "You don't really mean that. I know this because you told me you trusted me." With a saucy wink, she held up a spoon toward Rachel. "This is just the base. Would you like a taste?"

Rachel held back a groan. *Why is everyone asking me that today?*

"No, I trust you." For the second time tonight, she denied herself a taste of something she really wanted.

ALTHOUGH COLE HAD BEEN RUNNING SUBSTANTIALLY LATE, he'd actually arrived at the meeting before the other parties. Now, three and a half hours later, he stepped into the elevator that would take him up to his condo.

God, that was one mind-numbing meeting, he thought as he unbuttoned his coat.

Pressing the number twenty-six, he moved to the back of the elevator and leaned up against the wood-paneled wall, crossing his legs at the ankle and stuffing his hands into his pockets. When his fingers brushed over the square of wax paper, he reflected on the unexpected run-in from earlier.

He was in one hell of a predicament. He couldn't get that woman off his mind. She had denied him at every opportunity. *Well, isn't that the most intriguing part of all?* Instead of accepting her decision, he found the challenge of changing her mind a total fucking turn-on.

Rachel Langley. She was Josh Daniel's friend and his good friend's little sister. It wasn't the smartest idea he'd had, that was for sure, but it was the most intriguing one he'd had in a long time.

Rachel Langley. Yes, he even liked the sound of her name as it rolled through his mind, and there was no way he was changing course now. He wanted her, and he was going to have her.

Ever since that first moment in the club, he had become intensely fascinated by her. Add tequila in with that exchange, and he had been hooked. He had even gone back several nights after that, always looking for her but never finding her. Imagine his delight when Josh had invited him to Mason's Halloween party, and he'd walked in to see her dressed like some kind of ninja. And again, she had run from him.

Well, not anymore. The time for running was over—unless, of course, she was running straight to his bed. The only way he thought he could remove this fixation with her was to satiate his curiosity.

As the elevator came to a stop on his floor, it made the usual loud ding. He made his way out and turned left, passing by the closed doors of his unknown neighbors and several mass-produced floral prints on the walls of the cream-colored hallway. When he reached his corner condo, Cole pulled out his keys from his pocket, unlocked the door, and pushed it open.

Stepping into the small foyer, he dumped the keys on the wooden table at the entryway. He shrugged out of his coat and black suit jacket and then hung them both on the six-foot cherry wood coatrack situated in the opposite corner.

Rolling his shoulders, he stretched his neck from side to side, trying to ease some of the tension knotted up between his shoulder blades and the top of his spine. Making his way across dark hardwood floors into his kitchen, he opened a cabinet and grabbed one of his crystal tumblers. He reached up to loosen his tie as he walked over to where he kept his liquor. At the opposite end of the kitchen, he'd had a wine fridge installed on the bottom half of a separate cabinet, and above it was where he kept his old friend, a bottle of twenty-five-year-old Macallan.

Moving over to the sink with the bottle and tumbler, he uncorked the scotch. He turned on the tap, got his fingers wet, and then proceeded to pour himself a single neat before he flicked a couple drops of water into the liquor.

Lifting it to just under his nose, he inhaled deeply and closed his eyes. In the complete silence, he thought about the unobtainable for a moment—the one thing he currently desired more than anything, even more than the drink he now had in his hand.

How long has it been since I was so focused on a woman? A damn long time, he thought, moving around the kitchen counter. He walked toward the French doors that opened onto his balcony. The night was dark, and the lake was too, he mused as he stepped outside. He finally brought the glass to his lips and took a slow sip, the fiery liquid warming a path down his throat to his belly. He reached down to where his crisp white shirt was tucked into his black tailored pants and pulled it from its confines. Lifting the glass again, he took another sip as he started to undo the bottom buttons.

How can I find her again? That was the main question that was currently bothering him. He knew he could go down to Exquisite, but he also knew he would have to get past her brother. While the thought of dealing with Josh's friend Mason didn't bother him at all, Cole wanted his next meeting with Rachel to be private. He wanted to get her alone, and he wanted it to happen soon.

Downing the rest of the scotch with a deep swallow, Cole walked back inside and placed the empty tumbler on his coffee table. First, he needed to relax. Unbuttoning his shirt, he made his way down the hallway, passing his office and library, through to his bedroom. When he reached the top three buttons, he stopped, pulled the tie over his head, and threw it on the end of his bed.

Opening a drawer in his large bureau, he pulled out his swimwear, and then he grabbed a towel from the linen closet before he headed to the pool upstairs. It was time to decompress. Only then would he be able to really focus and work out a plan—a plan that involved Rachel and himself in a room together, alone.

RACHEL PUSHED through her apartment door at approximately one in the morning. After kicking it shut behind her, she threw her bag on the floor, toed her black flats off, and walked barefoot down the hall to her kitchen. Opening the small fridge with a yawn, she pulled out the almost empty jug of milk, poured herself a glass, and then threw the container in the trash.

She headed into the living room and flopped down onto her old, comfy leather couch. Unbuttoning her coat, she pulled her feet up under her as she looked around the sparse living space. *God, when did my life become so lonely?* she thought, moving her head back and forth against the couch.

When her phone rang, she wasn't surprised. She pulled it out of her coat pocket and then grinned as she looked at the caller ID. *Casanova.*

"I'm here, and I'm alive. No one mugged me on the way home."

"You're home then?"

"Yes, Mase, I'm here, safe and sound." She sighed before she quickly added, "Thanks for checking on me."

Her brother chuckled. "I don't know why I feel the need to check on you. I mean, with your kickboxing moves, you could probably fight off a mugger better than I could."

Rachel laughed. "Yeah, you're probably right. See you tomorrow, brother."

"Night, Rach," he said before she ended the call.

Placing her phone down beside her, she closed her eyes, trying not to feel sorry for herself. Letting pity and self-doubt creep into her mind was becoming a nasty habit of hers whenever she was alone at night, and that was why she had finally decided to venture out to Whipped several months ago. It was the place where she had unintentionally caught the eye of a man who reminded her of things she'd thought she had buried the day her father had been laid to rest.

Cole. That was the only name she knew him by. To avoid the possibility of being set up, she hadn't bothered to ask Josh anything else. After the Halloween party, Josh had dropped the case—*thank God*—and she hadn't seen or heard from Cole since. *That is, until today, nearly two months later, and holy mother of God, did I see him and every last inch of his tall frame.*

Just thinking about the uptight, perfectly tailored suit made her palms itch. As her skin started to heat, she found herself sitting up and shrugging out of her coat. Throwing it beside her on the couch, she leaned back and closed her eyes, picturing Cole's short blond hair, his scorching hazel eyes that were so focused and so intent, and that damn mouth that had licked and sucked that stupid piece of candy.

Apparently, it also totally destroyed my brain cells, she thought as she opened her eyes and sat up on the couch.

Standing, she stretched her arms above her head. She removed the elastic from her ponytail and shook her hair out, causing several blue tips to fall over her shoulder. *Yeah, I'm sure I'm exactly who his mother wants him to bring home. Then again, I can't imagine a man like him giving a shit about what anyone thought.*

Either way, it didn't matter. The likelihood of her seeing him again was not very high. Even if they were to run in to one another at the club, they had similar tastes, which meant one thing. They were certainly *not* compatible for each other. That was exactly the point she had been trying to stress each time they had met. *He just wasn't listening*, Rachel thought as she walked into her bedroom.

She pulled down the zipper from the back of her black leather pants and then peeled them off her body. After removing her shirt, she looked herself over in the full-length mirror in the corner of her room.

The blue-and-black demi cup bra had cost her a little over a hundred dollars. When she'd added in the matching strip of blue lace that had been sold as a thong—*but looks more like a small piece of string*—the cost had jumped to one-fifty.

Placing her hands on her waist as she cocked her left hip, Rachel decided that the money spent had been worth it. If there was one thing she indulged in, it was her lingerie. She loved the feel of lace and silk against her skin. She also loved how the boutique sets made her feel sexy. It was like she had her own little secret under her clothes. *Well, it's one of many*.

As her long black hair draped over her shoulders, she could feel the blue tips tickling the upper curve of her breasts. She gazed in appreciation at the new silver navel ring she had bought yesterday. As it winked back at her, she could see the edge of the script writing she had tattooed down her ribs on the right side of her body.

Rachel knew she was outside of the box. She was okay with that; she had people in her life that loved her *because* of that. Mason, Josh, Wendy, and now Lena and Shelly all loved her just the way she was, but when she was alone in bed late at night, she found that it wasn't enough anymore.

As she made her way past the small dresser, she looked at the framed photo of her parents who were both gone now, and she felt that same stab of loneliness deep inside her heart. *Everyone is moving on.* Mason had moved on with Lena, and now, Josh was moving on with Shelly.

Crawling between the covers, Rachel closed her eyes and pictured a tall, blond-haired man sucking on a piece of candy. She almost laughed at the absurdity. *God, I really am lonely if I'm dreaming about him.* Rolling over, she tried to let go of the heaviness that had recently started to weigh on her heart.

CHAPTER 3

Eight o'clock the next morning, Cole stepped off his work elevator and made his way toward Jane's desk with a smug feeling of victory. *I have a plan.*

Unbuttoning his coat with one hand while holding his black briefcase in the other, he smiled down at his paralegal as he stopped in front of her desk. Jane had been working for him for six of the eight years she had been with the firm.

As she sat there, staring up at him, he could tell she knew something was different about him.

Taking the envelopes she held out to him, he inclined his head as she greeted him with a warm smile.

"Good morning, Mr. Madison."

"Good morning, Jane."

"Apparently, it is. You seem positively upbeat this morning."

Cole knew not to take that the wrong way. Jane was one of the few people who ever told him the truth on a regular basis, so it wasn't out of the norm for her to point out when he was being a miserable asshole.

"I think today is going to be a very informative day."

Jane chuckled as she adjusted her wire-rimmed glasses on her nose. "Is that right?"

Tapping the envelopes on the edge of the desk, Cole lifted his briefcase and gave her a rare smile. "Oh yes, Jane, that *is* right. Can you do me a favor?"

"Of course, what—"

Just as she was about to continue, her phone rang. Cole gestured for her to take it as he turned and moved toward his office door.

"Good morning. This is the law office of Mitchell & Madison. Jane speaking."

Opening his office door, Cole walked in and closed it behind him. After placing his briefcase on the black leather couch sitting against the wall by the door, he shrugged out of his coat and hung it on the rack. Walking to his desk, he undid the two buttons securing his gray pinstripe jacket. He tugged the bottom of the vest that accompanied the outfit into place as he looked down at the documents Jane had deposited in his inbox.

On the very top of the stack, he noticed a small yellow memo note that had two words: *Call Becky*.

Damn it. That was the last person he wanted to deal with today. *Why can't it be Friday already? That way I could go up there in person.* Instead, he had two more days to push through before he could take off.

Cole sat down and ran a frustrated hand back through his hair. He let out a deep breath, and for a moment, he forgot the reason for his good mood. Looking at the day planner on his desk, he figured if he got Jane to move a few of his meetings around, he could leave the city by three o'clock tomorrow afternoon.

"Jane," he called.

Immediately, she popped her head in and looked him over, her smile turning to a frown. She made her way into the office and stopped in front of his desk. "You got the memo, I see."

"Yes." Cole sighed as he stood with his eyes still on his calendar. "Is there any way you can shuffle around tomorrow's meetings? Maybe get Harrison in here at ten and Fogerty at noon. I'll skip lunch and see Gallagher at one. I want to try to be out of here by three. Three thirty at the latest."

"Yes, that shouldn't be a problem." Nodding, Jane scribbled down a few notes. "Do you still need that favor?"

Cole thought about it for a minute. Really, he should wait until next week, but he got the impression that if he did, he would somehow lose the upper hand in the scenario. And, this was a scenario he very much wanted to have his hands in.

"Yes." Pulling a Post-it note from the stack on his desk, he wrote down two words of his own: *Rachel Langley*. "Her family owns and runs that restaurant Exquisite, downtown."

"Oh yes, I've been there a few times with Gary. Isn't that the one run by Mason Langley? He was in all the gossip magazines for a while."

"Yes, that's the one, he's her brother. Well, she also runs a flower shop. I'd like the number to that shop." Cole sat down again and leaned back in his chair.

Jane looked him over with a small smirk tugging at her lips.

"What?"

"Nothing, sir."

Jane turned to walk out of the office, but Cole wasn't letting her leave without knowing what that was all about.

"Jane?"

"Yes, Mr. Madison?"

"Jane Markham. I'm positive I have told you to call me Cole when you're in here. Now, what was all of that?"

"All of what?"

Rocking back in his leather chair, Cole placed his elbows on the armrests and steepled his fingers. "That smirk."

"There was no smirk, Mr. Madison."

"*Cole*, Jane. And there was a smirk." Sitting forward, he placed his arms on the desk, waiting patiently for her to answer.

"Oh, fine." Jane told him slightly exasperated, and stepped back across the room to place her hands on the desk. "In the six years I have worked for you, not once have you asked me to get you a woman's phone number."

Cole looked up at his paralegal. He was about to deny that statement wholeheartedly, but he found he couldn't bring himself to lie, so instead, he shut his mouth.

"Don't worry. Your secret is safe with me." She smirked again.

"There is no secret, Jane. Maybe I just want to order some flowers."

Straightening, Jane adjusted her glasses again and then wiped her hands down her prim skirt. "I'm sure that's all there is to it, Mr. Madison."

Arching his brow, he shook his head. "I think you are placating me, Jane."

Jane spun on her heel and made her way to his door. She opened it and then turned back to him with a smile. "And I think you are omitting the truth, Mr. Madison."

Chuckling, Cole conceded, "Perhaps, Jane, perhaps."

"I'll have the number for you as soon as I locate it," she told him. "So you can order those flowers." She gave him a huge I'm-on-to-you grin before she turned and closed the door behind her.

Damn perceptive woman. With a grin of his own, Cole opened the first envelope on his desk, conveniently pushing aside any thoughts of Becky.

"MR. MCCLUSKY, how many times do I have to tell you? I don't go out for coffee with customers," Rachel said to the little old man standing on the opposite side of the cash register. "Even the charming ones."

"One day, young lady, you will change your mind."

Mr. McClusky had been stopping by every week since Rachel had reopened the store. One morning, he had come in and told her a wonderful story about how his wife loved fresh flowers in the house. So, every week, he would show up and buy her a bouquet of bright blooms. The man was full of interesting stories, and he was an incorrigible flirt. If Rachel had to guess, she'd place him mid seventies.

"And what would Mrs. McClusky have to say about that? Hmm?"

"Oh, don't you worry about her, Rainbow. She doesn't have to know you took an old man out for coffee."

Laughing at the nickname he had given her, Rachel handed him the large bouquet. "But I would know, and I just wouldn't feel right."

"Well, at least tell an old man something fun. What color is next week?" he asked, gesturing to the blue tips that were curled over her shoulders this morning.

Rachel cocked her hip and placed a hand on it, pretending to think it over carefully. "You know what? I haven't thought about it yet. Any suggestions?"

She had to hold back a full-on giggle as the old man in the green tweed coat looked her over very seriously.

"Red. I see you with red."

Rachel thought about that for a moment as she walked around the counter toward the man she now absolutely adored.

"Red, huh? That's bold."

With a mischievous grin, he held out the crook of his arm to her. Rachel couldn't help the wink she gave him as she slipped her arm through his. He patted her hand as they walked toward the front door.

"Don't try and tell me you aren't an outgoing young lady. I see that twinkle in your eye."

"Oh, you do, do you?"

"Yes, missy, I do. My Clara has that twinkle, too."

Stopping at the front door, Rachel reached out and twisted the handle. When she pulled it open, the bells chimed above. She leaned down and laid a gentle kiss on the man's cheek. "Well, I will take that as a compliment. Your Clara is a very lucky lady."

"So, red?" he suggested again as he let go of her arm. He made it down two steps and then turned back to look at her standing in the doorway.

Rachel nodded and waved. "Come back next week, and see for yourself."

"I think you just asked me on a date."

As he turned and pushed his free hand into his pocket, Rachel couldn't help the warmth that spread in her chest. *Incorrigible indeed.*

Making her way back into the shop, she headed over to the counter where Tulip was lying beside her laptop. She now kept it handy for orders and to update the website she had designed for the store. This morning, she had placed an ad for some part-time help, providing her email address and the shop's phone number for applicants.

Clicking open her inbox, she was happy to see she had received six emails since the ad had been posted two and a half hours ago. *Good. Maybe I'll find some half-decent help*, she thought as she opened the first inquiry.

Bonnie Sampson. Work experience: McDonald's and babysitting. Education: high school diploma, currently enrolled at Midwestern University. Looking for morning part-time position.

Okay, so that one could work, but I really needed an afternoon person, Rachel thought as she closed it and moved to the second email on the list.

Kate O'Neal. Work experience: O'Malley's Pub. Education: high school diploma, currently attending the University of Chicago. Looking for a part-time job in the afternoons.

This one looks like a good possibility as well, she thought. *So far, so good.*

She wrote down two numbers on her notepad. Rachel clicked on the next message, and she was about to read it when the shop phone started to ring. Minimizing the screen, she answered the phone with the usual greeting.

"Precious Petals. This is Rachel. How can I help you?"

~

You can come to my office, and let me take off all your clothes, Cole thought as he stood. He stared out the large window in his office as Rachel's smooth voice flowed through the phone.

When he didn't say anything, she repeated, "Hello? Can I help you?"

"Hi. I'm here. I'm actually calling about the ad that's posted online."

"Oh yes, the part-time position."

Cole imagined her smiling. It was an expression he had seen a couple of times although it had never been directed at him.

Not really believing his ridiculous behavior, Cole almost hung up until her voice came through the phone again.

"You're the first guy to call about it actually. Huh, I didn't expect that—a guy working in a flower shop."

"Excuse me?" Cole questioned, not knowing if she expected an answer.

"Oh, nothing. I'm sorry. Of course, the job is open to both males and females. I'm in no way sexist."

Biting back a laugh, Cole found himself enjoying her rambling for the moment. "Well, that's good. I might have had to call a lawyer."

"Ugh. Don't do that. I can't stand lawyers," she admitted good-naturedly.

That interested Cole immensely. Turning his chair to face the window, he sat down and leaned back, crossing his ankle over his knee. "You don't like lawyers? Why's that? Bad experience?"

Rachel seemed to forget that he was a potential employee candidate as she began to talk his ear off. "Well, they always turn up at such horrible times, don't they? Divorces, accidents, deaths." Her voice faded out, but then she muttered, "Reading of wills."

Cole could understand her aversion, but it would make it that much harder to get her in his bed.

"I'm sorry. You're calling about the job, and here I am, going on about something not even remotely related."

"Yes, about the job, I'm wondering if the position has been filled yet. Or can I come in for an interview?"

There was a pause, and he wasn't sure, but he could have sworn he heard her whisper, "Tulip."

"Yes. I mean, no. No, the position hasn't been filled, and yes, you can come by for an interview."

Cole wasn't sure why he was so surprised she was all over the place. From the beginning, he'd known she was anything but ordinary, and that was one of the reasons he was so intrigued. Another was the fact that she tried to contain all her wild energy whenever she turned up at that club.

He thought she needed to be free, free to be *this* woman on the other end of the phone. She could be free to be all over the place as long as she had someone like him there to anchor her and pull her back in when needed.

"I need a name first," she pointed out and waited.

Shit. He hadn't thought that far ahead.

"C.J.," he told her, giving his first and middle initials. He could hear her moving around, and he presumed she was writing it down.

"C.J.?"

Last name. She needs my last name. Well, I hope she doesn't know it, or if she does, I hope she doesn't put it together.

"Madison," Cole said, waiting for an accusation to be hurled through the phone.

Instead, she just said, "Okay C.J., when do you think you can stop by?"

"Today?" he asked without any thought or hesitation.

She's so close. She was so close to being right where he wanted her—in a room alone with him.

"Today?" she repeated back, like she hadn't expected him to come by so soon. "Umm...well, it depends on what time you're thinking. I have to be downtown by seven tonight. Do you think you could stop by here around four?"

Cole felt a self-satisfied smirk cross his face. "Yes. I am positive I can be there by four...Mrs.?"

Rachel laughed loudly at that. "Oh no, please. I'm not married. You can call me Rachel."

Oh, I plan to call it—when I'm deep inside you while you're screaming my *name.*

"Okay, Rachel, I will see you at four. Is the address on the website correct?"

"Yep, all the info is correct."

"I'll see you at four then."

"Yes, I will be there. See you soon."

After disconnecting the call and placing his phone on the desk, Cole wondered just how congenial Rachel would be when he arrived as one C.J. Madison.

THREE FIFTY ROLLED around quicker than Rachel had expected. She was happy to have several interviews lined up throughout the week. Right now, she needed to step into the back room and do a quick touch-up on her makeup since her four o'clock would be here any moment.

Well, she hoped he would be punctual. After all, it would show he gave a shit. *Oh hell*, she thought, realizing that had sounded very much like Cole. She groaned at the thought that he was rubbing off on her in any way.

In the small bathroom, Rachel looked herself over in the mirror. Fluffing what was left of her black curls, she pouted at her reflection. She pulled out her cherry red lip-gloss from her pocket and slicked her lips. Just as she decided that she was happy with the result, the bells from above the front door chimed. *Yes*, she thought as her blue eyes stared back at her, *this is presentable for an interview. Time to go and meet the potential lifesaver.*

She wiped her hands on the red apron looped over her neck and tied around her waist. She turned and made her way up the back aisle to the front of the shop. As she walked through the doorway between the two areas, she came to a complete stop as her eyes connected with broad shoulders covered by a black wool coat.

No, no, no. Rachel's mind screamed. *It can't be him. He hasn't turned around yet, so maybe there is a slight possibility—oh hell, who am I kidding? I'd know that rigid backbone anywhere.*

Glancing up at the clock, Rachel watched as the big hand moved in slow motion to make that final tick to the twelve, confirming it was now four o'clock. She had missed locking him out by only ten minutes. *Why didn't I lock the damn door before?* He was the last person she wanted to deal with when C.J. turned up. *Well, better get this over with. Keep it professional, Rachel.*

Clearing her throat, Rachel made her way behind the counter. *Best to have something between us.* He turned to face her, and just like that, she was reminded of exactly why she needed an obstacle to separate them. *Those damn eyes* were serious and far too perceptive as they looked her over, like he was studying her for later consideration.

Pushing his hands into his pockets, he took several steps forward. Rachel was certain to track those steps with absolute focus. After what felt like an eternity, he finally stopped directly in front of her, standing on the opposite side of the counter, as Rachel allowed herself to look up and meet his eyes. She reached out to grip the edge of the counter as the heat between them increased, threatening to melt her on the spot. *Holy shit, this guy is something else.* She knew she needed to get rid of him quickly, so Rachel steeled herself against the sizzling once over he was giving her. She decided to go with cocky. With a bit of luck, she hoped that maybe her attitude would get rid of him.

"Well, I don't know about you, but I'm almost positive this falls under the stalking category."

~

COLE TOOK a moment to look around the small flower shop. He was surprised to find that she really fit in here. Bursts of color were everywhere in the form of red roses, a rainbow of tulips, and bright yellow sunflowers displayed in a large aluminum can.

With her colorful hair and bright persona, this place seemed exactly right for her. *Now, it's time to get that wild side to come out and play.*

"You'd be wrong," he stated matter-of-factly.

He removed his hands from his pockets and began to undo the buttons of his coat. When her eyes dropped directly to his hands, he had to stifle a laugh as she watched him intently.

What exactly is she thinking? Better yet, why should I guess when I can just ask? "You don't mind if I unbutton my coat, do you?"

Her eyes shifted directly back to his as she moistened her painted bottom lip and shook her head. "No. I mean, no, I don't mind...not no, you can't."

After undoing the final button, Cole shrugged a little to let the material part and relax around his body.

"What are you doing here?" she demanded, finding her footing again.

Cole lifted his arm and made a show of pushing it forward, so his silver watch appeared from beneath his coat and sleeve. Looking down at it and then back to her, he allowed himself a moment of enjoyment. He then turned to look at the clock on her wall. "Well, I'm sure I was told to be here at four."

He could see the wheels turning behind those annoyed blue eyes of hers. He decided he didn't care how long it took her to come to her final conclusion. He was happy to stand there for a minute, just looking at her.

Her hair was down today, hanging in loose curls over her shoulders. Her eyes had been enhanced with what looked like blue and silver glitter across the lids. Instead of looking ridiculous, it just made her more appealing, like a shiny toy he wanted to touch.

She'd colored her fabulous mouth a sinful red that made Cole think about how good that color would look smeared all over his —*Yeah, well, best not to think about that at the moment.*

While he couldn't see much of what she was wearing, the apron that was wrapped around her waist made him want to untie it. He liked undoing things, and the thought of undoing her was extremely appealing.

"*You* were told to be here at four?" she asked in a tone that screamed *bullshit*.

"Yes, definitely four today. I never miss a meeting."

"You're insane." She muttered in frustration as she ran her hand through her hair. "The only person who should be here at four is C..."

Ahh, the penny has finally dropped, Cole thought as he tilted his head to the side. "Who?"

"You presumptuous jerk." She stormed around the counter.

Well, I'm not going to argue with that.

Cole turned and met the feisty woman head-on. As she stopped in front of him, he became immensely satisfied when she had to crane her head back to look up at him.

"You set this whole damn thing up. C.J. my ass," she hissed like a pissed-off wet cat.

Cole admitted to the accusation without a shred of remorse. "Guilty. And as for your ass...well, I am definitely open to discussing it."

Her cheeks flushed as her annoyance and irritation began to overwhelm her, and then there was the fact that she had been duped.

"Your arrogance is unbelievable," she fumed, turning to storm away from him.

Cole decided it was now or never. He reached out and took ahold of her arm in a firm but gentle grip. She stopped where she was, like her feet were glued to the ground, but she didn't turn around.

Okay, Miss Langley, let's get all the cards out on the table.

BREATHE. *Just breathe.* That was the mantra Rachel was repeating over and over in her mind as she felt the heat of his tall body move in close behind her. The hand that had firmly grasped her left arm had still not let go, and just as she was about to request her freedom, she felt a second hand wrap around her right arm.

Closing her eyes against what she knew was about to happen, Rachel wasn't surprised when she felt Cole's strong body brush up against her back.

Why did I ever go to that damn club? Oh, that's right. I was lonely. Well, look at what that got me.

The man standing behind her now wanted something she was not willing to give. Oh, she was human. She wanted companionship, and she craved to be touched, but Rachel wanted the control. She *never* wanted to be the helpless one again—*ever*.

The only problem with this scenario was the way she melted at the thought of giving it all over to a suit named Cole.

"Where are you going, Rachel?"

His voice, dark and seductive, slid down her spine.

"You need to take your hands off of me." She was proud of herself for getting even that much past the lump in her throat.

Immediately, he released her arms.

Instead of fleeing the way she had imagined she would, she stayed frozen and waited.

"They're off. I won't touch you again until you ask me to," Cole whispered.

Rachel couldn't help the ridiculous noise that escaped her throat. She tried to convince herself that it was somewhere between a laugh and a cough, but she knew it ended up sounding more like a bark.

"Well, don't hold your breath," she retorted.

"Why? Are you worried for my health?"

"No," she denied emphatically.

This time, she turned her head to look over her shoulder, forgetting how close he was. Her mouth was now only a whisper from his, and as their eyes collided, Rachel felt her heart almost thump right out of her chest.

"In that case, I repeat, I won't touch you again...until you ask me to."

Rachel blinked and clenched her jaw as she watched his eyes trace what felt like every line of her face. Finally gathering her nerve, she pivoted around to face him. He stood back up to his full height, which caused him to look down at her, as he waited with what seemed like infinite patience.

"And what if that's never?" she countered.

"It won't be," he answered with far too much confidence.

"I hate to be the one to tell you this, but I don't want to date you."

Rachel studied him as he moved his coat aside. He pushed his hands into the snug pockets of his pants, which automatically drew her eyes to his crotch. She instantly became infuriated because she knew that had been his goal.

"I don't remember asking to date you," he said matter-of-factly, taking a step closer.

Rachel refused to back up. With men like him, she knew she needed to stand her ground.

"I want to touch you, Rachel, *all* of you, but I won't until you ask me to."

Rachel was finding it harder and harder to breath. *The man is too fucking much—cocky, arrogant, sexy, and bad.* Oh yeah, and it didn't help that the look in his eyes and the tone in his voice screamed all the bad things he wanted to do to her. He was making it impossible for her to think rationally.

How can I be getting all hot and bothered over a man wearing a three-piece pinstripe suit? He is my exact opposite. Think, Rachel, think.

"There's one small problem here, don't you think?" she questioned.

She watched his light brown brow arch while his serious mouth twitched with what she could only guess was some form of humor.

"And what's that?" he asked with a smile.

Rachel swallowed and decided it was now or never.

"We both want to be on top."

COLE COULDN'T HELP the wicked thrill he felt snake up his spine at her words.

"I'm not averse to being underneath you, Rachel, not in the least."

She placed her hands on her hips as her eyes moved from his face, to his body, and then back up to meet his eyes again.

"You'd never let someone control you," she accused.

"Is that what you want? To control me?"

As she licked her lips, Cole felt a delicious bolt run straight to his cock.

Fuck, she just might be able to control me with the way my body is reacting to her.

"I won't lie. I wouldn't mind getting you out of that suit. How many layers do you have on anyway?"

Cole considered her question before he extended an invitation. "Come closer, and find out."

Shaking her head, she finally took a step back. "No, thank you, not here and not now."

Following her retreat, Cole pushed. "When and where then?"

It wasn't fair, he knew that, but as her back met the wall, Cole kept up his approach until his shoes met hers and their clothes were touching. He knew she had no idea, but every time she looked up at him from under her lashes, it made him want to lean down and take her mouth with his.

"When, Rachel?"

Her glittering eyes were conflicted, and her breathing was coming out hard enough that her breasts were brushing against his chest with each exhale. Pulling one hand from his pocket, he was shocked when the desire he saw in her dampened, and he was sure a hint of fear appeared. Moving back a few inches, Cole brought up his hand to show her he wasn't doing anything more than unwrapping a piece of candy.

Her eyes shifted to his fingers before returning to his with questions. As he started to unwrap it, he asked again, "When and where, Rachel?"

She remained silent as he brought the small square to her mouth. Pressing it against her bright red bottom lip, he wasn't surprised when she opened immediately, taking the candy into her mouth.

As she sucked it between her lips, Cole leaned down to her ear and informed her smoothly, "Caramel. You asked me the other day what I was sucking. I love caramel. In fact, I will do just about anything for it. Now, tell me, Rachel, when and where are you going to get me out of my suit?"

He could hear her sucking on the caramel square as she turned her head and met his eyes.

With the smell the sugar emanating from her breath, she whispered, "Tomorrow night. Eleven o'clock at Whipped."

Cole winced. "I can't."

"More like won't." Rachel shook her head, breaking the spell.

"I said that I couldn't. I never lie. You should know that about me right now."

Cole thought about what he needed to do tomorrow. Knowing

there was no way out of it, he came up with a compromise "How about tonight?"

"I work, hotshot. Now, can you move? I need to close up and head that way. You snooze, you lose."

He stepped back, letting her walk away from him, but not before he warned her. "Rachel, I never lose. What about after work?"

"Tonight?" She stood behind the counter again, effectively protecting herself.

"Yes, after your shift at Exquisite. If you're feeling brave, tell me where to be, and I'll be there."

He watched as her hands gripped the counter, her knuckles turning white.

"It's not a matter of bravery. It's about you keeping a promise. Will you be able to do that?"

"If I tell you I will do something, I will do it, no matter what it costs me. So, what will it be?"

He stared at her as she moved the caramel in her mouth, and he found himself fighting the urge to go and take a taste.

"Okay, tonight, but not at Whipped. Meet me here at one."

Cole looked around the small shop, assessing the space. He wasn't about to argue with her. The plan had been for him to be alone in a room with her. He didn't care which room, and as she shook her head, letting her hair fall down her back, he found he didn't give a shit about anything other than that.

If she wanted him naked, that was fine by him. The next stop after that would involve her minus her clothes, so however they got there didn't bother him as long as they got there.

"I'll be here," he told her. When she gave him an amused look, he added, "And, Rachel, this better not be some trick of yours. If you don't show, I will find you, and when I do, you best believe that *this* offer will be off the table."

As her face turned serious, Cole tilted forward in a mock bow and then turned on his heel. Moving to the door of the shop, he couldn't help the immense feeling of satisfaction he felt when he heard her mutter, "Know-it-all jerk." All he could think was, *Got you.*

CHAPTER 4

He's not insane. I am, Rachel thought as she stood with an arm wrapped around the pole in the center aisle of the train. *I've lost what is left of my mind. The dye has finally seeped through my thick skull and penetrated my brain.*

She hadn't even bothered with the earbuds as she made her way downtown with the rest of the rush hour crowd. She was too busy trying to decipher exactly what had happened this afternoon. Cole Madison had happened, and he had happened to make her want him between her thighs. She thought back to his words that had seductively stroked over her.

"Is that what you want? To control me?"

Hell, I am insane. Nothing could control a man like that, let alone her. *But what's the alternative? Let him hold the power? No way.*

She had this. *Just get it over with, and then he'll be out of my life. Itch scratched.*

Plus, it wouldn't be a hardship for her to rub all over him. Maybe she could ask him to keep the suit on. She found it hard to believe that anything could top that look, but apparently, she was willing to risk her sanity to find out.

The train pulled up to her stop, and as she stepped onto the platform, she was immediately reminded of her run-in with Cole yesterday. She thought back to when he'd accused her of playing a part. Deep down, she knew he was right. The problem was she wasn't sure which part was truly her, or maybe it was more that she just hadn't found out yet.

Ugh, the jerk is already in my head. Shaking it like it would clear away all the confusion, she wrapped her arms around the coat tied at her waist as she pushed her way through the evening crowd. Maybe if she tried really hard, she could block out the wall of a man she had stupidly dared to challenge.

~

COLE HAD JUST MADE it back to his office when Jane popped her head around the corner.

"So, did you get those flowers?"

Cole looked over his shoulder at his paralegal. "I did actually. They have nice stems," he told her without missing a beat.

Jane smiled back at him with a look of pure mischief. "I'm sure they do, Mr. Madison."

"*Cole*," he reminded as she walked out of sight.

Cole shrugged out of his coat and draped it over his arm as he walked around his desk, looking at the notes Jane had put there.

God, Becky called again.

Placing his coat over the back of his chair, he looked down at his watch. There was no point in calling now. First thing tomorrow morning, he would call and let her know that he would arrive in the evening.

Incompetence at its finest. Yeah, well, that shit is not going to fly anymore.

Besides trying to distract himself, he couldn't do anything about it tonight.

Cole sat down and looked at the papers in front of him. *God, I need a vacation. How long has it been since I truly took one? Years? It has to be years.*

Glancing up at the clock, he noticed it was now approaching six thirty.

"Mr. Madison? Will that be all today?" Jane's voice drifted into his office.

Turning to face her, he gave her a nod. "Yes, Jane, that is all. Please go home to Gary."

"Only if you promise you will go home soon. You work far too hard."

Picking up the paper in front of him, he waved it once. "I need to look this over for tomorrow, and then I promise to leave."

"You promise?"

"Promise."

She gave him a warm smile and bid him good night. "See you tomorrow, sir."

"*Jane*," he warned with a low voice.

She moved away from his desk with a wave. "Night, Cole."

At her departing two words, he chuckled.

CLOSING time rolled around much quicker than Rachel had expected, especially considering she had spent every minute of the last several hours thinking, panicking, and collectively freaking out about what she had gotten herself into this evening.

Shit, I'm stupid.

No, I'm not. I'm strong. I can be in control. Just remember, Rachel, he chased you.

"Rachel."

Spinning around with a piping bag midair, she came face-to-face with Mason. He was standing at the entryway to the kitchen, looking at her with a frown on his face. He moved between the two large stainless steel tables and made his way toward her.

Rachel looked around and saw that most of the kitchen had emptied out. A few people were at the sinks, and a couple more were out in the dining room, but essentially, it was her and her perceptive brother.

"I've been calling your name for nearly five minutes." He stopped in front of her and leaned against the table.

"You have?" she asked, trying to appear clueless.

"Yes, I have. What's going on with you lately?"

"Nothing."

"You're lying."

"Am not," Rachel fired back. *Yeah, real mature.*

"Rach, if something's wrong, you can talk to me." Mason reached out to squeeze her shoulder.

She looked up into eyes that mirrored her own and replicated their father's. Those eyes made her heart ache at times, and this was one of them. Looking away from the confusion and compassion in Mason's eyes, Rachel tried to pull herself together.

What else can I do? Tell him I'm going crazy, and the best way to forget how lonely I am is to lose myself in sex? Oh, and I could mention that I don't like men to control me, so I make sure they don't touch me. Yeah, that would go over well.

"I'm fine, Mason, really. I've just been a bit stressed out lately with working at Precious Petals in the morning and then coming here at night."

"Well, let's do something about it," he suggested, a frown still present between his brows.

"Stop worrying about me, would you? I already placed an ad for part-time help. You have a wife to worry about now. I'm good."

Cocking his head to the side, he gave her a thorough look over. "Okay, I'll let it go for now."

"Gee, thanks," Rachel sassed, turning away from him.

He moved around her, heading toward the fridge. She watched him disappear inside, and then she closed her eyes, exhaling a deep breath. Between Mason, Lena, Josh and Shelly, she had a hard time hiding anything, but she wasn't ready to talk. Honestly, she had no idea what she would say anyway.

COLE MADE his way down the dark street with his hands burrowed inside his pockets. The wind was whipping around tonight, and the bite from the cold air was harsh. He was glad the cab had dropped him only a few feet away from the small flower shop's front door.

Stepping up to the entryway, he knocked twice and waited. He was surprised she had left on the small light overhead. It was currently illuminating the snowflakes falling silently to the ground.

Reminding himself of the promise he'd made, he bit back a curse. No touching was going to be difficult. The door to the shop opened with the sound of bells, and when Rachel appeared, covered in leather, he thought difficult was the wrong fucking word.

"Right on time," she announced as she stepped aside, inviting him in.

Brave woman. "I try to be."

"So, you're never late? What else do you try *never* to be?"

Standing right beside her, he took a moment to take in the full impact of her outfit. "Something I'm not."

Annoyance flashed across her face at his not-too-subtle jab.

What the hell? I told her I don't lie, and I'm not going to start sugarcoating shit for her benefit.

Taking several steps into the dimly lit shop, he noticed only the lamp by the cash register was on. *Makes sense really. She doesn't want anyone to know she's here at one in the morning.*

Hearing the door shut with a lot more force than when it had opened, he turned to face her.

Fucking hell. She sure is something to look at right now. He let his eyes wander over every inch of soft black leather that seemed to mold to her body. She was wearing a pair of pants that were held together only by the crisscross of black satin ties running down the outside length of each leg from her hip to her ankle. It showed off smooth skin he wanted to lick. With that thought, his cock started to throb inside his pants, and that was before he took the time to admire the black strapless corset that perfectly completed the ensemble.

Oh yes. Here was the woman who had intrigued him ever since the first time he had seen her.

He reached up and loosened the gray scarf he had wrapped around his neck as he kept his eyes on her, daring her. She accepted the challenge by taking a couple of steps toward him in heels that screamed, *don't fuck with me.*

It was such a shame really, because fucking with her was exactly what he wanted to do.

~

RACHEL COULD FEEL her blood starting to boil. She had known this was a mistake the minute she had opened the door and seen him looking up at the snow. For a moment, she had almost forgotten what an insufferable jerk he was, and then he had opened his mouth, giving her a much-needed reminder.

Stepping forward, she placed her hands on her hips. She felt her breath catch as Cole slid the gray scarf away from around his neck.

I can do this.

I. Can. Do. This.

He's just taking off his scarf for God's sake. How can that be so fucking sexy?

He turned and placed the scarf between the lamp and the cash register on the counter. When he looked back at her, Rachel took great satisfaction in the way he couldn't seem to take his eyes away from her.

This is your chance. Take it.

"So, are you trying to say I'm fake? Is that it? That's kind of insulting, considering what you want from me."

Rachel concentrated on his large hands as they unbuttoned his coat, just as they had done earlier in the day. Once the buttons were undone, he shrugged out of his coat, and she allowed herself to look up into his eyes. He was assessing her with a shrewd stare that was filled with so much fire she was surprised Precious Petals hadn't burst into flames.

His short dirty-blond hair was sticking up in the front. Rachel couldn't be sure, but she figured, as pedantic as he was, he had probably styled it that way.

"I don't think you're fake." He threw the wool coat over the counter without turning away from her. "I think you are hiding."

That pissed her off. She wasn't hiding jack shit. She just didn't want some control freak trying to hold her down—literally. That was why her ex, Charlie, had been such a great choice. There was a mellow guy if she had ever met one.

Now, the man currently in front of me? Anything but mellow. More like a dormant volcano waiting to erupt.

Raising her chin, she tilted her head to the side. "I'm not the one who wears five layers of clothing everywhere."

"This is an image. *That,*" he told her, looking over her leather-clad body, "is a costume."

Shaking her head, Rachel asked incredulously, "Are you really stupid enough to think that I would remove any of my clothes after this conversation?"

Calm and so annoyingly casual, he went about undoing his suit jacket without hesitation. His remaining ensemble—gray pinstripe pants, a perfect white shirt, and a matching pinstripe vest—was all neat and precise, positioned exactly where they should be.

The damn man even has cuff links.

So busy caught up in her inspection of him, Rachel hadn't even noticed he had taken a step toward her until his voice cut through the air.

"As far as I was aware, you're not supposed to remove your clothes. You're supposed to be removing mine."

For the first time this evening—and she was sure it certainly wouldn't be the last—Rachel lost her footing. She couldn't seem to formulate the words to tell him to get out even though that was exactly what she should say.

At every turn, the man had been rude and insulting. Begrudgingly, she had to admit that he had also been more honest than she had been.

Suck it up. Come on, show him he's wrong.

"You're right. I am," she agreed.

"That's what I said."

"Do you always have to have the last word, Cole?"

Fuck, there it is—my name on her tongue. Finally.

"Say it again," he demanded softly, taking the final step he needed to put them only inches apart.

"Say what?"

Angling his face down toward her, he repeated, "My name. Say it again."

That was when she realized she possessed a new weapon in her arsenal, and Cole found it fascinating to see the wicked calculation flash in her eyes. He tracked her gaze when she deliberately dropped it to his mouth as she considered the request as if it were a life-or-death decision.

"Make me," she challenged, raising her eyes back to his.

You have no idea what you just invited, Cole thought as he let a devious smile finally spread across his lips. Then again, when his teeth appeared, the look that crossed her face seemingly showed that perhaps she did realize what she had gotten herself into.

Yes, teeth. Get a good look at them. I am going to eat you up.

"Remember this moment, Rachel, because I don't plan to forget it until you're screaming my name so loudly that every single person within a ten-mile radius knows what it fucking is."

Her painted lips parted as she bravely raised a hand, laying it on the left side of his chest.

"You know, for a man so immaculately dressed, your mouth is filthy, and your manners are terrible."

Looking down at her hand, Cole watched as it moved to the buttons of his vest. "I don't really think it's my manners that you're interested in."

"Well, obviously not since you lack even the basic ones," she fired right back, flicking the first button out of its hole. "You promised you wouldn't touch me," she stated, looking up at him. "Will you keep that promise?"

Cole acknowledged her question with a slight nod as he placed his arms behind his back. "I will. But are you ready for what is about to happen here?"

Her eyes narrowed as she freed the second button. "And what exactly is that? I get you out of your suit and do what I like. It's not rocket science, is it?"

Opening the final button, she boldly placed both hands against his stomach and spread the vest apart.

That was when Cole cautioned her for the last time. "No, it's not rocket science, but be careful, Rachel. Everything isn't always as it appears."

~

SOLID—THAT'S what he is. Solid, tight muscle under this perfect white shirt. Huh, who knew?

"Stop talking in circles. What are you saying? You aren't as you appear?" Rachel quipped as she moved around behind him. "You aren't the man in a three-piece suit and shiny shoes?"

"I am," he admitted, turning his head to follow her as she removed the vest down his left arm. When their eyes met, in a voice so seductive it set off alarm bells, he added, "But I'm also so much more."

What the hell is that supposed to mean? Rachel thought when she finally removed the vest and placed it with his coat on the counter. Coming back to stand before him, Rachel cocked her head to the side with more attitude than was probably wise. "You want to back out?" she asked undaunted.

"Not even a little bit. I'm just trying to play fair," he informed.

His expression made Rachel nervous. The man was so confusing. Maybe he was trying to tell her he didn't believe he could keep his hands off her.

"Are you sure about this? Because if you touch me, I'm out of here."

"I told you, Rachel. I will *not* touch you until you ask."

Satisfied, she smoothed her hands across his tight abdomen again as she inched toward the buttons of his shirt. Looking at him from beneath her lashes, she tugged the material, freeing it from his pants, and she smiled when she heard him take in a breath.

"Nervous?" she asked.

"No, but would you like to remove my tie? It makes taking off my shirt that much easier."

Rachel released the shirt and gripped the end of the tie. Wrapping it around her hand, she pulled on it until he was leaning down, just an inch away from her, and then she decided to tell him exactly what she was thinking. "I like the tie. I've never fucked a man in a tie."

COLE OBSERVED her as she stood perilously close to him with his tie secured around her palm. It was amusing that she believed she held the control in this scenario.

"And you aren't going to tonight either."

"No?" she asked, licking her bottom lip that was now very close to his.

"No. I said you could take off my clothes, not fuck me. What kind of man do you think I am, Rachel?"

Her sultry eyes connected with his as she moved in even closer.

Finally, she pressed her lips right beside his. "Bet I can change your mind," she murmured.

He turned his head, so their lips were now aligned, and he could smell her sweet breath and cherries. "I bet you can't."

Annoyed with him and possibly herself, she pushed him away, releasing his tie.

"So, why are you here then?"

Cole reached up and loosened his now mangled tie. "I told you that I would come back here, so you could get me out of my suit."

She let out a frustrated sound as Cole added the tie to the pile.

"Would you like me to leave? I didn't misunderstand the whole point of this meeting, did I?"

"You're enjoying this, aren't you?" she accused.

Shrugging his shoulders, he started to undo his shirt buttons one at a time.

"You came all the way down here at one in the morning to strip for me and not put out? Oh, now that's a laugh. Do you get off on this?" She spun around and marched to the other side of the shop in her click-clacking heels.

"On what?" he asked calmly as she continued to fume. He was now halfway through with undoing his shirt buttons.

"Playing with women? Teasing them? 'Oh, I'll be there at one, and then you can take off my suit,'" she mocked, throwing her hands up in the air. "What else was I supposed to think? I mean, forgive a woman for jumping to conclusions." She finally turned around to face him.

That was when her mouth snapped shut, and her eyes widened.

"I haven't even begun to play with you, Rachel. Want me to start?" Cole asked as he lifted his arm and threw his shirt on the pile of clothes behind him.

He was now naked from the waist up.

~

OH MY FUCKING GOD.

Yes, Rachel admitted, that kind of language was not usually her style. But as she stood across from Cole, who was now minus every last scrap of material covering his upper half, Rachel felt justified in her choice of words.

The man is a fucking god.

If she thought he had been dangerous with clothes, removing them had just made him lethal. Underneath that carefully put together suit was a whole new beast, a beast covered in tattoos and —*Are his nipples pierced? Fuck.*

Suddenly, her mouth was dry, and her palms were sweaty as she was confronted with something she had definitely not seen coming.

Okay, okay. I can do this. He is still the same man he was five minutes ago.

The problem was she had been having enough issues dealing with this man. Throw in all of this, and she was...*yep, fucked.*

"I asked you something," he said.

His voice penetrated her insane thoughts, and finally, it brought her out of her stupor as she stood in what she could only guess was shock. Running her eyes all over him, Rachel couldn't find any words. She was too busy looking at everything he had just uncovered.

"Rachel?" he queried again, taking a step toward her.

Brain, kick in, run. Brain?

"Are they both pierced?" she blurted out before she could help herself.

"Would you like to take a closer look at them?"

Shaking her head back and forth, she knew that answer. For her sanity, the only logical response came out of her mouth. "No."

He chuckled deeply as he continued forward.

Nowhere to go. I have nowhere to go. Damn wall.

"I think you do," he told her. "You even want to touch them, maybe even lick them."

Rachel could feel her clit throbbing incessantly between her thighs as her brain continued thoughts all on its own. *A wolf. That's a goddamn wolf on his right pec.*

Closing her eyes, she tried to block out everything, but all she could see were tight, hard rippling muscles, tattoos, and silver.

The tattoo of a wolf on his chest smacked her between the eyes, but there was so much more. He also had some writing on his forearms and down his left ribs. Not to mention, he had what looked like a sterling silver bar through each nipple.

Had not *seen those coming.*

"Rachel?"

Looking up at him, she finally found her tongue. "I'm fine. You're, uh..."

As she trailed off, she watched a very—yes, she was always going to think it now—wolfish grin appear across his mouth.

"Not as I appear to be?"

Suddenly, everything fell into place, all his clues and frustrating riddles. Before she could say anything, the wall was flush against her back, and he was close to being against her front.

"You promised no touching," she reminded him, feeling more panicked than ever before.

This man, *this* stranger, who was now directly in front of her, was definitely a man she had no chance or hope of ever controlling.

"I'm not going to touch you," he promised, leaning forward. "But I am going to kiss you."

And before she could protest, his mouth was pushing hotly against hers.

YES, Cole thought as he pressed his lips to hers. *Gotcha.*

Swiping his tongue against her bottom lip, he felt a scorching jolt of arousal as she immediately parted for him. Instead of pushing his tongue straight in to tangle with hers, he took a moment to trace her ripe, succulent mouth. He could feel her shaking as she stood with her back pressed against the wall, but she wasn't backing down either. She wanted him, but she was stubbornly clinging to her resolve.

Nipping her bottom lip, he soothed it once more with his tongue, teasing her, playing with her. When a small moan escaped her, Cole couldn't help his own groan. Keeping his arms firmly behind his back, he lifted his mouth from hers and moved it to her ear.

"I can't touch you, Rachel, and *god*, I want to. I want to undo these sexy leather pants and slide my hand inside. Or maybe, I could lick the skin that's peeking out between the laces, but I can't. You said no."

Flicking her right lobe with his tongue, he bit it gently, causing a second shudder to rack through her body.

"You like how I look, don't you? Unexpected at first, but now that it's sunk in, now that you know, I bet you're wet from just thinking about playing with my piercings."

Nibbling his way along her jaw back to her mouth, Cole looked directly into her eyes. "They aren't the only piercings I have either."

As her eyes glazed over and her breathing accelerated, he lowered his mouth to hers, making another promise. "Maybe if you let me touch you, I'll let you see the other one, too."

From the words that were coming from his mouth, she was panting now, and he could see her breasts rising and falling rapidly. He wanted to fuck her so badly, and he was positive his cock had never been harder.

Obstinate as ever though, she shook her head.

"No? Okay then." He crushed his mouth down onto hers.

Pushing his tongue deep into the warmth of her mouth, he felt her suck on it immediately, and he almost lost his own footing. Like a piece of his candy, she sucked him in deep as she tilted her head to the side, angling their mouths, so he could get even deeper inside her.

Growling in the back of his throat, he fisted his hands behind him as she continued to take what he was willingly giving for now. As he kept his hands away from her, he felt her arms reach down between their lower bodies.

At first, he was certain she was about to touch him, and he just hoped he could rein in his reaction. But as she moaned against his lips, he realized he didn't feel her hands on him. He leaned back to glance down between them, and what he saw made him feel as though she had cut him at the knees. The little minx had one of her hands grinding down hard between her thighs while she looked him over as though he were her latest dirty magazine.

"Stubborn, stubborn woman. Just say the word," he muttered, lowering his head. Pressing his mouth to hers, he promised, "Say the word, and I will make you come with my hands *and* my mouth."

"No. No touching." She panted desperately as her hand rubbed against herself.

"Fine then. Show is over." He abruptly removed his mouth from hers and turned, making his way back to the pile of clothes.

He quickly got dressed, and when he turned to face her, he was shocked to find her in the exact same spot with her hand burrowed between her thighs. As he headed toward the door, he took a good look at her and arched a brow.

"I suggest you lock the door after I leave. It's late, and you wouldn't want anyone to come in and find you with your pants around your ankles and your fingers deep inside yourself." Gripping the handle of the door, he nodded once. "Have a good evening, Rachel. It's been interesting."

With that, he walked out into the night.

CHAPTER 5

Rachel pushed through her front door and slammed it shut. Leaning back against it, she rested her head on the wood and closed her eyes.

Cole had been wrong. She hadn't taken care of herself after he'd left. Oh, she had been tempted, but knowing he'd suggested it grated on her nerves.

So now, she was standing in her apartment at two in the morning, frustrated and alone.

Pulling out her phone from her bag, she then dumped it onto the floor. As she moved straight to her bedroom, she checked her phone for any messages.

Four missed calls. No surprise they're from Mason, Mason, Josh, and—yep, I knew it—Mason.

Sighing, Rachel ran a hand through her hair and hit play to listen to the voice mails.

"Rach, just calling to make sure you got home okay. Call me."

Shaking her head at Mason checking in on her, she hit delete and listened to call number two.

"Rach, call me."

Kicking off her heels, she trashed another one of Mason's messages and hit play on Josh's message.

"Mason told me to call you to tell you to call him. So, please, Rach, call him. It's one forty-five in the morning. You know he'll worry until you do."

Looking at the photos on her dresser, she focused in on the one of her and Mason at his wedding. She had to laugh a little. *Surely, one day, he'll quit worrying, right?* Playing the final message, she felt her heart warm at Mason's concerned voice.

"Okay, Rachel Langley, I know you're an adult, but it is now one fifty in the morning, and you left at eleven fifty. Shh, Lena...she knows I hate that she has to catch a taxi so late at night...I know she's an adult."

There was a pause, and she could hear him sigh and rustle. It was probably from the bed he was lying in.

"I am not going to sleep well until you text me. I'm worried. Love you."

She typed a text to both her brother and Josh.

I'm home, safe and sound. I was not mugged, accosted, or taken by a sex addict (I should be so lucky). GO TO SLEEP. —R

Standing, she unzipped her leather pants and peeled them off her body. *I thought I would be doing this in front of Cole. Guess not.* Apparently, that man had decided on a different agenda. It was a pity he hadn't filled her in on it before she got herself all worked up.

Once she was naked, she slipped between the sheets, closed her eyes, and immediately drifted off to sleep.

~

"Turn around," his voice commanded in her ear.

Obediently, Rachel turned, so she was facing the wall in their bedroom.

"I got a little gift for you today," he said as he unzipped his jeans.

He had called her earlier and told her she should be naked by the time he got home because he needed to fuck her. At first, she had been hesitant, especially after their argument last night, but she knew if she didn't do as he suggested, the evening would be that much worse.

"I just love your ass. I'm going to have it one day, I promise you."

Rachel shivered. He knew how she felt about having his cock near her ass, but he constantly liked to push. Instead of protesting though, she kept her mouth shut, just as he preferred it.

"Maybe tonight?" He planted his palms against the wall by her head and pushed his erection against her bare crack.

Being this close to the wall, Rachel felt cross-eyed, so she shut her eyes and turned her head, laying her right cheek against the wall. Lately, it was becoming more and more obvious she needed to end things with him. But every time she approached the subject, he would turn the tables, and she would end up apologizing before she took off her clothes.

That was the problem with their relationship. He never listened, and she couldn't help the way he made her feel. What the fuck is the matter with me? How can I get off on the way he treats me? *To be more precise, it was the way she* let *him treat her.*

In the beginning, it had all been fun, having a little kink in the bedroom, but over the last year, he had become more aggressive, more demanding. When he would be in the right frame of mind, it would turn her on more than she had ever imagined. Lately though, his moods and disposition had become volatile, and that frightened her.

"Hands behind your back, Rach."

Slowly, she moved and rested the backs of her hands against the curve of her waist right above her ass. That was when she felt the cool hard snap of a handcuff encircle her right wrist. Automatically, her shoulders stiffened, and she raised her head from the wall.

Looking back over her shoulder at him, she locked eyes with hot, annoyed ones.

"Handcuffs? I don't think that's a great idea."

His lip curled in a cruel twist as he lowered his face close to hers.

"I don't remember asking for your opinion. Now, turn around, and shut your mouth."

Biting down on her bottom lip, Rachel lowered her eyes and tried to control the shiver that racked her body. Something didn't feel right. The way he had looked at her with a glint in his eyes that hadn't been there before felt evil.

"Spread your legs," he demanded, his warm breath skating along the skin at the top of her spine.

Opening her eyes, she slowly spread her legs as she felt him snap the left cuff around her wrist. Rachel could feel her heart beating faster, and despite her growing fear, she could feel herself becoming more and more aroused.

When she heard him removing his jeans, she closed her eyes again, waiting for whatever he was about to do.

"I ran into your brother today," he said, his voice cutting through the air.

The words were so unexpected and so inappropriate that she had no idea what to say or if she was supposed to say anything at all.

"He's such a player. He's always got a new piece of pussy on his arm. Wonder what he does to make the women flock to him."

Rachel stiffened. Turning around, she was ready to tell him to get lost. As she faced him, he reached out, and with a strong palm to her breastbone, he pushed her hard against the wall. Looking up at him, she could feel her breathing accelerate as fear fully replaced any kind of arousal she had been feeling. Her arms hurt as he moved in close and crushed her against the wall, forcing the metal cuffs to bite into the skin on her wrists. Sliding his hand up to her neck, he squeezed as his eyes narrowed.

"Your precious Mason told me to let you know he heard from a friend of his."

Rachel's brain was trying, trying to catch up, but nothing was making sense. "You're hurting me. Can you please move?"

"No, I can't fucking move, and you aren't going anywhere either. Who's Josh?"

Josh? What the fuck is he talking about?

"Josh, an old family friend, according to Mason. He told me you used to have a big old crush on him."

Rachel swallowed, trying to think, willing her brain to catch up. Josh? *She hadn't seen or heard from Josh in years. Yes, she'd had a crush on him in high school, but that was fucking high school.*

The man in front of her had completely morphed, and there was no way he was going to listen to her. Changing before her eyes, he had gone from a man she had found comfort with to a man she no longer knew. He had become a man who terrified her.

"Let me go. You're being ridiculous, and I don't think this is the time for me to explain anything."

"You're not going anywhere." He took a step back and removed his shirt.

Rachel looked him over as she stood there, shaking. "Well, I'm not staying here with you." She moved to push past him and leave the room, but she didn't get far.

Before she knew it, he grabbed her shoulders and threw her on the bed. She landed on her back, and as he straddled her body, crushing her hands beneath her, the pain in her arms ricocheted up to her shoulders.

"Get off me," she yelled as she thrashed underneath him.

"No. You're going to fucking lay there while I show you exactly who you belong to," he growled. He held her shoulders and pinned her down, leaving her utterly helpless.

"Get the fuck off me, Ben."

She bucked her hips up just as he raised his right hand, and he slapped her hard across the cheek. Closing her eyes to the pain that blasted up the left side of her face, she felt the tears sting her eyes as they escaped down her cheeks. As the weight on her shifted, she turned her head, hoping to block out some of what she knew would follow.

Preparing herself for a second blow, she was shocked when she felt fingers lightly graze her stinging face, wiping away her tears. A strong grip took hold of her chin, pulling her face back, as a voice filtered through her throbbing head.

"I know I shouldn't touch you, Rachel, but I wanted to."

Her eyes fluttered open and met with heated hazel.

Naked from the waist up, Cole straddled her hips as she realized her hands were suddenly free and clasped together above her head of her own volition. Her core clenched while she stared up at exactly what she wanted.

His mouth pulled into a tight smile as he reached forward with a large hand. Automatically, Rachel flinched, but it didn't deter him. He gently pushed a piece of her hair behind her ear as he lowered himself down until his lips were against hers.

"Keep your hands right there above your head for me."

After nipping her bottom lip, he shifted and brushed a kiss against her cheek. "I won't touch you again until you ask."

Rachel felt her mouth part as he moved away from her. She was about to ask. She could feel it. And that was when...

She woke up.

THREE MEETINGS LATER, Cole glanced at his watch as he stood, stretching his neck. Finally, he could head out. It was a shame he had to go out of town. He wouldn't have minded a follow-up visit with one Rachel Langley, but this was something he couldn't put off.

Moving to the coatrack, he fastened his suit jacket, pulled on his thick coat, and draped his scarf loosely around his neck.

"Heading out for the weekend, sir?"

"Yes, *Jane*," he told her, stressing her name, as he walked over to her desk.

"Well, you drive safely."

Cole shook his head with a small smile as he turned and walked to the elevators. He pressed the button and then faced his paralegal. "I have been driving for years. I'm sure I will be okay."

Jane looked at him with a serious expression, and he was surprised at the frown that creased her brow. That look was usually reserved for him.

"Yes, but you are preoccupied. Try not to worry. Check out the situation before you fly off the handle."

A loud ding sounded behind him, signaling an elevator's arrival.

Nodding once, Cole told her sincerely, "I will endeavor not to lose my temper unless it is warranted. How's that?"

"Very good, Mr. Madison."

Cole turned, stepped onto the elevator, and pressed the parking garage button. Just as the doors started to close, he called out, "Go home early, Mrs. Markham."

He chuckled as "Yes, sir," met his ears.

~

THE DRIVE to Lake Forest took approximately forty-five minutes to an hour, and as Cole finally drove down the main road, he tried not to feel annoyed at himself. He hated leaving her here, but it seemed like the best solution.

Heading off the main road and making his way through several streets, he finally saw the sign for him to turn up ahead. Making a right, he drove past two entrances and turned at the third. Pulling his black Peugeot 907 into one of the parking spaces, he climbed out and shrugged into his coat. He didn't bother to button it as he made his way briskly across the parking lot to the front door. Taking a deep breath, he raised his hand and opened the front door to Tranquil Lakes, the retirement home he had been visiting every Sunday for the past three years.

"Good evening, Mr. Madison."

Cole moved to the front desk. Resting his arms on it, he clasped his hands together as he looked down at Gillian, the petite blonde who had been greeting him since he'd been coming here.

"Evening, Gillian," he greeted. "Is Becky around? I told her I would be arriving by five."

Gillian nodded and looked at the clipboard that was in front of her. "Yes, Nurse Parnell just went down to your mother's room. Do you want me to page her?"

Cole shook his head. "No, don't worry. I'll meet her down there."

Turning to his left, Cole made his way down the first hallway, leading to the east wing of the facility. Pushing his hand into his pocket, he tried for a smile as he passed a nurse in the hall, but he knew it came off more as a grimace. He was too preoccupied with the fact that he had not been contacted immediately about the incident that had occurred after he had left last Sunday night.

His mother had accidently burned herself during a cooking exercise. The activity had been supervised, but apparently, during a moment when eyes were not focused, his mother had placed her hand directly on top of the hot burner.

Cole wouldn't have been so infuriated if he had been informed immediately. Instead, he had found out about it only after he had called. Becky, his mother's nurse, had claimed she hadn't wanted to needlessly worry him. *Well, too fucking late for that.* It was bad enough that he couldn't look after his mother himself, but when shit like this happened, he felt completely useless.

As he reached the end of the hall, he stopped at the open door and rested his shoulder against the jamb. Looking in the large room, he could see his mother sitting in her favorite rocking chair in front of one of the large windows overlooking the lake.

The room was decorated with all her beloved knickknacks, and a single painting was displayed on the wall. She had bought an abstract of the Eiffel Tower on her honeymoon with his father.

On one of the shelves were various photos, ranging from when he was a baby up until now, and sitting by her bed was a small music box with a hand-painted rainbow on the top. Her father had given her the box when she was a child, and to this day, it still faithfully played.

He stood there, quietly watching his mother. Tipping the chair with her slippered foot each time it rocked down, the little lady softly hummed to herself. She was wearing a blue robe, and her wet, bobbed gray hair was brushed back from her face. She looked peaceful while he felt anything but. The nurse was nowhere in sight, so he decided to visit with his mother first before hunting down Becky.

Pushing away from the door, he knocked gently and coughed softly to get her attention. His mother stopped her movement and turned in her chair to look at him. Her eyes roamed over him before coming up to meet with his.

"Hello, young man. Are you looking for someone?"

Cole stepped into the room slowly. "Yes, I was, but I can't seem to find her. Would you mind if I sit with you for a while just until she comes back?"

His mother smiled at him, and as the warmth of it met her hazel eyes, the same color as his own, he felt his heart break at the lack of recognition in them.

"Oh, of course, please. Just pull that chair over here, and we can have a chat until she comes back. I love visitors."

Cole shrugged out of his coat and pulled up the plush sitting chair beside her. Taking a seat, he watched her as she fussed for a minute with her hair.

She straightened her robe before she turned to face him. "So, what is your name?"

Cole grinned at the same question she would ask him every week. "Cole. My name is Cole."

"Oh, what a lovely name. It's strong."

"Thank you. My mother thought so. What's your name?"

"My name is Lydia."

Looking out to the snow falling silently onto the balcony railing, Cole whispered softly, "That's a beautiful name."

"What's that?" she asked, not hearing him.

"I said that's a beautiful name. My mother's name is Lydia."

"Really?" she asked with a warm expression that always reminded him of happiness, safety, and home. "What a coincidence."

"Yes, it really is." He chuckled as he pushed his hand into his pocket and pulled out two caramels. "Do you like caramel, Lydia?"

She looked at the white wax paper in his hand before raising her eyes back to his. "Why, yes; yes, I do. How funny." She giggled like a little girl as she got up from the chair.

Cole knew exactly where she was headed.

After picking up the music box, she came back to him and sat down. "I keep my caramels in here, but I ran out this morning. Are you sure you don't mind?"

Cole shook his head and handed her one of the candies. He watched her unwrap it as he undid his own. Just as she popped it into her mouth, she gave him a grin that made all his annoyance at Nurse Becky Parnell melt away.

"My little boy loves caramel."

"Does he?"

She nodded as she sucked the candy and closed her eyes. "He would eat them all day if I let him. He can be such a naughty little thing."

As she started to hum again, Cole also closed his eyes as he tried to remind himself it was good to talk to her about these things. He had been told it would keep her mind active. It was something he could do to help her.

It was a pity though that no one had an answer on how to make *his* heart and mind stop hurting. That was something he had no control over, and that made him feel absolutely fucking helpless.

CHAPTER 6

It was amazing how long two days could drag, Rachel thought as she woke up on Sunday morning.

She had not been sleeping well. Between the nightmares of her past and dreams revolving around a man she had begrudgingly decided she *needed* to see again, she was surprised she hadn't fallen asleep at work on Saturday night.

Pushing back the covers, she swung her feet over the edge of the bed and stretched as she ran a hand through her hair, pulling it off her face. Quickly, she secured it with a hair tie before she got up and made her way to her closet.

Once she was dressed in her baggy red gym shorts and tight black sports bra, she sat back on the bed to lace up her shoes, and then she grabbed her black hoodie and put it on. Moving in front of the full-length mirror, Rachel looked up and down at her reflection as she picked up the tape and spread her fingers. She wrapped it first around her wrist and then her knuckles. After her hand was bound the way she had been taught, she lifted the dangling tape to her mouth, used her teeth to cut the end, and secured it in place before she repeated the process on the other hand. Flexing her fingers, she jabbed her fists out in front of her a couple times and smiled. *Oh yeah, it's time to go and kick some ass.*

With her boxing gloves shoved in her gym bag, she opened the fridge, grabbed a protein shake for breakfast, and ran past the side table on her way out the door. She never missed an opportunity to beat up the bag.

~

A COUPLE OF HOURS LATER, Rachel was stepping out of her class when she spotted Shelly and Lena getting off the treadmills. Waving at them, she made sure she plastered on a wide smile as she stopped in front of the girls.

"Well, well, if it isn't the late-night streetwalker," Lena quipped as she swung a small towel over her shoulder.

Rachel gave Lena a shocked look and tried to hide her grin. "Honestly, Lena, how am I ever going to have a successful sex life if I have to check in with Mason every night?"

Shelly let out a laugh and shook her head as they all moved toward the front doors. "Well, at least he doesn't know about Whipped. If he ever found out, he'd never back off."

Rachel looked over at the perfectly put-together blonde with the shit-eating grin.

How did I end up being so close to these two women? They were the furthest things from herself that she could have found.

"I'll have you know that I haven't been there for quite a while."

"Oh, and why's that?" Lena uncapped the water bottle she was holding and took a gulp.

"Did a certain someone run you off your stomping grounds?" Shelly teased.

Resisting the urge to punch her in the arm, Rachel zipped her jacket as she glared at Shelly. "Can it, Georgia. Cole Madison did not run me from anywhere. I just haven't been in the mood, and I haven't been sleeping well lately."

"Why not?" Lena asked, concern showing in her green eyes.

Rachel turned to Lena and thought about how close they had become, as though she were her own sister. "I keep having dreams. Well, they're nightmares actually, but that doesn't matter. That's all they are." Slinging her gym bag over her arm, Rachel turned to Shelly. "Are we still going to your place for lunch?"

Shelly nodded and pulled her sweater over her head. "Yeah, Josh said to remind you to pick up the beer."

Rachel rolled her eyes as they pushed open the doors and walked out into the cool air. "Of course he did. Those two never could watch Sunday football without beer."

Rubbing her arms, Rachel promised to be there at two. She waved once and made a dash down the street. Luckily for her, even if the rent was too high, her place was only a hop, skip, and jump away from the gym they all worked out at.

~

It's official. I hate football, Rachel thought as she sat on the couch. She started to zone out while Josh and Mason yelled at the TV, and Lena and Shelly talked about work. As much as she hated to admit it, she had started to feel like the fifth wheel lately.

Who would have ever thought these two would end up so committed? Certainly, not me, she thought incredulously.

It wasn't as though she begrudged anyone a happy ending, but the way both Mason and Josh had become so domestic almost mystified her. All they needed were a pair of rug rats to complete the picture of domestic bliss.

Oh, who am I to be sitting here, envying them their happiness? They all deserved it. It wasn't their fault she was feeling the way she was and at the rate she was going maybe she could be the old single aunt with the bright hair.

Hell, I knew I should've stayed home and dyed my hair today, I'm even annoying myself.

Standing, Rachel excused herself and made her way down the hall to the bathroom. As she passed a room that Shelly must have converted into what now looked like an office and gym, Rachel smiled and moved across the space to the punching bag hanging from the ceiling.

This is what I need installed in my place. The only problem was that she didn't own her place. She rented, so bolts in her ceiling beams were not allowed.

Turning to leave for the bathroom, she walked past the old desk in the corner and happened to glance down. There, sitting on the desk, was an official-looking piece of paper that had *Mitchell & Madison, Attorneys at Law* written across the top.

Cole.

Rachel felt her pulse accelerate as if he were in the room with her. Gingerly, she let her fingers creep onto the paper as she pulled it closer to the edge of the desk. Ignoring the contents beneath the header, she peered at the writing across the top, focusing on the address and phone number printed boldly under the firm's name.

Before she could even think about it, she took out her phone and snapped a picture of the letterhead. She dashed out of the office, ran straight into the bathroom, and locked the door behind her. Moving to the edge of the tub, she sat and stared at the number.

It's Sunday. He wouldn't be there today. Would he? What if he is?

Quickly, she dialed the number before she could change her mind. After three rings, just as she suspected, a recorded message came over the line.

"Hello. You have reached the law office of Mitchell & Madison, and we are currently closed. If this is an emergency, you can reach Logan Mitchell at 312-555-1467 or Cole Madison at 312-555-7173. Thank you, and have a good day."

Rachel hung up and stared at the phone. She thought about what she was going to do for less than two seconds before she hit redial. She quickly typed the digits following Cole's name into her contacts. After she ended the call this time, she stared at his number like it would bite her.

Should I or shouldn't I?

Oh, what the hell.

~

COLE WAS halfway home from Lake Forest when his phone began ringing, the sounds coming through his car speakers. Glancing at the display, he didn't recognize the 773 area code number offhand. Pressing the button on his steering wheel, he was about to answer as a car cut in front of him.

"Jesus," he cursed as he slammed on the brakes.

He noticed there was silence in the vehicle, and he realized no one had said anything on the other end of the line. "I'm sorry. Hello?"

More silence. "Hello?" he greeted again.

That was when the call ended.

He stopped at a red light and decided to call the number. With the unprofessional way he had answered, maybe the caller hadn't realized it was him. As the call connected, he waited for a greeting. When nothing came, he decided to speak up. "Hello, this is Cole Madison. You just called me. I wasn't sure if you had the wrong number."

The light turned green, and he slowly pushed his foot on the accelerator, letting his Peugeot purr as it began to move.

"It's Rachel."

Immediately, his eyes glanced at the number on the display. *Rachel? Well, now, isn't this interesting?*

"Hello, Rachel." Tapping his finger on the steering wheel, Cole finally cleared the traffic and let the car power forward. "Rachel? Are you still there?"

"Yes, I'm here," she replied, like she was annoyed that she was.

Cole couldn't help the twitch of his lips at her tone. "Okay, I was just checking. This is a surprise. How did you get my number?"

"Do you really care?"

"No, not really. But you don't seem to be saying much, so I thought I should fill the silence."

"With questions you don't really care about?"

"Well, it was that or ask you *why* you are calling, but I've figured out that answer already."

He thought he heard her scoff softly before she spoke again.

"Oh? And why did I call you?"

Surprised at the feeling of satisfaction he felt at that moment, Cole replied, "Because you want to ask me something obviously."

"Is that right?"

"Oh, come on, Rachel. I hardly think you hunted down my number to make sure I got home alright after Thursday night. It's Sunday. That's a wide window of time for something to have happened to me."

"Okay, you're right. I didn't even think about you after you left Thursday night."

"Liar."

"Am not."

Cole chuckled. "Did you just stick out your tongue as well? You're lying, Rachel, but that's okay. You'll tell me the truth soon enough, and I'll enjoy every minute of it."

~

Oh hell. This man was god-knows-where, and he had her locked in a bathroom with her hand pressed between her denim-clad legs.

"And how do you plan to do that?" she whispered, surprising herself by how much she *wanted* to know.

"Rachel, I am not going to sit in my car and talk you into an orgasm. If you wait and show me that you have some kind of self-discipline, I'll give you one in person."

Immediately, she removed her hand. She clenched her teeth and shook her head. She hated that she was already doing what he asked.

"Aren't you forgetting something?" she questioned as she clutched the phone tightly.

"No, I don't think so. Are you?"

"No, I'm not, but you promised not to touch me."

During the silence that followed, she felt her heart start to thump faster with each second she waited. *One, two, three*, and then his voice slid through the phone with a carnal promise.

"I don't need to touch you to make you come, Rachel. You have hands, don't you? Just wait, so I can watch. Tonight at ten. I'll see you where we first met."

She was about to reply, but as her mouth parted, the call ended.

Then, there was a loud banging on the bathroom door.

"Rachel. You okay in there?"

She jumped up as though her ass was on fire. Clutching the phone to her pounding chest, she moved to the door and unlocked it to find Shelly standing in front of her, her brow arched.

"Yep, I'm great. Look, I've got to run," Rachel said quickly as she brushed past Shelly.

She briskly walked through the hallway into the living room. Rachel picked up her bag, slung it over her shoulder, and then waved to everyone before she headed to the front door.

"Rach, wait up," Mason called to her as he got off the couch.

He followed her out the door to the elevator. Pressing the button, she looked up at her brother and tried for a genuine smile. It was best not to let him see the holy-shit feelings currently pumping throughout her entire body.

"Rach? What the hell?" Mason asked, stopping beside her. "You've been acting so strange lately. Are you sure you're okay? I mean, I know things have been stressful, but...well, you're acting a little more—"

"A little more what, Mase? Crazy? Harebrained?"

Shaking his head, he reached out and pulled her into a hug. "No, none of that. You just seem so different lately. I can't put my finger on it. Even your usual crazy has been different."

Leaning back, Rachel looked up at him and patted his chest. He smoothed a comforting hand down her hair and picked up the ends.

"What color is this going to be tomorrow?"

Without missing a beat, she told him, "Red streaks."

When the elevator arrived, Mason reluctantly released her. "That's a vivid choice."

Stepping into the empty space, Rachel hit the lobby button and wiggled her brows. "I'm feeling particularly daring. See you tomorrow, Mase."

"Night, Rach. Be careful."

As the doors swooshed closed, she promised, "Always."

IT WAS nine fifty in the evening, and Rachel was exactly where she had been the first time she had met Cole at the bar in Whipped.

After rushing home from Josh and Shelly's, she had spent the afternoon dyeing her hair. She loved the final look. Throughout her black hair, chunks of red were loud and flashy. It reflected the way she was feeling right now.

Rachel had pulled her hair back into a sleek tight ponytail. She had a deep crimson gloss on her lips with smoky dramatic eyes to match. All afternoon, she had debated on what she would wear to meet up with Cole again.

Do I want to make him work for it? Or do I want this to be an easy conquest?

In the end, she had decided on her black leather miniskirt with the silver zipper that ran from top to bottom in the center, and she had paired it with a red-and-black lace corset.

Sure, the outfit was minimal, but in the end, it gave off the right message. *What exactly is that message? Well, that's easy.*

You think you can keep your hands off this, Cole? Prove it.

~

THE MINUTE he stepped into the club, Cole let his eyes move over the sea of people. It was amazing how not one of them even registered as being worth his time. Focused on one thing only, he searched for the reason he was here tonight.

He moved deeper into the main crush, and that was when he spotted her. He thanked every fucking entity he could think of because she was standing there, expecting him. The alternative would have been to just drag her off somewhere and introduce himself in the most intimate way imaginable. His tongue in her mouth came to mind.

That wasn't necessary though because the woman standing at the bar with her elbows resting on it was staring directly at him. Like a magnet, her smoky eyes pulled him through the gyrating bodies until he reached the other side. He was now only steps away from her. Letting his eyes run down over her, Cole had to consciously hold himself back. The woman standing in front of him was just his type. *And I plan to show her I am hers*. The only thing that would have made the situation better was if everyone in the room would get the fuck out.

She was dressed in the same tiny black skirt she had been wearing the first time he had seen her and a corset that looked more like an expensive piece of lingerie.

She seems to like those.

That wasn't what was killing him though. Around her neck was a pretty little piece of black satin. She had tied it into a small bow, making a choker out of it.

Fuck.

Clenching his hands by his sides, he finally brought his eyes back to her provocative stare. That was when she arched an insolent brow, like she wasn't affected by him at all, and then she turned to face the bar, giving him a fantastic view of her backside. Her long legs were encased in sheer black stockings with a bold seam running up the center of each leg and ending somewhere beneath the skirt that was barely covering her ass.

Moving up beside her, Cole rested his arms on the surface of the bar and turned to face her. *If she wants to play games, then let the games begin.*

~

RACHEL WAS TRYING to regain her composure.

Watching Cole stalk through the crowd toward her while she remained where she was, trying to appear cool, calm, and collected, had taken every ounce of her concentration and willpower.

All black. He was dressed in all black, and when contrasted with that sexy blond hair, the impact was so effective that Rachel had to remind herself not to beg him to take her.

Turning to face him, she saw he was resting against the bar, staring at her. As their eyes collided, she felt the thrill of anticipation zing up her spine. Without a word, he moved closer, trailing a finger along the cool surface. It drew her eyes, distracting her, just as he knew it would.

He moved to stand behind her, and without touching an inch of her skin, he spoke clearly and concisely into her ear. "Come."

Rachel turned her head as he moved away from her. Narrowing her eyes, she watched him walk around the bar without a backward glance. Taking a deep breath, she tried to gather her wits as she followed. She rounded the end of the bar and saw the corridor that led down to the private rooms at Whipped. Although she'd known about the rooms, she had never been in them.

Do I really want this? Do I even know what the hell I'm doing? This all started from what? Fear and boredom. I'm not sure I'm ready for someone like him.

As she took two tentative steps into the dim hall, she heard The Pretty Reckless overhead singing "Make Me Wanna Die" from the speakers.

God the guitar at the beginning gets me every time. So damn sexy, add in my current ache and—Jesus where did the man go?

She gathered her courage and took several more steps. She was shocked when Cole appeared from a side alcove, making her take a step back. He didn't touch her, but with each forward step he took, she took one step back until she was in an alcove opposite from the one he had been standing in.

Rachel's back came up against the wall, and even though he still had not touched her, she recognized the stirrings of fear as Cole moved closer. He raised his arms and placed his hands by her head, his palms resting on the wall, as he locked eyes with her in an all-too-familiar stance.

Oh shit. He really isn't going to touch me, Rachel thought as she looked him over.

Just as she was about to confirm it, she thought better and decided to just take. Keeping her eyes on his, she reached out and ran her index finger from his neck to the buttons of his black shirt. When she got to the center of his chest, she trailed her finger over to his nipple and the bar she now knew was under there, running her finger against the fabric and the hard piercing beneath.

That is such a turn-on, she thought, raising her eyes to his. As she continued to play with it, she asked, "You aren't going to talk?"

"Oh, I plan to talk," he acknowledged.

He shifted his feet as she reached up with her other hand and pressed her finger to his other nipple.

"You like them, don't you? It's okay to admit it now that you're about to come, and I'm about to watch you while you do."

"Are you always so sure of yourself?"

"Yes," he replied without a moment's hesitation. "Undo my shirt, Rachel. Stop playing this coy little game, and take what you want."

"Is that what you do?"

"Play coy? Never," he confirmed.

Her eyes dropped to her fingers as they rapidly started undoing his shirt. "You're very clever at twisting and playing with my words."

"That's what I do. My job requires me to twist words and to know when someone is trying to bullshit me."

When she reached the final button, she pulled his shirt apart, biting her bottom lip between her teeth. Seeing him was such a sinful shock. Being this close to him, she couldn't stop herself from staring, but now wasn't the time to look. It was time to act.

Placing her hands on his stomach, she smoothed her palms up his body until she reached the small metal bars. "And that's what you think I'm doing—bullshitting you?"

His jaw flexed as she ran her fingers over his nipples.

"I think you're confused."

Fixing her eyes on his, she pinched one of the nipples she was playing with. "Oh? And what am I confused about?"

Lowering his head, Cole warned her, "Be careful with what you're doing there. Do you really think that hurts or bothers me? If you twist it a little harder, you might not like my reaction."

"You told me to," she pointed out.

"That's right, Rachel. I *told* you to do it. I *allowed* you to touch me, didn't I?"

As what he was saying sank in, her frustration and annoyance caught up with her, and she twisted his nipple harder. Instantly, he crowded in, standing against her so close that her hands were pressed between his bare chest and her breasts. His hands were still by her head, and as she looked up at him, he stared down at her with feverish eyes.

"That wasn't very nice. Why did you do it?"

"You said you wouldn't touch me," she blurted out, feeling trapped.

"I'm not touching you. My hands are on the wall. Your hands are actually touching me. Now, Rachel, answer me. Why did you do that?"

"Do what?"

"You know what. Don't make me repeat the question again."

"Or what?" she asked incredulously.

"Answer me, Rachel," he growled.

"I was annoyed that you tricked me. I'm frustrated," she spat out.

"Good. So am I," he pointed out. "Stop playing this silly fucking game with me, and tell me what you want."

Rachel could feel her rapid breathing pushing her breasts against her hands and his bare chest. Licking her lips, she stood frozen. She knew what she wanted, but she couldn't find the courage to voice it. That didn't seem to be a problem for Cole though.

"I only want to give you what you want, Rachel." He rubbed his chest against her arms. "Don't you want to get what you want?"

Blinking up at him, Rachel parted her mouth as he lowered his head. She felt the tip of his tongue tracing her lips while he kept his hands planted by her head, still not touching her.

"I want to do *that* down between your legs. Don't you want that?"

~

COLE WAS SO FUCKING HARD that he was surprised he hadn't busted through the zipper on his pants. Rachel's face was a study of hunger and longing. Her mouth parted, she looked ravenous, yet she couldn't seem to say one damn thing.

He could tell she was aroused because her breathing had accelerated, pushing her hands up and down more rapidly against his bare chest. He would also bet all his money on the fact that she was now wet and warm between those sexy thighs. He wanted between her thighs so badly that his cock was actually starting to hurt.

"Have you ever been in one of these rooms, Rachel?" Cole almost laughed from the expression that crossed her face, but he didn't want to lose the moment they were in. "You want to know a secret?" he asked, lowering his mouth to her ear. "Neither have I. I don't want to tie you to a bed or strap you to a cross. I want you to willingly *want* every single thing I plan to do to you. I want you to keep your hands behind your back because you want to." Biting her earlobe, he then added, "And I want you to swallow because you love the fucking taste. Play with me, Rachel, so I can play with you."

Moving back to her mouth, Cole greedily followed her tongue with his as she licked her lips. She groaned and pushed her body forward. She wasn't trying to dislodge him; she was trying to get closer.

"How close are you?" he demanded, biting her slick lower lip as he rubbed himself against her. When no answer came, he released her and confessed, "You smell so fucking tempting. I can't wait to get between your legs."

"Oh god." Moaning, she closed her eyes.

Squirming against him, she extricated a hand from between them and slid it down. Moving back a few inches, Cole let his gaze drop, and he cursed when he watched her pull the zipper on her skirt from the bottom up.

She pushed her hand up under the leather and hissed as she obviously got her fingers where she wanted them. "Yes. I agree."

"Clarify." He moved back in close to her, trapping her eager hands between them.

She raised her other hand to his nipple and twisted the piercing.

"Rachel," he growled. With his hands still against the fucking wall, he glared down at her. *Goddamn it.*

"Yes," she keened.

"Yes to what?"

"Yes to my orgasm, and yes to whatever else you just said," she agreed desperately. Closing her eyes, she began fucking her hand as she played with his nipple.

Cole almost found the situation humorous as Rachel tipped her head back and came with a loud scream.

Un-fucking-real. She is totally uninhibited, he thought. *This is going to be fun.*

As her eyes opened, she focused on him, giving him a lazy self-satisfied smile. She released his now tender flesh with a condescending pat over his wolf tat on his chest.

As though she had broken the orgasmic spell she had dragged him under, he softly asked in a menacing tone, "Satisfied?"

She gave him a smug look. "Very."

Cole dropped his hands from the wall and pinned her to it with his stare. "Good. Now, it's time to negotiate."

CHAPTER 7

"Negotiate?" Rachel asked, managing to push the word past the lump that had suddenly formed in her throat.

Her eyes tracked Cole's movements as he began to button his shirt from the top down.

"Yes, negotiate. You didn't think this was over, did you?" he inquired, gesturing between the two of them.

Rachel didn't know what to think as she stared at him, slack-jawed. All she could remember was his voice offering to do dirty, sexual things to her, and it was making her nerves start to tingle all over again.

Is a possible second orgasm on the table? If so, count me in.

"No, I can see that you're starting to know me better than that. You see," he informed in a voice that sounded far too calculating, "I never leave a negotiation until I get what I came for."

Rachel finally removed her hand from between her thighs as his perceptive eyes glanced down there.

"Did it feel good?" Now that his shirt was in order, he took a step back toward her.

"Well, it certainly wasn't awful," she told him in a caustic tone.

Placing his left hand on the wall by her head, he raised his right hand to where she could see it. "I can make it feel even better. Let me touch you."

Rachel couldn't control the shiver that racked her body.

"I'm only asking you out of common courtesy. I figured I owed you that since your first agreement was given in the midst of an ear-blistering climax. So, what will it be, Rachel? Will you stick to your original decision? Or will you renege?"

Rachel's brain was screaming, *Renege, renege, renege.* That did not, however, have any impact on the way her thighs tightened as Cole bent his head and licked the shell of her ear.

"Plus, there is one promise I haven't kept tonight, and it goes hand in hand with my hands on your body."

Turning her head up, Rachel looked into eyes that seemed to see and know everything. "And what would that be?"

The look on his face was so devious and alarmingly sexy that Rachel felt her nipples harden.

He revealed, "I promised you'd scream my name."

Rachel didn't remember that promise, and surely, that wasn't something she would forget. "I don't remember you promising me that."

"Who said I promised you? I promised myself. Now, tell me what I want to hear, Rachel."

Slowly, he moved his free hand toward her, and his index finger touched the satin ribbon around her neck. When she offered no complaint, he continued to stroke it.

"I want to take this and every other piece of material off you and start fresh. I want a blank canvas to play with. I want *you* to play with. I have from the moment I saw you. So, was that yes real, or should I go back out there and find a willing participant?"

Rachel considered all the erotic possibilities as his words began to tempt her, but before she could offer up an answer, Cole removed his finger from her throat and stood to his full towering height. He crossed his arms and took a step back from her, allowing his eyes to run down her body, and Rachel felt them like they were his hands touching her.

Hell, who do I think I'm kidding? I want his hands on me, his tongue in me, and that body naked and covering me. ASAP.

Rachel finally decided. "Don't go anywhere. Stay here, and let's negotiate."

~

Cole wouldn't have left if the building were on fire, but he wasn't about to tell her that. "Okay, let's negotiate. Well, obviously, you have issues with men—"

"I don't have issues with men."

Cole lifted his right arm and index finger in the universal hang-on sign. "For this to work, you need to listen until I am finished, or you will jump to the wrong conclusion. So, do you think you can hold your tongue for a minute? Or would you like me to?"

He watched her carefully as she pouted her lips.

"Thank you. Being interrupted isn't something I enjoy. It would be a smart thing to remember."

Re-crossing his arms, he remained silent as she straightened up against the wall. He could tell she was annoyed by his tone and getting ready to leave, but the look in her eyes belied her internal conflict. This was a woman who wanted the same thing he did. She was just too scared to admit it or chase it.

Good thing for her that I'm not.

"Now, as I was saying, obviously, you have issues with men controlling you or touching you. As I'm sure you know, I want to do a lot more than just touch you, Rachel, so maybe we can start slow. One hand, and if I prove to you that you can trust me, we'll renegotiate."

As she stood there, headstrong as ever, Cole stepped forward to her.

"Being petulant won't help your case either. Tell me, Rachel, do you really want this? Because I need to know that you are in all the way before we go any further here."

When her tongue came out to moisten her lips, Cole couldn't help but reach out his hand, allowing his finger to follow the path it took.

"What *exactly* is it that you want from me?" she finally asked as she raised her eyes to his.

Cole re-crossed his arms and bent at the waist, so his face was hovering over hers. "I want you to give yourself to me."

As he watched her pupils dilate, he knew the idea was as appealing to her as it was to him.

"For how long?"

"See? Now, you're negotiating. Let's start with a week."

"A week? So, we meet here?"

"No." He shifted, pressing his mouth to the corner of hers. "You come with me for the week. You stay with me, sleep with me, eat with me. You *be* with me."

When a moan slipped free from her lips, Cole couldn't help himself from kissing her hard and quick.

Then, quietly, he demanded, "Say yes."

~

YES, yes, yes. Rachel's body was screaming, but nothing was coming out. Her stupid brain had to make sure this was a choice, not a takeover. So, of course, it had demands of its own. "I don't think this is a negotiation right now. It feels a lot like coercion."

She experienced a small slither of delight in the humor that tugged at the corner of his serious mouth.

"Very good, Rachel. You are right. I'm trying my hardest to coerce you without becoming physical. So, in my book, I am not actually stooping as low as I could."

"This isn't physical? It feels pretty physical to me." *Time to give him some of his own medicine.* "My nipples are hard, and the ache between my thighs—"

"Could all be taken care of with one word."

Raising her hand, she recklessly pressed her index finger to his lips. She was starting to fantasize about those lips that had just sent a jolt of pure lust through her. "Shh, it's rude to interrupt during negotiations."

"Rachel," he cautioned.

"Yes?"

She watched him close his eyes for a moment, almost as if trying to calm himself physically.

"Nothing. Continue. Your terms?" he asked.

"You said one hand. As in, you will only touch me with one hand?"

"Yes. If you agree and come with me, I will not touch you with more than one hand. When I prove to you I can be trusted, we will renegotiate."

Rachel shivered at the thought. "Will you use your mouth?"

Cole gave her a look filled with so many hot, dirty promises that it melted away any resistance she thought she had left. That was the moment their two lives became soldered together by mutual desire and understanding. Whether it would go beyond a week was anyone's bet, but it was one she wanted to take.

"If you agree, I will use my mouth, tongue, and anything else I need to make you whisper, groan, and scream my name."

"Okay. I agree, but no straps and no..." She paused, looking away. "Handcuffs?"

A strong hand lifted her chin, so her eyes were directly on his.

Sincerely, he replied, "There will be no physical restraint, just your free will."

"No pain?"

"Rachel, I don't know who hurt you in the past or what kind of relationship you were in, but with me, no pain, no humiliation, and no harm will come to you. I want to please *you* as much as I want *you* to please me. I want to use my body and yours to bring you the most pleasure you have ever felt, and after it's through, I want to start all over again."

Rachel felt her body shake at everything he was saying. She finally realized it was everything she had ever wanted, and she could have it for a week.

One week of perfection.

"Why me?" she asked.

She felt him remove the hand he had at her chin, and slowly, he wrapped it around her waist as he tugged her forward. She could feel the full length of his muscular body pressed tightly against hers.

"From the minute you walked in, it was you. I'd been coming to this place for months, looking for someone—not someone who wants gimmicks, not someone who wants to act a part in the bedroom. This is me and my life, Rachel. I'm bossy, I'm arrogant, and I can be an asshole at times, but I also crave the power to control my surroundings. So, that is what I ask of you. Will you let go and give me the power to make you happy? To make you scream when your body finally explodes around mine? I want the power to make you smile and curse at me, so if you want to try that, then come with me. Say yes, and come home with me."

Really, it's a no-brainer, she thought as she said, "Yes."

~

One silent cab ride later, Cole found himself staring at the woman standing opposite him in the elevator as it ascended to his condo's floor. She hadn't taken her eyes off him the whole ride up. He liked that about her. She was daring, just like her bright red hair and tattooed spine He might want someone to let him hold the reins, but he'd be damned if he wanted someone meek and mild who wouldn't give him a challenge.

This woman is definitely going to be a challenge, he thought, *and I can't fucking wait.*

"What are you thinking about?" he asked as she shifted against the opposite wall and crossed her legs.

He had discovered that once she made up her mind, she was the kind of woman who didn't back down. It was the moments in between, the uncertainty, that made her the most vulnerable.

"I was wondering what else is hiding under your clothes."

Cole admired her blunt no-nonsense response.

"Amazing. I was just thinking the exact same thing. What will I find when I unzip that skirt, Rachel?"

"Guess you'll find out in..." She looked at the lights on the panel above the doors as they lit one at a time with each floor they passed. "Six floors."

Cole pushed his hands into his pockets as their eyes met once more. "Yes, I will."

Silence filled the space between them as the elevator passed the final four floors.

When it came to a smooth stop, Cole pushed away from the wall and gestured with his hand. "After you."

Rachel moved away from the other side and stepped out into the hallway. She stopped when her black heels hit the cream carpet. Cole got off the elevator and came up behind her. He ran one finger down her neck and along her shoulder and felt her shiver.

She looked back at him. "Which way?"

"Left. It's the last door on your right."

She pivoted to the left and made her way down the hall. He watched her take in the paintings on the walls. When she reached the last door, she turned, so she was facing him as he walked toward her. Her eyes devoured him as he came closer, and when he pulled the keys from his pocket, she parted her lips and licked them as if she were ready to take a bite.

"Ready?" he asked, looking directly at her, as he inserted the key.

"For?"

He turned the key, and the snick of the lock was as effective as a starting gun.

With absolute certainty, he said, "Me."

Rachel was absolutely positive she was *not* ready for him, but she wanted him anyway, so she conveniently pushed that thought aside. She turned to where he was now waiting for her in the doorway. Stepping into the entryway, she felt a strong hand firmly grip her upper right arm from behind her.

"Let's see how well you follow direction."

As his breath ghosted over her spine, she allowed herself a moment of reflection.

How long has it been since I've given in to this side of myself? Years? Four at least.

She was pulled from her thoughts when his tongue touched the base of her neck where her tattoo began.

"Be sure this is what you want. Walk all the way to the door at the far end of the hall. Do not look around. When you get there, go inside, and you will see a large wooden trunk at the end of my bed. When I get there, I want you to be standing on it, facing my headboard, minus this sexy fucking skirt."

Rachel swallowed and nodded once.

"Good. Oh, Rachel, leave the stockings and heels on. I'll be in shortly. Now, go," he instructed.

She felt a slight pressure from one of his hands on the curve of her back, urging her forward. Straightening her spine, she decided that she might as well give him a show, so she strutted down the hall of his very impressive condo. She wished she had a moment to look around, but she knew if she did, he would see. Rachel could feel his eyes on her, watching her closely, and she still didn't know him well enough to try and play him.

Her heels clicked as she moved farther along the hardwood floors.

From what she could see out of the corner of her eye, she passed two closed doors. When she reached the one at the end of the hall, she extended a trembling hand and gripped the silver knob. Turning it, she stepped inside, and she was immediately surrounded by the dark masculine vibe that was all Cole.

On one side of the room was a large bureau made from a deep cherry hardwood. It perfectly matched the enormous bed pushed against the wall on the other side of the room. A wooden clothes valet sat in the far corner, and just as he had told her, there was a large wooden trunk at the end of his bed.

Rachel didn't know how much time she had until he joined her, so she quit gaping at her surroundings and kicked her ass into gear. She unzipped her skirt, and with a smirk, she moved to the clothes valet where he had a perfectly pressed suit all neatly laid out. She draped her leather over it with a little chuckle.

Walking back to the end of the bed, she noticed a small cream rug on the floor in front of the trunk. She bet that rug would feel good under her slightly achy feet right now. The room was so lush and rich, all cream and dark woods, yet it was so extremely manly at the same time. It smelled amazing, and then she realized it smelled liked him.

Stopping in front of the trunk, she removed her heels and placed them on top. Then, she hitched herself up onto it. While standing on the trunk, she put the heels back on. Facing the headboard, Rachel shifted her legs a little bit apart, so she was steady, and then she took several deep breaths. Just as she had her nerves almost under control, she heard the handle of the door turn. Closing her eyes, she told herself to let go.

Just let go. Surrender.

~

COLE TURNED the doorknob to his room and pushed the door open slowly. He had been curious about what he would find when he walked in, and what greeted him couldn't have pleased him more. She had done exactly as he'd asked, and what had been hiding under that little skirt was definitely worth the fucking torture of waiting outside.

After walking through the door, he shut it with a resounding thump, and when she didn't look over her shoulder, he felt a moment of pride for her. He knew she had to be dying to turn around. Moving into the room, he looked around. He did a double take when he saw her skirt lying over the suit that was hanging on his valet.

Mischievous woman.

As he walked toward her, he rolled up his sleeves to his forearms and glanced down at the writing on each arm: *Tålmodighet av en saint. Sinnet til en synder.*

How very appropriate it is tonight, he thought. *Patience of a saint. The mind of a sinner.*

As he looked at the long legs slightly spread and wrapped in those fantasy-inducing thigh-high stockings, he found he was praying for patience as he was definitely thinking like a sinner. *No question about it.*

He stopped directly behind her, and with her perched in her heels, she was the exact right height for what he had in mind. Her smooth pale ass, separated by a tiny strip of black lace, was at eye-level and calling to him.

"Very nice, Rachel," he finally said. "Your legs should always be in these stockings. This seam..." he murmured, reaching out a finger and touching the black line that began at the back of her right ankle. "It makes me want to trace it..." He ran his finger up the seam and then leaned in to the opposite leg. "With my tongue."

~

RACHEL CLENCHED her hands in front of her as Cole's hot, wet tongue ran a line from the back of her left knee up to the lace surrounding her upper thigh. When his mouth continued to the curve of her bare cheek, she bit down on her bottom lip to avoid making a sound as his teeth nipped at her. His finger made its way up her other leg and crossed over to the lace separating her ass before he slid it down and pushed it between her thighs.

"You're so quiet up there."

His voice traveled like a hot caress from her legs up to her burning ears.

"I didn't realize I could talk."

As he stroked his finger along her embarrassingly wet panties, his voice permitted, "Oh, you can talk if you like, but I'd prefer you to sigh, moan, and perhaps scream."

With that, he licked her bare rounded flesh, and then he removed his hand and mouth from her body. "Turn around, Rachel," he instructed in a voice that demanded she obey.

Is he naked? Will I get to touch him?

Slowly, she turned, wondering what she would find. When she was facing him, she looked down to see him staring up at her with eyes that were focused, determined, and burning. He hadn't removed one item of clothing, and although she thought that would disappoint her, she was so mesmerized by the look in his eyes that she couldn't find any disappointment whatsoever.

All she found was intense desire. *Desire, lust, and want.*

"You're exactly the way I imagined...only better. I could stare at you all day." He lifted his left hand to trace the lace at the top of her right thigh. "Take a step forward. Come closer to me."

Rachel moved as requested. His jaw ticked as he took a deep breath, and she knew he could smell her arousal. Hell, at this stage, she could smell her arousal, and his nose was much closer.

"One hand. That was the deal," his sensual voice promised.

He ran his fingers up to the crease between her legs, stopping at her throbbing hot mound. His eyes wouldn't release hers as his fingers crept under the lace and pulled it aside. Knowing what he was about to do was driving her insane, but what he said next just about made her entire body combust.

"ONE HAND AND MY MOUTH. That was the negotiated arrangement, I believe."

Cole finally tore his eyes away from the blue ones that were making it hard for him to think. When his eyes landed on what he had just bared, he almost fell to his knees to thank whichever god had sent him a woman like Rachel fucking Langley.

There, shining at him like a prize, were two sterling silver studs in a wicked vertical hood piercing.

It seems someone else is keeping a few dirty little secrets.

"What do we have here?" He leaned in to blow against the glistening metal. "You didn't tell me about this," he accused, peering up at her, an inch away from the most vulnerable part of her body.

"You...ahh—"

She broke off as he blew against her sweet swollen flesh again.

"Yes, Rachel?"

"You never asked."

"No, I don't suppose I did. Seems you and I have a lot more in common than I thought."

His eyes moved back to the piercing, and he shook his head in disbelief before firmly holding the panties aside.

"Rachel?" he asked again without looking up at her.

Her hands were by her side, but he could see her fists were clenched.

"While you are here, this is mine."

With that, he leaned in and swiped his tongue in a delicious hot lick against the two silver studs beckoning him.

RACHEL COULDN'T BELIEVE her knees hadn't given out on her yet. What Cole was currently doing with his tongue ought to be illegal. True, he was only touching her with one hand, but his mouth and tongue—tracing, flicking, and sucking her piercing—was destroying her.

She couldn't help the moan that slipped free from her throat as his finger joined in on the action as he moved it down to rub between her slick, sensitive lips. Finally feeling her stance becoming perilous, she reached out to gently grip his hair. He lifted his eyes to hers, and she should have been scared from the intensity she saw in them, but she wasn't. She was buzzing and high on the lust coursing through her body like a raging inferno.

"Lift your left leg, Rachel, and put it over my shoulder."

Oh fuck was all Rachel could think as she moved to drape her leg over his strong shoulder. She was suddenly grateful to all her kick-boxing training for giving her great balance because she knew she would need it the minute he lifted his hand and tugged her thigh further over him. Her piercing brushed against his rapacious mouth, and all Rachel could do was hold on and hope for the best.

"You look..." He licked. "Smell..."

Oh god, another lick.

"And taste...Jesus, Rachel...too fucking good," he murmured against her heated flesh.

Rachel could feel the scrape of his stubble against her bare thighs as he finally moved his mouth from the piercing to her clit. Without hesitation, he sucked it between his greedy lips.

"Oh, God," she groaned as she started to push her hips toward him, getting herself as close to that dexterous tongue as she could. She gripped his hair and tightened her leg over his shoulder, trying to pull him in closer to her.

That was when she felt a finger move up and slip through her juices, slowly pushing into her needy body. Crying out at the top of her lungs, Rachel let her head fall back as he fucked her with one hand and sucked her to the most spectacular climax she had ever had.

As her orgasm hit, like a wave crashing down upon her, she gave him what he had asked for. She screamed his name like her life depended on it.

When she opened her eyes, he promised, "Now, it's my turn."

CHAPTER 8

Rachel gazed down at the man who had her thigh propped up on his large shoulder. His face was tilted up to her, and the expression in his eyes told her things were about to get a whole lot more intense in a matter of seconds.

His decadent mouth was glistening from where he had just had his lips. As a smug smirk—which were the only words Rachel could think to call it—curled his lips, she almost lost her balance.

She could feel his right finger drawing lazy circles up the outside of her left thigh that was still draped over him, and just like he had promised, he had not used more than one hand. The other remained in a fist by his thigh. When he reached the edge of her lace panties, he ran the tip of his finger under it, and with a swift and concise move, he snapped the material in two. Feeling her breath catch, she tried to hold back a moan as he dragged them from her overly sensitive body, leaving her bare from the waist down. He dangled the material out to the side before dropping them onto the rug he was standing on.

Releasing her hold on his hair, Rachel moved to reclaim her leg, and he let it go reluctantly. When she finally had her feet steady under her, he held up both hands and moved quickly, grabbing her hips and tugging her forward. She stumbled a little and reached out to grip his shoulders to balance herself.

"I kept both promises. Time to renegotiate," he told her, sliding both palms around to cup her bare ass. "Hang on," he instructed.

Gripping her tightly, he took a step back and lifted her from the trunk.

Rachel let out a soft gasp as she was hauled against him, her body flush against his. He lowered her down his body, her heated skin rubbing all along the material of his clothes. When her aching mound slid against his hard cock, she took a moment to push against it, squirming like a cat in heat.

"Stop it," he admonished as he gripped the tops of her arms.

Looking up at him, Rachel found herself complying.

Amazing, she thought as she stared into calm, steady eyes that immobilized her. *This is what I have been looking for.*

It was what her body had been craving all those years since *him*.

She wasn't the Super Domme that Shelly had drunkenly labeled her. She just hadn't wanted to end up on the wrong end of a man who wanted to control her by using his fists ever again.

This man though—this man who was watching her like a hawk—had kept his word. He had done everything she had asked, and he was still waiting on her to make some kind of move to show him she was on board.

Slowly, she licked her lips as she locked eyes with Cole.

Cole released her arms, took a step back, and then walked around her. He was impressed when she didn't turn her head to follow his movements. In fact, he was pretty much impressed with everything she had done, including her ability to still be standing and breathing after the orgasm he had just given her.

He was so unbelievably hard right now that he had to take this moment to calm the hell down. She was standing on his cream rug in her black heels, stockings, and corset with no panties in sight, and she looked damn inspiring.

When he was standing behind her, he stepped forward and gripped the ends of the bow tied at the sway of her back on her corset.

"So, with the original agreement up for discussion, I would like to petition to now use both of my hands. Come on, Rachel, you know you want me to, so just say the word."

He tugged the laces free as he worked his way up the back of her top. When she glanced over her shoulder, Cole made sure his eyes met with hers.

"Do I get to make a demand of my own?"

Cole arched a brow. "Well, that's not usually how I work, but I'm feeling generous tonight."

"Oh, how kind of you," she muttered.

When he finally reached the top of the corset, he separated and removed it before dropping it onto the trunk. He fingered the top of the tattoo at the base of her neck and stroked his way over the repeated Chinese symbols down her spine. He was familiar with the characters, and he read each mark as his finger passed over it. *Pride, Strength, Hope, Love.* They repeated down her back, like a mantra. He also noticed a verse in script along her rib cage, but he couldn't make out the words from where he was currently standing.

"I'm not being kind, Rachel. I just figured the more lenient I am tonight, the more likely you will stay." Leaning forward, he pressed a kiss to her right shoulder. "You know what I want—both hands, your free will, and you with me for a week. Can I have that?"

His tongue came out to flirt with her skin. He dragged it seductively along her shoulder to her neck while still stroking his finger up and down her spine. "Will you give me that? Will you swallow your pride, show me your strength, and find the hope that this person took away from you?"

Her spine stiffened under his fingers. "With you?"

"Maybe, but for now, all I'm asking is that you let me prove to you that not all men are like him, that *I* am not like him." Cole took a deep breath just behind her right ear. "Turn around."

She held her head high and proud as she turned to look directly at him, letting him know she didn't care in the least that she was standing before him completely naked, save for her heels, stockings, and the black ribbon around her neck.

Cole made sure to keep his eyes on hers even though his whole body was screaming at him to look down. *Look down and see the rest of what you have uncovered.*

"My final negotiation is this: You with me every night this week and every morning when I wake up. I get to touch you with *all* of my body, no restrictions."

He saw her sway a little, and he wondered if she even realized she did it. As her eyes dilated, it was obvious how turned on she was, and the thought of being with him in that way was pressing a button she didn't even seem to recognize.

"What do I get?" she finally asked.

Cole wrapped an arm around her waist so fast that she didn't even see it coming. Tugging her body forward toward his, he made sure to press every hard inch of himself up against her as he leaned her slightly back and loomed down over her. "You get ten seconds to ask for two things, and then you get me."

RACHEL FELT her pussy clench as she stared into eyes that had flashed to fire. He was incredible as he hovered over her. She could tell he was wound tight because his cock was pulsating against her body, like a second heartbeat.

Everything he'd said and done to her had been designed to drive her out of her mind, and it had worked. As she stood there, wrapped in his strong arms, she found it difficult to think, let alone think of two things to ask for.

"So, what will it be, Rachel?"

Rachel squirmed against his clothing, enjoying the feel of her flesh rubbing against the material. Finally, she came up with something she wanted more than anything at this moment. "I want you to take off your shirt and pants."

She watched as an expression close to triumph crossed Cole's features.

Ever the lawyer, he clarified, "So, that's a yes then?"

Rachel nodded. "I said yes before, but to be crystal clear now, yes, I accept."

"Done," he agreed, sealing her fate. Releasing his hold around her waist, he told her, "Go and lie down on my bed. I'll be right there."

Rachel took a deep breath and went to move past him, but then his hand shot out to grip her arm. Glancing down, she saw a glimpse of writing on his forearm before he drew her attention back to his face.

"Leave on your stockings. I want to take them off."

Stepping around him, she made her way over to the large bed and crawled up onto the cream duvet. As she went to lie in the center, she removed the tie from her hair and fluffed it out around her.

Turning on her knees, she noticed he hadn't moved at all. His back facing her, he was still standing at the foot of the bed where she had left him. Placing a pillow behind her head, she tried to remind herself to breathe as she reclined, but somehow, the message was not getting to her brain. Her heart started to beat erratically as she watched his large shoulders shifting slightly.

What the hell is he waiting for?

Her question was answered almost as soon as she thought it. Cole shrugged and let his black shirt fall down off his back and arms, revealing one of the most elaborate tattoos Rachel had ever seen. In the center of his shoulder blades was a circular but jagged pattern with intricate details. From where she was lying, Rachel couldn't quite make out what exactly it was, but she thought it looked like several pitchforks or tridents. They were all joined in the center by what looked like a cog, and woven around it was what she thought could be rope.

Now, that has to tell a story of some sort. Rachel found herself anxious to hear it. *Holy shit, this guy is one surprise after another,* she thought, squeezing her thighs together.

He seemed to be cracking his neck while he stretched it from side to side, and Rachel kept her eyes fixed on him as he dropped the shirt onto the trunk. She really wanted a closer look at his ink, but she didn't dare move. Quite honestly, she didn't think she could if she wanted to.

Once again, she caught a flash of the writing on his arm. It looked like it was in another language, and she was dying to ask him what it said. It was probably something stuffy, like *I know everything, just ask me*. At that thought, Rachel let out a small giggle.

He looked over his shoulder, and as soon as their eyes locked, her mirth disappeared, complete and utter lust replacing it. He let his eyes finally trail down over her breasts, taut stomach, and navel ring until she felt it land between her thighs, which were currently squeezed tight together.

Raising his eyes back to hers, he turned fully, and she caught a glimpse of another bold black ink design on the right side of his ribs.

She couldn't tell what it was, but as he started to unbuckle his belt, she didn't think much beyond that.

"Why are your legs squeezed so tightly together? It's going to be difficult for me to get between them if you have them shut like a vise."

Of their own volition, Rachel's thighs parted until she knew he was getting a perfect view of her piercing and the moisture made evident from her desire.

"Hmm, that's much better. Whenever you are waiting for me, always wait as though I'm above you and about to slide inside you. Always be ready for me."

Rachel felt her breath catch in her throat, and she realized then that she didn't stand a chance in hell of resisting all that was Cole.

RACHEL WAS LOOKING at him like she was going to come just from seeing him undress. He liked that, but he had other plans in mind, and just in case she had any ideas, he made himself perfectly clear.

"For the next week, you don't touch yourself unless I ask you to. Your orgasms, keep them all for me." He pulled the belt from its loops, and when she didn't respond, he pushed. "Got that?"

She nodded, seemingly at a loss for words, as he toed off his shoes and began undoing his pants. Cole finally pushed them off his body, revealing a pair of black Calvin Klein boxers. Meticulous as ever, he bent down to pick up the pants, and then he placed them on the trunk.

Removing his socks, he threw them on top of the pile before walking around to the side of the bed. Pressing one knee down on the mattress, he climbed up onto it, moving to the foot of the plush bedspread. When he got to her feet, he kneeled between her ankles and looked up her body.

Fucking hell, her breasts are perfection, he thought as he continued raising his eyes until blue met hazel. Trying to stay on track, he chose not to comment.

"Give me your left foot," he demanded.

She raised her foot to him, and he placed it against his shoulder. He noticed she couldn't tear her eyes from his as he reached forward and rolled the stocking down her thigh, over her knee, and off her calf and ankle. He tossed the silk behind him as he placed her foot back down on the bed. He didn't even have to request the second foot. Rachel automatically raised it, and he repeated the move. When he was done, she was completely naked, except for that pretty ribbon around her neck.

Through a choppy breath, she asked, "What about you? You didn't meet my requirements."

He raised his right arm to push his fingers through his hair. "Yes, I did."

Rachel seemed to think about that, but she couldn't stop herself from arguing. "No, you didn't."

Ahh, brave and daring. That will get her into trouble every time.

RACHEL SHOOK HER HEAD, thinking back to their conversation. *I asked him to remove his shirt and—*

Her thought was interrupted as two large hands suddenly gripped her ankles, hauling her down the mattress. Her eyes automatically focused on the large frame now moving down over her. Fitting his hips in tight against hers, Cole pushed hard as he placed both palms on each side of her head.

"You asked me to remove my shirt and pants," he reminded her.

Rachel was trying to remember how to string a sentence together with so much of him around and over her. All she could manage to say was, "You cheated."

The feral smile he gave her sent a thrill directly to her clit as he rocked his hips against her naked flesh.

"I never cheat, Rachel, but I do pay attention to the details."

Raising her hands, she gripped his biceps as he continued to rock his hard-on against her.

"So, this is it?"

Cole leaned his head down to her ear and bit the lobe. "Why so impatient? Isn't the wait half the fun? Just think how good it will be when I'm finally deep, deep inside you."

Rachel raised her hips up, chasing every thrust of his. "So, you're a tease then?"

Her eyes zoomed in on the flexing muscles and veins popping out along his biceps as Cole pushed himself up over her. Beneath his tamed and polished exterior, Cole was a fucking animal, and she wanted to be devoured by him.

"I'm not teasing you *yet*. You've come twice. I haven't come at all. I'm merely giving you incentive to stay the full week."

Rachel raised her thighs to each side of him and squeezed his hips tightly. Pulling herself up against him, she rubbed her piercing against his cotton-covered cock as she parted her mouth. All her efforts were an attempt to alleviate the building pressure between her thighs.

"It's not going to work," he informed her as she continued to rub herself all over him. "And, if you come before I do, I'm not going to fuck you tomorrow either."

Immediately, Rachel stopped.

"Ahh, that got your attention."

As she released her thighs from around his waist, she stretched them out beside his. "You said it was your turn. If not this, then what?"

"It's my turn to come." Lowering his mouth to hers, he softly promised, "And I'm going to mark what's mine."

Rachel's eyes widened as she watched him move his right hand down her body until she felt it between her thighs.

"And what's mine, Rachel?"

She was about to tell him when his fingers zeroed in on her piercing, and instead, she just moaned.

"THAT'S RIGHT. This. *This* is mine." Cole ran his fingers between the two little studs. *This is so fucking sexy.* "Look at me," he demanded as her eyes started to close. "You keep your eyes on mine."

Moving his hand off her body, he pulled down his boxers over his ass and thighs, and then he moved to thrust his *finally* naked cock against her bare skin.

With his teeth clenched, he let out a hiss of sheer agonizing pleasure at the feel of her skin against his engorged hot flesh. He felt her tense against him, and he knew the minute she felt his own piece of metal slide against her skin. When she shifted, he could tell she was about to try and look down between them.

"Eyes on mine, Rachel. You can look and touch some other time," he promised gruffly.

He wanted to get inside her so badly that he almost gave up on this insane moment of self-inflicted torture, but the way she was looking at him made him continue. Her eyes were filled with a sense of awe. He didn't know the source of it though. *My body? How she is feeling? Or maybe the way I'm making her feel?* In any case, the force of her approval drove him to continue.

"Hands above your head."

Completely in the moment, she showed no hesitation as she reached back over her head and clasped her hands together. As he let his eyes finally drop to her beautiful breasts, he promised himself that they, along with her navel ring calling out to him, were next on the list. Right now though, he needed release, and he needed it now.

Reaching up to where her hands were tightly clenched together, his right hand circled her small wrists as his left palm ran down her side to her hip. He slid his left hand under her ass and pressed her hips up to meet his.

Lowering his forehead to the pillow beside her, he asked, "Do you remember when you were young and inexperienced and holding hands was a thrill? That moment when your date would drive you home and maybe start to kiss you, touch you?"

Rachel groaned and lifted her hips, but he made sure to keep his just out of reach.

"I do. God, I wanted to rub my cock against everything I could find back then, just to make it feel good. That's what I want to do right now. I want to take you back to before someone hurt you. I want to pretend we're in the backseat of a car, and I want us to rub up against each other until it's so fucking good that we just have to come."

With that, he started to rock his hips against hers. While he sucked her earlobe between his lips, she whimpered as her legs spread farther apart, and she arched up against him. He could feel her juices coating his cock as he slid it back and forth, generating an intimate hot, wet body rub.

"Cole," she cried out.

She strained against his grip, but he held her wrists tightly as he slid his body against hers. He could feel her hard nipples against his as his piercings abraded them, adding a delicious new thrill to the full body rub, and he could feel her navel ring against his abs. Every single move they made together created a friction that was burning him up to the point of maximum heat.

Finally, he looked down at her to see her blue eyes were watching him closely. Her mouth parted as he thrust against her.

"Please," she requested on a breathy sigh.

"This is my turn, remember? *You* have to wait for *me*," he reminded as he felt his body tightening from her plea.

"Cole, please," she begged again.

And that was all it took.

He closed his eyes, grinding hard against her. As he replayed her voice seeking permission, he felt his climax hit him hard, making his body tense and his spine tingle. He threw his head back and groaned as he came all over her mound and abdomen. When he opened his eyes, he saw two mesmerized blue orbs looking back at him.

Reaching down between them, he ran his fingers over her needy flesh, lubricating them with their juices, as he played with her hood piercing. When he slipped his fingers inside her, she arched her back beneath him, and he lowered his mouth, finally taking one of her nipples between his lips. She thrust her hips against his hand, and within seconds, she came with a loud cry as her body gripped his fingers tight.

Leaning down over her, he bit her bottom lip. "Who does this belong to for the next week?"

Without any hesitation, Rachel replied on a sigh, "You."

RACHEL AWOKE with a start as her dreams finally caught up to her. Sitting up quickly, she looked around and realized she was not in her own bed.

What the—

Cole. I'm at Cole's.

She was lying between silk sheets, and she had the most comfortable pillow under her head. Looking around the luxurious room, she noticed it was empty. The sun was peeking through the closed heavy navy curtains, and as she looked at the black alarm clock on the side table, she noticed it was six thirty in the morning.

Yawning, she stretched her arms out over her head and thought back to last night.

Shit. Now, that was an experience.

Cole Madison sure hadn't been a disappointment in any way, and he still hadn't even...well, taken her. No, the stubborn man had given her three mind-blowing orgasms if she included the club, and then dry humped her to one of his own.

Is it really dry humping when things got so wet and sticky? Ahh, now, there is an important question, she thought with a small laugh.

She wasn't complaining. The sheer eroticism of that act with the way he had been staring down at her had elevated the whole you-scratch-my-itch-and-I'll-scratch-yours to exceptional proportions.

And that reminded Rachel. *Where the hell is he?*

She pushed back the covers, swung her legs over the edge, and got out of the king-size bed. She was halfway to the bathroom when the bedroom door opened, and the man in question strode in. Already dressed for the day, he was immaculately put together in black tailored pants and a pressed white shirt. His hair and stubble were all ideally groomed, and around his neck was a bright red tie knotted to perfection.

His eyes zeroed in on her, and she was sure, any moment now, her brain would provide her with the ability to move. However, as it was, she was a prisoner to her fickle mind as he made his way toward her.

As he got closer, Rachel tried to remind herself that he hadn't done one thing last night to hurt or scare her, but that didn't stop her from backing up until her naked backside hit the wall. He continued until he was only inches away from her. In the way he seemed to like, he placed both hands on each side of her head.

"Good morning."

Rachel tilted her head back to meet his gaze full-on. "Morning."

"It's not good for you?"

Trying for nonchalance, she shrugged. "Semantics."

"Semantics, I care about, so I'll ask you again. Is it a good morning?"

Deciding to go for honesty since she was standing there butt-ass naked, she nodded. "One of the best in a long time."

"I'm pleased to hear it," he admitted as he stepped back. "So, what time should I expect you tonight?"

Rachel quickly went over everything she had to do, but she found it was difficult to concentrate while she was so...*jeez, naked.*

"Uh, would you mind if we have this conversation after I'm dressed?"

"Yes, I do mind. I actually prefer you naked."

Rachel scoffed, "Like that's a huge surprise."

"So? What time?" he pushed as though she hadn't even asked a question.

"Well, I only work at the flower shop today until four. Exquisite is closed on Mondays, but I do need to call Mason and tell him I won't be able to make dinner." Thinking about that for a moment, she winced at the twenty questions she knew she would get. "Actually, maybe I'll call Josh."

"Why Josh?" Cole immediately questioned.

Rachel warily lifted her gaze to him. He seemed to notice her reaction because he rephrased the question.

"I was just curious why you would call him. I didn't realize you were that close."

Rachel nodded. "He's like a brother to me." She then raised her chin. Challenging him, she asked, "Is that going to be a problem? Because if it is, we might as well forget this whole thing right now."

Cole moved away and walked over to the clothes valet. He lifted his wallet and slid it into his back pocket. He turned and walked back to her, holding out his phone. "No problem. Why don't you give him a call?"

Rachel took the phone and looked him in the eye. "I feel weird calling him with no clothes on."

Cole gave her a look, conveying to her that her lack of clothing was the least of her worries, as he dropped down on his knees before her. "Then, you're going to feel really weird with what I have planned. Call him, Rachel."

~

LOOKING up at her from where he was kneeling, Cole wondered what the fuck was the matter with him. He needed to get out the door and to the office. But when he had walked into his room to say good-bye, he had seen her standing there, naked, except for the little black ribbon, and his cock had different ideas.

He needed one more taste.

He heard her dial the number, and as she waited, resting up against the wall, she glared down at him. He reached up and flicked the little hood piercing he was now fascinated with. He knew he was a perverted fuck, but as the phone must have connected, he couldn't help the grin that pulled at his mouth when she realized what just happened.

~

RACHEL STARED down at the man at her feet. He was such a contrast, kneeling there in his perfectly tailored suit, and she had to admit the sight completely turned her on. She was so lost in her thoughts that she hadn't realized what the sneaky jerk had done until the call connected and Josh's voice came over the line.

"Cole? Really? You're calling me at six thirty in the morning? Man, you need to get a life."

Fuming, Rachel pulled Cole's phone away from her ear and aimed furious eyes down at the man who was now blowing a warm breath between her thighs. Reaching down, she gripped his hair and tugged his head away from her body. Unrepentant, he grinned at her and raised a questioning brow as if to say, *What do you want me to do about it?*

Pulling the phone up to look at it, Rachel quickly hit the end button. She was about to toss it on the bed when it rang like a fire alarm in her hand. Cole chuckled as she glared at him.

Against her flesh, he whispered, "I dare you."

"I don't care. If I answer this, it is going to cause mass chaos."

"And do you really want *me* to answer it?" he asked her calmly.

Good point. There was no telling what he would say. *Nope.* It could go straight to voice mail. She hit the off button and threw it on the bed.

Cole kissed her hard between her legs. Then, rising to his feet, he gave her a kiss that almost blew her mind.

Who knew the suit would have such a dirty side?

"You need to tell them, so they don't worry."

"I will."

"Where's your phone?" he questioned.

"It's in my bag by the front door."

Cole nodded once and gave her another quick kiss. "Wait here."

As he left the room, Rachel was shallow enough to take a moment and think he looked just as good leaving as he did coming. *Literally*. So, she stood with her back and ass against the wall until he walked back in. He handed her the phone and waited patiently for her to dial the number.

Bossy man.

When the phone connected, Josh answered for the second time.

"Rachel? Jesus, what's with everyone this morning?"

She laughed at the grumble in his voice. Even as a teenager, he had never been a terrific morning person.

"Sorry to wake you, Josh."

"You didn't. Someone else did."

Her eyes flew to the larger-than-life presence standing in front of her with his arms crossed.

"So, um...I'm not going to be able to come to dinner tonight, and I was wondering if you could let Mase know."

There was a pause. As she stood there naked, she felt as though he could see her through the phone, and her guilt made her think he was about to call her out.

"So, why not tell Mason yourself?" he asked, his voice groggy.

"Well, um...that's a great question," she hedged.

She locked eyes with Cole's. Rolling his eyes, he reached out and grabbed the phone from her. Rachel squeaked as she slapped at his hand and tried to get it back. In hindsight, she realized she must have looked extremely ridiculous, but that didn't bother her one bit. What bothered her was the fact that Cole was about to—

Yep, too late.

"JOSHUA?" Cole waited for his friend and business associate's brain to catch up.

"Cole?"

"Yes. Rachel is here with me."

He waited for one, two, three seconds, and that was when the question came.

"What the hell is she doing with you at six thirty?" Josh paused. "Is she in jail?"

Cole chuckled. "No, she is not in jail. Although, considering the way she is currently glaring at me, I think she wants to murder me."

"Hang on, hang on. Rachel is *there*...with *you*?"

"This is her phone."

"Madison, what are you doing?" his friend finally demanded.

"Now, if I told you the answer to that, *you'd* likely want to kill me, too. Anyway, be a good friend, would you? Tell her brother something to get her out of tonight."

"Like what? That you're fucking his sister?"

"Careful," Cole warned. He looked at the woman who had given up the fight for her phone as she was now standing naked and vulnerable in front of him. "You wouldn't want to say something you would regret. Just know that she's here with me, and she's safe."

"Cole," Josh growled his own warning through the phone.

"What?" Cole barked back at Josh. He felt like a possessive dog, and he knew Josh was feeling it, too, but they each had different reasons.

"Don't hurt her."

Cole let his eyes run over her once more. "I don't plan to."

And with that, he ended the call.

CHAPTER 9

Three hours had passed since Cole had bundled her up and sent her home in a taxi. Rachel now found herself staring down at Tulip who was in a snit over not being fed on time.

"You do know that before I let you in here, you slept outside, right?" Rachel asked the obnoxious animal as she stepped over Tulip.

Heading into the small office at the back of the flower store, Tulip followed and then jumped up on the worn desk with an irritating meow, letting Rachel know that she didn't really care about all of that.

"I know, I know. I'm your human can opener."

Reaching up to the top shelf of the cabinet pushed against the wall, Rachel grabbed a can of Fancy Feast. She was about to open the can and serve the furball when the bells above the door sounded.

Looking down at the meowing noise machine, she scratched the cat's head. "Hold that thought."

Making her way out of the office and down the small hallway, she felt a twinge of annoyance skate up her spine at the sight of Mason standing in the store with his back facing her.

Of course, Josh told him. Traitor.

"Good morning, brother. You're a long way from home. How are you?"

Mason turned to face her with a frown. Wearing jeans and a black sweater with a blue scarf wrapped around his neck, he stood there and stared at her like he was trying to work something out. "I'm good, Rach. How are you?"

Rachel glanced down at herself to make sure her appearance matched her wellbeing, and then she looked back to the brother she loved more than anyone in the world. "I'm fit as a fiddle," she told him as she made her way around the counter.

She was determined to not make this easy for him. If Mason wanted to know something, then he could be the one to bring it up. *Ha. Good luck making that smooth transition.*

"Yeah, so I see. That dress is cute."

Leaning back against the counter, Rachel crossed one leg over the other as she clasped her hands in front of her. *Really, Mase? My dress? Come on. Oh well, two can play at this game.*

"Really? You think so? It's a '50s bebop dress. I made it myself. First, I had to sew the bodice, and I couldn't decide if I wanted it as a halter neck or two straps, but obviously, I decided on the two straps. Then, I had to get all this black tulle for the underskirt to give it that kick, and that was such a hassle to sew on. It took me at least—"

"Rachel," Mason finally interrupted.

Raising innocent eyes to his, she batted her lashes as he shook his head.

"You know why I'm here, don't you?" he asked, sounding exasperated.

"I have my suspicions, but if you confirm them and say you heard from Josh this morning, then I can't promise you his safety."

Mason stuffed his hands in his pockets and took a step toward her. "He told me you called him from Cole's house at six thirty this morning. Is that true?"

"Oh my god," Rachel grumbled as she threw up her hands. "You two are worse than gossipy old women, you know that? Overprotective jerks," she muttered.

"We're just worried about you."

"Why? Because I spent the night with someone? Give me a break, Mase. You didn't act like this when Charlie was on the scene."

Mason clenched his jaw and turned away from her. "That's because Charlie was different."

"Really? How? How was he different? I was sleeping with him, too, you know," Rachel threw out.

When Mason turned on her with a pissed-off look on his face, she thought she might have gone over the top just a little bit.

"You slept with him already?" Mason thundered, pulling his hands out of his pockets. He moved back in front of her and gripped her arms. "Do you know anything about this...this Cole guy? From what Josh says, he's pretty shady."

"Shady?" Rachel laughed. "Josh does business with him. I hardly think Josh would use Cole as his lawyer if he didn't trust him."

Mason released her arms and raised his right hand to his eye. He pressed his fingers to his brow, like he was trying to control a twitch that had started there. "Just because Josh trusts him with his money does *not* mean Cole is a good guy. Lena told me you wanted nothing to do with him before. What changed?"

More than a little annoyed at this point, Rachel pushed away from the counter and stalked around behind it. Placing her hands on the surface, she glared at her brother. "So, everyone's discussing my private life now? Did you have a conference call with Shelly and Josh this morning as well?"

"No, Rach, it wasn't like—"

"You know what? I don't care," she said, effectively cutting him off. "I know you love me, Mason. I *know* that, but I need some time to myself."

"Because of him?" her brother questioned, placing his hands on the opposite side of the counter.

"Maybe?" she hedged. "Would that be so bad? You don't even know him."

"Do you?"

Rachel thought about that for a minute before she shrugged. "No, not a whole lot, but I'm starting to. Isn't that how things usually happen?"

Mason pushed back from the counter and ran a hand through his dark hair as he shook his head. "Usually, you get to know someone before you stay the night."

Rachel raised an eyebrow at him before she laughed a little. "*Okay*, Dad."

"You've just seemed so unhappy lately, Rach. I don't want you to do something you'd regret." Mason stepped behind the counter and took her hands in his. "You'd tell me if you needed anything, wouldn't you?"

Rachel decided it was time to at least admit there were things going on with her even if she wasn't a hundred percent sure what they were yet. Squeezing her brother's hands, she looked up into eyes that mirrored her own and reminded her of the father they had both lost. "I just need some time to myself."

Mason's eyes creased on the sides as they focused on her. "I don't understand."

Rachel took a deep breath and blew it out, trying to think of how to word what she wanted to say. "I don't know. Lately, I've been feeling like the fifth wheel, like I don't belong, you know?"

"We've been making you feel like that?" he asked, concern covering his face.

Rachel shook her head and tried to explain. "No...well, not intentionally. Honestly, between you and Lena and Josh and Shelly, I'm just feeling a little bit...lonely."

The expression that crossed her brother's face almost broke her. He looked pained, like someone had ripped out a part of him and told him he couldn't have it back. Pulling her to him, he wrapped his arms around her as she hugged his waist.

"I had no idea you felt like that," he confessed against the top of her head.

"Why would you? I never told you."

Pulling back from her a little, Mason nodded and held her for a moment. "Do you need me to sing?"

Rachel let out a small laugh. "No. No, I don't need you to sing."

"Are you sure? Because I think you do. It always helps." He made a small production of clearing his throat, and then he began to hum before he started to sing, *aww hell the entire chorus of My Girl*, a song that was achingly familiar as he moved them around the flower store.

~

RACHEL RAN through the front door, slamming it behind her. Stupid dance, *she thought as she reached up, tugging the hairpins from the French twist she had pulled her hair into. She knew it wouldn't go the way she had wanted it to. Nothing ever did.*

When Josh had told her he would take her to the winter formal, she had been so excited and, not to mention, a little nervous.

Being sixteen and having a senior take you to a dance was a big deal, but the fact that it was Josh—Rachel thought of him with a sigh—made it that much better.

She had spent hours picking out her dress, and she had finally decided on a light pink strapless one. It was made up of soft silk material that swept down around her knees, and for the first time in her life, Rachel felt like everyone else —pretty and not awkward.

At first, her father had been reluctant to let her go, but knowing that Josh was going to take her, her parents had relented and decided she could attend.

Now, I wish I never would've left the house, *she thought as she ran up the stairs to her bedroom. She pushed through the door, moved over to the bed, and sat down, dropping her face into her hands.* What an idiot. *She kept repeating over and over in her head. She couldn't believe what a giant moron she had been.* How am I ever going to look at Josh? Or Mason? *This was the worst night of her life.*

As she sat there, berating herself, her door pushed open, and Josh poked his head inside.

"Can I come in?"

Rachel quickly wiped her tears, and looking away from the door, she mumbled, "Whatever."

She heard him come into her bedroom and close the door behind him. Her heart started to speed up. Josh Daniels is standing in my bedroom, and we're alone. *How long had she been mooning over him? Yeah, well, that was officially over now since he probably thought she was a major loser.*

"Why'd you run inside, Rach? I would have walked you to the door."

Turning back to face him, Rachel glared up at the boy who held all her attention whenever he was around. "I'm pretty sure you know why, Josh."

He took a step farther into the room and looked around. He looked uncomfortable.

Well, good. So am I, *Rachel thought, feeling her embarrassment all over again.*

"Look, there's nothing to be upset about. We had a nice time, didn't we?" he asked.

Rachel looked down at her hands clasped in her lap. Shaking her head, she felt the tears starting again. He looked so cute, standing there in his suit, with his shaggy brown hair pushed back. It was normal to do what I did, right? *At least, she thought it had been until he had said no and pushed her away.*

"Sure," she murmured, reaching up to wipe another stupid tear off her cheek.

That was when she felt the bed dip beside her. Oh my god, Josh is sitting on my bed. *Sitting as still as she could, she almost jumped out of her skin when he reached over and took her hand in his. Looking over at him, her mouth went dry as he smiled at her with the grin that every girl in school could not resist, including her apparently.*

"You didn't do anything wrong tonight," he reassured.

Rachel tried to look away but found she couldn't.

"It's just...I'm with Lisa, and...well, you're Mason's little sister," he explained.

Looking away to try and hide her shame, Rachel felt like an even bigger fool. When Josh reached out and cupped her chin, turning her face back to him, she was in shock.

"You took me by surprise," he admitted.

Yeah, well, you and me both, pal, *Rachel thought as she tried to pull her face away.*

"Would you hold still?" he asked with a chuckle.

Immediately, Rachel found herself calming down when she did as she was told.

"Have you ever kissed a boy, Rachel?" he asked, his kind brown eyes searching her face.

Rachel felt her heart speed up as she stared at the boy she had known for most of her life.

"No answer?" he pushed.

Rachel couldn't tear her eyes away from his mouth or make her lips move to speak as he leaned in toward her.

"Then, let me give you what you wanted. Let me be your first."

After that, she didn't remember much, except for the feel of Josh's lips against hers. His kiss was so sweet that she felt it all the way down to her toes. He was her first kiss, and it was absolute perfection.

When he pulled back from her, he gave her a huge grin that warmed her heart and made her feel like she was glowing.

"There. Now, you've been kissed."

Rachel sat still on the bed, trying to think of something to say, but for the next few minutes, she was content to just stare at him.

Right around the time things were about to turn from dreamland to the usual awkward world, she turned to the radio to switch songs. "My Girl" by The Temptations started to play through the speakers. It was the song her father had been singing to her for years, and everybody knew it, including Josh. Her father took any opportunity to embarrass her with impromptu serenades at birthdays, bedtime, and when he would dance her around the kitchen.

Josh stood and held out his hand to her. "You ran out on the last dance, so how about dancing with me now?"

Rachel stood and put her hand in his.

He pulled her forward and swayed with her as he sang in her ear, "My girl," while he moved her around the small bedroom. Rachel closed her eyes and dreamed of her future, hoping it would include this boy.

~

I'M GOING to kill Josh and his big mouth, Rachel thought as she stared up at her brother.

"My cat is begging for you to stop," she told Mason with a small grin.

He doesn't need to know Tulip is hungry.

"Oh, is that why she's meowing? I figured she was joining in."

Rachel laughed and pulled away from her brother. "No, she was trying to drown you out." Resting up against the counter with her arms crossed over her chest, she reiterated, "I just need some space. I need to be on my own for a bit. I love you all, but lately, I just need—"

"Space," Mason answered for her. He pushed his hands back into the pockets of his jeans and nodded. "Fair enough, Rach. But the suit? Really?"

Thinking about Cole for a moment, Rachel had a flash of everything beneath the suit. She gave Mason a swift nod. "Guess we'll see. He's not that bad."

"Yeah, he seems like a real barrel of laughs," Mason muttered, moving out from behind the counter. "Okay, I'll leave it alone. For now."

When he got to the door, he reached out and put his palm on the handle, but then he turned, looking back at her. "Leave your phone on, would you?"

Rachel quirked her eyebrow. "Only if you promise not to call me every five minutes."

Mason nodded. "See you tomorrow night?"

"Yep, I'll be there. Oh, Mase?"

"Yeah?"

"Don't worry, okay? It's not you guys. It's me. I'll work this out."

Mason didn't look all that convinced, but he tried for a smile before he opened the door and stepped out into the cold air.

Rachel looked down at Tulip, sitting by her feet, as Tulip looked up at her as if to say, *Uh, hello? You still haven't fed me.* Rachel stepped over the hairy annoyance and made her way to the back.

Feeling calm for the first time in a long while, she decided to really look at her life choices. She was going to take the week to not only be with Cole but to hopefully also be with herself. By the end of the week, maybe she would have some sense of direction and know exactly what it was she wanted out of life.

And if not? Well, at least, I'll have a hell of a time getting to that final conclusion.

~

AT THEIR WEEKLY MONDAY MEETING, Cole sat in the boardroom with the other lawyers of the firm, looking down at his watch. Logan was running through the usual points of interest at work while flirting his way around the table as each attendee discussed the cases he or she had acquired. It wasn't until the room fell silent that Cole realized everyone was staring at him.

"Cole, would *you* like to contribute in any way to your business and the running of it?" Logan questioned, his voice dripping with saccharine sweetness.

Cole sat up in his chair and frowned over at his partner. "Sorry, what was the question?"

Logan, who was usually the easygoing one, narrowed curious eyes on him. "Nothing. Don't you worry your brooding self about it. Okay, everyone, that'll be all. Go and win. Oh, and have fun crushing your opponent, of course."

They all laughed as they filed out of the conference room one at a time, leaving Cole where he was sitting with Logan at the other end of the boardroom table.

"What's up with you today, Madison? You've been a virtual space cadet."

Cole shook his head and pushed up from his chair to stand. He straightened his suit and picked up his file.

"Is it your mom?" Logan asked.

"It's nothing. My mind was just somewhere else."

Logan gave him a shit-eating grin. "Really? I hadn't noticed."

"Logan?"

"Yep?" he replied, still aiming his smug, superior face in Cole's direction.

"Shut up."

"Aww, don't be like that. It just isn't like you to zone out. It's more like me."

"I'm sorry, boss. It won't happen again," Cole told him, making his way over to the door.

Logan got up and followed Cole, clapping him on the shoulder. "I'm just concerned."

Cole glared at the other man. "Bullshit."

From behind black-framed glasses, Logan's blue eyes were laughing at him.

"You're not concerned. You're nosy."

Logan moved away from him, and when he was halfway down the aisle to his office, he chuckled and shouted back, "Well, I'm always here for you when you want to talk, *dear*."

Cole held back what he really wanted to yell in response as he walked back to his own office. As he was about to pass Jane's desk, he stopped and tapped his fingers gently on the cool polished surface.

She looked up at him with a smile. "Is there something you need, Mr. Madison?"

"Yes, actually. For the next week, I would like all my meetings scheduled to end before five. I want to be walking out of the office at 4:59 p.m., and no later. Can you do that?"

Jane frowned, but she assured him, "Of course. Is there anything else?"

Cole thought about it for a minute. "Yes. Any calls that come in late should be directed to Logan. I'll let him know I'm unavailable this week."

"Okay, I'll get the outgoing message switched." She paused for a moment. "Will you still be attending the dinner for the new District Attorney on Thursday night?"

Oh shit, Cole thought with a groan before he had a thought. "Yes, I'll still be there. Please let them know I will have a plus one."

When he saw Jane's mouth twitch, Cole took a moment to tease her. "Is something amusing you, Jane?"

"Not at all, sir."

"I'm glad to hear it. Please hold my calls until I let you know otherwise."

He moved past her and into his office. Closing the door behind him, he walked over to his desk, picked up his cell, and sat down. Twisting his chair around, he looked out the window. He couldn't stop thinking about her. Ever since he had watched the cab pull away from his curb this morning, he had wondered if she would show up tonight. Not knowing was driving him insane.

Usually, he was the one consumed by work, not by a woman with huge blue eyes and multicolored hair. As he tapped his phone against his knee, he considered the possibility of her not returning, and then he found himself devising a plan to get near her again.

Convincing himself he had a good reason to call, he scrolled through his phone, and when he found her number, he hit call. After the second ring, she picked it up, and he felt his mouth pulling into a grin at her greeting.

~

"WELL, well, well, if it isn't Cole Madison." Rachel leaned back against her couch and played with her skirt.

She had closed the store at four and made her way home, wondering when she would next hear from him. When his number had flashed on her phone's screen, she had felt her stomach jump and her thighs squeeze together at the thought of talking to him again.

"So, it would seem," he confirmed.

His low voice sent a delicious thrill of anticipation through her.

"And what can I do for you this afternoon?" she teased, tongue-in-cheek.

"I'd like to see you again. I thought I should let you know."

Rachel had to stop the small giggle that threatened to bubble out of her throat. *Is he ever anything other than formal?* The only time she could recall was when he had removed his clothes, and even then, he had exuded an air of formality, or maybe that was just his authoritative manner.

"Oh? Well, you were so unclear about it all last night, and this morning, I wasn't really sure," she replied sarcastically.

"Rachel?" he questioned in a cautionary tone.

And didn't that just push her buttons. "Yes, Cole?"

"Meet me at six thirty, and I will make sure I am very clear with what I want from you."

Rachel tried not to envision all the scenarios as she quickly asked, "At your place?"

"Yes. And Rachel?"

Swallowing slowly, she managed to respond, "Yes?"

Silence greeted her from the other end, and just when she thought she would scream in frustration, his voice came across the phone with a seductive warning.

"Don't be late."

CHAPTER 10

S*ix thirty in the evening, and I'm right on time,* Rachel thought as she pulled open the door to the lobby of Cole's condo. As she made her way across the dark marble floor, she took a moment to take in her surroundings. *It really is an impressive space.*

A large fireplace and several couches were to the left of her, and in the center of the room was the security desk. Sitting there, a short bald man smiled at her in greeting as she walked toward him.

"You new to the building, miss?"

Rachel shook her head, her hair brushing against her shoulders now that she had removed her coat. "Oh no, I wish. I'm Rachel Langley, and I'm here to see Mr. Madison."

The little man looked down at a list he had in front of him and then smiled back at her.

"Oh, yes. He called down a little bit earlier and told me to let you up."

"Thank you. This place is lovely. So cozy."

"Yeah," he agreed, looking around. "It's not too shabby, is it?"

Rachel let out a small laugh. "No, not at all. It's beautiful. That fireplace is amazing. I could sit by it all day with a good book."

"Well, you are welcome to come and sit by it anytime you like, miss."

Rachel grinned back, enjoying the man's jovial nature. She made her way over to the nearby elevators and reached out to press the button to head up to Cole's condo. As an elevator arrived, she turned back to the security guard. "Well, that's my ride. See you later—"

"Ed, miss. The name is Ed."

Rachel took a step into the elevator and turned around to face him. Pressing number twenty-six, she waved. "Have a good night, Ed," she called out before the doors swooshed shut.

As the elevator made the climb toward her fate, Rachel smoothed her hands down her black-and-white skirt. Suddenly experiencing an attack of nerves, she took a deep breath as she tightened the black satin bow at the side of her waist.

When she reached her destination, she stepped out into the hall and made her way down to the left. When she arrived at Cole's place, she noticed a folded piece of paper taped to the door. Across the front of it, her name was printed.

Ripping the note off the door, she decided that if he'd stood her up, she was going to break into his condo and cut up all his ties. She opened the note and frowned as she read it: *Level 28.*

Heading back to the elevators, she refolded the paper. She waited for an elevator to open and then stepped inside. Looking at the panel, she hit the button for the twenty-eighth floor. As it ascended, her nerves slowly crept up again. *Where the hell is he? And what is on floor twenty-eight?* Trying not to let her imagination get the best of her, she held her breath until the doors opened.

As she stepped out onto the floor, the first thing she was hit with was the smell of chlorine. She spotted a single plastic chair and draped her coat across it before turning to look at the full-length pool in front of her. Taking a hesitant step forward in her silver-buckled black Mary Janes, she looked down to the white concrete floor where she was now standing.

Glancing around, she found the space was completely empty, and then she heard a splash in the water. Moving her eyes back to the pool in front of her, she watched as a man powered with perfect form through the water toward her. His arms sliced through the surface with absolute precision on each stroke, and as he glided closer to her, Rachel could do nothing but stare. She knew she was looking at Cole, but she just didn't know if her heart could handle what she was seeing.

When he reached the end of the pool, he came to a stop and gripped the edge. Taking a deep breath, he reached up his right hand to remove the black goggles protecting his eyes. After tossing them aside, he ran his hand through his hair, making it stick up in wet spikes all over his head. Blinking a couple of times, he finally looked up to see her standing there.

She hadn't moved an inch as she remained frozen, staring at him as he caught his breath. She was about to question her own sanity for not going toward...*well, all of that*. Then, he placed both palms on the edge of the pool and hauled himself up and over the edge.

Oh, thank you God for giving me this moment, Rachel thought, sending up the quick prayer. Her eyes went crazy as she tried to take in every inch of wet skin Cole had just put on display, and there was a whole lot of damn skin.

While his body came into view, the water slid over his strong muscular arms, ran down his powerful chest and rippling abs, and finally, dripped from his tight black swim shorts, sitting extremely low on his hips. As if that sight alone wasn't hard enough to comprehend, throw in his hard nipples that were adorned with silver bars and tattoos that were screaming for her to trace with her tongue, and she was surprised she hadn't started to drool.

When his eyes locked with hers, he took a step toward her, and Rachel decided there was no way she was going anywhere. She wanted a piece of that, and she wanted it now.

As Cole walked over to Rachel, his eyes took her in. She looked like a sexy pinup girl who had strolled directly out of the 1950s. Her hairstyle was parted off to the right and swept softly to the side where curls framed her face perfectly. Her red highlights interspersed throughout kept the style modern. Her dress was black with white musical notes all over it, and a black silk bow wrapped around her waist where the skirt kicked out. She was the very image of the women who had been plastered all over the magazines back in that era.

Cole felt his cock stiffen, and he didn't care one bit that he was pretty much *all* on display. He raised a hand and ran it through his hair again, trying to get himself under control. He really wanted under her skirt.

When he stopped in front of her, he looked down into guileless eyes as she stared up at him.

"Hello, Rachel. I see you got my note."

Her lips parted but nothing came out.

That's just fine with me, Cole thought. He wrapped a wet arm around her waist and pulled her in tight against him. Pressing his body flush against hers, he lowered his head. "You don't mind if I get you a little...wet, do you?"

She gripped his biceps hard as she shook her head without saying a word.

"Good because I *need* you wet for what I have in mind."

Lowering his head, he pressed a kiss to the corner of her mouth, and when she parted her lips, he ran his tongue along her bottom one, teasing her. As her nails bit into his arms, he sucked on her lip and then released it. Finally, he slid his tongue deep inside to rub against hers. As she sighed against his mouth, her eyes closed, and he felt her right palm slide down his arm until it gently landed on his waist.

Angling his head to the side, he closed his eyes and deepened the kiss. He groaned when he felt her tongue chase his back into his mouth. He loved this aggressive side of her that simmered under the surface. As she pushed closer against him, he felt that sneaky right hand of hers smooth around his back to the top of his black swim shorts.

Lifting his mouth from hers, he opened his eyes. "What do you think you're doing?"

Silently, she curled her nails into the top of the elastic and dragged it down until his left ass cheek was bare. She scraped her nails up and over his cool flesh before grabbing him tightly, pulling him as close as she could against herself.

Clenching his jaw, Cole brought up his left palm to her covered breast where he cupped her and squeezed, pushing it up, as he pressed his cock in closer to her. He could feel her breathing coming quicker as she remained completely focused on him. One set of her nails dug into his arm while the other set gripped his ass.

"I want to see," she finally said.

Cole rubbed her breast through the material again as his other arm held her immobile. "You want to see what?"

Blue eyes zeroed in on his mouth as Rachel told him fearlessly, "I want to see your *other* piercing. I want to see what is mine for the week."

~

RACHEL WAS LOSING her mind if she thought she was the one making demands. *But damn, his ass is hard as a rock*, she thought as she gave it another squeeze while she waited for his answer.

His expression right now could only be described as ravenous. He released her and took a step back, watching her intently. Rachel was just about to give up, thinking she would be denied.

Then, he sensuously instructed, "Take off my swim shorts."

Caught up in the sexual energy swirling around them, she took a step forward, and without thinking, she reached out to slip her fingers into the elastic. That was when his hands came out and gripped her wrists. Looking up at him with questioning eyes, she was about to ask what the problem was.

"On your knees," he added.

Feeling thrilled at the order, she lowered herself in front of him, and when she was eye-level with his impressive hard-on, she stroked her finger over the wet material. Making sure she was allowed to do that, she raised her eyes to his, and she almost lost her train of thought from the view above her.

Cole had placed his palms behind his head, and she now had a completely unobstructed view of the tattoo covering his right ribs. It looked like the side profile of a silhouette. Inching upward, her gaze drifted over to the tufts of hair under his arm, which were slightly darker than the hair on his head, and then the writing on each of his arms drew her attention again.

The man is so fucking hot I'm surprised steam isn't coming off him.

Just as the thought entered her head, he looked down with sharp, intelligent eyes, and Rachel found herself moistening from the look he aimed her way.

"Is there a problem?" he inquired.

His tone was so arrogant that Rachel should have found it annoying, but instead, it made her want to hike up her skirt and beg him to take her. Rather than doing that though, she shook her head and rose up on her knees. Slipping her fingers into his swimwear, she pulled it down over his hips and let them fall to the floor where he stepped out of them. That was when she found herself face-to-face with his *very* impressive erection and a bold Prince Albert piercing.

Knowing, feeling, and *seeing* were three totally different experiences, and in this moment, Rachel was paralyzed. The straining hard flesh in front of her was tipped with what looked like a ten-gauge curved stainless steel barbell that was currently glistening from the pool water and a small bead of pre-cum.

Just as she was about to lean forward and flick her tongue over it, she felt a hand cup the back of her head and grip her hair. Cole pulled her head back, so she was looking up at him.

He shook his head at her. "Your request was to see it, and the promise was you could look at it. I believe both have been met."

As his words penetrated her lust-addled brain, she felt him tug gently on her hair.

"Stand up," he instructed.

After getting to her feet, she almost stumbled as he walked her back to the wall where he pushed the button beside her for the elevator. That was when it hit Rachel. *Oh shit. Roles are reversed. I'm completely clothed, and Cole...well, he is one hundred percent gloriously naked.*

As he stood in front of her, pinning her to the wall with his stare, he didn't seem to notice or care at all.

COLE WAS BARELY KEEPING it together as he waited for the elevator to arrive. He was taking a gamble that no one would be in it, but at this stage, he didn't really give a shit.

"Uh, you're naked," Rachel pointed out cautiously as the elevator arrived.

He couldn't help the insolent grin that came across his face as she wriggled out from between him and the solid surface. When she scurried into the empty lift, he sauntered in behind her and pushed the button to his floor. He turned to rest against the back wall and tugged her in front of him.

"Good thing this dress has a full skirt then, wouldn't you say?" He gripped her hips and pulled her back, so her ass was pressed up against his stiff cock. He blew a gentle breath against her ear and smoothed a palm around her to play with the bow at her waist. "What do you have on under this skirt?"

Taking a swift breath, she revealed, "Nothing."

Cole's hand tightened on her waist as his cock flexed. He was dying to get inside her. "Really?"

He watched her silky black hair as she nodded.

"You told me to always act like you are above me and about to slide inside me, so I figured you'd prefer nothing in your way."

She is going to fucking kill me, Cole thought as he felt his chest tighten.

Thank God his condo was only two floors down. When the elevator reached his floor, the doors opened, and he shifted his hand to where the skirt covered her bare mound.

Pressing his palm to it, he promised her, "As soon as we're inside my front door, I am going to lift this skirt, and I am going to fuck you. Before we get there, is there anything I should know?"

He released his hand and urged her forward into the hall. When he realized she hadn't yet replied, he asked, "Rachel? Do I need to get protection?"

She finally glanced back over her shoulder. With eyes as dark as a stormy night, she shook her head. "I'm safe and on birth control."

Watching as her eyes took in his tense body, he pushed off the wall and stepped out of the elevator. He pulled her back against him again.

"Good because I can't wait to feel you hot and tight around my cock. Now, stick close, would you? I don't mind the whole floor seeing my ass, but *this*," he emphasized, pushing himself hard against her skirt-covered ass, "I'd rather keep between us."

~

BREATHE. I have to remember to breathe, Rachel told herself over and over as they made their way down the hall. She could feel Cole's overheated body pressed to every inch of her back, and she was still unable to comprehend that the man was walking down the hall completely naked.

More to the point, I'm missing out on seeing it.

When they got to his door, he reached around her and turned the doorknob. He had obviously left it unlocked while he had been upstairs. As he pushed it open, Rachel's eyes zoomed in on the door, wooden side table, and wall. Suddenly, she found all the oxygen had left her lungs.

Where? Where is he going to take me?

"Three steps forward, eyes front."

His commanding rumble penetrated her thoughts. In heightened anticipation, she licked her lips and made her feet move. Three steps in, she heard the door shut behind her before a large hand immediately grabbed her right forearm and spun her around.

With her breath stuck in her throat, her eyes found Cole's as he yanked her to him. He marched her backward until her ass hit the side table. Reaching around her, he swept his arm across it, and several things—she couldn't have said what they were—clattered to the ground.

His eyes, blistering and possessive, riveted hers as he gripped her hips and hitched her up on the table, pushing his way between her thighs. With a hand around her waist, he pulled her close to him and crushed his mouth down on top of hers.

Parting her lips on a guttural moan, Rachel gripped his shoulders while he continued to press himself directly against her heated core. He squeezed her waist and then trailed his left hand down to her naked calf. He slid it back up over her knee and moved effortlessly under her skirt. His fingers burrowed deeper between her bare upper thighs, urging them further apart.

Raising his hungry mouth away from her, he kept his eyes on hers as he drew her knees wide. Following his lead, Rachel spread her legs without uttering a word. When he took his other arm from around her waist and slid it up her other leg, Rachel leaned back against the wall and let her eyes slide closed in ecstasy.

Pushing the skirt up and out of his way, he slid his large palms around to her naked hips, letting out a low curse. Her eyes flew open as he gripped her tightly and tugged her right to the edge of the table. Clenching his jaw, he removed his hand from her waist to fist his cock. He lined himself up, and with one solid thrust, he finally slid deep inside her.

With a loud moan, Rachel cried out as he wrapped his right arm back around her waist. Gripping her leg in his other hand, he hitched it up and over his naked ass. Not releasing her from his molten gaze, he flexed his hips, and as the force of his thrust pushed into her, Rachel felt the wall behind her. With her skirt rucked up around them, Cole's muscles strained and bunched as he pounded into her.

As her eyes slid closed, Rachel's last thought was that she was losing her mind. Enjoying the ride, she held on for dear life.

~

COLE'S COCK had found heaven, and it never planned to leave.

As Rachel sat, spread wide apart on his foyer side table, he couldn't help the way he went at her like a starving man.

With her skirt up around her waist and those prim little shoes thumping against his ass with every thrust he made, his brain was telling him that this was everything he had ever wanted. As he continued to power into her, he wanted to scream, *Mine, mine. You are fucking mine.*

He could feel her nails digging into his shoulders, and he welcomed the pain as he quickly found himself losing his grip on reality. He moved the hand around her waist to slide in under her skirt. Tightly squeezing her bare ass, Cole lifted her up to get his other hand under her as well. Once he had a firm grasp on both her ass cheeks, he quickly pulled her down onto his cock, and then he stilled, waiting for her to open her eyes.

It didn't take long. The minute she realized he had stopped moving, her eyes snapped open, and he nodded once.

"I just wanted to make sure I had your attention and that we are now clear about me wanting you here."

With that, he crushed his mouth back down on top of hers. He pulled out of her slowly and then tugged her hips forward, sliding back inside. Penetrating her deeper than before, she cried out against his lips while Cole firmly held on to her ass. Her thighs clenched around his hips as she pulled herself forward to meet every thrust. Using his cock in the most delicious way, she got closer and closer to that moment when—

Her eyes flew open, locking with his, as he felt her pussy grip him like a hot silk fist. She screamed his name, and that was all he had been waiting for. Cole steadied his legs and then hammered into her as her fingers came down over his chest, tracing the outline of the wolf tattooed on his pec.

Her sultry eyes came up to meet his, and while his hot cock pounded inside her, the sex bomb arched her brow. Licking her glistening lips, she gave him a smile so full of sex. He almost cried as she reached out and twisted hard on one of his nipple piercings. Clenching her ass, Cole threw his head back and came with a loud shout as he thought to himself, *Who the fuck won that round?*

CHAPTER 11

Rachel stood in front of a glass sliding door that opened out onto a balcony. The night had closed in on downtown Chicago, and lights were twinkling in the distance on the lake.

Cole had told her to make herself at home as he had walked down to his bedroom to put on some clothes. *He probably meant a three-piece suit*, Rachel thought, feeling a mischievous laugh leave her swollen lips. It's not that she was complaining about anything because when that suit came off... *Wow. Just wow.*

The man was a walking contradiction. During the day, he was completely put together, not a single blond hair out of place, but after hours, she was finding that there was a lot more to Cole than she had originally suspected. The tattoos, five in total as far as she was aware, were enough of a shock, but the piercings were what made Rachel's mind spin.

"I brought something more comfortable for you to change into, only if you would like, of course."

His persuasive deep voice broke through the silence. He sounded closer to her than she had expected. Rachel steeled herself for what she would find as she looked over her shoulder. In the middle of his living room, he was standing behind her, dressed in a simple white cotton tee and an expensive pair of jeans that fit his long, lean legs perfectly.

Damn it. Even in jeans, the man has me thinking dirty, salacious thoughts.

Her eyes moved to his arm extended out to her, and she saw he was holding a white shirt. Walking toward him, Rachel let her tongue come out to touch her abused top lip. When she was standing directly in front of his raised arm, she fingered the cool material. Bringing her eyes back to his, she questioned, "*Just* a shirt?"

As she took it from him, he moved to stand behind her. She felt his hand softly graze her back as he swept her hair over her shoulder. Slipping his fingers into the top of her dress, he methodically undid the hook-and-eye clasp and unzipped her zipper.

"It's not *just* a shirt. It's *my* shirt," he admitted against the base of her neck with a soft kiss. He lifted the left strap off her shoulder and drew it down over her arm. Running one of his fingers down her spine, he continued, "I want you to wear something that is mine."

Rachel looked over her now bare shoulder and met his covetous gaze. "Is that so?"

His lips tugged into his version of a grin as he leaned forward and kissed her. "It is."

Facing forward, Rachel reached up to remove her other strap and slid it down, letting the dress fall over her waist to pool at her feet. She was about to put on the shirt when Cole stepped around in front of her.

He fingered the front clasp of the only remaining scrap of lace on her. Raising his eyes to hers, he deftly unsnapped the bra and parted it. He permitted himself to look down at her as he discarded the bra on the ground.

"Next time, I want you like this—completely naked."

As she stood naked in his house, she didn't know where her courage came from, but she couldn't help herself from pointing out, "Well, if you hadn't been so impatient—"

"On the contrary, I've shown immense patience." He flicked her silver navel ring. "I've been waiting to get you here for months."

Rachel parted her lips with a sigh. "I can just walk around your place naked if you like."

"No, I can't have that, or I'll never actually learn anything about you. I'll just end up keeping *your* mouth busy and *my* hands full. So, for now, wear my shirt."

Cole chuckled as he turned and headed over toward the kitchen. Rachel kicked off her shoes and slipped the shirt on her arms. She buttoned it down the center, and as she bent over to pick up her dress, she angled her body to give him a good look at her bare ass beneath the shirt.

"Behave yourself, Rachel," he told her from behind the counter where he had placed two tumblers.

Straightening, she draped the dress over the black leather couch and made her way around it and over to him. Standing on the opposite side of the kitchen island, she took a moment to really look at him. He seemed so different, standing there in his kitchen. He was almost approachable, almost easygoing.

"What are you thinking about?" he asked, his voice calm but inquisitive. Turning to a cabinet, he pulled out a bottle of liquor.

When he was facing her again, she noticed it was Macallan.

"I was just thinking how different you seem here."

As he uncorked the bottle, he placed it on the granite counter. "How? How do I seem different?"

Rachel shrugged as she suddenly lost her nerve.

"No, don't do that," he admonished, pouring himself a glass. "Would you like one?"

Shaking her head, she declined. She needed all her wits about her when dealing with him. "Don't do what?"

After putting the bottle away, he leaned up against the far counter, crossing his legs, as he stared her down. "Don't cop out."

"I'm not."

"Yes, you are. You made a statement. Now, back it up."

Rachel pursed her lips at him. "You're really aggravating sometimes."

"I know. It's one of my most endearing qualities."

Through an indignant snort, Rachel demanded to know, "Who told you that? Your mother?"

With his glass halfway to his mouth, he paused and narrowed his eyes at her over the rim. In a voice that seemed removed, he said, "No, not my mother." He downed the rest of the scotch in one gulp, pushed off the counter, and placed the tumbler down. Stepping over to the island where she was standing, he asked her again, "How do I seem different?"

Rachel crossed her legs at the no-nonsense tone. "Well, I *was* going to say that you seem more approachable."

~

Cole knew he wasn't doing a good job at hiding his emotions. Her mention of his mother had made him think about how useless he was when it came to *that* whole situation, and that thought completely pissed him off.

Trying to forget about something in which he had no control over, he instead decided to push for the power where he knew he could find it. "You were going to? But now, you've changed your mind. Why?"

Letting out an exasperated breath that shifted her black hair against the side of her face, she gave him a look that should have been captioned, *Really?*

"Jeez, Cole. What is this? Twenty questions?"

"No, it was three. Are you going to answer them?"

"Are you going to loosen up?"

Raising his right hand to his chin, he rubbed it. "Now, that's something I have never quite gotten the hang of or saw the need for."

"What? Loosening up?"

Cole walked around the island and stopped beside her. "Answer me, and I'll answer you."

Gritting her teeth, she turned to him and raised her hands in defeat. "Fine. You win. I was just going to say that you appeared more approachable here, more easygoing in your kitchen.

"But not now?"

"No. Now, you're all up in my face, being your usual overbearing and intimidating self."

Cole felt his mouth twitch as he held back a full-on laugh. *Damn, I like this woman.* "You think I'm intimidating? That's kind of harsh."

She rolled her eyes as her feet shifted on the hardwood. "I hardly think I've hurt your feelings."

"You're right. You haven't. I'm choosing to take it as a compliment." Reaching forward, he took her hand, bringing her closer to him. "I think you're intriguing, and I want to know everything about you."

Her eyes lowered as she seemed to slowly hide and disappear inside herself. "There's not that much to know."

Cole wondered about what was really going on in her head. "I disagree. Look at me."

As she did, he pulled her left hand up to his chest.

"The minute I saw you, I wanted you. I *still* ache for you, and I had you a little less than fifteen minutes ago. Everything about you makes me want to know more," he confessed as he stroked her hair with his free hand. "This hair is so sleek yet so fucking eye-catching. Why do you do it? And what about this tattoo you have printed down your spine like some kind of self-religion? Plus, the two shiny secrets, which are hidden away for a certain someone to find." Lowering his head, he pressed a soft kiss against her ear. "For *me* to find. Take note, Rachel. I'm officially intrigued, and my attention is usually very hard to acquire."

~

RACHEL TURNED her head and moved a fraction closer, unable to stop herself from pressing her lips up against his. He didn't seem to mind though as he released her hand and wrapped both arms around her waist, pulling her in tight against him. Parting her lips, she shivered as he slid his tongue in against hers, stroking the roof of her mouth.

This man is going to unravel me. She could feel it in her blood, and she knew it somewhere in her brain. Rachel was aware that she should be working out how to build a wall around herself, but as his hands drifted down, sneaking under the shirt to stroke her bare ass, she couldn't find the fortitude to start.

Pulling his head back, his piercing hazel eyes met hers. "Take the week off," he suggested.

"What?" She laughed. She couldn't quite believe what had come from the mouth of the man who never stopped working.

"The week—can you take it off?"

Gripping his arms, Rachel shook her head. "Not really. I have to work at Precious Petals in the morning and Exquisite at night."

"How late?"

Rachel winced. "Usually, I get home around one."

"Shit," he cursed as he released his hold of her. "Well, that doesn't work at all."

"I'm sorry, but I need money to pay for bills, like my rent," Rachel quipped sarcastically.

Pushing a hand up through his hair, Cole nodded absentmindedly. "I know, I know. I'm just trying to work out how we can make this happen. Your schedule is a disaster."

"Yeah? Well, your ability to try and understand is poorly lacking as well," she mumbled.

Cole seemingly ignored her as he started to pace back and forth.

Rachel couldn't help herself as she asked, "Is this your thinking dance?"

He stopped and looked over to her. "Huh?"

She pointed to his bare feet as her fingers followed the trail of his motions. "The pacing? Do you do that whenever you are thinking?"

Almost as though he hadn't realized he was doing it, he frowned. "Huh. I suppose so. I've never really thought about it. Now, you say you start over at Exquisite when?"

"I didn't, but I start at six."

"Right. Well, I'll be there at six thirty."

Rachel laughed incredulously. "What? Why?"

When she realized he wasn't laughing with her, she noticed he was instead looking at her very calmly as though he had come to some master plan.

Rachel shook her head. "No."

As he walked back toward her, she started to shake her head more furiously.

"No, Cole. You are *not* going to come and eat at the restaurant every night. That's insane."

Stopping before her, he did something she had never seen him do before. He shrugged, and she thought it was completely out of character for him.

"I don't care. It's the best plan there is," he said.

"No, it's *not*," Rachel stressed. "It's the worst plan there is."

"Why?"

"Why?" she repeated back to him.

"Am I talking in another language?" he questioned, crossing his arms.

Rachel glared up at him. "Ugh, you are so frustrating. Why? Because Mason will be there, which means Lena is there, and that's usually followed by Shelly and Josh being there, too."

"Ahh, yes, the two ladies from the club. That'll be fun to explain."

"There will be no explaining. This has only been something for two nights. Why are you determined to tell everyone about this? First, Josh, and now, you want to just turn up at the restaurant."

"Why are you trying so hard to keep it a secret?" he countered.

"I'm not."

"Yes, you are. What's wrong, Rachel? Do you think I'll embarrass you?"

"No," she denied as she thought, *I'm more concerned with how* I *will react to* you *than anything you will do.*

"Then, what is the problem?"

"Nothing," Rachel fumed as she stalked past him over to the couch.

Grabbing her dress, she was about to storm into the bathroom and change when his voice cut through the air, halting her as effectively as his hand.

"Where do you think you are going?"

Looking at him over her shoulder, she hated the fact that he looked so damn good standing there.

"I'm leaving. You're nuts."

"No, I'm not," he told her calmly as he undid the button on his jeans. "And you're not going anywhere. What are you so afraid of?"

Rachel clutched her dress to her chest as he unzipped his jeans. While moving toward her, he reached over his shoulder and pulled the T-shirt up and over his head, baring his upper half to her greedy eyes.

Dumping the white cotton on the floor, he tilted his head to the side and ran his eyes over her, examining every inch of her. For one crazy moment, she thought that it was quite possible he was seeing right through her.

"It's not me you're running from. We've established that. Your past maybe? But that doesn't explain why you don't want everyone to know about us. Or maybe you're just running from yourself?"

When he stopped directly in front of her, he bent down, so they were eye-to-eye. "It's a little bit late to worry about all that, don't you think? By now, I'm sure that Josh and your brother know all about this. Put down the dress, Rachel, and come with me."

~

COLE HELD out his hand to her and waited. Her wary eyes met his as she finally relented and placed her palm in his hand. Without another word, he tugged her along behind him as he walked down the hallway to his room.

When they reached the cream rug in the center of his room, he let go of her hand and moved around to the right side of the bed. After turning back the covers, he looked over to the rigid spine of the complicated woman in his room.

He hadn't been lying. She intrigued him, and he wanted to know all of her. *That's only part of it though,* Cole thought. As he moved back over to her, he now found himself fighting another need that was clawing at him. *I need to look after her. I need to protect her.*

When he stopped before her, he started to undo the buttons of her shirt. He kept his eyes fixed on hers until he reached the top. Sliding both his hands along her collarbone, he removed the material from her and let it fall to her feet.

In the moonlight that was shining through the window, Cole thought Rachel had never looked more desirable. Completely naked and one hundred percent vulnerable, she left him speechless.

Reaching out to the script that was written along her ribs, he finally read the passage: *At any given moment, you have the power to say this is not how the story is going to end.*

That was when everything started to make sense. This woman—with the loud hair and the even livelier clothes—was sad.

Removing his finger from her skin, he pushed his jeans off his body, baring himself to her in the same fashion, as he held out his hand. "Let go, Rachel. Let go, and lie down with me. Close your eyes, and forget everything. Tomorrow will be here soon enough, and you can argue with me then."

When she placed her fingers in his, he squeezed them and led her to his bed where they both got in quietly. Moving in close behind her, he wrapped an arm around her, placing it under her breasts, as he formed his body against hers. *We fit like two pieces of a puzzle finally coming together,* he thought.

As her body gave in and relaxed into sleep, Cole closed his eyes and wondered how to go about making Rachel his.

CHAPTER 12

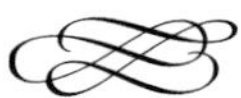

"I think tonight went well, don't you?" Rachel asked as she removed her hat and unbuttoned her coat.

Ben pushed in through the door behind her, closing it with a lot more force than was necessary. "What part exactly were you thinking went well? The part where your brother asked me a million questions about our plans? Or the part where your father glared at me all night?"

Rachel chuckled as she shrugged out of her coat. She had known Ben had been uncomfortable, but she didn't realize just how upset it had made him.

Poor guy. Meeting the family for the first time is always hard.

"Oh, come on, Ben. You can't be serious. Mase was just trying to be polite, and...well, dads always glare at boyfriends."

Ben spun around to face her as he threw his jacket on the couch. "Just how many boyfriends do you have, Rach?"

Rachel pulled off her gloves and smiled as he walked closer. He knew she hadn't dated before him. He was being ridiculous. She tilted up her head, thinking he was about to tell her he was kidding. Instead, his hand whipped out, strong fingers gripping her chin.

"Ouch. Ben, you're hurting me," she told him, trying to tug her chin free.

Rather than releasing her, Ben tilted her head back farther and leaned down toward her. "I don't care how many guys you dated before me, and I don't want to hear about them either. You might find it amusing, but I don't."

"Ben," Rachel pleaded. "I didn't mean anything by it."

"Then, why say it?"

Releasing his grip with a cruel flick of his wrist, he turned away from her. As he walked to their bedroom, the last thing Rachel heard him mutter was, "Stupid bitch."

~

RACHEL AWOKE WITH A START.

Sitting up in a panic, she scooted up to the headboard, clutching the sheet to her chest. As her eyes locked on the bedside table clock, she saw that it was two forty-five.

"Rachel?" a low, calm voice cut through the air and reached her ears.

Looking across the bed on the opposite side from her, she saw Cole propped up on his elbow, staring at her with wary eyes.

"Are you okay?" he questioned cautiously.

Trying to calm her breathing, she reached up and pushed her hair behind her ear. Nodding, she lowered herself back down on the bed. When she was flat on her back, looking up at the ceiling, she felt the bed dip, and she knew Cole had moved closer.

Turning her head on the stark white pillow, she stared through the darkness to a man she had never thought she would trust, let alone sleep beside.

"Bad dream?" he pressed gently.

Rachel blinked twice, just to make sure he was real, and for a brief moment, she closed her eyes. When she opened them, she saw he was still there beside her, larger than life, and she nodded.

"Do you have those often?"

Finding it easier not to look at him, she turned her head back to stare up at the ceiling. "Sometimes," she whispered.

She was surprised when she felt tentative fingers on her naked shoulder.

"Want to talk about it?"

Feeling a tear escape her right eye, she reached up to brush it away. "Not really."

"Rachel?"

Turning her head back toward him, she allowed herself a moment to really give in, to really see at him.

"You can trust me," he promised.

Reaching across her chest to the fingers on her shoulder, she pressed them closer to her cool skin as she rolled to her side, scooting in close to him. As his strong arm slid around her body, she found herself tracing the writing on him.

Before drifting back to sleep, she softly muttered, "I know."

~

WITH THE ALARM BEEPING INCESSANTLY, Cole woke up a few hours later with his arm still wrapped tightly around Rachel. Reluctantly, he released her and rolled over onto his back to hit the snooze button.

How is it that we have moved forward so far in only one night?

As he shifted and turned back to her, he was surprised to see her wide blue eyes open, staring back at him. Giving him a shy smile, she pressed a small palm to his chest and pushed him down on his back.

Cole raised a brow at her as she moved to her side. As she propped herself up on her elbow, the sheet fell down around her waist.

"Not that I'm complaining, because this is affording me one hell of a view, but what are you doing, Rachel?"

Taking her bottom lip between her teeth, she reached out a delicate finger and traced the wolf tattooed on his right pec. "I want to see you."

"See me?" he queried.

"Yes, see you," she replied.

She lifted her hand and whipped the covers all the way off of him, leaving them both naked in his bed.

Never one to be ashamed of his body, Cole craned his neck to look down at their bodies. Turning his head, he brought his eyes back to her. "Well, now, you can definitely see me." He chuckled as he fingered one of her hard nipples. "And I must have done something right because I can see all of you."

"I know." She grinned impishly as she scooted up to her knees beside him. "I want to know all about this," Rachel informed him as she made a gesture to his piercings and tats.

Cole thought about the request for a moment. "Why are you so brave this morning?"

She leaned down over him with her hands behind her back, and he enjoyed her full round breasts as they swayed forward to graze his chest while she kissed him softly.

"Because I trust you," she admitted.

As she sat back up, Cole was surprised to feel his heart warm at her admission. *Damn, it didn't only make my heart happy, but it's also making my cock hard.*

"Okay, Rachel, what do you want to know?"

He studied her closely as her eager eyes looked over his body. When they zeroed in on his morning erection, he waited for the question that he figured was obvious, but in usual Rachel fashion, she marched to the beat of her own drum.

"When do I get to taste you?" she asked, her gaze lifting back to his eyes.

As he met her stare, Cole replied, "When I say so."

She pouted at him as he raised his arms and placed them under his head. Suddenly, he was liking this game of hers very much.

"Not now?" she double-checked, letting her eyes fall back to his Prince Albert.

"No, not now."

"Why not?"

"Because I said no."

Rachel scoffed, "What guy says no to a—"

"Rachel?" He waited for her to look at him. "Not. Now."

"Fine. Your loss though." She shrugged before she pointed to his arms. "What do your tattoos say?"

Feeling a smug smile cross his lips, Cole reached out and took one of her arms. Tugging her down over him, he shifted and rolled them over, so he was lying on top of her. As she parted her thighs, he snuggled between them and placed his palms on each side of her head.

"Not going to answer that either?" she guessed as she reached up to trace the bar through his left nipple.

"I'm going to answer," he told her, pressing his hardness against her warm mound, "but you keep interrupting me. That's not very nice."

As Rachel's eyes met his, he thought he saw some hesitation for a moment, but as he continued looking down at her, he felt the hesitation disappear as her mouth curved and her lips parted.

"No, it's not. So, what's my punishment going to be?"

Playing with the red-and-black hair that was spread out on the pillow, Cole rocked against her. As a small moan left her lips, he leaned down to her ear.

"Patience of a saint. The mind of a sinner. That's what my tattoos say."

She let her eyes drift to his arms, and as he ground his hips into hers once more, she pouted and sighed.

"What language is it written in?"

Cole nibbled the shell of her ear down to the lobe. "Norwegian."

She pulled her head away and turned it on the pillow. "Is that your heritage?"

Enjoying her curiosity, Cole continued to assault her ear as he murmured, "Part of it."

"As in big blonde Vikings?" she asked, her voice catching in breathy excitement.

Cole lifted himself up on his arms and pinned her to the bed with a stare. "That seems to excite you. Do you like the idea of being ravished by a Viking?"

Her hands came up to grip his upper arms as she arched her back, pushing herself against his cock. "Maybe I want to be punished by one, for not being very nice."

"I don't want to punish you, Rachel."

As she raised her thighs to his hips, he brushed his mouth on hers.

"But I am going to show you why I have that written on my arms." With that, he rolled off of her. Getting out of the bed, he made his way to the bathroom, and just as he stepped through the door, he heard her call him.

"Cole."

Looking over his shoulder, he saw that she had turned her head on the pillow to face him, and she was now moving her hand down between her thighs.

"Don't," he warned.

She bit her lip hard. "That's it? You're just going to leave?"

"Yes. You need to learn the reward that comes from patience. I have it in abundance. While you are practicing that today, remember the other half of the saying. Because when I'm sitting behind my desk at work, I will be thinking of all the ways I can sin with you." Cole turned and continued into the bathroom, and just as he was about to shut the door, he called out, "And do not touch yourself today, Rachel. Don't you dare come before I get to you."

"And how would you know?" she shouted in response.

Cole strolled back over to the door, staring at her in his bed. "By the time I get to you, I promise you will be begging for it. In fact, I should just be able to look at you, and you will want to come. If your greedy little hands have done the deed, you won't need me now, will you?" Turning on his heel, he said, "I'm taking a shower. Keep your hands off of what is mine."

As a frustrated groan met his ears, he couldn't help but smile as he turned on the water.

RACHEL PUSHED through the back door of the restaurant at six fifteen. She rushed in and made her way straight to her office. *Late again, damn it.* When she spotted Sarah, Rachel gave her a quick wave and a smile. She shrugged off her jacket and pulled the bright red beanie from her head.

"We ready to go for tonight?" Rachel asked.

Sarah was hot on her heels. "Yes."

After Rachel hung up her jacket on the back of her office door, she removed her turtleneck pullover and threw it on her chair before picking up her smock. Fastening it quickly, she reached back to braid her hair. She stopped when Sarah gave her a soft laugh.

"Lena showed up around forty-five minutes ago, and we have not seen or heard...well, much from Mason since. They're in his office."

Rachel screwed her nose up in an exaggerated *eww* look and shook her head. "I don't even want to know," Rachel joked, walking out into the kitchen to the stainless steel prep table. "As long as the pears are cored, wrapped, and ready to bake, all I care about is that the weekly special is ready to go."

Sarah nodded. "Of course, of course. He's just so funny when Lena's here. He goes from Mr. Business Smooth to a dopey-eyed, lovesick—"

"Fool?" Rachel suggested with a grin. "Yeah, I know. They are sweet and all of those great adjectives. Let me know when you see them emerge. I don't really want to be—"

"What? Ambushed?" her brother's voice called from behind her.

Groaning, Rachel shut her eyes for a moment as she raised a hand and rubbed the bridge of her nose. "Surprised, Mase," Rachel told him, turning to find both Lena and Mason standing behind her hand in hand. "I didn't want to be surprised."

"Of course, you didn't," Lena said, coming to the rescue, as she stepped forward. "I was leaving anyway. I'm meeting up with Shelly for a movie. Hey, when's your next day off? We should all get together."

Rachel creased her brow and glared over at Mason as he raised his eyebrows. Obviously, he hadn't told his wife about their little chat, so Lena didn't know that Rachel wanted some time away, making this all the more difficult. Lena was such a sweetheart, and lying to her never felt good.

"I'm pretty busy right now with the flower shop and all. I'm in the middle of hiring someone, so maybe next week?"

There. That wasn't a full-on lie.

Mason wasn't buying it though. She could tell by the disapproving look on his face, and Rachel felt her guilt creeping in.

"Oh, okay. Well, that sounds good. I have a really busy schedule this week anyway."

Good, Rachel thought.

Just when she stupidly assumed she had gotten away without any kind of uncomfortable conversation, Lena added, "But we need to get together soon because you need to tell me all about Cole."

Oh, fantastic.

"Cole? Who's Cole?" Sarah asked with a curious smile.

Rachel lifted her eyes to her brother's to find they were fixed on her.

"No one, Sarah. He's just a mutual acquaintance. He works for Josh."

"Oh, gotcha."

"Who works for me?" a deep voice said into the kitchen.

Rachel cursed under her breath as she glared over at Josh—*the traitor*—who had just appeared in the door of the kitchen.

"Last time I checked, you don't work here. So, what are you doing back in my kitchen?"

As the staff made their way around them, like they weren't even there, Josh gave her a look that screamed, *Since when do you care?*

"I'm dropping off Georgia. These two are going to a movie." He nodded to Lena.

Rachel looked around him, but she couldn't see the blonde bombshell anywhere in sight. "Then, where is she?"

As the side of his mouth curled up, Rachel had a fleeting fantasy of socking him one right in the kisser.

"She's in the bathroom, fixing her already perfect hair. What's the problem, Rach? Trying to get rid of me?"

Through clenched her teeth, Rachel managed to say, "No. I am trying to get everything I need together before it gets insane back here."

"Well, most of it is done. We just need to mix the caramel sauce, and we are good to go. Prep is finished."

It was normally such a blessing to have an organized worker, but in this instance, Rachel really wished Sarah had been an incompetent mess. Rachel wanted an excuse to flee, any excuse to get away from familiar eyes piercing into her.

"That's great, Sarah, but I need to—"

"Um, excuse me, Rachel?"

Like some horrible comedic scene, all five of them turned to the main window, dividing the dining room from the kitchen to see Wendy. The restaurant manager was standing there with a grin so wide that there was only one thing that could have possibly prompted it.

Oh, please. Not now. Not right now.

"There's someone asking for you in the dining room," Wendy said, looking at Rachel.

Before Rachel could say anything, Mason jumped in, speaking up. "Who, Wendy?"

"Don't answer that," Rachel countered as she glared at her brother.

"It's him, isn't it?" Mason pushed.

With her pulse pounding and blood ringing in her ears, Rachel glared and stormed past him. "It's none of your business. Stay here."

"Hang on a minute," Josh finally piped up. "Cole's out there? Waiting on you? That guy doesn't wait for anyone."

Aiming annoyed eyes over her shoulder at Josh, Rachel warned, "Don't even start. As of yesterday morning, I am not talking to you."

"What did I do?" he asked, having the gall to act offended.

"You have a big mouth," she accused, looking from Josh to her brother. "Now, both of you, *stay here*."

With that, Rachel rushed around the prep tables and over to the doors to the main dining room. Pushing through the frosted double doors, it took her only seconds to spot Cole.

He was seated at a table in the center of the restaurant, facing her, and he was dressed in the same immaculate black suit, white shirt, and blue tie he had left the condo in this morning. He had one arm resting flat on the white linen tablecloth, and the other, his left, was propped up on his elbow with his fingers and thumb at his chin. He looked like he was in deep thought, and as his eyes met hers across the dimly lit dining room space, she knew she was at least a part of those musings.

After he had seen her home this morning, which was completely out of his way, Rachel had changed into a pair of flared black dress pants and a purple turtleneck pullover. Now that she was at work, she was dressed in her purple smock and black pants.

Smoothing her palms down her sides, she thought, *Breathe. Remember, you were just with him this morning.*

The only problem with reminding herself of that little tidbit was the fact that she was still completely frustrated, and she wanted his hands down her pants pronto. He had been spot-on about one thing: Just his look alone was bringing her perilously close to the edge.

Walking through tables that were starting to fill, she was aware of him tracking her every move. Pushing her shoulders back, she walked as confidently as she could to his table. She stopped behind the seat that was opposite him, placing her hands on the back of the chair.

"Good evening, Mr. Madison. I heard you requested to speak to me."

~

TAKING a good long look at the woman standing on the other side of the table to him, Cole decided he liked what he saw. He was almost positive that most chefs wore black-and-white checker pants with a white top, but not Rachel. No, Rachel, as usual, was making a statement, and on her, it worked.

"I did." He replied, tracing his fingers along the pattern in the tablecloth.

"Well, here I am. What can I do for you?"

Cole tilted his head to the side. "Well, first things first, how are you feeling right now, Rachel?"

She looked around to make sure no one was within hearing distance. With a tight-lipped smile, she informed him, "I feel like if you touched me, I'd explode."

"Is that why you are all the way over there?"

"Yes," she confirmed quickly. "I thought, for the time being, it was the safest place to be."

"You're probably right, especially with how I'm feeling." Sitting up straight in his seat, Cole had to hold back a laugh at the way she gripped the back of the chair she was using as a shield. "Relax, Rachel. Despite how hungry I am, I'm not into *sharing* my meals."

He was about to add something else, but then he spotted Josh and the man he knew was her brother, making their way through the restaurant toward them. Shifting his eyes to just behind them, he also saw the two women he had seen at both Whipped and the Halloween party.

Ahh, I see the women are smarter than their men, Cole thought as the two finally flanked by each side of Rachel.

Immediately, he noticed Rachel's spine stiffen as her fingers grasped the chair to the point of turning her knuckles white. Cole wasn't quite sure what she was so worried about. As far as he was concerned, this was just a blip on his radar, and his radar was fixed directly on her.

"Evening, Josh," he greeted his friend and colleague first.

Cole couldn't decide what emotion had crossed his usually easygoing friend's face, but he didn't look pleased, so Cole decided to focus on the tall, dark hair guy who had an expression Cole knew very well. That look screamed, *Meet me outside. You and I need to talk*.

Cole decided he needed to be on equal footing, so he pushed his chair back from the table and rose. He was pleased his stature met with Rachel's brother as he held out his hand toward him across the table. "You must be Mason. I'm Cole Madison."

Cole studied the look that flashed over the big guy's face as Mason reached forward and shook his hand.

"Yeah, I'm Mason, Rachel's big brother."

At that announcement, Cole removed his hand as it seemed the silently seething Rachel lost her shit.

~

"ARE YOU KIDDING ME?" Rachel demanded as she turned on her brother. "My *big* brother? What am I? Fifteen?"

Mason was about to say something when Cole's voice interrupted smoothly.

"You are *definitely* not fifteen, Rachel."

"Cole, cut it out," Josh warned in a voice that shocked even her.

Rachel was surprised by the attitude Josh was throwing off, especially since he had originally wanted to set them up.

Turning to face Cole, Rachel was about to tell him he wasn't helping the issue, but the way his eyes were focused on her rendered her speechless. *Always so flipping intense.*

Instead, she tore her gaze from his and looked at Josh, who was also glaring at Cole.

Stupid men and their testosterone.

Spinning back to her infuriating brother, she clenched her teeth. "I thought I told you both to wait in the kitchen."

"Well, I wanted to meet the man who has all your attention these days, Rach," Mason told her, eyes still focused on the man standing opposite them all.

What an absolute nightmare. Three guys standing around a table, all glaring at one another, ready to engage in a pissing match.

"Well, great, Mason. You've seen him, met him, managed to embarrass me, and have now drawn all of our customers' attention."

Mason still hadn't bothered to look at her. His eyes were still on the calm and put-together Cole, and Cole now had his hands in his pants pockets and was refusing to drop his own eyes from her brother's.

"How did you two meet?" Mason probed.

"Mason," Rachel exclaimed. She swung her eyes to Cole's, pleading with him to keep his mouth shut.

The message must have been received because cool-as-you-please Cole replied, "I don't think that's really any of your business unless Rachel wants to tell you. Now, is this over with? Or should I go and grab my dueling pistols and meet you out back at high noon?"

"Cole," Josh warned again.

"Yes, Joshua?" Cole questioned.

Rachel was just trying to keep up with everything that was going on.

"Cool it, man. Mason's just worried about his sister."

Cole nodded slowly before he asked pointedly, "And you? Who are you concerned about? His sister, your friend, or your business partner?"

"You know what?" Rachel finally cut in. "You two are acting like overprotective jerks. I am a grown woman, and if I want to date someone, I do *not* need permission from either of you. And as for you," she stressed, turning to look at Cole across the table.

She had been feeling extremely confident until she saw an expression that screamed, *Remember who you are talking to,* cross his face.

Deciding she was already screwed, she thought, *To hell with it*. Bluntly, she stated, "You promised me *something*, and I want it."

"Rachel, calm down," Mason muttered.

Spinning on her brother, she poked him in the chest and glared up at him. "I will *not* calm down. I asked you for space, and I asked you to wait back there. I did not ask you to come out here and act like my father—who, by the way, would have never embarrassed me."

"That's not true, Rach. He was just more discreet than Mason. He pulled me aside and read me the riot act before I took you to the formal that year."

As those words left Josh's mouth, Rachel's eyes flew to Cole's to see how he would react to this new information. His eyes had shifted to Josh and narrowed slightly, but other than that, he did nothing else.

She could feel her heart thumping hard in her chest as she thought about the way Ben had reacted to the mere mention of Josh, and Josh hadn't even been in the same state as them then. Her worries were laid to rest though when Cole began speaking again.

"Well, it's a good thing Rachel is no longer fifteen or sixteen, and she is now woman enough to make her own decisions. I actually don't understand the issue here, Josh. You had originally told me you'd be happy to introduce us."

Just as Josh was about to answer, Rachel hissed, "Stop it, all of you. You two leave now. No more words, or I will walk out of this restaurant and leave you screwed." She pointed to Mason and added, "And I will *not* cook you any more beignets for a whole year."

The minute the threat was out of her mouth, both men told her in unison:

"Aww, come on, Rach."

"Rach, we were just worried."

"Just. Leave. Us. Alone," she gritted out between her teeth.

Without any more words spoken, the men she had grown up with turned and walked away, leaving her to stand alone, opposite Cole, with most of the dining room watching them.

She hurried around the table, so she was standing beside him. Looking up at Cole, in a lowered voice, she said, "I'm sorry about that. I told them to—"

"Rachel?" he interrupted.

"Yes?"

"I don't care about that, and now, it's done and over with. I have, however, lost my appetite."

She didn't blame him one little bit.

Stepping to her, he cupped the back of her neck, tugging her forward. As he lowered his head, she thought for sure that he was about to kiss her in the middle of the dining room and under the judgmental eyes of Mason, Josh, Lena, and Shelly.

Instead of doing the expected though, he moved his lips to her ear. "I've been patient all day, and now, I am very ready to sin. Be ready for me. I'll be back to pick you up."

As he let go of her, Rachel felt her knees go weak. He straightened to button his suit jacket, and he gave her a smug look that told her he had accomplished *exactly* what he had set out to do tonight. Then, he turned and made his way over to the hostess to retrieve his coat.

As he left the restaurant, Rachel realized she was still standing exactly where he had left her. Making herself move, she turned on her heel and stormed back to the doors where Lena and Shelly were both standing with huge we-knew-it grins on their faces.

Rachel glared at them both as she stopped in front of the doors.

"Not your type, huh?" Shelly asked.

"Not interested?" Lena reminded her.

Rachel shook her head, but she couldn't help the small tug at the corner of her mouth as she pushed through the large double doors. "Oh, shut the hell up, you two."

And as the doors swung shut behind her, she heard the two women laugh, and she couldn't help chuckling a little to herself.

CHAPTER 13

Several hours later, after the final customer had eaten and the last drink had been drained dry, the head chef, Ryan, walked through the dining room to lock the front door. "I'm getting ready to leave," he informed Rachel.

Rachel was busy making sure everything was ready to go in the morning when she heard his familiar voice closer this time.

"Front doors are locked, but I found this guy out there. He said he was picking you up."

Rachel poked her head out of the walk-in fridge to see Cole in her kitchen leaning back against a stainless steel prep table. His long legs were crossed, and he had a neutral expression plastered on his face.

As their eyes collided, she felt the air crackle with immediate sexual tension, and she knew he had come for her. *Yes, I'm honest enough to admit that I can't wait to come for him.*

Belatedly, she remembered they were not alone, and she pulled her eyes away from his to nod over at the head chef.

"Yeah, that's right. He's here for me."

"So, you're good if I leave then?"

Rachel found her eyes had, unconsciously, moved back to the silent man who was dominating the kitchen more effectively than the man speaking.

"Yes, you can leave," she replied dismissively.

Feeling Ryan's eyes on her, she turned to see him looking back and forth between her and Cole.

One last time, he asked, "Are you sure, Rach?"

Rachel turned back to face Cole, and her eyes didn't waver as she watched him pull a hand from his pocket with what she now knew was a caramel. He slowly unwrapped it and put it in his mouth.

Without a second glance at Ryan, she confirmed, "Yes. Positive. Go."

As the words left her mouth, she noticed the left corner of Cole's lips twitch as though he wanted to smile, but at the last minute, he held back.

It would have been comical to Rachel if she wasn't so damn annoyed with all the men in her life who were suddenly taking an inordinate amount of time in securing her safety around the man she couldn't currently tear her eyes from.

So, maybe it wasn't just her that sensed who he really was. With all of that hidden strength simmering just beneath the surface of that pristine suit, he was giving off a sense of barely restrained control.

When I look at him, I swear I can feel the power radiating from him. It isn't that he is trying to project it; it's just such an innate part of who he is, Rachel thought as she felt his eyes watching her intently. *At least I know I am not imagining it.*

When the back door shut loudly, signaling that they were now alone, Rachel shut the fridge door and leaned her back against it. "I won't be long," she assured him. She walked to the prep table with a towel in her hand and put the utensils back in their proper locale. As she moved efficiently around the kitchen, she knew he was tracking her moves. *Damn. The man still hasn't said a word.* And that made her nervous as hell. *In my own domain, no less.*

Several seconds passed until he spoke finally. "Don't rush on my account. I like seeing you here. I'm only disappointed that I didn't get to try any of your desserts."

As soon as the words left his mouth, Rachel's feet stopped moving, and she turned her head. She let her eyes zero in on the immaculate suit, covering what she now knew was a wicked work of art, and Rachel found that all she could think about was what they had discussed this morning—*a taste*. Suddenly, she had a brilliant idea.

"So..." She moved closer to where he was standing. "You have a real sweet tooth, don't you?"

Stopping in front of him, Rachel threw the small towel she was holding onto the bench. Removing his hands from his pockets, Cole pushed himself up tall, and she kept her eyes trained on him, tilting her head back.

"Yes, I suppose I do. You could call it a vice of mine."

"Your only vice?" Rachel probed, stepping closer.

Raising her right palm, she placed it on the middle of his chest, directly over the blue tie that was hanging there. He glanced down at her hand for a moment and then lifted his gaze back to hers. The look that came into his eyes lit a fire deep in the pit of her belly.

"Definitely not, but it's one of the few I am able to admit to in public."

"I see," Rachel murmured. She traced her hand down his chest to his abdomen where she then began to finger his belt buckle. "So, are you going to continue to deny me and yourself *this* for the second time today?" Leaving no question as to what she was referring to, she boldly ran her finger down over the hard bulge that was now pressing against his perfectly tailored pants.

"Technically, it's not really the same day, and no, I was thinking that if you were still interested, I'd be up for the discussion."

Rachel couldn't help the sultry smile that spread across her mouth as she daringly flattened her whole palm against him and squeezed. Just the thought of getting her mouth around him was making her body heat and her thighs clench. "Well, you're definitely up. I'm starting to wonder if you're ever down."

COLE WAS TRYING to remind himself that this was not the time or the place, but as Rachel leaned into him and squeezed his rapidly growing cock, he was having a hard time remembering anything at all.

Reaching down to cover her hand with one of his own, he pressed her palm harder against his throbbing frustration as he flexed his hips forward. "Around you, Rachel, I'll admit that I find it close to impossible to remain decent."

"Who said I wanted you to be decent?" she challenged as she

licked her plump bottom lip, reminding him of exactly what she wanted to do to him.

Removing his hand from hers, he reached out and cupped the back of her neck, tugging her forward. "Go and get your coat or whatever else you need before I forget my manners."

Still stroking him, Rachel let her eyes fall closed. "What are you doing to me? I can't seem to think of anything but having you naked against me."

Cole had no idea, but he knew she was doing it to him, too. He was a second away from bending her over the prep table and taking her, but that wouldn't happen. He wanted her in private, and he wanted it as soon as possible.

Placing his mouth on hers, he licked her top lip and sucked it between his lips. As she continued to palm him through his pants, he groaned against her mouth and released her lip. "Get your things, and I'll meet you in the dining room." With that, he stepped away from temptation and moved out into the empty space, gathering and hanging on to what little control he had left.

~

RACHEL WAS LEFT STANDING in the kitchen, aroused and shaking. She didn't know how he did it, but Cole had the ability to make her lose her ever-loving mind. All he had to do was glance in her direction, and she'd forget that she had specific plans for him or ideas of her own when it came to getting naked. *Yep, one look from him, and I'm a useless, horny mess.*

It should have bugged the hell out of her, but the more she gave in, the more she was learning to enjoy that side of herself again. It had been a long time since she had given herself permission to do that.

Moving back into her office, she stripped out of her smock and grabbed her sweater, tugging it on over her head. After she picked up her bag and switched off all the lights, she ran over to the fridge and pushed the large stainless steel door to the side. Reaching in to the third shelf, she grabbed a small clear container, and with a grin, she put it in a brown paper bag and closed the fridge.

Oh yes, this will be just perfect.

WHEN THEY REACHED the condo at around one thirty in the morning, Cole let her in and took her coat from her. He couldn't help but admire the tight fit of her purple turtleneck as she moved down his hall into the living room. It fit her like a second skin, and he wanted to see what was under it sooner rather than later.

Shrugging out of his coat and suit jacket, he hung them both on the coatrack and walked through the room to find her over by his microwave.

"Do you mind if I use this?" she questioned as she pushed the button to open the door.

Frowning, Cole moved to the opposite side of the island and took a seat on one of the bar stools. "Go right ahead. Did you bring home a late-night snack?"

She placed a microwavable container in the center, closed the door, and hit the button to start it, and then the microwave hummed to life. She turned back to face him, and without answering, she crossed the kitchen area toward him. He found his eyes slide down from the high neckline of her sweater to her firm perky breasts and tight abdomen.

"See something you like?" Her tone of her voice indicated that she knew he liked everything he was looking at.

Oh yes. If his rigid cock was any kind of indicator, it would seem this feisty side of her worked for him quite a lot.

"I don't know why, but that top is really flicking my switch right now," he admitted as he reached up to tug his tie loose.

"No, don't," Rachel told him as she rounded the kitchen island.

Keeping his eyes focused on the woman moving closer to him, Cole reminded her in a firm tone, "I don't think you have been paying attention to how this works, Rachel. If you want something from me, ask me. Nicely."

As she stopped in front of him, Rachel raised her eyes to his. She seemed to realize she had overstepped her line. "*Please* don't take off your tie. I like it."

Cole wrapped an arm around her waist, pulling her forward. "What's in the microwave?" he asked again, more curious now than ever.

"A surprise. Where's that patience of yours?"

"So, you aren't going to tell me then?"

Giving him a mischievous look, she shook her head. "Nope."

"Troublemaker," he accused lightly before reverting back to the statement she had made just moments ago. "What do you like about my tie?" As her breathing came harder, he pushed, "The fact that it makes me look—" He had been about to say *educated*, but she interrupted with a word that just about had him falling off the stool.

"Civilized."

Cole felt his shoulders tense at the implications she was throwing his way. *So, what is she trying to tell me? That she knows I'm not really civilized? Fuck, she is going to kill me.*

"Lift your arms, Rachel," he ordered in a tone that was almost a growl as he released her.

Immediately, she did as she was told, raising her arms above her head, and then she stood there, waiting for him. He gripped the hem of her sweater, peeled it off, and tossed it to the side, leaving her in a tiny black tank top, and from what Cole could tell, a lacy bra.

As she lowered her arms, Cole fingered the strap. "You don't think I'm civilized, Rachel?"

Her breasts began rising and falling more rapidly, and as he stroked a finger down her right arm, she jumped as the microwave beeped loudly.

He gave her a look that screamed, *Well? Answer the question.*

She swallowed deeply, and with a slight tremble in her voice, she replied, "I think you can be."

Cole lowered his head until they were eye-to-eye. "That's an interesting choice of words. You think I can be...but? That is definitely an answer that is screaming for further explanation. Lift," he instructed again. Gripping her tank top, he tugged it up and pulled it off of her as well.

Tossing it aside, Cole kept his eyes on hers as he brought his finger down to trace the see-through material cupping the curve of her breast. "So?" he pushed, his voice calm while his cock pounded between his legs. "You think I can be civilized, but—"

Her mouth parted, and her eyes were starting to glaze over in that delicious lust-crazed way. "But I don't want you to be," she admitted.

RACHEL BIT back a whimper as Cole's fingers pulled the black lace away from her sensitive breasts. As he sat on the bar stool with his long legs spread apart with her standing between them, she felt her pussy tighten and her body moisten at the picture he made. He was so refined in his black pants, shirt, and tie, but he was looking at her like he wanted to fuck her into next week, and Rachel couldn't help the way her body was responding.

When her breasts were free, he cupped her in his palms and lowered his head. Without any teasing at all, he took one of her hard nipples between his lips and sucked. Gripping his head, she pulled him tight to her chest as he repeatedly flicked his tongue over the hard tip.

She groaned loudly, pushing her flesh harder against his lips. "Cole," she sighed as she spread her fingers through his hair, massaging his scalp as he continued his sensual torment.

She could feel his other hand as it slid up her back, and suddenly, her bra was loose and free. He pulled it from her and threw it behind him. Moving back a little, he reached up with both hands, plumping her breasts up to him like a meal, before he lowered his mouth to the neglected tip. He made sure to keep their eyes connected as he licked the tight, hard flesh. The sexy dark glint in his eyes was just as effective as if his fingers were sliding between her thighs. She felt her panties grow damp from his seductive play.

"Your breasts are fucking perfect, Rachel." He sat back and pushed them together again. "I want to slide my cock between them."

Rachel couldn't help the small gasp that came from her mouth at the image of his hot thick cock pushing between her breasts while that piercing brushed close by her lips with every thrust he would make.

Oh yes, please. Can we do that?

Although she said nothing, her thought must have been stamped across her face because Cole's talented lips stretched into a taut smirk. She knew his next words would be nothing short of a hot, sensual promise.

"You like that idea. I can tell." With a clever finger, he flicked her hard nipple. "Some other time. Right now, if I'm not mistaken, you asked to taste."

~

RACHEL STOOD motionless as Cole got up off the stool and reached forward to the four buttons on her pants.

As his big hands undid them, he asked her again, "What's in the microwave, Rachel?"

Blinking once, she was brought back to reality and her original plan. Taking a step back, she asked him *nicely*, "You're like a dog with a bone, aren't you? May I?"

Cole frowned, clearly intrigued, as she stepped away from him. He nodded, and Rachel couldn't help the grin that hit her lips, knowing what was about to follow. Naked from the waist up, she moved back to the microwave, opened it, and pulled out the container.

When she turned around, she found that Cole had moved, and he was now on her side of the island. In fact, he was standing right behind her. Almost running into him, Rachel squeaked as he looked down into the container.

"What is it?" he questioned like a curious boy.

But this is no boy. Oh no, this is one hundred percent man, and I want to lick him all over.

"It's my caramel sauce from the special this week."

She watched his face carefully as his eyebrow winged up. Placing the container on the bench beside her, Rachel dipped her finger into the warm sticky mixture. Bringing it up to his lips, she whispered, "I wanted you to taste it since you are something of a caramel connoisseur."

As his full lips parted, Rachel pushed her index finger between them, and she almost collapsed from the pleasure of him sucking on her finger. His wet tongue swirled all around her flesh as he reached up and gripped her wrist tightly.

After nibbling her finger and finally sliding it free, he demanded, "More."

With smug satisfaction, Rachel dipped two fingers into the sauce and brought them back to his mouth. This time, she painted his lips with the thick mixture before pushing her fingers in between his lips.

As his eyes slid closed, she felt his tongue slip between her fingers and glide around them before nipping at the ends. He so erotically cleaned them with his tongue that she found herself reaching down with her free hand to cup her aching sex.

When her fingers were free again, no words were spoken as she loosened his tie just enough to unbutton his shirt. With a flirtatious look from beneath her lashes, Rachel pushed his shirt apart, leaving the tie in place, and then she slid it down his muscular arms, dropping it on the counter. Reaching between them, she unbuckled his belt, and he stood perfectly still and let her. He remained that way as she unzipped his pants and pushed them and his boxers off his hips.

As her eyes climbed back to meet his, he didn't smile or frown. He just continued to watch her every move with unflinching focus.

Rachel knew exactly what she wanted as she felt herself inching closer to what she had been imagining ever since this morning. When she had him exactly the way she wanted him, she dipped her fingers into the caramel and gave him a sultry wink before she finally dropped to her knees.

~

COLE'S HEAD and cock was pounding as he stared down at the vixen at his feet.

Fucking caramel.

This woman never ceased to amaze him, but when she'd whipped out that little surprise, he very nearly raised the white flag in surrender to her brilliance. He was glad he hadn't though as she knelt down on the kitchen floor and fisted his cock with her sticky palm.

Fuck. Between her at his feet and her small hand around his cock, Cole couldn't remember ever being this turned on in his fucking life.

She coated his shaft in the sweet, syrupy confection, and he couldn't help but reach over to the small container beside him. As his fingers dipped into the thick amber liquid, he groaned from that erotic feeling alone.

It was wet and warm, and it reminded him of exactly where he wanted his cock to be. Glancing down to Rachel who was silent and kneeling on the floor, he gripped her chin with his clean hand and tilted up her face to him.

"Open your mouth," he ordered in a gruff tone even he had trouble recognizing.

As her lips parted, he brought his other hand over her, letting the caramel drip from his fingers onto her waiting tongue and lips. As it coated her mouth, her tongue came out to flick over her glistening lips, and her eyes closed in pleasure from the sweetness that hit her taste buds.

Reaching back over to the caramel-filled container, Cole scooped up some more of the liquid, and this time, he let it slide down his fingers onto her naked breasts and nipples.

Jesus, she looks fucking edible, he thought with a groan, *and I plan to eat.*

Not being able to resist, Cole lowered his fingers to her lips, and as she parted them, he slid them deep into her mouth as she was still kneeling on the floor before him.

"Fucking hell," he cursed as she sucked on his fingers in a way that made his cock jealous. When he finally pulled them free from her mouth, he released her chin and gripped her hair firmly. "Suck me, Rachel. Put those sticky lips around my cock and suck it good."

As her eyes fluttered down to the task at hand, Cole couldn't help but dip his fingers back into his favorite candy. As he lifted the dripping sweetness to his own mouth, she knelt up tall and finally flicked out her sticky tongue over his piercing.

RACHEL WAS a hair trigger away from climax, and as she fisted Cole's cock in her palm, she couldn't help but lean forward and flick her tongue over the studs that pierced him. As she licked the bulbous head and sucked the tip into her mouth, she raised her eyes up his body, and what she saw made her orgasm teeter on the brink.

Cole was leaning back against the kitchen counter with his legs slightly parted where she was kneeling, and his blue tie was hanging down the center of his naked chest, like an arrow pointing to her prize.

That wasn't the only reason her panties were completely soaked and her nipples were rock hard. The man who had the ability to render her speechless with just a look was currently staring down at her and sucking on his own fingers, presumably after coating them with the caramel sauce.

He had a look of such pure sexual ecstasy on his face that it was making Rachel want to stick her hands in her pants and her fingers in her hungry pussy. Instead of doing that though, she took her left hand and ran it up and over his rippling abs, past his navel, and as high as she could until her arm was stretched up across his body. She began fingering his nipple piercing as she fisted his cock.

Removing his fingers from his mouth, he reached down and gripped the counter behind him as he pushed his hips forward. "Quit fucking around, Rachel, and suck my fucking cock."

Usually, a demand like that would have her pulling back as she thought about the tone and if she should be frightened, but as caught up as she was in the eroticism of the moment, all Rachel felt was turned on. Feeling playful, she tsked him and twisted his nipple. As she removed her hand, she leaned down to wrap her lips around the head of his impatient erection.

Lowering her lips an inch at a time, she took him as deeply as she could, and when she brought her mouth back up on a delicious drag, she made sure to rub the underside of him with her tongue. She reached the tip of his aching flesh, and she flicked his piercing with her tongue. As she removed her mouth, she followed it with a stroke of her fist up over his shaft.

"Rachel," he groaned.

She raised her eyes to him, and bravely, she told him, "Stop being so civilized."

And that was all it took.

~

COLE LOST IT.

Reaching down to the woman in front of him, he thought, *Fuck messy hands,* as he pushed them into her braid. Gripping her head hard, he tugged up her face and told her, "Open your mouth."

As soon as her lips parted, he moved the tip of his cock against them, and he groaned as he pushed his hips forward, sliding inside against her tongue. When he was in as deep as possible, he looked down to see her eyes aimed up at him. As he held her stare, he slowly rolled his hips back and pulled his shaft free from her mouth before reversing the throttle to thrust back inside. Over and over, he pushed between her lips, holding her head exactly where he wanted her, as he watched her take all he had to offer.

He was about to stop and pull back when he felt her fingers grip his ass cheeks, pulling him forward. Parting his own sticky lips, he grunted as she swallowed, the motion squeezing the head of his cock.

"Fuck Rachel. Your fucking mouth," he muttered as she sucked and licked with every thrust he gave to her.

He had thought he wanted to finish in her mouth. He had thought he wanted to watch her swallow every part of him, but he had been wrong.

Pulling himself from her abused swollen lips, Cole grabbed the container from the bench and went down to his knees beside her on the cool kitchen tiles. Dipping his hands into the sticky sauce, he brought his fingers to the lips that had just been wrapped around his cock, and he smeared them with the taste he craved. When her mouth was shining and wet, Cole pounced.

Wrapping an arm around her waist, he gently lowered her to the tile and kissed her mouth as though it were his last meal. Licking her lips with his avaricious tongue, he captured her moan as she thrust her hips up against his very hard and naked cock. All Cole could think was, *More*.

Dragging his hands down over her chest, he didn't even care that the caramel was ruining his tie as he rubbed his body against hers while his tongue continued to plunder her mouth in a soul-destroying kiss.

He felt her hands drag up his stomach and over his nipples before they desperately gripped his biceps. She raised her hips up to him with a throaty cry as she gripped his tie with one hand. Pulling his naked chest to hers, she rubbed her sticky nipples against his.

"God, Cole, do *something*," she pleaded as he started to yank her pants down her hips.

Tugging them down over her ass, he lifted his mouth from hers and moved so he could suck one of her sweet nipples into his mouth. *Fucking hell, she is the best thing I've ever tasted.*

Reaching into the container, for what he knew would most definitely be the last time, he raised his coated hand beside her. Her eyes locked on to his dripping fingers, and she didn't even seem to care that he had just turned the tables on her.

Slowly, he brought his hand to his lips and sucked his thumb into his mouth, and as she kept her eyes on his, he pulled it free and then pushed it between hers, for her to finish the job. But Cole's patience had run thin, and his thumb wasn't the only thing crying out to be inside something hot, tight and wet.

He pulled his hand away from her and sealed his mouth over hers in a brutal kiss. As their tongues tangled in an erotic dance, he slid his hand down to cup her breast, letting his caramel-coated fingers slide all over her tight nipple. The sheer decadence of what he was doing was not lost on him, and if he could be certain he wouldn't die from not putting his cock inside her, he would have taken a moment to lick her clean.

As it was though, with the way she was moaning and thrusting her hips up against him, Cole knew that his time was up. Pulling his fingers from her, he lowered his hand and shoved her tiny excuse for panties aside, lined himself up with her pussy, and firmly thrust his cock home.

The minute he was lodged deep inside her, she cried out, arched her hips, and screamed as he gripped her bare ass with his sticky hand and placed his other palm by her head.

"Rachel?" Although he was trying to get her eyes to refocus, he was putting forth more energy into trying to get his body under some type of control.

When her eyes opened and she looked up at him, he gave her a slow smile and leaned down over her.

Next to her ear, he whispered, "Thank you for my surprise. Now, I won't be able to eat a caramel without thinking about being balls deep inside your sweet, warm pussy."

As he bit her ear, he felt her core grip his cock tight as she screamed and pulsated around him. That was when he finally let go and pounded inside her. He lost himself in the sublime as she fell apart around him, dragging him down deeper into her soul. Nothing had prepared him for the way she destroyed his control with every glance, every action, and as he finally came on a loud roar, every breath she took.

She had crawled under his skin, and he knew he would never be the same.

~

After a warm shower, Rachel was naked and lying in bed beside Cole as she ran her hand down over his chest to the tattoo of the wolf.

This man, who she was currently pressed up against, continually threw her off balance. Tonight, she had expected that she would be on the giving end of the equation, but unlike Ben, she was finding that Cole had the ability to change and adapt.

He was capable of letting go of his rules and demands if something felt better. He also gave her the opportunity to explore her own desires without the pressure of punishment if she didn't *obey*.

This whole relationship they had entered into felt different, yet it still evoked the same side of her that Ben once had. While Ben had been cruel with the power he wielded, Cole used his to persuade, arouse, and ultimately, bring her the most pleasure she had ever felt.

Cole was a man who exuded confidence. He projected strength and determination in every aspect of his life, and it only made sense that he would carry it over to the bedroom. This wasn't a man who was playing at anything; this was a man who lived the only way he knew how. Yes, it just happened to roll over into the sexual aspect of his life. *And aren't I the lucky one?*

She rolled over to her side, so she was looking down at him. "Do these all have some specific meaning?"

Cole looked down at her finger tracing over his skin. With a question of his own, he answered, "What do you think?"

Lifting her eyes from her finger's path, Rachel stated plainly, "I don't think you do anything without some kind of motive or meaning."

"Well then, you have your answer, don't you?"

Frustrated with him, Rachel lifted her hand and pinched the nipple near the wolf.

Almost immediately, one of his large hands came down on top of hers. "Careful," he cautioned.

"Well, answer me. Why do you always deflect?"

"Why aren't you more specific?" he countered, still pressing her palm to his piercing.

"Fine. What does the wolf mean? Even though I can probably guess."

Cole lifted his hand and placed it back under his head. "Well, that sounds interesting. I want to hear your thoughts on it."

Rachel pouted as she stared down into his twinkling eyes. "So, you can laugh at me?"

He reached out one of his hands and twisted a piece of her hair around his finger. "No, I want to see what you think you know about me."

Rachel went back to her imaginary finger painting over the dark ink. The tat was of a wolf facing forward. With his tail in the air, his snout and two front paws stalked toward her.

"I think this has something to do with your personality and how you see yourself—possibly as a lone wolf. For me, I see it as stealth and power." She stopped and stared up into burning eyes. "An alpha male."

She knew she hit the nail on the head because Cole made a show of smiling at her while baring his teeth.

"All the better to eat me with?" she questioned with a small giggle.

He hugged her in close. Instead of answering, he asked, "Aren't you tired, Rachel? I don't know how you do all that you do."

Rachel rubbed her cheek against his side as she ran her fingers down the center of his chest and then over to where the silhouette was intricately inked down his ribs. Shifting in the bed, Rachel scooted away from him to really look at the side profile of the lady. She was so delicate yet strong, etched forever into this complex man's skin.

"Don't deflect. What about this one?"

"No theories?" he pushed.

Rachel didn't really want to voice the one thing that came to mind, so she remained silent.

"Really? Nothing comes to mind?" he pushed as he stroked a finger down her scrunched up nose. "I think you're thinking of something. Tell me. Nothing you say will annoy me, and nothing you say will make me mad."

Rachel took his finger in her hand and looked up at him with cautious eyes. "A girlfriend?"

Shaking his head, Cole swore solemnly, "Nothing on my body is a souvenir of long-lost love, Rachel. I don't believe in making something permanent unless I am one hundred percent sure I won't regret it."

Reaching up to the back of her head, he stroked a palm down her hair. "That being said, this is for my mother, whom I love very much."

Rachel felt her heart swell at Cole's intimate confession.

"Is she..." Rachel paused, not quite sure how to ask the looming question.

"Alive? Yes, but she's no longer with me."

Frowning, Rachel was confused by his answer. She pulled herself up, so she was hovering over him. Daring to cup his cheek, she turned his face, forcing his eyes to fixate on her instead of the ceiling.

"What do you mean? Did she leave you?"

Cole's eyes took on a haunted look, fracturing a part of her that she hadn't realized she had taken him into, as he whispered, "Yes, and she's never coming back."

Before Rachel could ask more, Cole wrapped his arms around her and pulled her against his chest. "No more questions tonight. Sleep, Rachel. Sleep, and have peaceful dreams for the both of us."

Closing her eyes, she rested her cheek on the wolf and placed her hand on his chest, trying to soothe the beast. As she drifted off to sleep, she found herself wondering if Cole Madison knew that he had somehow managed to infiltrate her body, mind, and soul.

CHAPTER 14

As Rachel waved good-bye to Katie, a potential new employee for Precious Petals, she felt as though a weight had been lifted off her shoulders. Rachel liked Katie, and if no one else bothered to show up for interviews, she would be more than happy to hire her.

Moving around her shop, Rachel stopped in front of a bouquet of colorful tulips and took a moment to picture her mother tending to her garden back at the little yellow house that currently sat empty. The house had once been so full of life, and it still held all her most important memories, so it always amazed Rachel that it was now lifeless and sitting for sale.

Shaking her head, she turned away from the tulips and reminded herself that this week was all about finding a way to move forward and to decide what she wanted in life, not to let herself be overwhelmed by the loss she had been feeling for quite some time now.

Naturally, the thought of moving forward automatically made her think of Cole.

Now, there is definitely a welcome distraction. Who knew?

He had marched into her life and demanded she let him in, and with that, he had reintroduced her to a side she had tried to deny.

When Cole had dropped her home this morning, he appeared like the professional businessman he was. It was hard to imagine him as the lover who had taken her on his kitchen floor. Then, he'd leaned over, kissed her, and pressed his card into her hand with the suggestion to come and find him for lunch.

Looking up at the clock, she saw it was two forty-five. She had told him she could just close the shop a little early and be there at three thirty. If she wanted to make it into the city and on time, just the way he liked it, she needed to leave now.

Grabbing her purse, she glanced in the mirror and blew her reflection a kiss, making herself a promise to just go with it, follow her instincts, and let it take her where it would.

And, right now, that was to Cole.

COLE WAS across town and seated behind his desk in the middle of a much longer than expected conference call. As he glanced up at the clock, he clenched his teeth as the big hand shifted to three forty-five. *Shit.* He was late for lunch with Rachel.

As Mr. Fogerty, one of their top clients, continued on about how he was not responsible for the fact that one of his employees was suing him for wrongful termination, Cole looked over to Logan. Logan was sitting on Cole's couch, examining his nails and looking exceedingly bored. He finally raised his eyes and rolled them behind his glasses.

Cole gestured him over and continued taking notes, giving Mr. Fogerty noncommittal answers. Logan stood, smoothed his jacket, and walked over to Cole's desk. Switching to a separate page, Cole scrawled: *Woman in lobby. Name is Rachel. Go get her.*

Logan picked up the paper and read its instructions. As he glanced down at Cole, he tapped the note with his opposite hand. "What does she look like?" he asked in a hushed tone.

Looking him dead in the eye, Cole whispered, "Like a woman you will only ever dream about but will never have the balls to take."

Logan chuckled as he made his way to the door. "That good, huh?"

"Yes, that good. And Logan?" Cole hissed quietly as he covered the mic to the speakerphone. "Hands and eyes off."

Opening the office door, Logan turned back at the last moment just to irritate Cole. "How am I going find her if I can't get a good look at her?"

"Mr. Fogerty?" Cole interrupted his client.

"Yes, Mr. Madison?"

"Can you hold for one minute?"

"Sure, Madison, but don't keep me waiting too long."

Cole pressed the mute button and glared over at his partner, who was currently giving him a what-did-I-say look.

"Keep your charm to yourself, Logan. There are plenty left in the world for you to choose from. Just go get her, and don't ogle her."

Logan laughed as he held his hands up in mock surrender. "Alright, alright. It's refreshing to realize you still acknowledge that I have more charm in my little finger than you do in your whole body."

"Just get her, would you? And don't try anything."

"Okay, message received. No need to be so possessive."

"Logan," Cole warned in a voice that was low and slightly more annoyed than even he expected. "I mean it. Don't try anything. She's with me."

As Logan moved through the open door, he turned back to Cole for one last jab. "Does she know that?"

Logan left, and Cole hit the speaker button and let Mr. Fogerty know he had returned. Distracted, Cole thought back to last night. He was certain of one thing: Without a doubt in his mind, Rachel knew exactly who she was with.

~

RACHEL WAS SEATED, along with several other people, in the very impressive lobby of Mitchell & Madison's Law Firm. As she let her eyes move around her plush surroundings, she reminded herself that there was no need to feel intimidated. It was one thing to tell herself that, but in reality, the marble floors, leather couches, and expensive paintings on the walls were all *very* damn intimidating.

Pulling out her phone, she glanced down at time: 3:46 p.m. He was late, which was very unlike him.

Maybe he changed his mind? No, the perfectly put-together Shelly look-alike behind the mahogany desk had buzzed through and told Cole she was here. *So, he must just be busy.*

Rachel pushed her loosely curled streaked hair behind her shoulders as she crossed one leg over the other. Leaning back into the soft leather couch, she glanced down at her black cheetah leggings with a grimace. She had paired them with knee-high leather boots and a black dress that stopped near her upper thigh and molded to her body like a second skin. Lastly, she had coupled the outfit with a long cream cardigan. *Yep, I definitely do not fit in here.*

Just as she was starting to have serious doubts about being there, one of the large glass doors to the left opened, and a man dressed in a gray pinstripe suit came out into the lobby. The receptionist immediately perked up and smiled at him as she nodded in Rachel's direction.

The tall man turned on his heel and looked around at the people waiting on each of the couches. Framed by expensive-looking, black hipster glasses, his eyes landed on her before he moved across the lobby. Rachel got the impression he was sizing her up. He was at least six feet tall with dark hair buzzed down close to his head, and he had the perfect amount of stubble lining his cheeks and jaw to look fashionable. When he stopped in front of her and looked down, she could see curious blue eyes surrounded by thick dark lashes.

"Well, now. I knew Madison was a lucky bastard, but parading you under our noses is just mean-spirited, even for him."

Rachel felt her mouth twitch as the large yet-to-be identified man unbuttoned his jacket and took a seat beside her. Crossing one leg over the other, he placed one of his arms across the back of the couch behind her and turned to face her.

"You are Rachel, correct? Otherwise, this will be very embarrassing."

Rachel couldn't help the sarcasm that slipped into her voice as she quipped with a smile, "Oh? And if I'm not, will you go and find her and deliver that same line?"

The man beside her placed a large palm over his heart. "You wound me. That was the absolute truth, not a line."

Rachel pulled her bottom lip into her mouth to stifle a small laugh.

"See, you doubt me. I can tell," he accused.

Shaking her head at his playful tone, Rachel replied with a full-blown grin, "You can, can you?"

"Yes. You definitely doubt my sincerity, yet I was telling the truth, the whole truth, and nothing but the truth, so help me God."

"Well, maybe I would be more open to believing you if I knew who you were," Rachel informed him in a conspiratorial whisper.

The man gave her a smile that was just this side of naughty as it met his mischievous eyes. "But then, all the mystery is gone."

Unable to hold back the laughter any longer, Rachel chuckled as she tilted her head to the side. "Obviously, you know Cole."

"Yep, I have had that mostly fortunate pleasure since we were tearing up the college campus together."

Rachel looked him over, noting that he was just as put together as Cole but far more relaxed. As her eyes came back to his, his dark brow quirked up behind the dark-framed glasses.

"So? Do I measure up?"

"I wasn't checking you out," she sputtered.

"Yes, you were. It's okay though. People can't help themselves."

Letting out a bark of laughter at his easy arrogance, Rachel raised a hand to cover her mouth. "Are you serious?"

"Very. I mean, look at all of this."

Rachel looked around to see if anyone else was paying attention to the outrageous words spilling from this man's mouth, but no one else seemed to be looking at them, including the receptionist.

"I still don't know who you are," she pointed out, choosing to ignore his last comment.

"That's right, you don't, do you? Allow me to introduce myself. I'm Logan Mitchell."

Rachel ran the name through her mind several times. *Logan Mitchell. Mitchell.* Her eyes moved to the wall behind the receptionist where the name of the firm, Mitchell & Madison, was announced to incoming clients and guests in large block lettering.

Oh shit, this is Cole's partner, she thought, turning back to him.

He winked at her and pointed out, "See, I was telling the truth. People find me irresistible when they look at all of *this*."

Rachel wasn't really sure what to say to that, but as she stared at him, he lost some of that flirtatious shine. She thought that there was probably a lot more to that comment than what he had said.

"Well, Mr. Mitchell—"

"Oh, come on, Rachel. I think you can call me Logan. We're practically long-lost friends now," he said as he slid closer to her on the couch.

Rachel held her ground as she looked up at him. "Okay, Logan.

Obviously, you know that I'm here to see Cole. So, do you know where he is?"

Logan nodded and replied vaguely, "Yes."

Rachel rolled her eyes with a small laugh. "Wow, why am I so surprised that you are just like him?"

"Oh no, that's where you are very wrong, Rachel. Cole and I might both be apples, but when we fell from the tree, we fell further apart than expected. That's all."

Rachel frowned as she tried to read between the lines. When she came up with nothing, she told him, "Well, like him, you are very good at deflecting and acting vague, Mr. Mitchell."

"Logan," he corrected.

"Yes, okay. Sorry, Logan. So, are you going to tell me where Cole is?"

"Why? So, you can leave me all alone?"

Rachel reached up and scratched her brow. "Now, why do I find it hard to picture you ever alone?"

Logan's smile fell back into place as he stood, holding out his hand to her. "Because I'm so incredibly charming?"

"If you have to point it out yourself, I believe the charm is negated by arrogance."

Logan laughed loudly then, a full-on belly laugh, as she took his hand and stood.

"I can see exactly why Cole has grabbed on to you. Come, I'll take you to him."

"How very kind of you." Rachel muttered as she followed him across the lobby,

When Logan opened the door to the offices and she moved to walk past him, it became clear that she hadn't been as discreet as she hoped or he must have had supersonic hearing.

"I'm never kind, Rachel, but I'm also not stupid. If I don't take you to Cole in the next...oh, let's say five minutes, he's likely to go apeshit, and that would ruin my lunch as well as yours."

Rachel stopped and looked up into Logan's now very serious expression.

"And why would he go apeshit?"

As he looked down at her, she thought the answer she would get would scare her, make her want to leave and never come back, but instead, the answer she got sent a delicious thrill up her spine.

"It's simple really. He'd go apeshit because you are his."

And apparently, that was that.

~

COLE LOOKED up when he heard a light knock on his door. Logan pushed it open, and as Rachel appeared, Cole was shocked by the immediate sense of calm that washed over him. As she moved hesitantly into his office, he glanced at Logan as his partner tilted his head down with a smirk as if to say, *I see exactly what you meant.*

As Mr. Fogerty was wrapping up, Cole gestured to the couch, and Rachel immediately took a seat. Logan closed the door, and even though Cole couldn't greet her, her stare made him feel her *hello* more eloquently than if the words had left her lips.

"Well, Mr. Madison, I believe that is all I can tell you right now, but I will be sure to send you the paperwork with the written statement as soon as possible."

Cole watched Rachel as she slid back into his couch and crossed her wildly covered legs. All the while, she was watching him like this was the first time she had seen him.

"That sounds fine. As soon as I receive it, I'll be in contact."

Leaning back in his chair, he remembered the way she had looked last night, staring down at him as she traced her fingers over his body.

"Terrific. Listen, Madison, will you be at the function for the new DA at the Shedd Aquarium tomorrow?"

"Yes, I'll be there. In fact, I'm hoping my lunch date today will be accompanying me."

Through the speaker, the man chuckled. "You mean, you're going to bring someone? Well, I'll be damned. That's a first."

Cole's eyes moved up to see Rachel's blue ones staring back at him with questions.

"Well, I've never found someone worth bringing before," Cole admitted, sitting forward as he rested his arms on his desk.

The man on the other end told him, "In that case, maybe you should give the little lady my number, so I can warn her all about you."

"I will see you tomorrow, Mr. Fogerty, and you can warn her then."

"*If* she says yes, my man. You still have to ask her."

"She'll say yes. I won't let her say no."

"That's the way, Madison. See you tomorrow night."

"I will see you then," Cole replied and reached out to hit the end button on the speakerphone. Leaning back in his chair once more, Cole quietly requested, "Come over here, Rachel."

Almost as though he were watching her in slow motion, he let his eyes track down her tight black dress and loose cream cardigan to her tall black boots, and he couldn't help the tightening he felt between his legs.

She moved toward him but stopped on the opposite side of the desk.

"Here," he said, patting his lap.

"I'm not doing anything in here, in your office," she sputtered out almost hesitantly.

Cole tilted his head to the side and raised his gaze to hers. "Did I ask you to?"

"You want me to sit on your lap," she pointed out.

"And that automatically means I am going to spread you across my desk and take off your tights?"

Looking around as if to make sure they were alone, she whispered, "The way you were looking at me—"

"Yes?" he coaxed. "Go on."

"The way you *are* looking at me makes me question your motives."

Cole stood then and watched as her hands gripped the back of the leather chair she was standing behind. Moving around the desk, he walked up beside her, and he was slightly amused that she continued to stare out the window behind his own chair, instead of facing him.

He reached out and traced her hand that was still clenching the chair, watching her closely as she sucked in a deep breath.

"Are you more scared of what I will ask you or that you won't be able to deny me?"

Turning her head, she looked up into his eyes, and he could tell she was fighting some kind of internal battle.

"What's going on in there?" he asked.

"Nothing," she denied too quickly before looking away.

"You're lying to me," he pointed out. "Rachel, I will never make you do anything you don't want to." Leaning in close, he placed his mouth to her ear and whispered, "I suspect that's the problem here, isn't it? You want to."

Cole continued watching her as she stepped away from him and moved over to the window to stare out at downtown Chicago.

~

RACHEL COULDN'T DESCRIBE to him how she was feeling.

After Logan had told her so matter-of-factly that she was Cole's, she had experienced such a rush of arousal and acceptance that when she had stepped through his office door, she had been hard-pressed to sit down on his couch and wait for him.

Then, he had sat there, running his eyes all over her, and he'd said words that had only ramped up her feelings.

Am I ready to let a man have such a hold over me again?

Whether or not I am ready doesn't seem to matter though, does it?

He already had a hold over her, and as she stood staring out at the buildings surrounding them, she reminded herself that it was time to surrender to her feelings, not to second-guess them.

Time to give in, to trust.

"My father used to work in a building like this," she told him as she glanced over her shoulder.

Cole slid his hands into his pockets and moved over to stand behind her. He didn't touch her anywhere, but she could feel the heat emanating from his body.

"Did he? What did he do?"

"He was an accountant." Rachel laughed softly. "A boring numbers man, he would say."

"You say *was*. He passed away then?"

Rachel felt her heart ache as she nodded and wrapped her arms around her waist. "Yes. Both my mother and father have passed away."

He didn't touch her, and Rachel wondered how he knew that if he did, she would crumble to the ground. Instead, he offered condolences.

"They must have been amazing individuals to raise such a unique and beautiful woman."

Rachel felt a small smile touch her lips. "My dad always encouraged us to be ourselves—hence the crazy hair and the fact that Mason loves to cook, which isn't the manliest occupation."

Without touching her, Cole's mouth was by her ear. "I love your hair. It was the first thing that drew me to you...well, that and your miniscule skirt. As for your brother, he seems to be doing okay for himself."

Rachel agreed, "Yes, he is. He's a wonderful man, just like our dad was. It's almost funny how similar they are. Dad used to teach us how to cook, and he would dance with me around the kitchen."

She felt two large hands on her shoulders as they gently turned her, so she was looking up into concerned hazel eyes.

"How is it that you make me want so many things I had sworn I could do without?" Cole asked her.

Rachel felt a lump form in her throat as he reached out to cup her cheek.

"I don't ever want you to change, and I will never make you do something that you don't want to."

Leaning down, he pressed his firm lips to hers, all the while keeping his eyes locked with hers.

"And, Rachel, for the moment, I am yours. And you? *You* are mine."

As she stared up at him in breathtaking silence, he asked softly, "Well, now that I know you had the best dancing lessons available, will you come to a function that is being held for the new DA tomorrow night?"

Is there even a need for him to ask? Of course, I'm going to say yes.

But like he had said just a moment ago, he would never make her do something she didn't want to.

With a warm smile, she placed her hand on his chest and spoke the only words she could think of. "I'd love to."

CHAPTER 15

Toward the end of her shift that night, Rachel moved up to the service window to hand one of the waitresses the dessert for table twenty-three, and that was when she caught a glimpse of Cole out of the corner of her eye.

Sitting by himself in the same seat he had been in the night before, he was looking up at Meredith the youngest server on staff, smiling at her as she scribbled notes down on her pad. Rachel noticed that Meredith was paying a little too much attention to the lone man at the table, but Cole...well, he seemed to be just ordering.

Rachel rested her hip against the stainless steel counter and continued watching, not out of jealousy but more curiosity. She supposed she was watching to see if Cole had the same effect on others that he did on her.

And God knows, he has the ability to reduce me to someone with one thing on my mind: sex. Hot, sticky, kitchen floor sex.

As Meredith tipped back her bleach-blonde head and laughed—louder than one would think was necessary—Rachel had her answer.

Rolling her eyes at the sheer absurdity of a man wielding so much power over the opposite sex, Rachel pushed off the counter and moved to turn, only to come face-to-face with Wendy, who was looking in the same direction she had been.

With a smirk on her face, the restaurant manager made her way toward Rachel. When Wendy stopped on the other side of the window, Rachel waited, knowing what was coming.

"Two nights in a row? Since Meredith wasn't on shift last night, I guess she missed the memo on which staff member he belongs to. By the way, he must really like the food."

Rachel almost choked on the laugh she held back at the thought of Cole belonging to anyone, let alone her. Placing her hands on her hips, she tried to glare at the petite blonde with the sleek ponytail, but she knew she was failing.

"Really? I hadn't noticed," Rachel said nonchalantly.

Wendy laughed and leaned over the window as she whispered, "Well, honey, you better because every other single woman on staff has, not to mention the female customers sitting at the bar."

Rachel frowned and turned back to look in Cole's direction again, and this time, she found his smoldering gaze focused on her. Swallowing slowly, she felt her palms begin to itch as a smile so decadently sexual spread across his lips.

I'm going to melt into the floor.

It wasn't until Wendy spoke up again that Rachel realized the manager was still standing there.

"Yes, I can see you are completely unaffected."

Without breaking the heated stare she now held with Cole, Rachel responded absently, "Huh?"

When Wendy chuckled, Rachel finally pulled her eyes away from Cole's to look at the snickering manager. It also happened to be the moment Meredith reached them with a little extra pep in her step.

"Oh, Rachel, hey. You're just who I need."

"Oh?" Rachel responded without giving anything away.

"Yup. See the guy in the suit at table twenty?"

Rachel made a show of looking over at Meredith's table to where Cole was seated. He inclined his head slightly, just enough for her to notice but not enough to draw attention.

Turning her attention back to Meredith, Rachel nodded. "Yes, I see. What about him?"

"Well, first, look at him. Damn, that man is hot." Meredith turned around to get another look, but she quickly spun back when she realized Cole was looking in their direction. "Oh shit. He's looking over here." She giggled.

As Rachel noticed the waitress's cheeks flush, she had to try and hold back her own laughter. Wendy was obviously having the same issue because she couldn't even bring herself to say anything.

When did we turn into teenage girls?

"Yes, he is, isn't he?" Rachel replied, not actually knowing which statement—him being hot or him looking at them—she was answering. "You want to tell me what he wants?"

Meredith sighed dramatically and placed a palm over her heart. "I wish it was me."

"Oh my god. Rach?" Wendy finally busted up with uncontrollable laughter. "Please put the poor girl out of her misery before she goes on."

"Huh?" Meredith questioned, looking between the two of them.

"Shut it, Wendy," Rachel told her friend and manager with a fake grin. "Now, what does he want, Meredith?"

"Well, he said he knows it's not on the menu, but if he asked nicely, could you serve your caramel sauce a little different for him?"

Rachel felt her lips part and her thighs twitch as she thought about the things they had done with her caramel sauce just the night before.

Oh, the places I had my tongue and the places he had his fingers.

"He'd like a scoop of vanilla ice cream with the sauce served warm over it." Meredith stopped talking when she realized Rachel's attention had moved to the man across the room. Then, she prodded, "I told him that would be okay. Is it?"

Rachel grinned as she looked back to Meredith. "You can tell him it will be right out, and he can have my caramel sauce anytime and anyway he wants it."

Meredith's eyes widened before Rachel turned away, and then she heard Wendy hiss at the unsuspecting waitress, "They're dating, you idiot."

Rachel shrugged. *What the hell? He wants everyone to know. Well, now, they know.*

~

AN HOUR and a half after he had arrived, it was closing time. Cole waited patiently for Rachel, and when she finally stepped out into the empty dining room, he felt something he never had before.

His heart started to beat erratically...with nerves.

The woman walking toward him with her black hair and red highlights was looking him over like she was on a mission, and that mission was him. When she stopped in front of him, she showed no hesitation in reaching out and placing a hand against his chest. Cole wondered for a brief moment if she could feel just how hard his heart was thumping. As she raised her head and lifted her thick lashes, he had no clue how he had stayed away from her for so long. Then, he was struck with the realization that he couldn't imagine not seeing her every day.

Wait, what? Well, that had snuck up out of nowhere.

"I think I like you waiting out here for me every night," she told him, almost mirroring his thoughts.

Cole pushed a piece of dark hair behind her ear. "Do you? If I remember correctly, you didn't want me in your restaurant."

She gave him a sassy shrug and raised her brow. "Things change. I'm a woman; it's my prerogative."

"Oh, I see," he murmured as her hand smoothed across his jacket lapel to his tie. "So, *now*, I have permission to stalk you?"

He kept his eyes on hers as she wound his tie around her hand, the way she had done only a couple days earlier.

Has it really been only a couple of days?

Gently, she tugged on the narrow strip of material, and there was nothing Cole could do to stop himself from giving in to her at that moment.

Lowering his head, he closed his eyes as she pressed her lips gently to his. As her tongue came out to flirt with the seam of his lips, he reached forward and gripped her hips, tugging her in close, and that was when all the lights turned off in the dining room.

Pulling her mouth from his, she whispered against his lips, "You have permission to be anywhere I am."

He wasn't sure she knew exactly what she was saying, and as his eyes adjusted to the shadows, he wondered if she realized how much she had just revealed.

"I'll have to remember that," he told her as he released his grip on her. "Let's get going."

"Back to your place?"

Cole took her hand and entwined their fingers. "Yes. Back to my place."

He felt her fingers squeeze his as they made their way to the front door. When they stepped out into the cool night, another realization hit him.

This crazy, spirited, bright-haired woman needed to be his *permanently*.

He was starting to think he would do whatever he needed to make it so.

~

"SWIMMING? It's one in the morning," Rachel pointed out.

Cole opened the top drawer in his bureau and pulled out the small black swim shorts he had worn the other day.

Yes, it was late, and she was tired, but if she got to see him in those again—

Hell, who am I kidding? Of course my ass is going up to that pool.

Calmly and methodically, Cole started to remove his clothing, one item at a time. First, he undid his black belt, sounds of metal clinking against metal filling her ears, and then he pulled the thin strip of leather through his belt loops, creating a whoosh noise. Second, he sat down on the wooden trunk, the one she had stood on only days before, to remove his shoes and socks. Then, he stood back up and pulled his shirt from his pants.

That was when Rachel moved across the space between them and reached up to loosen his tie. Removing his hands, he let them fall to his sides.

In his voice that stroked her in all the right places, he asked, "What are you doing?"

Raising her eyes to his, she didn't smile or give him any kind of sassy response. She just held his inquiring gaze. "I'm undressing you, but unlike the time in my store, I want to take off *all* your clothes. May I?"

She watched him intently, her hand still holding the tie, as he moved his hands behind his back, like he had once before.

"You may," he confirmed, granting her the permission she requested.

Methodically, Rachel undid his tie, slid it from around his neck, and dropped the material to the floor. When she raised her eyes to his, she didn't falter once as she placed her hands on the sides of his abdomen. She smoothed her fingertips up over his chest to the top button where, one by one, she started to undo them. When all the buttons were free, she parted the crisp material. Slipping her palms inside, she moved her hands across warm tight skin. "How did you do it?"

Narrowing his eyes on her, he coerced gently, "How did I do what?"

"I was determined not to know you, yet here I am. How did you slip past all the walls I put up?" Rachel asked him curiously, almost like she didn't really expect an answer.

"Is that what I did?"

Pushing his shirt apart to his shoulders, Rachel leaned in to press a kiss on the wolf. From there, she confessed, "Yes."

Then, she felt one of his hands come up to cup her cheek, urging her to look at him. "I just went where you allowed."

For some unexplainable reason, Rachel felt tears welling in her eyes. *What the hell is going on?* He was making her think about things she had long left behind. He was making her *want* things she had decided weren't for her. As he stood before her, showing her an even softer side to a man she wasn't sure she fully understood, she took a chance. She gave herself completely over to him.

"I'm scared."

"Of me?" he questioned cautiously.

Shaking her head, she closed her eyes as she admitted, "I'm scared of how you make me feel."

As her confession left her lips, he reached out both hands to cup her face, and he leaned down to press a firm kiss to her mouth. There were no tongues and no open mouths involved, but the emotion behind the move rocked her to her soul.

When he pulled back from her, he told her, "Take off your clothes, Rachel. I want you in my bed."

Rachel ran her eyes over his face. "But I thought you wanted to swim?"

Shrugging out of his shirt, he threw it over the trunk. "Like you, I'm capable of changing my mind. I want you naked and in my bed, and I want it in the next two minutes."

"Or?" she pushed.

"Rachel?"

"Yes?"

"There is no or," he informed her as his serious eyes met hers. "Just do it."

~

COLE FOLLOWED her movements as he undid his pants and took them off.

There was no way he was letting this opportunity slip through his hands. She was finally opening up to him, allowing herself to admit to things she might not have acknowledged only days earlier.

This is the right time. I can feel it.

She'd taken off her shirt, bra, and pants, and she was about to remove the sexy scrap of pink lace covering his favorite secret when he stepped toward her. He caught her hand as her fingers slipped into the top of her panties.

Her eyes came up to his in question. "I thought you wanted me naked?"

"So did I," he mused.

He pressed the pads of his fingers against the lace and pushed them down between her thighs. Her mouth parted, and she sighed as he slid his fingers back and forth over the wet material covering her.

"But I really like these, especially the color."

As a soft whimper escaped her lips, she managed to ask, "You like pink?"

Cole touched her again through the damp material. "Yes, Rachel, especially your sweet pink pussy."

He watched her eyes close as her whimper turned to a moan, and she grasped onto his wrist, holding it where it was, as she pushed her hips against his teasing fingers. Cole allowed her a moment of self-pleasure before he pulled his hand away from her and brought it to his mouth.

He licked his fingers and then firmly told her, "My bed. Get in it."

Her lust-glazed eyes moved down over his body to where his cock was pointing at her.

"Now, Rachel," he demanded.

Quickly, she moved around him and climbed up onto his bed. When Cole felt somewhat in control of his body, not to mention his emotions, he turned to see her waiting for him exactly where he wanted her.

Walking around to the side of the bed, he got in and positioned himself next to her and turned her over to her side. She rolled to face him willingly, and as he moved in closer, her eyes looked down his body. He could tell she had different ideas as to where this would go, and he had a feeling his intentions were going to piss her off.

Reaching out to her, he ran the backs of his fingers over the curve of her breast, and then quietly, he urged, "Talk to me."

Huh? What? Talk? Is he insane? He has to be because talking is definitely *not on my mind right now.*

"Talk?" Rachel finally pushed out of her head and mouth.

Cole tweaked her nipple and nodded. "Yes, talk. I want to know about you."

Rachel tried to get her brain to catch up, but with all of him...well, naked and hard in front of her, she was finding it really damn difficult. "You want to talk?"

She watched as an amused look crossed his facial features.

"Yes, talk. You know, it's where you open your mouth and let words fall from your tongue. Are you familiar with that activity?"

Rachel felt her spine stiffen at the smart-ass remark. She was about to push herself up and out of his bed, but her face obviously gave her away because his hand whipped out and firmly gripped her hip.

"Uh-uh, no, you don't."

"Let me go, Cole."

She let out a shocked gasp as he pushed against her hip, and she found herself flat on her back. He followed her over and wedged his body between her thighs, propping himself up above her with his elbows by her head. She turned her head away from him, already feeling too vulnerable tonight, but the all-too-knowing jerk flexed his hips and brushed that delicious cock against her sensitive mound. After that, she couldn't help but look up at him as she arched to meet him.

"Talk to me," he cajoled.

Rachel shook her head on the plush pillow. "I don't want to talk."

His eyes dropped down her body to her heaving breasts and then came back up to hers. "That's a shame because talking is all that's available to you right now."

Rachel's eyes widened as she glared up at him. "That's not true. You're ready to—"

"Ready to what?" he questioned.

As he pushed against her again, she lost her train of thought.

When he seemed to realize nothing would come out of her mouth, he answered for her. "Ready to fuck?"

"Yes," she whined.

"I am ready, Rachel. I'm more than ready to slide between your thighs, but first, I want to talk."

Shifting underneath him, Rachel was about to reach down and take what she wanted, but then he pressed his body flush against hers. All of a sudden, she could feel every inch of his hot skin as he effectively trapped her hands between their stomachs.

"Cole. Please," she pleaded, deciding she wasn't too proud to beg.

"Talk. To. Me," he demanded in that infuriatingly calm tone of his.

Pressing her head back into the pillow, Rachel glowered at him, and she had to admit that the sheer strength in his arms, holding the top part of his body away from her, was fucking sexy. His tight abdomen and erection were twitching and throbbing against her aroused skin, and as his focus remained solely on her, Rachel found it hard to think, let alone talk.

But she managed through as she said, "You're a jerk."

He chuckled and nodded once. "That might be accurate, but I'm the jerk you want, so talk."

Gritting her teeth, Rachel finally relented, seeing it as the only way to get him inside her anytime soon. "Fine. What do you want to talk about? The weather?"

"No. I want you to tell me about Ben."

As that name left Cole's lips, it ricocheted like a gunshot through the silent dark room, and he felt Rachel stiffen right before her body kicked into flight. With more strength than he thought she possessed, she pulled her hands from between their bodies and pushed up to shove against his shoulders.

"Get off me," she demanded.

Cole had known she would flip out when he told her what he wanted to talk about, so being obstinate as ever, he braced himself and remained where he was.

"No. Talk to me."

"Cole," she warned.

He looked down at her with one thought: *I'm not moving, so if you want me to get off, make me*. Just as it entered his mind, she maneuvered herself, so her thighs were parted and wrapped up tight around his hips. Before he knew it, she pushed and rolled as she slapped at one of his arms, making him lose his balance.

He fell down on top of her with a grunt before he gripped her shoulders. He rolled with her until they tumbled across the sheets and fell off the edge of the bed, landing with a loud thump on the floor.

Jesus, that's going to leave a fucking mark.

She landed on top of him with an oomph before she began squirming all over him as she tried in vain to get away, but Cole wasn't letting her go anywhere. He just hoped her knees didn't connect with anything that would leave permanent damage. Holding her wrists, he struggled with her as he pulled her arms around behind her back and twisted his legs over hers, pinning her in place, flush against him.

"Let me go," she spat at him as if she were a trapped animal.

"No," he growled, holding her tight against him.

Ignoring the throbbing in his ass, back, and head, Cole leaned up, so he was nose-to-nose with her. Again, he demanded, "*Who* is Ben?"

Her blue eyes narrowed on his with as much heat as the center of a flame as she tried to glare him to death. "Why? Are you jealous?"

If he hadn't been so worked up, he might have found some humor in her accusation, but as it was, he found himself losing the control he relied on to keep him in check. "Do I seem jealous, Rachel? I'm fucking pissed off that I am lying on this hard fucking floor. But I'm not jealous."

Tightening his grip on her wrists, he continued in a softer tone, "I want to know why you yell his name out at night right before you wake up. You scream like the devil is chasing you."

He noticed she took a quick breath before she turned her head away.

"Was he the one who hurt you?" Cole pressed cautiously. "Was he the one that made you afraid to be touched?"

The silence in the room was deafening as he made himself wait. *Give her time, man. Give her some fucking space.*

But on the heels of that thought came, *Fuck that. I'm in her space now, and she is not getting rid of me.*

Cole waited for her to say something, anything, but it turned out that no words were needed. As she turned her face back to him, he could see tears in her eyes, and he felt his chest tighten.

Releasing her hands slowly, Cole wrapped his arms around her shoulders and pulled her down until her cheek was resting against his chest. He felt her back shake beneath his palms as she silently sobbed against him.

"Shh," he coaxed against her dark hair where he pressed a kiss. "It's okay."

He let his legs relax from around hers as she snuggled in closer to him and rested her palms against his chest. He could hear every deep breath she took, and before he knew it, his hands were gently smoothing down her back to try and soothe her.

"Talk to me," he encouraged again. He couldn't quite understand why it was so important to him, but somehow, he knew it was vital.

"I don't know what to say," she finally replied.

Cole continued to stroke her naked back, running his fingertips over her mantra—*Pride, Strength, Hope, Love*—and for the second time tonight, he thought that this woman needed to be his permanently.

"Just start at the beginning and tell me what happened. Nothing you say will make me think any less of you, and nothing you did will make me look at you any differently. But maybe if you tell me what he did to you, you will see *me* differently and realize that you are safe here. I am not him, and you do not need to be scared when you close your eyes at night."

Resting one hand on the curve of her hip with the other in her thick hair, Cole squeezed gently and pressed his lips to her head. "Let me in, Rachel. Let down that final wall."

~

"Ben, please don't do this," Rachel pleaded as she stood, shaking, in the corner of their bedroom.

Her tank top and denim cutoffs that she had worn to her mother's house made her feel practically naked as he moved toward her. She could feel her right eyelid starting to close from the swelling, and she was sure the cool liquid running down her chin was blood from her own lip. The worst part was that she was sure this wasn't over, not by a long shot.

Ben had come home drunk. This was a new thing he had started.

It had been bad enough when he hit her sober, but when he would get in a mood like this with the bottle behind it, it would usually be days before she could go outside.

As he rolled up his sleeves, his face blurred in front of her. Rachel was hoping she would pass out. Somehow though, she knew she wouldn't be that lucky. He'd always made sure to never give her a reprieve like that.

"I asked you a fucking question, so answer me," he shouted as he stepped closer to her.

Rachel swallowed and wrapped an arm around her waist as she licked her upper lip. She winced from the sting it caused in her bottom one. "I was over at Mom and Dad's until three. I was helping Mom plant her tulips up the main path to the hou...house," she stuttered the final word as she watched him unbuckle his belt.

"I expected you to be here when I got home," he told her, his voice seemingly coming from far, far away now.

Or maybe she was just wishing that were the case as she swayed back into the wall.

"I expected dinner, and I expected you.*"*

As his saliva hit her face, a shiver ran through her entire body at the venom he directed her way.

"I'm sor...sorry. I didn't think—"

"You never fucking think of anyone but yourself," he spat at her as he snapped the leather in his hand.

Rachel knew what he was going to do. Really, she had known it would only be a matter of time before things progressed from his fists to other objects, but as her eyes kept shifting to the leather in his hand, she couldn't actually bring herself to believe he would use it.

"That's not true, Ben. I...I was thinking about you. Tha...that's why I hurried home."

"You hurried home, so I wouldn't catch you, but you were too fucking late. I was here, and you weren't, and you know how that makes me feel."

She did know. Over and over, he had told her how he hated to come home to an empty house. It made him feel neglected and unloved, like his hard day at work meant nothing to her.

Oh god, when will I stop putting up with this?

As the thought entered her mind, she watched Ben's hand rise up above her, and with whiplike precision, he cracked the leather belt down hard across her bare upper thigh.

Screaming out in agony from the painful burn, Rachel had nowhere to go as he whipped his hand up a second time and brought it down across her other thigh.

Pulling back into the corner, Rachel closed her eyes tight, knowing there was nowhere to go. He was too big, too powerful, and he had her cornered. The best she could hope for would be the peace of blackness, whether that be from passing out or death. At this point, she would take either.

Closing her eyes, she made herself float away, letting her mind drift, as she numbed herself to the cuts that were forming over the raised welts on her thighs. If she survived this night and recovered in one piece, this was it. She would no longer do this to herself. She would no longer let him do this to her, and she would never, ever let a man control her or tie her down—ever again.

CHAPTER 16

Rachel placed a palm to Cole's muscular chest and pushed up, so she was looking down at him lying beneath her in the moonlight. Serious eyes peered back at her with so much intensity that they made her shiver as she tried to find the words she was desperately searching for.

However, "Can we go for that swim?" was what she blurted out instead.

"You want to go for a swim? Now?" he asked, double-checking, as she started to wriggle and make her way off his lap.

This was the only way she could think of to put some much-needed space between them. If he wanted answers, he wasn't going to get them while they were this close. She needed distance. She needed the ability to move and breathe, and here, on the floor of his bedroom, he was too close, and she was too vulnerable.

"Yes," she confirmed.

She moved to kneel beside him where he was now leaning up on his arm, staring at her with an incredulous look on his face.

"Okay," he told her slowly. He sat up, so they were now nose-to-nose. "But we go as is."

Rachel looked down at his naked body before raising her eyes to his. "I don't see a problem with that."

"Okay then, let's do this."

~

Cole stared at the woman kneeling beside him. She was covered only by a small pair of pink panties, and her crazy red-highlighted hair was flirting with her hard nipples. He had to remind his cock not to get excited. He had meant it when he told her he wanted to talk, and he had a feeling she was going to, but she just needed space. He hoped she didn't expect too much of it because her being nearly naked in a body of water was not going to be a great deterrent for him.

Pushing up to get to his feet, he watched her smoothly rise before she walked around him to the end of the bed.

"What are you doing?" he inquired as she picked up her shirt.

"I'm going to get dressed before we go upstairs. Unlike you, I don't fancy parading my naked ass up your corridor or for the camera in the elevator."

Cole had to try extremely hard not to smile at her smart-ass mouth. "I have robes. Want one?"

Cocking her head to the side, Rachel asked, "How many do you have?"

"Enough for us."

"His and hers?" she quipped.

"Try, mine and mine."

He strode over to where she stood beside his bed, the bed they had just tumbled out of. She never took her eyes away from his face, and as he got closer, she turned and moved a step back until her ass hit the edge of the mattress. Cole kept walking until he pressed his naked body up against hers, and then he placed his hands on each side of her on the bed, effectively caging her in.

"I haven't forgotten why we are going up there, so it's best you don't either. Okay?" he reminded her.

Rachel tipped up her chin and locked eyes with him. "This seems to be your favorite position."

Cole let his top lip curl this time while his eyes traveled down to where her breasts were heaving with each deep breath she took.

"This is definitely not a bad position," he agreed as he raised a hand and ran a finger over her nipple. "It's close, but it's definitely not my favorite."

Her eyes clouded over as her lips parted around two words, "What is?"

Rising to his full height, Cole turned and walked over to his closet. When he returned, she was still where he had left her waiting for an answer.

"Some other time, perhaps? Okay, let's go. The pool, it is."

~

RACHEL TOOK the robe from his outstretched hand, shrugged into it, and wrapped the tie around her waist. She watched Cole from out of the corner of her eye as he did the same, and just as she was about to walk by him and make her way out, he shocked her yet again. He held his hand out to her. Rachel looked at the large palm extended to her before she raised cautious eyes to his.

How does he do it? How has he made me feel so safe in just a few days? And nights. Don't forget the nights.

She reminded herself that she was here to move forward, to let go, and to find out who she really was. Taking a leap of faith, she reached out and slid her palm into his.

"Trust me?" he asked as he wrapped his warm fingers around hers and tugged her hand gently.

As she moved up beside him, Rachel whispered softly, "I do."

~

NOT TEN MINUTES LATER, Cole watched as Rachel dropped the robe she had worn up to the pool. She strutted to the edge and dived straight in. He had to give her props. She had great form as she glided through the water in a sleek freestyle up the length of the pool.

As he moved to the edge, his mind started to jump all over the place. *How can I keep her? How am I going to convince her to stay? Does she want to stay? Fuck asking.* Make *her want to.* That was what it came down to—making her *want* to.

As she came to a stop where his toes were kissing the end of the pool, the woman—who he was shuffling around all his plans for—looked up at him with large blue eyes and lashes sparkling with water droplets. As she moved effortlessly to her back, the smile that crossed her face was a combination of shy and sexy. Slowly, she pushed away from the wall, displaying her wet naked breasts to him.

Cole undid his robe and dropped it to his feet. Naked as the day he was born, he raised a brow. "Talk first, remember?"

She moved her arms out beside her, like she was making snow angels in the water, but with her fiery-highlighted hair and pink panties, Cole knew no angelic thoughts were going on in this room. From where she was, he watched her eyes drop to what he knew was throbbing proof that his cock wanted to do a hell of a lot more than talk.

"I remember," she acknowledged as she closed her eyes. "Do you?"

That was when he made his move. Diving into the water, he torpedoed through the heated liquid, and as he came up beside her, he grabbed her waist before she had a chance to evade him. With a shriek, her legs splashed the surface as they went under. Her hands reached out for purchase, and luckily for him, he was the only thing for her to hang on to.

As her palms gripped his shoulders, Cole wrapped his arm around her waist, pulling her wet warm body against his own. With a natural ease that showed years spent in the pool, he kicked out behind himself and moved her across the pool to the edge.

When her back met with the cool tile surface, Cole moved in, so his body was pinning her to it. Her mouth, wet and shiny, parted just as her legs did, and he could feel her hard nipples grazing his as she arched her body against him and wrapped those legs around his waist. Keeping his eyes on hers, Cole thrust his cock against the wet scrap of pink, the only barrier between them at the moment.

"I can do this all night," he informed her as he lowered his mouth to her ear. "You, me, the warm water, and your sexy body...almost naked but still not quite naked enough. And after the way you tumbled me out of bed, the water feels good on my poor aching muscles."

Cole flicked his tongue against her lobe and felt her shiver. She made a noise so soft that he would have missed it if he weren't so focused on her.

Yes, Cole thought, *that was definitely a moan.*

"I could easily keep you here, and I could just continue to..." He paused to rub his body against her. "Grind..." He punctuated the word with his hips. "My..." He gave her another delicious stroke. "Cock..." *Oh Christ, hurry.* "Against..." *Fuck, talk.* "You."

~

RACHEL COULD BARELY REMEMBER *how* to talk with Cole practically fucking her against the pool wall. The only thing hindering the process was her pathetic excuse for panties.

Just rip them off.

"Cole," she finally managed to push out of her mouth as her eyes searched his face.

"Talk to me," he growled between clenched teeth. "I know you trust me, so talk to me."

It's now or never, Rachel thought as she looked into unwavering, unrelenting hazel eyes. *He isn't going to budge. If I refuse, that's it. Whatever we have started will be over.*

Licking her wet lips, she relaxed her legs from around his waist and pushed gently against his shoulders. She felt his arm relax as she watched his eyes narrow on her.

"You need to move," she informed him softly.

"Rachel, let me in, and—" he started.

"No," she began.

"No? Well, if you aren't going to—"

"Cole?" she questioned, interrupting him once more even though she knew he hated that.

There was a steady pause.

And then, he replied, "Yes?"

"Not no, I won't tell you. No, I can't tell you, not while you're so close. You need to move," Rachel told the immense man before her.

It was funny to her. In a moment as intimate as sex, his strength, height, and power were what appealed to her most. Yet, right at this moment, it was what she needed the most distance from.

"You want me to move? Where?" he asked her in a calm voice, an exact opposite to the growl she had heard only moments before.

Rachel looked around and saw they were close to the ladder. Bringing her eyes back to his, she lifted her arm and pointed. "Over there."

He turned and looked to where she was directing him. Bringing his eyes back to her, he agreed, "Okay, I'll go over there. But, Rachel?"

Rachel blinked as he started to swim backward toward the agreed-upon spot.

"When this is over, you better be ready. I want to fuck you almost as bad as I want to hear what you have to say."

"You want to *fuck* me?" Her tongue traced her bottom lip as she stared at him while he rested against the ladder. "That sounds…rough."

She felt Cole's eyes on her as though he were touching her from across the pool.

"After wrestling with you in and out of my bed and then in this pool, my desire for a nice slow night of making love has suddenly disappeared." He moved his arm, so he could run a hand through his hair. "Plus, there's something extremely sexy about you trusting me, and it makes me want to get close to you." He paused and licked his lips. "Really fucking close. Now, talk."

~

COLE WASN'T LYING. He did want her, but first, he wanted words. He needed to know what chased her from her sleep every other night. He kept his eyes on the nearly naked and half-submerged woman pressed firmly against the tile wall. Her dark hair was sleeked back from the water, and even though he could see hints of red through it, this was the first time she looked completely natural. She looked vulnerable.

"I met Ben when I was seventeen," she started.

"Seventeen?" Cole couldn't stop himself from commenting. When her eyes came to him, he shrugged. "Sorry, I didn't realize. Go ahead."

Looking away from him, she continued, "It was the night I graduated, and Mason and Josh came home from college to see me. The graduation ceremony was over, and I was planning to go to the after-party with them."

"But you didn't?" Cole questioned, keeping a close eye on her.

"No, I didn't," she replied, shaking her head.

"Why?"

Turning to him, she asked him directly, "Do you promise not to get weird or pissed off?"

Cole was surprised by the question. He didn't have a clue as to why she thought *he* would get mad at her about something that happened years ago before they had even met. She seemed to need the answer though, so he nodded, wondering what she was about to reveal.

"I...well, I had a huge crush on Josh all the way through high school." She paused and glared at him, daring him to respond.

He had already suspected that there was history between her and Josh, so it wasn't that big of a surprise, but it was interesting information just the same. When he remained impassive, she pressed on.

"Well, I was going to go to the after-party that night, but I overheard someone talking...*Lisa*..."

She seemed to hiss that name, so Cole couldn't help himself. "Who was Lisa?"

She rolled her eyes and then tartly replied, "Josh's idiot girlfriend."

Realizing this was not a good time to laugh at her continued dislike of a girl from her teenage years, Cole remained silent.

"Anyway, she started talking about how *amazing* the...well..." Rachel stopped and bit her lip. Then, she blurted out, "You know what I mean."

"Sex? How great the sex was with Josh?"

Cole couldn't believe he was having this conversation about his business associate and friend. He would probably never look at Josh quite the same, but it was obviously very important to Rachel, so he tried to listen objectively.

"Yes. I got upset. It's stupid now, but back then, the thought of her with him pissed me off."

Although he knew the answer, Cole interjected there, "Does it still bother you?"

She turned so quickly he could have sworn her head almost flew off her neck.

"Definitely not. Josh is like a brother to me. That night still bothers me for many reasons, but none of them revolve around Joshua Daniels."

Cole nodded, believing her one hundred percent. "So, what happened?"

"Well, I went to a different party. I was determined to forget about the boy who broke my heart, so I did what all girls do to forget."

"Eat ice cream?" he quipped, trying to keep her from becoming too upset by her story.

"No," Rachel replied caustically. "I drank way too much."

Cole felt his stomach tighten as he thought about Rachel at seventeen—alone, heartbroken, inebriated, and meeting this Ben guy for the first time. "And then what?" he urged.

Rachel slid down the wall a little until half of her hair was in the water and her chin was touching the surface. "Then, I met Ben."

Cole told himself to stay where he was and keep his mouth shut. She just needed a moment, but it was quickly becoming apparent that his patience was running thin. He needed to let her know what he wanted. *And god, I want it.*

Softly, he encouraged her to continue, "Tell me your secrets, Rachel. I need to know you."

RACHEL TURNED her head to look at the naked man submerged in the water. All she could see were his broad shoulders and head as he leaned against the pool ladder. His eyes were focused on her with such ferocity that she felt he was pulling the information from her through sheer force of will alone.

"Ben was older than me," she found herself divulging.

"How much older?"

"I was seventeen, and he was twenty," she confessed.

"He had sex with you when you were seventeen? I'm going to beat this guy's ass."

Rachel couldn't help the small smile that tugged at her lips. "Relax over there, would you? We didn't do *that* until I was eighteen...a week later."

Cole showed his teeth in a fierce scowl. "That does not make me want to kick his ass any less."

"Oh? And how old were you when you lost your virginity?"

"We are not discussing me," he pointed out in a surly tone.

"Well, maybe we should."

"Stop stalling, Rachel. Tell me about Ben."

She nodded and took a deep breath, and suddenly, she wanted to be closer. First, she had wanted distance, but as she thought about the cruelty of Ben, she found herself inching closer toward Cole, closer toward safety.

"Everything started out fine, like normal. When we met, I was trying to forget about Josh, so I flirted outrageously with Ben. I hadn't dated anyone else, so I pretty much threw myself at him, and he took what I offered...over and over."

"Yes, I get the point Rachel. Move on."

As she got closer to him, she could see his eyebrow twitching, and she knew he was exercising immense control and patience.

"Things were great for a while. He was older, smarter, and to me, he was perfect. Plus, he made me forget about Josh until..." She paused, realizing she was now only an arm's length away from Cole.

"Until?" he asked.

Rachel looked him straight in the eye as she confessed softly, "Until he started to hurt me."

COLE WRAPPED his hands around the metal rails of the ladder. He had guessed it was something along those lines, but to hear the words come out of her mouth, entering the space between them, made him want to find the cowardly fucker and kill him.

She continued looking at him, and the significance of her moving closer was not lost on him. All of a sudden, he wanted to wrap her in his arms and promise her that no one would ever touch her again. That he would take care of her. That he would never let her go.

It was only the skittish look in her eyes, like she was about to bolt, that had him holding his tongue.

Gingerly, Rachel reached out as though she needed something to anchor herself. She placed her wet small palm against his chest and looked up into his eyes. "At first, it was for fun."

Cole looked down at the woman staring at him and tightened his fingers around the rails. If ever there was a time not to touch, this was it. He didn't know what he wanted to do—shake her and say, *No, you were completely wrong*, or hug her close and never let her go.

"At first?" he asked.

She attempted a flirty smile, but it didn't reach her eyes. "You know, in the bedroom. I'm sure you've—"

"Stop right there. Don't assume things you don't know for certain. It only makes a fool out of you and me."

She lowered her eyes, and he knew she was about to remove her palm from him, but Cole wasn't about to let her go anywhere. He raised his left hand and placed it firmly over her right.

"I'm not one to judge what others do behind closed doors, but know this. I have never hit a woman—ever. Not inside or outside of a bedroom, not in anger or passion. Is that something you want? Something you need?" He hoped to hell she said—

"No."

Oh, thank God. He knew he didn't have that in him. He enjoyed having the power in a situation, but he didn't want to take it with violence.

"I like being told what to do," she admitted, staring up at him again.

He could tell that this was her version of baring her soul. He was also aware that he wanted to wrap her up in his arms and never let her go.

"You like to follow orders?" Cole clarified, already knowing this.

Whenever they had been together, any small order he had given her turned her on, and her desire had doubled. This wasn't news to him. *But it is fucking hot to hear out loud.*

"Yes. I like to follow yours. It turns me on to please you. To do as you tell me to. To have you instruct me." Bravely, she kept her eyes locked with his as she continued, "Ben started out the same, but somewhere along the way, he changed. He became possessive, demanding..." She paused, and then she whispered, "Abusive."

"What did he do, Rachel? Tell me," he requested, now needing to know everything.

"We were together for a long time—five years."

Fuck, Cole thought. *Now, I really hate the fucker.*

"The first two and a half years were fine but casual. We dated and would sometimes stay over at the other's house. He was just as a boyfriend should be, and one night, as we were...intimate, he told me to do something, and he noticed the way it affected me. After that, he asked me if I wanted to do that more often. I didn't really understand everything he was talking about, but he convinced me that I should let him lead in the bedroom, and I should follow...or obey as he put it.

At first, it was fun, exciting...different. I had a secret no one knew about. I knew it was a good one because nothing that felt that good could be wrong, right?"

Cole couldn't talk. He wanted to hit someone—preferably Ben or maybe even Josh for not dating her when she was younger and letting her end up with this creep. But he knew that wasn't fair either. They all had pasts, but—*fuck him*—he was *not* enjoying hearing about hers.

"Then, things started to change. After he moved into my apartment, he began to get aggressive. We went to a family dinner one night, and when we got home, Ben got mad at me and pushed me into the wall. He hurt me and then called me a stupid bitch. I couldn't understand what I did. I didn't know why he was acting that way."

Cole could feel her little nails digging into his chest, and he relished the bite they brought because he was feeling murderous. Squeezing her hand where it rested against him, he silently pushed her to continue.

"After that, he became really intense. He started wanting to tie me up during sex. He'd use belts, ties, and handcuffs to hold me down, and while it was exciting, at the same time, his fucked-up mood swings scared the hell out of me. I was terrified to say no because I didn't want him to hit me. Then, it escalated one night. He came home and told me he had run into Mason. At first, I didn't understand where he was going with that because he had called and told me to be waiting for him, which meant I had to be naked. So, I waited for him, just like he had asked, knowing this would make him happy. Well, at least, I thought it would."

She stopped and took a deep breath. Bringing her second hand up to his chest, she gripped him just like she was doing with the other. Cole could tell she was as absorbed in the story as he was because not one part of him or her was focused on their lack of clothing and their intimate proximity.

"He told me to turn around, and I did as he asked me to. When I heard him pull out handcuffs, I knew that he was in a weird mood, and I did *not* want to be cuffed while he was acting that way. I told him no, but he didn't listen. Once he had me secured, he taunted me. Finally, he turned me around and told me that Mason had said Josh was back in town and he'd joked about Josh being my old *crush*," she spat the word like it was tainted, like it was poison.

When her eyes came up to his, she had tears running down her cheeks.

"I never even knew Josh was back. I didn't even care, but Ben didn't believe me."

Cole brought up his free hand and cupped the back of her neck where her wet hair was pressed to her naked skin. He was letting her know he was there, so she wasn't alone.

"He threw me on the bed, and I was on my back when he got on top of me. I promised him that Josh was no one and that I didn't even know he was back in town, but that wasn't enough. He straddled me and slapped me in the face, and as I lay there beneath him, I let him. I just *let* him hit me. But instead of that being the wake up call it should have been, I stayed. I stayed with him, naively believing that things would change. It wasn't until he took his belt to me one night that I knew, if I survived, I couldn't stay with him a day longer than I had to. I also promised myself I would never let a man hold me down or control me—ever again. "

Lowering his mouth to her forehead, Cole gritted his teeth. Against her cool skin, he whispered, "What happened? How did you leave? Mason?"

She pulled back abruptly and shook her head. "No. And you have to promise me to never tell him."

Cole nodded, but he knew that, like himself, if Mason ever found out about what had happened to his little sister, he would hunt the man down, and...*well, God help Ben. Or not.*

"Then how?"

"My father." She finally smiled up at him. "My wonderful, larger-than-life father. He came over the day I was kicking Ben out and found him hitting me." Rachel's smile widened. "He beat the ever-loving shit out of Ben."

Cole felt his own mouth twitch, but he couldn't bring himself to smile. "Your father sounds like a very wise man. He managed to stop. I probably would have killed him."

Finally, she nestled in close to him, and the enormity of trust she was extending was so overwhelming that Cole felt an unfamiliar knotting in his throat. With her hands trapped between them in the water, he stroked a soothing palm down her hair and under the water to the curve of her back where he pulled her in as close as possible.

That was when she softly said, "My father would have loved you."

Cole closed his eyes and squeezed her tightly. "I don't know about that. I'm not really the father-loves-me material."

She tilted up her head and gave him a shy smile he had never seen. "This time, Mr. Madison, you are wrong."

"Am I?"

"Yes," she murmured as she nuzzled close to him.

When her tongue flicked his nipple and piercing, he felt the familiar stirrings of desire.

"What do you think you're doing?"

She did it again and peered up at him with eyes now full of mischief.

"Well, I've finished talking. Do you still want to fu—"

"Shh," he interrupted. "No, I don't."

He watched a frown appear on her face as she made a move to push away from him, but Cole wrapped his arms around her waist and hauled her up so her mouth was level with his. He moved his face in close to hers and looked her directly in the eye.

"I want to take you up to my bed, lay you down in it, and slide so deep inside you that I have trouble remembering what it's like to be apart from you. And, Rachel?"

"Yes?"

"I want you to let me."

As he pressed his mouth to hers, he was happy to find that she had agreed.

CHAPTER 17

It was Thursday morning, and the sun was shining down through the shop window. If Rachel was honest, she was feeling pretty fantastic. As she stood behind the counter, arranging a vase of calla lilies, she thought back to last night with a smile.

When they had finally reached Cole's bedroom, he had made good on his promise, and he had effectively made her forget what it was like to ever be apart from him. He had also managed to chase all the demons from her sleep. She had no doubt it had to do with the fact that he had wrapped her up in his arms and held her all night.

The man has such a wonderful soft side to him—like that look I keep seeing, the one he shows when he thinks I'm not looking. Hmm...

Tonight was the night of the function down at the Shedd Aquarium. She'd already arranged with Mason to have the night off at Exquisite, so she was going to close the shop early to get her hair done.

She'd also decided to go ahead and hire Katie.

She's perfect. So what if it's quick and impulsive? I like her, so it's completely justifiable, she thought as she imagined Mason ruminating over the reasons for looking at several other candidates.

Placing the vase in the back display cabinet, Rachel moved around the shop, singing one of the old songs her father used to love. Of course, she was adding her own personal flair just for fun.

"Stars shinin' bright above me." She started as she hummed Dream a Little Dream Of Me.

Picking up the broom, she found herself twirling it in her hand as she was possibly—*actually, definitely*—dancing with it.

Oh god, Rachel thought as she stopped abruptly. *He's reduced me to moon-eyed teenage girl.*

"Ahh, the classics. Mama Cass. Don't stop on my account. Please continue."

Spinning around on her toes, Rachel snapped her mouth shut as she came face-to-face with Josh. She was not pleased to see him standing just inside the shop door, bearing witness to her horrible pseudo-singing audition. With his shoulder propped against a display stand, he was staring at her with one annoyingly amused grin.

"What are you doing here, Josh?" she demanded as she leaned the broom handle up against the wall. "And how did I *not* hear the bells on the door?"

"I'm stealthy?" he offered as he moved closer. "Or maybe you were singing so loudly and dancing around the place that you didn't notice?"

Rachel shook her head and placed her hands on her hips.

"Look, smartass, I'm in a really good mood, so don't come in here with another warning or lecture about Cole. Okay?"

Josh took his hands out of his jeans pockets as he moved closer toward her. Raising them in the universal sign of surrender, he chuckled and cocked his head to the side. "I come in peace, especially if he's the reason you're so happy. Relax, would you? Does Madison know how quick you are to defend him?"

Rachel tipped up her chin to face her lifelong friend, and then she finally gave him a slow grin. "No, and don't you tell him either. He doesn't need to know he's turned me into a silly girl."

Josh reached out and slung an arm around her in a one-arm hug, tugging her in close. "You? A silly girl? Never. You have always had impeccable taste."

Jamming a soft elbow to his side, Rachel laughed as she looked him in the eye. "Yeah, I do, don't I?"

"Well, definitely at first. I mean, nothing is as pure as a wide-eyed innocent girl's first love."

Rachel bumped her hip to his. "Is that right, Daniels? Who was Shel's first love?"

"That's different," he answered immediately.

As he removed his arm, Rachel made her way to the counter with him following.

"Really?"

"Yes. Shelly knew nothing before me."

"Oh, of course. How could she?"

Placing his hands on the counter, Josh leaned forward with a huge smirk. "Exactly."

Rachel crossed her arms over her chest and decided, *What the hell?* She dived right in. "Alright, Josh, what do you want? Did Mason send you?"

Rachel could just imagine the conversations surrounding her and Cole at the moment.

"No, no. This has nothing to do with Mason. I just wanted to stop by and see how you are doing. You know I have always worried about you, even before Cole."

Relaxing her arms down by her side, Rachel couldn't help the soft smile she gave to the man with the kind eyes, shaggy brown hair, and the warmest smile she had ever seen. "You're pretty special, you know that, right?"

Josh raised a brow as his lips quirked. "Special meaning?"

"Good, loyal, sweet."

"You make me sound like Mutley minus the dog slobber," he pointed out lightly.

"No, you sound like a good man, and that's what you are. Even as a kid, you were always good."

Josh shook his head as he rested against the counter. "Well, I think you must be forgetting about all the times Mason and I got our asses chewed out by your parents and mine."

"No, I'm not. You did both get into a lot of trouble though, didn't you? But what I mean is with me and other girls. You were always a good guy, a guy that girls could rely on to not be a jerk."

"Rachel, you're remembering me through the eyes of a teenage crush." He chuckled and shook his head. "There are plenty of girls who would disagree, I'm sure."

"God, I had the biggest crush on you," she admitted, rolling her eyes. "I was *so* into you. I even remember a day when we all went swimming down by the lake. I think I was thirteen, and Mom asked me if I liked you. I was so embarrassed."

Reaching across the counter, Rachel placed her palm over the hand he had left there. "She would be thrilled to see you so happy with Shelly. I wish..." Rachel trailed off and looked up at familiar understanding eyes.

"You wish what?" Josh urged.

Squeezing his hand, Rachel whispered, "I wish we all could have said good-bye."

Josh turned his hand over on the counter, and in a comforting gesture, he wrapped his fingers around hers. "Me, too, Rach. Me, too."

~

Rachel made her way up the grassy bank to where her mother was sitting, looking down at the two teenage boys who were currently splashing each other in the lake. When she stopped in front of the blanket, her mother patted the spot beside her, gesturing for Rachel to join her.

"Sit with me?" her mom asked as she smiled up at her.

Rachel kicked off her bright red flip-flops and kneeled down beside her.

"You didn't want to go in with the boys?" her mother questioned as she raised her hand to shield her eyes from the sun.

Rachel thought about that for a moment and quickly shook her head. There was no way she was taking off her shorts and top and getting in the water with him *there.* Why did Mason have to invite him anyway?

"Rach?"

Turning her eyes back to her mom's, Rachel tried for a convincing smile. "No, Mom. I don't want to swim today."

That's a complete lie. *As the sun kissed the back of her neck, there was nothing she wanted more. That had all changed though when the boys had taken off their shirts and raced each other into the water.*

Instead, Rachel found herself staring at the brown-haired boy currently roughhousing with her brother. She decided there was no way she was baring her flat-chested thirteen-year-old self in her bathing suit to him. She couldn't decide what was more annoying—the fact that she was still flat as a board or the thought that one day she'd have boobs. Some days, she hated being a girl.

"Are you okay?" her mom asked, leaning into her with a little shoulder-to-shoulder bump. "You've been really quiet, which is not like you at all."

Rachel turned to look at her mom and bit her bottom lip. It was so hard, not having a sister to talk to about boys, and there was no way she was bringing this up with Mase.

"It's Mason's friend, isn't it?" her mom whispered conspiratorially.

Rachel felt her eyes widen as her heart started to beat erratically.

"No," Rachel denied emphatically.

Her mother chuckled and reached out to push a piece of hair behind Rachel's ear.

"It's okay if it is, Rach. It's normal to look at boys and think they're cute."

"I don't think anything," Rachel stressed, becoming flustered. In the back of her mind though, all she could remember was the way he smiled at her. Oh yes, she definitely thought he was cute.

"Well, no matter if you do or don't, it's completely normal. But remember, he is Mason's friend, and he is older than you."

"Mom," Rachel whined, feeling her face heating up. Why is Mom still talking? Is she determined to embarrass me?

"Alright, alright. I will keep your secret."

Crossing her arms in front of her, Rachel pouted and rolled her eyes in the way all thirteen year olds do. "There is no secret, Mom."

"Sure there isn't, love. Is that why you giggle every time he talks to you?"

"Do not."

"Do too," her mom replied with a mischievous grin. "But don't worry. I won't tell."

Rachel looked back down to the river where her brother and his new friend were now climbing out of the water. She stared at the lanky boy beside Mason, and as he raised his hand to push it through his hair, she felt her cheeks redden. Rachel looked away only to see her mom chuckling at her.

"I promise not to tell," she repeated with a soft look as she brushed gentle fingertips over Rachel's cheek.

Rachel lowered her eyes quickly. Her mom always knew everything. Would there ever come a day when I will to? *She doubted it. As her mom reached across the blanket and squeezed her hand, Rachel thought about how lucky she was to have such a great mother. She couldn't imagine life without her.*

"Promise?"

"It's our secret, Rach. I promise."

That was the first time she fell for a boy.

"AND WHAT ABOUT YOU?"

Josh's voice pulled Rachel from her memory, reminding her of the reason they were talking in the first place.

"What about me?"

"Are you happy? With Cole?"

Rachel narrowed her eyes. "It's only been a few days, Josh."

Josh looked her over and waited patiently.

What is it with the men in my life? All of them are so damn patient. Well, except Mason.

"Are you seriously asking me this?"

"Well, do you blame me? You've been acting different lately, and Shelly mentioned how you all first met him."

"Oh, she did, did she? What exactly did she say?"

"Come on, Rach. Don't get mad at Shel."

Raising a brow, Rachel sighed. "Okay, okay. At first, I was unsure about him."

"At first?"

"Yes. At *first*," she stressed. "But now, I've gotten to know him."

"You have?"

"Yes. Why? Don't you know him? He's your friend," she decided to point out.

"Well, yeah, he's my lawyer and a friend, but I don't actually know him *personally*."

Rachel thought about the serious lawyer who had somehow crept deep inside her tightly locked heart and had pretty much broken down all her walls just the night before.

"Yeah, that seems like Cole. He's very..." Rachel searched for the right word and ended with, "Private."

"He's a cagey bastard," Josh retorted.

Rachel found herself chuckling. "He's composed."

"He's distant."

"He's just different from you and Mase, so you both feel like you have to stick your noses in."

"He's reluctant to let people in, Rach, and that makes me wonder why."

Rachel shook her head. "I told you. No gloomy warnings. I like him, and I want to see where that takes me."

Josh straightened and winked at her as he pushed his hands back into his pockets. "If it helps you to be less annoyed at him, Mason told me yesterday that he was happy to see you smiling last night at the restaurant. That has to mean something, right?"

Rachel watched Josh turn and walk to the front door.

"Josh."

He stopped and turned to face her.

"It helps, and I should have said this months ago, but I'm so glad you finally came home."

"To Chicago?"

Rachel grinned and told him sincerely, "No, Daniels. To us."

CHAPTER 18

Unbuttoning his wool coat with one hand, Cole made his way through the tiny foyer of the apartments where Rachel lived and pressed the button for the elevator. He had dropped her off at the front of the building several times, but this was the first time he was going up. When the old elevator groaned to a stop at the bottom, he had to admit he was slightly nervous about getting on it. Taking a step back, he waited as the metal doors parted, ready to move aside for any occupants. That, of course, was the plan before he looked inside.

Life is too fucking good to me right now, he thought.

The woman inside the death trap of an elevator stepped forward on a pair of heels so tall that they made her eye-level with him. Cole was trying to find the words, *Hello, Rachel*, but the only problem was he currently had no power to speak. She had rendered him mute.

She was wearing the most sensual dress he'd ever seen. It was held up—*barely*—by a thin strip of ivory-colored satin around the neck, and then it flowed down over her body to the tops of her heels. It showed off every sexy curve she possessed.

As she moved off the elevator, Cole watched the silky fabric part and split, all the way up to her right mid-thigh.

Fuck the function. Where's a bed?

As that thought entered his mind, he heard her finally speak.

"Wow. You look like one of those ads in a glossy magazine."

Cole was still too busy looking over every inch of her to respond, and for once in his life, he was truly speechless. The rich cream color of the ivory fabric made him want to reach out and touch because she looked so damn soft, but at the same time, so incredibly sexy. It was such an innocent color, yet the minute she moved, it had that wicked split that made him want to run his fingers up her leg and under the dress.

Yes—up, under, and inside her.

"Cole?"

Finally, he brought his eyes to hers. In a voice that demanded she obey, he told her, "Turn around for me."

Very slowly, she pivoted on her toes and revealed the back of the dress...or more accurately, the lack of it. And nothing could stop him from touching. Cole moved quickly and decisively, and before she could turn any further, his front was pressed so close to her back that his coat was almost surrounding her. In the middle of the small foyer, he gripped her hips and pulled her flush against him.

Placing his lips against her ear, he asked in a voice he barely recognized, "Are you trying to destroy every semblance of control I have?"

Turning his face slightly, he took a deep breath and inhaled her intoxicating scent, and then he noticed her hair for the first time. It was pulled back into a high top-notch bun, showing off her elegant neck and the perfect tattoos decorating her spine.

That wasn't what held his attention though. Her hair didn't have any bright color in it. It was sleek, shiny, and jet-black. When she turned her face toward him, those fascinating blue eyes locked with his, and Cole knew it was all over for him.

This is where the search stopped. This is the woman.

His heart was now in complete agreement with his head.

"I take it you like my dress?" she inquired in a tone that told him she already knew the answer.

Sliding his fingers over her waist, he let the silky fabric brush under his palms as he caressed the material covering her hips before moving to rest his hands against her lower abdomen. Cole gave himself a moment to enjoy her, and then it hit him. He couldn't feel any kind of panty line.

"What are you wearing under this, Rachel?"

Turning in his arms, she looked him square in the eye, courtesy of her heels, and gave him a sexy wink. "Two silver studs. Why?"

He knew it.

Fuck. This night is going to take forever.

~

APPROXIMATELY AN HOUR AND A HALF EARLIER, they had walked into the reception room at the Shedd Aquarium fashionably late. The fact that they had made it out of the car and into the reception at all was a testament to Cole's control, certainly not hers.

Rachel had wanted to ditch the function the minute she had stepped off the elevator and seen him standing in her dingy little foyer, looking like a runway model from a *GQ* magazine. She'd known Cole would look amazing in a tuxedo, but to see him in person in the black-and-white ensemble...*well, shit, that is a moment I will never forget.*

She wanted to undress him one immaculate piece at a time.

Yes, starting with the little black bow tie.

That would have to happen later though. Right now, she was seated in one of the most impressive function rooms she had ever been in. The tables were surrounded by large glass windows that looked into the stunning aquarium. The setup was simply breathtaking, and Rachel found herself smiling as she followed the colorful fish swimming over and under the coral before bringing her eyes back to her date.

Cole was currently standing across the room with a shorter bald-headed man, who Rachel assumed was a business associate. Although he was engaged in conversation with the man, his eyes hadn't left her where she was seated at their table.

"So, Rachel, how long have you known Cole?"

Rachel swiveled on her seat, reluctantly tearing her eyes away from their purchase. Seated beside her was a woman who had to be close to her fifties. She was smiling so warmly that Rachel couldn't help but return her smile.

"Oh, just a little while."

"Ahh, I see."

Probably not, Rachel thought. She decided against mentioning, *We decided to sleep together last week, and it seems to have turned into one of the deepest connections I've ever had. Please tell me what to do because I have no idea what I am doing.*

"He's a lovely man. Quiet and very serious, but always so charming," the woman told her as she stared across the room to the man in question.

Rachel wasn't quite sure what to say to that, so she moved on from there.

"Is that your husband with him?"

"Yes, that's Byron. They've been doing business together for years. He won't work with anyone but Mr. Madison. He trusts him one hundred percent."

Well, Rachel liked that answer. *Hell, that's a lie.* She loved it. She knew it was rare to hear in advance that the man she was falling for was completely trustworthy. Looking back at the two men, Rachel felt her heart start to thump as they moved back to the table.

The shorter man walked in front of Cole, but that by no means detracted from his approach. His broad shoulders and commanding stride made him stand out as if he owned the room, and the exhilarating part was he was looking directly at her. Not once did he look away as he drew closer, and not once did Rachel drop the connection. When he stopped in front of her and held out his hand, Rachel rose without any words and took it, moving in close to him.

"I don't know about you, but I'd like to take a look around," he suggested as he wrapped his fingers around hers.

Rachel nodded, wanting to leave the function area to be alone with him.

He smiled at the lady who had been seated beside them all evening. "You don't mind if I steal her away, do you?"

Byron, the man Cole had been talking to, clapped him on the shoulder and chuckled. "Of course not. You go and show this beautiful young lady around. We've taken up enough of your time already, and all the boring talk and ceremony is over for the evening."

Rachel felt a smile spread across her lips as Byron reached out to take her free hand. He brought it to his lips and kissed it gently.

"It's been a pleasure, Rachel, and a first, eh, Cole?"

"Oh, Byron," his wife admonished, hitting his thigh gently.

Cole merely tightened his grip on Rachel's hand and gave them both a perfect smile before he looked back to her.

"Let's go and look around then, shall we?"

As they made their way through the first and second exhibit, Cole had let go of her hand, allowing her a moment to look around. He admired the view as she strutted in her slinky dress and high heels. And then, she reminded him of a kid in a candy store while she traced her finger along the clear surface to follow the fish, giggling when they wriggled and came closer.

She was unlike anyone he had met before. One minute, she was fearless and sexy, and the next, she was almost childlike in her joy and exuberance. In that moment, Cole knew without a doubt that he loved her.

"Have you ever been here before?" he asked. He was merely reaching for something, *anything* to grasp on to as he stood several feet behind her, blown away by his own realization.

"Oh, yes," she responded, tracking a bright yellow fish along the aquarium tank. "Yes, I have. When we were little, my father would bring Mase and me down here on the last Sunday of every month. I think that was a 'Mom' day, but we loved it." She paused and seemed to think back on the memories she had just mentioned. "I miss him."

Standing up, she turned and locked heartbroken eyes on his. "I miss them, my mom and dad."

As she walked back to him, Cole watched her closely, feeling his own emotions swelling at the thought of his mother and how he, too, missed her. He noticed her eyes move down over him, and when they finally came back up to rest on his, he felt as though she had touched him even though she was still an arm's length from him.

"Byron's wife had lovely things to say about you," she informed him.

Cole was grateful for the topic change as Rachel finally stopped close enough to touch him.

"Did she?"

"Yes, but I disagree with most of them."

Unable to help himself, Cole reached out and placed his hands on her hips, urging her closer. She came without hesitation and smoothed her palms up his tuxedo jacket to his shoulders where she lopped them around his neck.

"And what, pray tell, did she say that you disagreed with?"

"She told me you were quiet, serious, and charming."

Cole nodded. "And which point did you disagree with?"

"All of them." She sighed in a breathy tone as her lips parted in pleasure. "I think you are smart, cunning, demanding, arrogant, and most definitely, the sexiest man I have ever met."

Her mouth split into a devious grin, and Cole watched her perfect teeth bite into her bottom lip as she titled her head.

"I like this," she informed.

"You like what?" he probed as he studied her carefully.

"I like being almost eye-level with you. I don't have to look up as much, and our bodies," she whispered, moving in as close as they could be with clothes on, "are perfectly aligned."

Finally hitting the wall of his patience and control, Cole wrapped his arms fully around her and walked them slowly backward in the exhibit room until they hit one of the walls. In the dark corner, they were shielded from anyone who might walk in, and only their faces were illuminated from the aquarium lights.

Without a word, Rachel turned her head, offering him access to the smooth skin that had been calling to him all night, and he waited no longer. Lowering his mouth, he pressed hungry lips to the junction where her shoulder met her neck while his hands moved down the silk dress from her hips to her thighs.

As he pushed in close to her body, nibbling and kissing his way up her neck, he bunched the silky fabric in his fists and drew it up her gloriously long legs, all the while loving the sexy-as-hell sounds that were coming from her throat. She gripped his jacket lapels and pulled at them frantically as if trying to get closer. When he reached her jaw, Cole bit it lightly and thrust his hips against hers.

"Oh god," she moaned. As her head rolled against the back wall, she arched out against him. "I want...want my dress gone."

She was breathing heavily, and Cole felt a shiver of desire snake up his spine as her eyes dilated.

She sighed. "I want *more*."

Bringing one hand up, he gripped her chin lightly with his thumb and index finger and tugged it gently. "Open your mouth, Rachel."

As her lips parted, he moved in close and traced the top one with his tongue. Keeping his eyes connected with hers, he almost lost it when she let her tongue come out to touch his. Instead of sealing their mouths together, he continued to flirt with her, tangling his tongue with hers until he couldn't stand it any longer. Finally, he lowered his lips to hers in a scorching possessive kiss.

As a throaty moan bubbled up from deep inside her, he felt her legs part, and she started to rub herself against the black material barely containing his engorged length. Pulling his mouth from hers, he stared into lust-crazed eyes and groaned.

"Jesus Christ, Rachel. We can't, not here."

Straining her hips against him, she ran her hands over his shoulders and down his arms. "Then, just use this," she suggested, taking his free hand in hers and entwining their fingers. She was obviously past the point of rational thinking.

In a clenched fist, his other hand was still holding the fabric of her dress halfway up her leg, and he knew exactly what she was suggesting. Looking around behind them, Cole decided, *Why the fuck not?* No one had walked in, and the place was closed, except for the function.

Turning back to her, he inclined his head in affirmation. "Okay. We can play this your way. But, Rachel?"

As her heavy eyes focused on him, he gave her a stern look and warned, "Don't you dare scream. I do not want to end up as tonight's gossip. But I do want to end up with some part of me inside you." Lowering his mouth to hers, he ended with, "It's just a shame it will be my fingers and not my throbbing fucking cock."

RACHEL WAS SO TURNED on she was ready to pull up her dress and ask him to just take her here in public. Instead, as usual, Cole's self-control prevailed, and he was currently trailing his fingers up between her thighs. Biting down on her lip, she made sure to keep direct eye contact with him as she felt the tips of his fingers finally stroke against her piercing.

"Ahh, there it is," he murmured against her mouth. "Warm, wet, and mine. This little piercing is so fucking sexy that I could spend days playing with it."

Rachel was slowly melting from the inside out as Cole continued to finger the little stud adorned on her aching mound.

As she pushed her hips closer to his hand, she replied on a soft pant, "So is yours."

"You like my piercing, do you?" he asked, his finger sliding deep inside her slick pussy.

Rachel's breathing kicked up a notch. "Yes."

"Which one? The ones in my nipples or the one that really wants to be in here?" He punctuated the question with the firm thrust of two fingers deep inside her.

Moaning loudly, Rachel clamped her teeth onto her bottom lip, reminding herself not to scream, as she gripped his jacket and started to grind against his hand. His blistering gaze was burning into her where she stood, and Rachel knew it wasn't going to be much longer until this was all over for her. She could feel the climax building to an all-time high.

Cole gathered her in as close as they could get, and he continued to shove his fingers in deep and then slowly drag them out.

"I like them both, but right now, I wish this one," she told him, reaching out and palming the hard-on behind his tuxedo pants, "was either in my mouth or my pu—"

"Fuck, Rachel," he hissed out before he slammed his mouth down on hers, effectively cutting off her final word.

She had only seen Cole lose it once before, and that had been the night in his kitchen. Right now, she was witnessing it for a second time, and it was sexy as fuck.

He ripped his mouth from hers and pulled his fingers from the tight, snug sheath of her body. He glanced around, and when he looked back at her, she felt his other hand leave her dress, and he quickly undid his pants.

Rachel stood with her back to the wall, panting in the dark, as her legs trembled and her core clenched, dying for him to sink his cock deep inside her. Watching him tug open his perfectly tailored pants, Rachel thought she might climax on the spot, but as he freed his impressive erection, she knew she would wait if it meant getting some of that.

Moving back in tight and close, Cole's voice washed over her, making her body tremble.

"Lift your dress, Rachel. I *need* to be inside you."

She hurriedly pulled her dress up her legs, and the victory was *so* sweet as he stepped between her bare thighs and dipped down to brush his pierced cock through her wet slit.

"Cole," she moaned.

As their eyes met, he gripped her left thigh and tugged it up to his waist. "No talking and definitely no screaming. Think you can handle that?"

At this stage, she was surprised she hadn't passed out from sexual overload. Instead, she nodded, and in response, he slammed his hips up and forward, impaling her with his full length in one swift thrust. Rachel gasped as his mouth took hers at the same time his cock did. She held on and sank her tongue deep between his lips as her thigh tightened around his hip and she felt her pussy contract around his rigid flesh. In and out, he pummeled her relentlessly as he devoured her mouth with his sinful tongue.

It didn't take long, maybe two minutes or so, before Rachel's entire body tensed, and she came with Cole in one of the most combustible climaxes of her life.

It was also the moment his phone started to ring in his jacket pocket.

CHAPTER 19

COLE INHALED SEVERAL deep breaths to calm himself as the phone continued to buzz in his jacket pocket. *Fuck. Not now.* Closing his eyes for a moment, he gathered what little control he could find and slid out from between the sweetest thighs he'd ever had the pleasure of being in. Licking his lips, he savored the lingering taste of her kiss.

"Are you going to get that?" Rachel asked in a tone that told him just how satisfied she was now.

Reluctantly, he let go of her dress and took a step back from her, stuffing his happy-for-now cock back into his pants. When he finally had them zipped and buttoned, he reached into his jacket pocket with his left hand as he brought the other to his mouth and licked his fingers. "Hmm...god, you taste fucking delicious."

Then, he looked down at the screen and frowned.

"Better than your caramels?" she questioned.

This time, she received no response. Cole was too busy staring at the number flashing at him. His thumb slid over the screen to accept the call, and he brought the phone to his ear, holding up a finger to Rachel.

"Hello, this is Cole."

"Mr. Madison? Oh, I'm so glad I caught you."

"Becky? What's wrong? Did something happen?"

Cole kept his eyes on the floor as he listened to the woman on the other end of the phone, hoping with every fiber of his being that this wasn't a call he could never come back from.

"I'm afraid so. Your mother took a rather bad fall around an hour ago."

"Is she going to be okay?" he asked, knowing that his voice was much cooler than it had been only moments earlier.

"I believe so. She has a very bad bump on her head, and she broke her arm. We've moved her to the hospital."

"Fuck," he cursed, shaking his head.

Spinning on his heel, he made his way to one of the aquarium tanks illuminating the space from the opposite side of the room. "Look, I'm at a function right now, but I'm going to leave right away. I should be able to get there in around..." He paused and lowered his arm, so he could look at his watch. "An hour. Yeah, I can get there in an hour, I'd say."

"Of course, Mr. Madison. After last time, we knew that you would want to know right away."

Becky was right. He did want to know. He just hated that he was so far away, and at this moment, it made him feel so fucking useless.

"Thank you for that, Becky. I do appreciate it." His voice was clipped, but that was all he could manage. "I'll be there soon."

He ended the call and stared at the blank screen in his hand. He needed to leave right now. Pushing the phone back into the pocket he had pulled it from, he turned to walk out, and that was when he saw Rachel standing only a few feet from him.

"Are you okay?" she asked cautiously.

"No. I have to leave," he replied absentmindedly.

"Okay."

There was something in the way she immediately accepted his response that pulled him from his thoughts long enough to look her in the eye.

"I—" he started.

"Cole?" she coaxed, taking a step closer.

He kept his hands by his sides. He was almost afraid that if he touched her, he might break down for the first time in his life. What he hadn't counted on was her reaching out to him.

Silently, she raised a hand to his cheek, where she gently cupped it, and then she took that final step toward him. "It's okay. Whatever it is, go and take care of it. I can catch a cab."

And just like that, he knew what he wanted. He covered the hand she held against his face with one of his own. "Come with me?" he requested.

He held his breath as he watched her blue eyes blink, her dark lashes kissing her cheeks. Once again, he was struck by how beautiful she was.

"Where to?"

That isn't a no. He felt relieved as he brought their hands down between them.

"Lake Forest."

Her fingers squeezed his as she asked, "What's in Lake Forest?"

Trying for a smile but knowing it was coming off as more of a grimace, Cole replied stiffly, "Not what. Who. It's my mother. She's in a home up there."

He could tell he had surprised her, but she still held his hand.

She inquired, "Is she okay?"

"No, she had a bad fall tonight, and she's in the hospital."

Rachel's face changed to such a look of despair that he was sure he would get an excuse of some sort, but what he got instead was a nod.

"Of course, I'll come with you. I'll call Mason from the car. Let's go. You can tell me more on the way."

She turned to leave, but before he could help himself, Cole pulled her back around and tugged her to him. She came without resistance, and as his lips met hers, she returned the kiss with a soft sigh.

"Thank you."

"For?" was her quiet response.

There were so many ways he could answer, but considering his feelings for her at this moment, he decided to go with something simple yet oddly profound.

"For finally saying yes and going on a date with me."

RACHEL GLANCED over at the man sitting behind the wheel of his luxurious car as they hit the freeway.

Since they had left and navigated their way out of the city, he hadn't said much at all, so she'd decided to leave him alone. That was the best way with men, she'd found. She'd learned that from her past experience with Mason back when...well, back when they'd lost their mother. *Let them battle their demons until they reach a point where they need a hand or a woman to crumble with.*

Discreetly, she looked Cole over as they sat in the confines of his vehicle. He had his left hand on the steering wheel at the twelve o'clock position, and the right was fisted against one of his tightly muscled thighs.

The five o'clock stubble framing his serious jawline made Rachel want to reach out and touch, to remember how it had felt against her skin back at the aquarium, but she kept that memory and her hands to herself for now. Now was not the time for inappropriate touching. As a matter of fact, she found she wasn't even interested in that way. If anything, she wanted to reach out to soothe him, to heal him.

Settling back into the plush leather seat, she peered around the dark interior at all the bright blue lights shining from the dashboard. Suddenly, a random thought crossed her mind as she realized this car was way out of her pay range. It also struck her that even though Cole was obviously wealthy, he didn't ever mention it, and he never made her feel like he was in any way above her on the social ladder. No, he might dress like a million dollars every day, but he had never held his prosperity over her or anyone for that matter. *Huh, add that to my list of things I find so compelling about him.*

Right on the heels of that thought, the radio switched songs, and one of her all-time favorites came on. It was a classic, and she was a sucker for the classics.

Automatically, she leaned forward to turn up the music, but at the last minute, she stopped herself. Turning her head to face him, she smiled. "May I?"

Cole looked her way with a curious expression. "Simon & Garfunkel? Now that is something I wouldn't have pictured."

Rachel chuckled. "What can I say? My father was into the classics, it rubbed off."

As she turned up the volume on the melancholy melody, Rachel sat back and started to hum "Bridge Over Troubled Water." The lyrics were so incredibly fitting for him at this moment, and they made her want to comfort him that much more.

While Rachel sat there, wondering how to initiate any kind of contact or conversation, Cole unclenched his fist and moved his arm across the console to her, offering his hand with his palm turned up. Rachel felt a lump in her throat at the simple gesture, and she slid her hand into his, entwining their fingers and holding them in her lap.

And just like that, words were no longer needed.

~

As soon as he pulled into the hospital parking lot, Cole cut the engine and sat for a minute, staring out into the darkness surrounding them. He was trying to absorb the calming presence of the woman beside him. He was discovering that, unlike any other person, she had the ability to truly soothe him. She was sitting, silent and unmoving, but because of her silence and her understanding that he needed it, he felt closer to her than ever before. Pivoting in his seat, he unbuckled his belt and reached across the space to run a finger down her cheek.

She turned to face him, and in the dim light peeking through the car window, he saw eyes full of compassion staring back at him.

"You're so much more than I ever expected. How did I not see that coming?" he asked, mystified.

Her lips tipped into a shy smile. "Because I was hiding," she confessed.

"And now?"

Taking his hand in hers, she brought it to her mouth. "And now I want you to see me."

Cole held his breath as she kissed the pads of his fingers.

When she had reached the last one, she looked up at him and whispered, "Let's go and see your mother."

~

Rachel held Cole's hand as they walked down the hospital corridor under the bright lights. She was aware of how odd they must have looked in their cocktail attire, but she didn't care. She was far too focused on the rigid man beside her.

So much had happened tonight. She felt as though they had moved beyond some magical line, and they were now far, *far* beyond it, entering territory that was completely foreign. Instead of retreating or hiding, she embraced it.

They came to a stop in front of a nurses station, and Cole asked her to wait a moment. Rachel nodded and released his hand. She walked over to the waiting area to take a seat, and just as she was about to sit, he was beside her, gripping her elbow.

"She's down here."

As they made their way, she could feel his grip tightening on her arm. Reaching across her body, she patted his hand.

"It'll be okay," she assured him.

He looked at her, and with a tight smile, he agreed, "Perhaps it will be."

When they came to a stop at Room 3003, Cole let go of her arm, pushed his hands into his pockets, and moved inside the single room. Rachel waited by the door, allowing him a moment of privacy. She watched the man she had only ever seen as strong and confident walk slowly toward the bed currently occupied by a small gray-haired woman.

When he reached the side, he took out his right hand and brushed it gently across the bangs resting on the sleeping woman's forehead. As he shifted to the left, Rachel watched the lady open her eyes and peer up at her son.

"Hi there, Lydia," Cole greeted.

"Hello," the woman responded.

Rachel found herself frowning, trying to work out why her greeting didn't seem familiar at all.

"How are you feeling? You had a nasty fall," Cole said, his voice drifting through the quiet room.

That was when Lydia looked over to where Rachel was standing just inside the door in her cocktail dress.

"Did I pull you from a date, doctor?" Lydia asked as she looked back up at Cole.

Cole glanced over his shoulder and gestured for Rachel to come closer. As she moved into the room, she gave a warm smile to the woman who was looking at her.

"I'm not your doctor. I'm Cole, and this is Rachel."

Lydia blinked familiar hazel eyes, *Cole's eyes*, as she frowned. "I have a son named Cole."

That was when it all fell into place. Cole's mother obviously had a very aggressive form of Alzheimer's. She didn't even recognize her own son, this complex man who Rachel was currently standing beside.

Taking his hand in hers, Rachel smiled down at the woman with a cast around her right arm.

"We were on our way to a function tonight when I..." Rachel glanced around the room quickly, looking for something, and that was when she spotted it. "When I saw this beautiful music box through the glass window."

"Oh yes, that lovely lady Becky brought it in for me. It's full of caramels, but don't tell anyone."

Squeezing Cole's fingers, Rachel couldn't help the small grin she gave him before she moved toward the small box resting on a tray by his mother's bed. On the top of it was a painted rainbow. Looking back to Lydia, Rachel picked it up, and a smile, so like her son's, lit the woman's face.

"May I?" Rachel asked his mother, pointing toward her bed.

"Please. Go ahead." Lydia patted the space beside her.

It didn't go unnoticed that Cole had remained silent this whole time. Rachel only hoped she wasn't crossing any lines with him, but she figured if she were, he would tell her.

Tipping up the music box, Rachel twisted the mechanism and then opened it on her lap. Inside, she saw at least ten white wax paper squares. *Caramels*. Rachel listened closely as the melody began, and immediately, she recognized it and started to sing.

"Somewhere, over the rainbow..."

As Rachel continued, Cole's mother beamed and began to hum along with her, occasionally slipping into the lyrics.

Amazing. Songs seem to live in the soul even when everything else leaves, Rachel mused with a heavy heart, thinking of all the wonderful memories this woman had lost of her son.

Lydia reached out to Rachel at that moment, taking her hand, as she sang, "Where troubles melt like lemon drops," Before they both burst into the chorus.

As the song wound down, Rachel felt a tear escape as she placed the music box back on the side table. When she straightened, she felt a large warm hand on her shoulder. Glancing back, she met Cole's look of astonished wonderment as he cupped her cheek.

With no hesitation at all, he told her, "I love you."

~

COLE HADN'T PLANNED to tell her here, and he certainly hadn't planned to say it now, but watching her with his mother had solidified all the feelings that had been brewing inside him all day.

Rachel still hadn't said a word, so instead of waiting, Cole moved away from her and walked around to the other side of his mother's bed.

Taking her hand in his, he said, "That was beautiful. I remember my mother singing that to me when I was a little boy."

"Really?"

Nodding, he squeezed her fingers. "Would you mind if we come and see you again tomorrow? Maybe around lunchtime? This has been nice."

As he waited for the answer, he felt his heart beating irrationally, but he knew that had as much to do with his mother as with the woman staring at him from across the bed.

"I would like that."

Half of the weight lifted as he released her hand. "Good. That's settled. We'll be here around lunch."

When Cole locked eyes with Rachel, he saw she was staring at him as though she had never seen him before. Instead of letting it bother him though, he decided to go with it. "Are you ready?"

Silently, she nodded as he moved to the end of the bed. He watched her turn and reach out to squeeze his mother's hand.

"Bye, Lydia. I'll see you tomorrow."

"Of course, dear. Enjoy yourself tonight. Your date, he's very handsome."

Cole couldn't help the way his heart warmed at the statement, and the look Rachel gave him over her shoulder told him that she agreed with his mother.

"He is, isn't he?"

"Yes, he is." His mother chuckled. "Have fun, you two."

As Rachel walked toward him, Cole let his eyes travel over her as though he, too, was seeing her for the first time. *Maybe I am.* When she reached him and took his hand, he looked around her toward his mother.

"We will," he replied softly before they turned and left the room.

They quietly walked down the hospital corridor. Not one word was spoken between them as they got on the elevator and took it down to the ground floor where they made their way to his car. When they reached it, Cole followed her to the passenger door, opened it, and let her inside. All was done in complete silence.

Maybe I was too quick to tell her? Well, it's too late now. He had said it, and he would be damned before he took it back. As he slid into the driver's side, for the first time, he found that he wasn't a fan of the cozy interior.

He looked toward her as she stared out the passenger window. Tearing his eyes away from her, he started the car and pulled out of the parking lot, driving them to the hotel he usually stayed at when he would visit his mother.

As the car drew to a stop, he expected something from her, but again, nothing came. With every passing minute, his anxiety level was growing, thinking that he had pushed her away. By rushing and not keeping his thoughts under control, he had screwed it all up. *Well, fuck.* She would just have to put up with him until tomorrow when he could take her home.

When they got inside the hotel lobby, she moved to the waiting area and took a seat, presumably waiting on him. With a frustrated sigh, Cole made his way to the front desk and booked a room. Once it was paid for, he took the key card and turned, surprised to see her standing behind him in the middle of the foyer.

It didn't escape his notice that several men were taking a long look at the elegant woman waiting for him, but for the first time since the hospital room, Cole felt everything fall back into place.

She wasn't annoyed or upset. She wasn't even pushing him away. No, the look in Rachel's eyes was telling him something completely different.

When he reached her side, Cole crooked his elbow, and as she slid her hand through, he wondered what was going through her mind, but she seemed to want silence, so he gave it to her.

~

Rachel's heart was thumping so loudly in her chest she thought it might very well burst.

When they finally reached their room, Cole inserted the key card and pushed open the door, ushering her in first with a gentle hand on her back. She entered the low-lit suite, and when Rachel looked at the large king bed, she knew exactly what she wanted.

Stepping farther into the room, she wasn't surprised or shocked to hear the door click and lock. Without looking behind her, she reached behind her neck and untied the bow securing the ribbon of the satin cream dress. As it shimmied down over her body, she released her high ponytail, and she swore she could have heard a pin drop. She was completely naked beneath the dress, and once it pooled at her feet, she stepped free of the material and turned to find him.

She was ready, ready to offer herself completely.

Open. Naked. Vulnerable.

Cole was leaning up against the wall, just inside the door, with his hands firmly lodged in his tuxedo pants pockets. His legs were crossed at the ankles, and he looked brooding and magnificent.

Without a word, Rachel kept her eyes connected to his as she stepped free of her heels and made her way to him. She watched him tracking her in silent concentration, and as those seductively possessive eyes traced every inch of her body, she noticed different emotions behind them. Earlier, there had been lust, hunger, and raw desire, but *this*, right here, the way he was looking at her was making her feel heated, mesmerized, and full of love.

When she stopped before him, he pushed away from the wall and moved until his shoes touched her bare toes. She now had to look up at him, and when she tipped her face to do so, his hands cupped her cheeks.

"I love you."

Rachel blinked away the tears that were gathering in her eyes as she finally spoke. "I love you, too."

Slowly, he lowered his mouth and pressed his lips against hers in a kiss that relayed every raw emotion he was feeling. His lips were strong, persuasive, and gentle as he coaxed her mouth open. Raising her hands, she placed them against his white dress shirt where she could feel his heart thundering under her palms.

"Your heart is beating so fast."

Raising his head, he placed a hand over hers as he walked her back toward the bed. "For the first time in my life, I find that I'm nervous."

As the back of her bare thighs hit the high mattress, Rachel slid her hands up to Cole's bow tie and tugged it free. "Nervous?"

"Yes," he confirmed, lifting her up onto the bed. "I'm only human, Rachel."

"Are you sure?" she flirted with a sassy smile.

"I'm positive, and tonight, I don't want anything to go wrong."

As she sat there, he reached up to the top button of his shirt and began undoing each one. Once he reached the spot where his shirt disappeared into his pants, he stopped and looked her over.

"Lie back," he requested in a low voice.

She had no hope of resisting him. Very slowly, Rachel pulled herself further up the bed and lounged across the ivory comforter as she watched him toe off his shoes and then remove his socks. Once they were gone, he straightened and started to pull the dress shirt from his pants.

Rachel couldn't help the way her mouth parted from the pleasure of watching Cole undress in front of her. Once all the buttons were open, he shrugged out of the shirt and dropped it to the floor. She had thought he was magnificent earlier, but that was nothing compared to him standing naked from the waist up in only tuxedo pants. Now, he was her every fantasy.

~

COLE EXAMINED the naked seductress who was looking up at him from under her lashes. Her mouth was slightly open, and as he moved his hands to the button of his pants, he felt a sense of pride as she licked those sensual lips.

This woman, this woman is mine.

Quickly, he released the zipper and pushed his pants and boxers free. When he stood back up, he moved to the edge of the bed. Placing a hand on her knee, he gently pushed, and he felt a smile cross his lips as she parted for him.

Cole stepped closer and moved up onto the bed. He lowered

himself over her until his entire body was pressed against hers. Placing his palms by her head, he kissed her hard.

"Wrap your legs around me."

She did as requested, and he rolled them both over until she was lying up on top of him. Smoothing his hands down her back to her curvaceous ass, he pulled her against his body as he arched up and rubbed his cock against her.

She placed her hands by his head on the plush bed and pushed herself up a little. "I like this."

"I thought you might." He continued rubbing himself against her, and then he placed his hands behind his head, giving himself over to her.

She ground down on him and spread her legs wide, so they were on each side of his hips. With one hand on his chest, she sat up until she was straddling his thighs, and his stiff shaft became a very obvious sign of how much he wanted her.

With his right hand, Cole stroked his fingers between her spread thighs, and as she pushed against them, he confessed, "You're the best fucking thing my eyes have ever seen."

As he moved his hand away from her to fist his raging hard-on, he watched Rachel smooth her hands up and over her stomach to cup her breasts.

"Rachel," he growled out as he watched her tongue swipe against her bottom lip while she writhed atop him.

"Still nervous, Cole?"

Nervous? Fuck no.

He was totally enamored by the woman blowing his mind with her version of a lap dance. *Hell yes*, he thought, fisting his cock a little faster.

As she pinched her nipples, he tugged the piercing at the tip of his cock and groaned, pushing his head back into the pillow against the hand he kept secured there.

"Nervous is not the reason my heart is beating so hard right now."

"No?" she questioned, running her palms back down her body. "Hmm, do that again. So sexy when you play with yourself. Finger the —*yeah*, just like that."

Following her movements with a sharp eye, Cole was convinced he might die of sexual frustration as her flirty fingers dipped down and started to finger her own piercing.

"No, not nervous at all," he finally answered. "God, no."

Sliding her fingers lower, she gave him a scorching look as she moaned. "Then, what?"

"Rachel," he warned or maybe pleaded as she arched her back, pushing her breasts out to him.

"What?" she managed to say.

When she brought that damn hand out from between her legs, he reached his limit.

Quick as a lightning bolt, his hand whipped down from behind his head and gripped her waist as he tumbled her across the bed, her black hair fanning out behind her. He crawled up over her and wedged himself between her thighs. Cole entered her body in one smooth, powerful stroke. With his arms resting by her head, he looked down into big beautiful blue eyes.

"It's beating hard because it wants the one it loves to feel it."

No words, Rachel thought as she wrapped her legs around Cole's waist. *He's left me with no words.*

As he began to move, she gripped his powerful biceps, and she continued to look into eyes that were telling her with every stroke of his body just how much he loved her.

"I had no idea," she finally said.

He brought one hand to her hip and trailed it up over her waist and rib cage to cup her breast. Lowering his mouth, he took one of her nipples between his lips and sucked before he let it go and came back to her mouth. All the while, he continued thrusting inside her greedy body.

"You had no idea about what?"

As his hips moved, she felt him pull slowly from her before deliciously sliding back inside, which was where she was now convinced he belonged.

"I had no idea it would be you," she admitted as she started to touch his face.

She felt him grip the pillow under her head as his hips picked up the pace.

"And I knew it *had* to be you."

Arching up into him, Rachel wrapped her arms around his neck and parted her lips to his tongue as he made love to her in a way no other man ever had before.

As she held on tight, he sent her spiraling into her second climax of the night, and from beneath him, she watched as he fell apart above her.

Yet, as powerful as that sight was, it wasn't until he nuzzled his mouth and nose in her hair and whispered once more, "I love you," that the moment felt complete.

CHAPTER 20

Rachel rolled to her side and placed her hands under her cheek as she stared at the man lying beside her. He was resting on his back, and the sheet was pulled up over their waists. As he lay there, staring at the ceiling, Rachel couldn't help but wonder what he was thinking about.

"Now. How do I keep you?" He turned his head on the pillow, so their eyes met.

Rachel couldn't help the silly grin that came to her lips.

"Keep me?" Laughing, she scooted in close, and flippantly, she joked, "Well, you could always marry me."

Without a word, Cole rolled to his side, so they were the mirror image of each other. Rachel couldn't help the fit of giggles that started to overwhelm her at the serious look crossing his face. *He can't actually be considering—*

"So, marry me, tomorrow."

Oh shit, he is.

Like a life-sized jack-in-the-box, Rachel sat up quickly and brought a hand to her mouth to try and stop any more ridiculous things from flying out of it.

"Are you insane?" *Yeah, obviously* that *didn't work.*

"No, I'm quite sane."

Uncaring of her nudity, she dropped her hands to her sides and shook her head. "You're nuts. I think you've had too much happen tonight. You're overly emotional."

Propping himself up on his elbow, he gave her a small shrug. "I'm very aware of what I just said, Rachel. No one made me say it. In fact, *you* suggested it."

"As a joke," she laughed incredulously.

"Well, I'm serious," he pointed out in a tone that did indeed sound serious.

Still unbelieving of what this *usually* sane man was saying, Rachel continued to open and shut her mouth in the hopes that something intelligent would come out at any minute.

"I know what I want, Rachel, and you're it."

"You're insane," she scoffed. "Off-your-rocker, certifiably mad."

"You already mentioned that."

Rachel saw a mischievous grin, unlike any she'd seen on him before, spread across his lips as he moved to sit up in the bed, the same bed she was currently scrambling from.

"Running away from me?" he questioned with a faux frown. "Now, I'm kind of insulted."

Standing between the bed and the wall, Rachel continued staring at Cole like he had lost his mind. "Well, you're acting a little crazy, don't you think?"

"No," he stated in a voice that was incredibly sane.

Grr. He's making me *sound like the crazy person.*

"So, you're telling me that you want to get married? To *me*?" Rachel asked, completely flabbergasted.

Cole made a show of looking around the empty hotel room. "Is there anyone else in the room that I don't know about?"

"Would you stop being so...so..." At this stage, Rachel knew she must look absolutely ridiculous, flapping her arms around and stuttering.

But none of this is making any sense. Especially the fact that I want to say yes.

"So smart? So intelligent? So sexy?" he offered arrogantly as his eyes twinkled at her.

"Calm," she finally got out. "So damn calm."

"You don't think I'm smart and sexy?"

"I think this is an outrageous conversation, and I am very naked."

"Yes," he muttered, letting his eyes wander down over her, "I had noticed that. So, say yes, agree to marry me, and come back to bed."

"You don't even know me."

"I know you better than you think," he replied quicker than she had expected. "I know that you are the little sister of Mason Langley, you run Exquisite with him, and he looks out for you whether you like it or not. You're an incredible pastry chef, yet I haven't had the pleasure of sampling any of your creations, except for the sinful caramel sauce that needs to be a permanent staple in my life."

Throwing the sheet off his body, he climbed out of the bed and made his way toward her, like a wolf on the hunt. As Rachel stumbled back to the wall, he continued, naked like she was.

"You had an *insane* girlie crush on my friend and business partner throughout, I can only assume, all your high school years. And because you have the biggest heart in the world, you both are still as close as any brother and sister could ever be. You've lost both your parents, and you now run your mother's flower shop even though your first passion is cooking."

He paused as she stood there, rooted to the spot. Staring up at him, she felt completely gobsmacked.

"How am I doing so far?"

Grudgingly, she had to admit, *So far, he is spot-on.*

~

COLE LOOKED down into the face that was the very reason for his—*yes, slightly insane*—behavior. Running his fingertips down her arms to her hands, he took a hold of them.

"You have people in your life who love you deeply, and for some reason, the entire week we've been together, you haven't wanted them around. This week, you spent your evenings alone with me, looking for something that none of them could give you."

Pulling her forward, Cole wrapped her arms around his neck and gripped her hips, lifting her, so she could wrap her legs around his waist. Turning, he walked them back to the bed.

"You've been hiding away, not dating, and for someone who craves to be touched, you've refused anyone's hands. And that is all *wrong*."

Cole studied her closely as her eyes, tinged with fear and excitement, searched his face.

"Oh? But what about you?" she asked.

With a smug smile, he placed his knee on the bed and laid her down on the crumpled sheets. "You didn't refuse me, and I am all that is *right* for you." He kissed her quickly and lifted his head. "So?"

"So?" She giggled from beneath him.

Nipping her bottom lip, Cole repeated the words he hadn't even known he had in him the first time. "Will you marry me?"

He felt her hand stroke up his back, and when it reached the tattoo between his shoulder blades, he arched into her touch.

"What does this mean?" she asked, momentarily trying to distract him.

"You want to know about it now? I think you're avoiding the question."

"Me? Deflecting?" she asked. "Hmm, I learned from the best. Tell me, please?"

"Then, you will answer me?"

Using some of his own tactics against him, she pretended to think on it for a moment as she stroked her fingers between his shoulder blades once more. "Perhaps."

Taking a deep breath, Cole stared down into the face that had somehow become essential to his well-being. "Okay. It's a Vegvísir. It's a symbol used by the Nordic people, an Icelandic magical stave. It's meant to guide the bearer through rough weather, like a compass of sorts. I got it done when my mother's disease started to rapidly progress. I felt helpless, like there was nothing I could do but hang on and hope we made it through. I'm still hanging on."

He felt her fingers tracing a circle around it, and as her eyes closed, he knew she was picturing the tridents all intricately interwoven with the Viking rope.

"You can hang on to me," she offered as her eyelids fluttered open.

When their eyes connected, Cole swallowed against the unfamiliar lump in his throat. "Can I?"

"I still think you're crazy," she muttered, "but you are very persuasive."

"So, is that a yes?" he pressed, needing to hear it.

"Yes." Laughing, she leaned up and then surrounded him in a

tangle of arms and legs. “Yes, you insane man, I’ll marry you. But *you* have to deal with Mason and Josh.”

With her legs wrapped around his hips, Cole pushed up from her. “And if I do? You agree to tomorrow?”

As her blue eyes sparkled, she released her arms from around his neck. “Is that even possible?”

Playing with a strand of her hair, Cole told her, “We can get the license tomorrow, but we will have to wait until Saturday to make it official.”

“I can’t believe we are even having this conversation. You do know that we have no excuse, right? Neither of us is drunk, and we aren’t in Vegas. What happens *here* won’t stay here.”

“Are you trying to tell me that you need to be drunk to marry me?”

Shaking her head against the mattress, she snorted, and he found it completely endearing.

“No, but I’m impulsive. You? Well, let’s just say, I don’t think anyone will believe that *you* agreed to this.”

Leaning down so his mouth was by her ear, Cole moved his hips against hers.

“So, you think people will say that you drugged me? Or maybe I was seduced?”

As her fingers slid through his hair, he groaned against her ear. Raising his head, he looked down at her and was surprised to see a serious expression fixed on him.

“I’m serious, Cole. People will assume I talked you into this.”

“People being Mason and Joshua?”

“And Lena and Shelly.”

“So?” he questioned as she massaged his scalp. “They can assume whatever the hell they like. The two people who matter are right here, and I will be more than happy to set the record straight.”

He felt her hand smooth down to his neck and squeeze.

“And if it doesn’t work and we hate each other by next week?”

“Such an optimist, Rachel.”

“I mean it.” She pouted.

Taking her hand from behind his neck, he pinned it to the bed and did the same with the other. “I can’t ever imagine hating you, but if *you* get sick of *me* and decide next week that you want nothing to do with me—”

"Yes?"

Lowering his mouth to hers, he informed her with nothing but devious intentions, "Tell me, so I can change your mind."

RACHEL AWOKE with the sun hitting her in the eyes as it was shining directly through the hotel window.

Oh shit. Did last night really happen?

It was quite possible that she had fallen asleep after they had tumbled into bed, and she dreamed the last half of the conversation, not that *that* was any less disturbing.

Fantasies about marrying Cole? Wow, now, I really am losing my mind.

Taking a quick peek over her shoulder, Rachel was almost relieved to see that the bed was empty, but by the looks of it, Cole hadn't been gone long because his pillow was still indented.

Stretching her legs under the sheet, Rachel rolled to her back and pushed her arms above her head. *Last night was an interesting evening, that's for sure.* She had gone into it believing she was going on her first date *ever* with him, and she had come out the other side—

"I was wondering when my fiancée would finally wake up."

Engaged.

Rachel watched the steam billow around Cole as he stepped out of the bathroom with a white towel wrapped around his waist, and yes, she realized the shock of him nearly naked still was not something she was over.

"Early this morning, I remembered that we have no clothes to wear, except the ones from last night, so I called around and had some things delivered. They should be here shortly."

As he moved toward the bed, Rachel was silent as she tracked a water droplet sliding off the bar in his left nipple. It started a slow, lazy descent over his rib cage and down his waist until it hit the towel secured around the sexy V of his hips.

Now was *not* the time, however, to think about where the water droplet had gone. Now was the time to go and visit Lydia and to maybe have her son's head examined.

"The hospital called earlier to let me know they are releasing my mother this afternoon. Do you mind if we stay and help with that?"

Rachel lifted her eyes to his and shook her head. "Of course not. I'm happy to help in any way that I can. I need to call Mason and tell him I won't be back until...when exactly are we going back?"

Cole climbed into bed beside her. "I know you remember last night."

"Ahh, which part?"

Reaching across the sheet, he looked down to where his finger was now playing with her pierced navel. "The part where you said you would marry me." Lifting his eyes to hers, he arched a brow. "Do you remember that?"

Rachel pretended to think it over while her insides were twisting from anxiety. "I seem to recall something like that being discussed."

As he moved closer, he questioned, "Oh, you do, do you? Well, that's good, but if you didn't, then I have a very convincing eyewitness."

Rachel was coming to find that she loved this side of him. This playful, lighthearted side he switched on was a complete contrast to the fire simmering in his eyes.

"Oh? So, if I chose to maybe...oh, I don't know...plead the fifth?" she asked as a giggle escaped her mouth.

He rolled on top of her with narrowed eyes and a growl. "Then, you will suffer the consequences."

Rachel wrapped her arms around his neck and pulled herself up to gently bite his bottom lip. "And what might those be?"

"A lifetime of sexual favors," he informed as he reached between them to remove his towel, "to be performed by you, for me."

"In that case," she teased, arching her hips to rub against his delicious hard-on.

"Yes?" he asked as he thrust against her.

Pressing her lips to his, she smiled. "I plead the fifth."

~

IF SOMEONE HAD TOLD him a week ago that he would be standing in an office while a little gray-haired man in a tweed jacket was punching in his information for a marriage license, Cole would have said, *You are out of your fucking mind.*

As it happened though, he was currently standing at an old desk in the county clerk's office with a man in tweed asking him his last name.

"Madison. Cole James Madison."

"And the young lady?" tweed asked.

Cole looked over his shoulder to see Rachel pacing with his phone to her ear. She was dressed in a pair of casual jeans and a red sweater that hugged every curve she had and made her inky hair stand out in stunning contrast.

"Langley is her last name. Rachel Catherine Langley."

As he said her name, Rachel turned to face him with a serious frown.

Cole knew Mason was giving her a hard time on the other end of the phone, and the funny thing was that he was upset she had gone away with someone she hardly knew without mentioning it to anyone.

Yeah, he's definitely going to go postal when he finds out exactly what is about to go down.

"Mason, listen to me. I am an adult. I had to leave suddenly. I called as soon as I could."

Cole turned back to the tweed and handed over his driver's license who took down his information and then handed it back. That was when he heard her say softly, "I love him."

Moving to face her, Cole felt his heart pound faster at her admission, but it was quickly followed by annoyance.

She replied into the phone, "Well, you better get over it and quick. I don't understand what the problem is. Do I need to remind you that you went missing for weeks, and I didn't give you shit until the very end? Look, we'll be back on Sunday. Have Sarah look after things for me. Give her a bonus out of my pay. I. Don't. Care. But work it out, Mase. Please?"

When Cole stopped in front of her and flashed his driver's license, she opened her purse and wallet and gave him hers.

He mouthed, *Everything okay?*

She smiled up at him and nodded, rolling her eyes, as she covered the mouthpiece. "Mason's just being Mason."

"Want me to talk to him?"

"No. I've got this, don't you worry. I think I'll leave the talking to you when we all meet Monday night for dinner, counselor. That's when things will get interesting."

Holding up a finger to signal Mason was back, she said into the phone, "I'll be back on Sunday, and I'll see you at dinner on Monday, okay?" She closed her eyes and nodded. "I promise. I love you, too. Give Lena a hug for me, would you?"

Looking up at him, she started to laugh. With a sassy wink, she promised Mason, "I won't hug Cole for you, okay?"

Cole shook his head, and before she hung up, he couldn't help but smirk at her last words to Mason.

"But I'll kiss him once for Lena."

As she quickly disconnected the phone, she let out her version of what Cole could only assume was an evil laugh.

His future wife was a little minx, and he loved her for it.

CHAPTER 21

Married. Wedlock. Matrimony.

A union between two people who love one another.

No matter which way it was described or how she looked at it, she was—

Oh, holy shit. I, Rachel Langley—

Scratch that. I, Rachel Madison, *am now a wife. And not just anyone's wife,* she thought as she looked over her shoulder to the large bed in her cramped bedroom. *I'm Cole's wife.*

Turning back to the mirror in front of her, Rachel examined the woman staring back. She didn't *look* any different...well, except for the bright purple streaks she had reapplied last night at Cole's request.

No, the woman staring back at her was exactly the same. Except now, she felt like she had found a missing piece, a piece that had been so well-disguised she had almost overlooked him.

Zipping up the hoodie she had pulled on to pair with her yoga pants, she walked around to the side of the bed where Cole was lying as peaceful as she had ever seen him. With his eyes closed and his dark lashes kissing his cheeks, his face took on a boyish quality that was lost when those serious magnetic eyes were open and focused.

Awake, he was a powerful force that she couldn't resist. Asleep, he was a peaceful picture she wished she could emulate.

This weekend had been a whirlwind of emotions for both of them, and just like Rachel, he seemed to be exhausted from everything that had taken place.

~

"This is you and Cole when he was five," Rachel told Lydia as she pointed to the little boy in the image holding a young woman's hand. He was peering up at his mother with a smile reserved only for the young and innocent.

It was incredible to look at the man standing on the other side of this virtual stranger and realize that the boy and man was one and the same.

"Cole was my son?" Lydia asked her.

Rachel felt a lump catch in her throat as she raised her eyes to silently offer Cole any comfort he might need. He, however, was focused on his mother, and Rachel could see the pain etched across his features.

"I don't remember," Lydia confessed, shaking her head.

Rachel watched Cole sit down beside his mom as she turned to face him. Rachel almost fell apart as Lydia voiced her confusion.

"Where is he? Is he okay? He's so little."

Cole reached out and took her hand. When he held it firmly in his own, he placed two white wax paper squares in her hand.

Caramels.

"It's okay, Lydia. He's okay. In fact, he is the happiest he has ever been."

Rachel looked over the older woman's gray hair, and when her eyes met Cole's, she could sense the heartache, but she could also see the gratitude and love he had for her.

"You like caramels, right?" he asked his mother as he tore his eyes from Rachel's.

"Yes. Yes, I do. How did you know?"

That was when the mischief came back into his eyes as he winked at both women.

"Lucky guess. After all, who doesn't like caramel?"

~

"Not worrying about tonight, are you?"

Cole's lazy deep voice jolted Rachel back to reality. Focusing on her—*wow, husband*, who was now sitting up in her bed—*Hang on, is it now our bed?*—Rachel watched him run a hand through his messy blond hair.

"Nope, not at all," she answered.

"You're a terrible liar, Mrs. Madison."

Hearing him say her new name out loud sent a shiver down her spine, and looking at him naked in her bed for the first time made her thighs tighten.

"I'm not lying."

"Yes, you are. When you lie, you get a frown line here." He indicated the center of his forehead.

Rachel felt herself doing exactly that.

"It's okay to be nervous about telling everyone," he assured her as he moved out of the bed and walked toward her. "These are the people you love and care about."

Scoffing a little at that, Rachel shook her head while she wrapped her arms around his neck as he encircled her waist.

"These are people who are going to not only give *me* hell, but they'll also possibly kick *your* ass," she said as seriously as she could.

Rachel felt Cole's chest shake as she looked up into his laughing eyes.

"I'm glad you find this so amusing, *husband*."

"Oh, I like that," he drawled.

"Yes. I can tell," Rachel sassed, pushing her clothed hips against his naked ones.

"Say it again."

"I'm glad you fin—"

Rachel was cut off as he slid his hand into her hair and gripped it tightly, pulling her head back. Her mouth parted slightly on an excited exhale.

Oh yeah, there it is—that undeniable sex factor. God, the man has it in spades.

"Not. That," he said with a feral smile, enunciating each word.

Swiping her tongue across her parted lips, Rachel smoothed her palms down his back, and as the arm around her waist pulled her closer, she let out a soft squeak.

"Husband," she said on a sigh.

Lowering his mouth to her ear, he lasciviously demanded, "Again."

"*Husband.*" She panted as the hand at her waist moved between her thighs.

"Again."

Rachel closed her eyes as Cole stroked back and forth against the flimsy yoga material while his fingers in her hair flexed and tightened. She thrust her hips forward, brushing against his naked cock.

As a familiar piece of knowledge asserted itself in her mind, she took the opportunity to have a little *fun* with him. "My *husband* is detaining me, thus making me late for work, which is something he once told me shows such a lack of dedication to my final destination."

Rachel felt sharp teeth nip her earlobe.

He explained, "I only care about your dedication if *I'm* your final destination."

Just as she was about to retort, she felt a low moan bubble from her throat as his fingertips began to circle her piercing.

"Cole, I need to go to work, and so do you."

"I don't care," he mumbled against her hair before he took a deep breath in.

"Yes, you do. You told me last night you had to wrap up a few things."

As Cole's lips found hers, he kissed her fiercely, sinking his tongue deep inside her mouth. Rachel tried to hold on to her emotions as they swirled and her desire heightened. She did need to go to work, but right now, she didn't want to go anywhere, except back to bed with her husband.

As he pulled his mouth from hers, he looked down at her with such intensity and love that Rachel found herself tumbling back as she remembered the way he had looked at her this past Saturday morning.

~

"I, Cole James Madison, ask you, Rachel Catherine Langley, to stand beside me through the toughest battles and harshest critics, namely your brother, and to lie beside me through the calmest of nights. I ask you to continue being the exact person you are today and to never be anyone but the woman who turned me into this impulsive man who stands before you here today."

Cole squeezed her fingers in his, and his gaze stayed locked onto hers. He was intent on only one thing, and that was the woman in front of him.

"I was not expecting you, and that's what makes me so sure. Nothing this perfect could be anything other than right. So, Rachel Catherine Langley, will you be my wife?"

~

COLE COULD FEEL his chest rise and fall against the most beautiful breasts he had ever seen, and Rachel—*ahh, yes, my wife*—was staring up at him, her eyes shining with all the desire and love he craved from her.

"Look, I don't want you to worry about your brother, okay? I don't think it's funny that Mason and Joshua will be upset tonight because I know how that will hurt you. I do find it amusing that you are concerned for my safety."

Her eyes narrowed quickly, and he was surprised to see the annoyance that flashed into them. The look made him instantly stop what he was doing with his active hand as he released his hold of her hair.

"What's wrong?"

"You think it's amusing that I'm worried about you?" she ruminated.

"No, I suppose amusing is the wrong word. I find it endearing but unnecessary. No offense, Rachel, but Mason doesn't really strike me as the type who fights with his fists. As for Joshua, he pays me, and we have a working contract. I'm far too valuable to him alive, and he needs me on his side, so he wouldn't beat me up and risk losing my business."

She remained silent as she stared at him. She was still unconvinced by the looks of it.

"Plus, Joshua knows I am quite adept in martial arts. I could put him down in three seconds flat."

That's it. That was obviously what she had either wanted or needed to hear because a huge grin slid across her face.

"Does that mean you'll come and spar with me at the gym later?" she prompted.

Deciding things were all back on course, Cole made his way to the tiny bathroom connected to her bedroom. When he got to the door, he looked over his shoulder.

"I'd love to spar with you, anytime and anyplace, you choose. Just promise not to damage my pretty face."

As he continued into the bathroom to take a shower, he was happy to hear Rachel's carefree laugh.

"Arrogant jerk," she called out loud enough to ensure he heard her.

~

RACHEL FIDGETED NERVOUSLY with a piece of string hanging from her bright blue sweater that she had paired with black leggings.

It had just turned seven o'clock when Cole pulled his car into the small parking lot behind Exquisite. As he turned off the ignition, he shifted around to look at her, and she could feel the heat of his stare. Taking a deep breath, she glanced his way. She was about to open the car door and get out when he reached across the console and placed his hand on her arm.

"Wait just a minute, please?"

Rachel froze. "What's wrong? Did you change your mind?"

He gave her a slow easy smile that seemed to warm her from the inside out.

"Never," he assured as he reached into his navy jacket pocket.

When he pulled out a small ring box, Rachel's mouth dropped opened at what she knew was inside.

"You know we didn't have time to buy rings in Lake Forest."

"Cole, really, you didn't have to do this."

Rachel fell quiet as he cupped her cheek with his palm.

"Yes, I did. Now that my name is by yours, I want my ring on your finger."

Giving her a swift kiss, he pulled back and snapped open the box.

Rachel gasped as three rings nestled in black velvet came into view.

"Cole," she whispered, placing a hand over her mouth, "it's too much."

"Rachel, it's hardly enough. I want everyone to know you belong to me."

With a grin she couldn't seem to help, Rachel arched a brow. "Do you really think there will be any confusion?"

Cole chuckled softly. "Not if you're wearing my ring."

"And answering to Mrs. Madison?"

"Stop it, or you will become intimately acquainted with the interior of this vehicle."

He placed the box in his lap, and as he took her left hand, Rachel watched with a mixture of awe and excitement. Raising her hand to his lips, he pressed a gentle kiss on the back of her knuckles, and then he raised his eyes to hers as he pulled out the first piece of jewelry. It was a simple platinum ring with four round diamonds embedded across the top of the band.

As Cole slid it on her finger, he whispered, "I want you to be mine. My hope is that you wear this ring first, so it will always be closest to your heart and remind you of how much I love you."

Rachel could feel a tear slide free and run down her cheek.

His eyes met hers as he asked, "Will you?"

Is there really any doubt? Rachel thought as she stared at the wedding ring on her finger. Somehow, this man had bulldozed his way into her life, and now, only a week later, she couldn't imagine going minutes without knowing he would be there permanently.

"Yes, of course. Cole, it's stunning."

When the ring was firmly in place, he brought it up to his mouth and kissed it where it lay on her finger. He then reached down and pulled out the second ring. This one was a beautiful platinum band that sparkled with twinkly diamonds surrounding the largest cobalt sapphire Rachel had ever seen. Slowly, Cole slid the ring down the same finger until it locked in place with the wedding band.

"This is to remind you that every time I look into your eyes, the color of this stone, I fall in love all over again."

Blinking back several tears, Rachel wondered how the heck she had ever gotten so lucky. All she'd had to do was say yes, and then she completely belonged to this magnificent man. It was, she realized, simply because Cole had never taken no as an answer.

Leaning across the console, Rachel cupped his face and kissed him with as much love as she could. His lips parted for her tongue, and she showed no hesitation in pushing deep into his mouth.

Nothing could ruin this night, absolutely nothing.

Knock...knock...knock.

Rachel pulled away from Cole and looked out of the car window. When she could see Mason glaring right at her with a frown, Rachel took it back.

Well, nothing, except for that.

COLE QUICKLY SLIPPED the final band on his wedding finger and unlocked the car doors. "You ready?" he asked.

Before Rachel could respond, the passenger door was pulled open, and he could hear Mason.

"Were you two planning on coming inside? Or were you going to sit out here all night?"

Cole had several retorts just on the tip of his tongue, but he didn't think Rachel would appreciate any of them. So, he climbed out of the car and shut the door with a firm hand, choosing to let Rachel decide how she wanted to proceed.

"We just got here. Jesus, Mase. Relax, would you?" she grumbled as she slammed the door in the same manner he had.

Cole tried not to wince as he reminded himself the car had been built to withstand much worse.

"Mason," a soft voice chimed in.

Cole turned to see one of the women Rachel had been with the night they had all met at Whipped. Due to the way she was frowning at Mason, he had to assume it was Lena, Mason's wife.

"What?" Mason snapped, looking over the car roof in her direction.

As he did, his eyes came to a halt on Cole's, and as they glared at one another, Cole found himself in a pissing contest with his wife's brother.

"Excuse me?" Lena questioned in a tone that showed how much she did *not* appreciate being talked to that way.

As she marched forward, Cole had to admit that he was impressed with the confident, pissed-off demeanor she had going on. This was a woman who knew her mind, and she was certainly not afraid of anything, including her annoyed husband.

"Don't snap at me, Langley."

Immediately, Cole noticed Mason's mood shift. Mason tore his eyes away from him to look where his wife was now standing beside Rachel.

All three of them stood on the opposite side of the car to Cole, and as he studied the close-knit family, he could definitely see the resemblance between the siblings. Although he had spoken to Mason that first night he'd visited Rachel in the restaurant, he hadn't had long to get a good look at him. Now, as the other man mumbled something to his wife and scowled occasionally at Rachel, Cole could really see it. The dark hair, the blue eyes, and as they all finally turned to look at him, he saw the same frown as well.

Wow, Cole thought, *someone in their family had strong genes. These two could pass as twins.*

As they all stood silently in the frigid night air, Lena rolled her eyes as she came around the trunk of the car. When she finally reached him, she held out her hand. "It's time we were formally introduced. I'm Lena, Mason's wife and Rachel's sister-in-law. You must be Cole."

Cole liked her immediately. Her mass of brown curls spilled down over her shoulders, and as he took her hand in a gentle grip, he was shocked at how firm her handshake was. She was definitely confident, just as he had first suspected.

"It's a pleasure to finally meet you, Cole."

Cole gave her a genuine smile, and then he realized she still hadn't let go of his hand.

"It's not *that* much of a pleasure," Mason called out from across the car. "I'm telling you, if she really liked you, she'd be yelling at you right now."

Cole was surprised when Lena winked up at him.

Then, she turned her head to lock eyes with Mason. "Langley, you know I only enjoy arguing with you. It gets me all hot and bothered."

As she turned back to Cole, finally releasing his hand, she told him softly, "He'll come around. Just give him time."

Cole thought that was probably good advice, but as he looked back to the brother-sister pair glaring at one another, he thought it was a shame he'd never been one to take good advice.

"Well, I hope so since I just married his sister."

What is that phrase? Oh yes, there it is, Cole thought with a shit-eating grin aimed at the tall Langley currently glowering at him. *If looks could kill.*

CHAPTER 22

It's official, Rachel thought as she stared slack jawed at Cole from across the trunk of the car. This man is fucking insane.

"What did you just say?" her brother practically growled.

The sound was so foreign coming from her usually congenial brother that Rachel lost the words she was about to yell at Cole, and instead, she spun around to face Mason. That was when she heard Cole's reply.

"I said I married your sister on Saturday."

"Oh my god," Lena muttered.

"Not helping, Cole," Rachel pointed out as she faced her seething brother.

If she had been worried at all about her dealing with Mason's wrath over the matrimony, she needn't have bothered. All of his annoyance and anger was solely focused on Cole.

"Mase, come on, calm down," Rachel tried to reason with him.

"I will calm down when you tell me that what he just said is bullshit."

Um, not going to happen. What he said is all true.

"If you just listen, may—"

"Maybe, what?" Mason finally demanded, turning to pin her with a look full of anger, confusion, and something much worse—disappointment. "Maybe you'll finally tell me why you've been acting so distant lately? Or why you have decided to stop talking to everyone? Or maybe you will explain to me how you ended up married to a guy you don't even know."

Rachel took a deep breath and balled her fists at her sides. She tried to remind herself that this was Mason, her brother. He was the one person in the world who loved her unconditionally. Well, he used to be the only one.

As she glanced across the car to where Cole was standing next to a shocked face Lena, Rachel felt herself calm. Cole was looking at her with such certainty. He believed in her and trusted her to do the right thing here.

Looking back at Mason, Rachel squared her shoulders. She was never one to back down from any argument, and so she simply replied, "I love him."

"Excuse me? You just met him," Mason exclaimed, pointing his finger at her.

Rachel reached out and gripped his finger. "And you haven't even bothered to meet him."

She watched as her brother's blue eyes narrowed on her, and he dropped his hand.

"You never bothered to introduce us, Rachel. Or did you forget that?"

"Of course, I didn't forget. I didn't bother introducing you because the one night he turned up at the restaurant, you acted like an idiot. And you're doing the same right now."

"I'm acting like an idiot? Oh, that's rich. I don't know what you expect from me," Mason told her through clenched teeth.

"I expect you to quit acting like an ass, and instead, be the supportive brother I know and love."

Mason shook his head and pushed his hands into his jeans pockets. "Yeah? Well, when the sister I know and love shows up, maybe she'll be able to find him."

Rachel felt her heart physically ache as Mason turned on his heel and marched to the back door of Exquisite where he wrenched open the door and stormed inside. When it slammed shut behind him, she turned to face Cole and Lena, who were both staring at her silently. Lena's expression was contemplative, and Cole's—damn him—was proud.

With a quick nod and a fake smile, Rachel announced, "Well, that went well."

~

COLE WATCHED Lena as she moved around the car to where Rachel was standing. The two women whispered back and forth before they both turned to face him. Knowing he was the topic of conversation, he raised his left hand and gave a quick wave.

Well, that little reveal to Mason had not gone well, not that Cole had expected it to. The man had taken the pissed-off brother act to brand new heights. Mason was raging mad.

The cool air started to bite, and as Cole made his way toward the women, he heard Lena assuring Rachel.

"He'll come around. He's been so worried about you lately. And this? Well, this is a bit of a shock."

When Cole stopped at the end of the car, Rachel looked to him and gave a small smile.

"Want to head inside?" he asked as Lena also turned to face him.

He waited for accusations of coercion, but instead, he got a huge grin.

"Come on, it's time to meet the rest of the family, brother," Lena announced.

Rachel let out a small laugh as she moved toward him. She slid her hands inside his jacket and around his waist, laying her cheek on his chest. "You ready?" she whispered, looking up at him from beneath dark lashes.

Cole removed his hands from his pockets and smoothed them over her hair. "As ever. You?"

"No." She chuckled nervously.

Leaning down, he kissed her on the forehead.

Glancing up, he noticed Lena was watching them closely. Her eyes softened, and she mouthed, Thank you.

That's an odd thing to say, Cole thought.

As Lena turned and made her way to the back door, he pulled away from Rachel and took her hand in his.

"Come on, let's do this."

~

WELL, this is awkward, was all Rachel could think as she sat beside Cole at their family table in the dining room of Exquisite.

Mason was seated at the head of the table where he always sat, and Lena was off to his left. Beside her were two empty chairs—one for Shelly and one for Josh—who, of course, hadn't arrived yet because they were running late. Great, just when I'd kill for some of Shelly's over-the-top attitude, she's nowhere in sight. And that left the seats to Mason's right where she was sitting with Cole.

Mason still hadn't said a word to her. Instead, he was staring...no, glaring at Cole.

"So, Cole, what do you do?" Lena finally asked, attempting to break the arctic ice surrounding the table.

"He's a lawyer," Mason answered before Cole had the opportunity to open his mouth.

Rachel tensed, knowing how much it annoyed Cole to be interrupted or cut off in a conversation, but instead of saying anything, Cole took the much higher road than her pouting brother.

"Yes, Mason's correct, I'm a lawyer. In fact, I'm the lawyer for Joshua's company."

"Oh, that's right." Lena gave a forced laugh. "I knew that."

"No problem. I don't mind you asking or getting to know me," he pointed out, turning shrewd eyes on Mason.

The man has a death wish. Of that, Rachel was certain.

"You know," Mason replied in a frosty tone, "that's the kind of thing a man does when he introduces himself to the family before he dates or marries a woman."

"Mason," Lena hissed.

She wasn't even getting through to the imposter that had taken over Rachel's usually levelheaded brother.

"Well, in my defense, the last time we met, you didn't seem very open to getting to know me," Cole said.

Rachel could feel her heart hammering inside her chest while her head was pounding with the headache she could feel coming on.

"That's because Lena and Shelly told me that Rachel would never date a man like you—ever."

"Mason." Both Lena and Rachel shouted as they glared at the man who was usually so loving, usually so open.

Rachel wanted to hit something—Mason, in particular—as she shot a death stare in his direction.

What a complete disaster.

Thinking she would have some major explaining to do, Rachel turned to see Cole was looking at her with a mixture of amusement and annoyance. She liked to imagine that the amusement was for her and the annoyance for her brother.

Under the table, she felt a hand move to her thigh where Cole squeezed gently before he looked past her to Mason.

"Good thing I don't ever take no for an answer then, isn't it? And while your point is valid, technically, we didn't even finish our first date." Cole paused and looked back at Rachel with a smirk injected with a healthy dose of irritation.

The look almost made Rachel want to wince.

"When was that?" Cole asked Rachel conversationally before turning back to Mason. "Oh yes, Thursday night. A week after Rachel began, hmm...seeing me. Yes, our first date was definitely Thursday night, marriage license was Friday, and the wedding Saturday. You've got to love the efficiency of the county clerk's office, don't you?"

Like a missile being launched, Mason shot out of his chair. Just as he was about to open his mouth, the back door swung open, and Shelly sauntered in, dressed in a black pencil skirt and blue blouse. With a bottle of wine in one hand and Josh holding the other, she gave them all a warm smile.

"Sorry, we're late, guys. We got held up in traffic," she announced.

Josh dropped her hand and swatted her gently on the ass. "I don't remember there being any traffic."

Shelly laughed with Josh as she placed the bottle on the table beside the one they were all seated at...well, except for Mason who was still standing. She finally glanced at the other people in the room, and when her eyes moved to the man sitting beside Rachel, her mouth fell open. Not being the shy or retiring type, Shelly stepped up to the back of the empty chair with a sly smile.

"Well, well, well," she muttered as she let her eyes move back and forth between Rachel and Cole. "Isn't this an unexpected treat? Rachel brought a date to dinner."

Josh, wearing his usual jeans and T-shirt, stepped up next to Shelly and looked at Cole. Cole nodded in acknowledgment to Josh before turning to look at Shelly.

Rachel knew it only took Josh a second to sense the mood in the room, and as he looked to where Mason was standing at the head of the table with a clenched jaw and a pissed-off expression, she could see his mind whirling.

"Cole," Josh greeted cautiously as he pulled out his seat.

Before Josh could sit, Mason started to laugh like some kind of lunatic. His eyes shut, and he held his stomach as the hilarity of whatever he was thinking seemed to get the better of him.

Rachel watched as Shelly turned to Lena, who was silently shaking her head.

Then, in true Shelly style, she asked, "What the hell have you been smoking, Mason?"

Mason finally got himself under control and sat down.

Turning to Josh and Shelly, who were now both seated opposite Rachel and Cole, he finally spoke. "Let me introduce you, not to Rachel's date, but to her husband. Josh, I believe you already know him."

COLE KEPT his eyes focused on his friend and employer, Joshua. As the news seemed to finally make its way past the shock factor, Cole saw his friend look immediately to where Rachel was looking back at him and Shelly.

"Married?" Shelly shouted, slapping her hand on the table. "Shut the fu—"

"Shel," Josh interrupted the stunning blonde while still looking at Rachel with an expression of worry and confusion.

"What?" Shelly demanded on a laugh.

Well, hell, Cole thought, at least someone is amused.

"This is priceless. I've been waiting for Super Domme to finally admit she liked this guy, and here she is married to him." Leaning back on her chair, Shelly reached around Josh and poked Lena in the side. "You owe me fifty bucks."

"Hang on. You took a bet about this? That they would get

married?" Mason asked as he glared at his wife.

"No, I took a bet that they would end up dating," Lena muttered.

Cole sat back in his chair and watched the chaos unfold. He had to admit he was extremely curious about Shelly calling Rachel Super Domme. It was a point that Mason had obviously missed, or he would have—

"And why are you calling her Super Domme?"

Okay, no, he didn't miss it.

"Mason, I think you need to calm down," Lena advised as she reached across to where his palm was clenched on the table.

"I think someone needs to start fucking talking," Mason shouted as he turned his eyes to where Rachel sat silently, watching everything swirl around them.

Cole was going to let her answer. He was sure of it, but then the look on her face told him she had no idea what she wanted to say, and he hated that she felt so cornered. So, he stepped in.

"I think you should calm down, Mason. If and when Rachel wants to talk to you about it, I'm sure she will."

"Cole, I think you should probably let them talk."

The low warning came from Joshua, and as Cole zoomed in on him, he asked, "Is that the advice of my friend or from a man who once kissed my wife?"

"What?" Shelly sputtered, her mouth falling open.

"Oh, that's really mature, Cole," Joshua pointed out.

"I don't particularly think anyone is acting very mature at this table, so why should I?"

"What does he mean you kissed Rachel?" Shelly asked again, looking back and forth between Rachel and her fiancé. Then her face split into a grin as it dawned on her. "Oh, you mean when you were teenagers? I think it's sweet."

"Oh. My. God. Would you all just shut up?" Rachel finally yelled as she stood and glared at everyone.

Cole sat in silent admiration as she turned on Mason.

"You owe Cole an apology."

"I will not—"

"What?" she demanded, interrupting him. "Act like an adult? Right now, you are acting like a teenager who wants to beat up my boyfriend you disapprove of. And if I remember correctly, you never did that to him," she accused, pointing at Josh, who was now sitting back in his chair with his arm slung over the back of Shelly's chair.

"You dated Josh?"

This question came from Lena, who looked like she was trying to hold back a grin. Cole noticed the side of her mouth twitching, and he knew she was struggling.

"No, I didn't date Josh. I had a crush on him in high school."

"A huge one," Shelly added with a smile.

"Awww." Lena finally lost the battle, and the grin broke free. "That's very sweet. I bet he was a real sweetheart in high school."

"He was her first kiss," Shelly interjected, receiving a frosty glare from Rachel. "What?" Shelly feigned innocence. "It is sweet. And I have it on good authority that he is an excellent kisser."

Cole could tell Rachel was close to losing her cool as she let her eyes move over everyone sitting at the table.

"This must be so much fun for you all, and I get it. I used to give you all shit when you brought someone new in. I don't have any issue with that, but you..." She paused, turning to her brother. "I expected so much more from you."

Cole saw the way that comment hit Mason. His eyes clouded, and Cole could sense the anger draining from him, but Rachel wasn't finished. She leaned down until she was nose-to-nose with her brother.

"You haven't only embarrassed me, which I expected and probably deserved, but you have hurt and humiliated me tonight. I never thought you would ever do that."

Pushing the chair back, Rachel threw her napkin on the table and looked across to where Josh was silently staring up at her.

"Nothing to say? I'm surprised. I figured since you and Shelly must have had a fantastic laugh about me behind my back that you would be full of comments right now."

"Rach, it's not like that."

"Save it, Josh. I thought at least you would be on my side."

Cole glanced over to his friend, who was now frowning.

"I would like to leave," Rachel requested softly.

Standing, Cole buttoned his jacket and nodded to the table. "It's been...interesting."

And with that, he took Rachel's hand, and they left the table, heading out the same way they had come in.

~

THE ENTIRE DRIVE HOME, Rachel had been running through everything that had just happened, and she felt numb. Going in, she had known that Mason would be annoyed, but she had at least expected him to calm down enough to listen. His reaction had been unlike anything she had seen before. It was like he was a powder keg, and someone had lit the fuse. Rachel was still blown away by the ferocity of his anger.

"Hey," Cole said, his voice sliding through the interior of the car.

"Hey."

"Mason will come around," he tried to reassure.

"Honestly, I'm so angry at him right now that I don't care if he does."

"Yes, you do."

"You're right," she admitted begrudgingly as she stared out the window. "I do care. I just don't understand why he is so mad."

There was a long pause, and then she felt Cole's large palm on her thigh.

"Strange emotions can take over when a person no longer feels needed."

Rachel placed her hand over Cole's and looked at his profile in the dark confines of the vehicle. "Huh. You think that's what was going on tonight?"

Cole shrugged a little before he responded softly, "Perhaps. I get angry about my mother's situation, and it's usually because I feel unable to do anything about it. It's like I am suddenly no longer necessary."

As they pulled into the parking garage at his condo, Rachel turned in the seat to face him. "But that's not true. By you going there, you help her. You give her moments of happiness."

"I guess. Maybe Mason feels like he's lost you."

"Well that's ridiculous, and it doesn't excuse his moronic behavior."

"No, it doesn't," he agreed.

He unlocked the doors, and they climbed out to head inside.

Making their way through the lobby, they got into the elevator silently and Rachel leaned back against the far wall, staring at the numbers lighting up in front of her.

4, 5, 6, 7...

Cole remained beside her but touched her in no way. For a moment, she worried that he had changed his mind after witnessing the chaos that was her family.

11, 12, 13, 14...

"Don't change your mind," she blurted out into the silent space.

There was a second of silence.

"Look at me."

Turning her head against the back wall, Rachel found Cole facing her.

"I'm not going anywhere."

Blinking once, Rachel looked away and closed her eyes on a sigh. As the elevator climbed, she heard nothing, except for the whisper in her ear.

"Tell me what you need."

She knew the whisper was real, and she knew he could give her the one thing she wanted more than anything right now—to feel. When she opened her eyes, the elevator dinged and lit up number 26. Rachel pushed away from the back wall and turned to face her husband.

"I need you to make me forget about tonight. Take me someplace new."

Stepping up close to him, she placed her hands on his chest. As the doors swished open, Rachel felt Cole's fingers trace her cheek.

"That, I can do. Let me show you my office."

His office?

It must have been behind one of those shut doors she hadn't been in yet.

Silently, she took his hand and trusted him to make good on his word.

CHAPTER 23

Cole followed Rachel into his condo, and he was shocked to find he was excited that they would soon call this *our* home. It amused him on some level that when he had left this place last Thursday, he had been heading out on his first date with her, and now, here they were, walking back inside his—*scratch that, our*—home as a married couple.

As she stopped by the table in the foyer, she looked over her shoulder, letting her eyes run down him where he stood just inside the door.

"Which door?"

Cole unbuttoned his jacket and shrugged out of it. Placing it on the coatrack, he undid his left cuff and began rolling it up his arm as he made his way toward her. "Second to the left. It's my office and library."

When he stopped behind her, he let his eyes travel over her elegant back to her tight ass that was encased in those black leggings. Quickly, he undid the right cuff and rolled it up and out of his way. Without touching her, he leaned down and placed his mouth by her ear. "Let's go."

Placing a hand on her lower back, Cole heard her breath hitch, and he saw her shoulders shift as she started to move forward. Following her closely, he took a deep breath and reminded himself that tonight was about making her forget. It was about making her feel again, and he had the perfect idea in mind.

When they stopped by the door, he reached around her and grasped the handle. He felt her lean back into him, and Cole took the moment to breathe her in. The shampoo she used was mixed with the lingering scent of her hair dye, and it was one hundred percent Rachel.

Pushing the door open, Cole stood back and gently nudged her inside. She moved into his office and stopped in front of his desk, running a finger along the mahogany wood. Leaning his shoulder against the doorjamb, Cole watched her as she silently looked around the space.

There was a large window that overlooked the lake, and on the far side of the room were bookshelves that spanned the entire length of the wall and ran from the floor to the high ceiling.

Over the years, Cole had collected hundreds of hardbacks, both fiction and non, and he had stored many of them here in his private office. He loved to read, and as Rachel moved toward them, he realized they had yet another thing in common.

Looking over to him, she gave a small smile as she pointed to the books. "I didn't know you were such an avid reader."

Cole raised a brow as he reached up and undid his top button. "I'm sure there are many things you don't know about me yet."

Turning back to the books, she nodded, obviously giving that statement some thought. "Yes, I suppose you're right." Reaching out in front of her, she ran a finger down the spine of one of his books. "I love to read also. This is an amazing collection."

Keeping his eyes locked on her, he watched her walk down along the wall, trailing her fingers over the books as she went. When she reached the ladder he had installed so he could reach the books on the top shelves, Cole had a stunning vision. Immediately, he felt all the blood in his head drain south as Rachel stopped in front of the ladder and looked up.

"Wow, I love this." When she tugged the side of the ladder, it started to roll to the right. Laughing, she did it again, and the ladder smoothly rolled along the brass bars it was attached to.

Cole felt his breathing speed up as she pulled on the ladder once more, bringing it farther into the center of the wall.

"Rachel?" he managed to say as X-rated images continued to flash through his mind.

Her name didn't come out as a statement. It came out as a question, and as she looked back at him with her hand still resting on the smooth polished wood, she froze in place. He knew she could see it. She could sense the need that was suddenly clawing at him like a caged beast.

"Yes," she whispered.

Cole pushed off the doorjamb and walked over to the desk. Leaning his backside against it, he let his eyes finally drop from hers to the tight sweater molded to her magnificent breasts. He saw them rise and fall with every breath she took, and he found it difficult to pull his eyes from them.

"I want you to take off your clothes slowly."

Her breathing quickened at his suggestion, and he could see the lust as it entered her eyes. It was the same desire he was now feeling. Opening her mouth, she was about to speak until Cole lifted a hand and raised an index finger to his lips.

"Shh, no talking."

Instantly, Rachel closed her mouth.

Cole added, "You aren't to make a sound, or you will wait until tomorrow morning to come."

As her eyes narrowed on him, he felt his lips twitch, but he didn't let the grin appear. Instead, he stood and moved around to the leather chair behind his desk. He sat down, barring her from any view of him from the waist down.

Lifting his chin slightly, he raised a brow in a gesture that shouted, *Begin.* Leaning back in the chair, Cole settled in to enjoy the show.

WHAT IS HE DOING? Rachel thought as she kept her eyes on him.

He looked so incredibly attractive right now as he sat behind his desk with his shirt rolled up his arms, baring his tattoos to the naked eye. Add in the way he had undone the top two buttons of his shirt, and the man looking back at her, her husband, was the sexiest man she had ever seen. His eyes were focused on her, and his mouth was pulled taut into a neutral expression.

Well, let's see if I can change that with what I do *since I can't talk.*

Rachel fingered the bottom of her sweater where the wool had come loose. With a smile meant to seduce, she took the loose piece between her thumb and forefinger, and gently, she started to pull on it. More and more wool came away, and as Cole's eyes dropped to her fingers, she let it go and began to flirt with the edge of the blue wool resting against the top of her thighs. Slipping her fingers under the sweater's edge, Rachel gripped the fabric and swiftly tugged the material up and over her head, bringing into view her creamy white skin and breasts encased in black lace with a pearl at the center clasp.

Keeping her eyes fixed on him, Rachel toed off her black heels and kicked them aside, and when her feet touched the hardwood floor, the firm surface felt good and solid as though it would never be pulled out from under her.

"Leave the bra. Now, take off the leggings. And, Rachel? Keep your eyes on me while you do it."

Dipping her hands into the waist of her pants, she made sure to do as she was told. She peeled the tight fabric down her legs. Bending in half with her neck arched back, she made sure she never lost eye contact with the man who was currently undoing his shirt buttons one at a time.

When her pants hit her ankles, she took one step toward him, leaving her pants where they lay. Even though she was dying to drop her gaze and look at the skin he had just revealed, she kept her eyes locked on his.

"Christ, Rachel. Do you have something you'd like to tell me about this lingerie fetish of yours?"

She parted her lips to answer, but then she caught herself at the last moment and remained silent.

"Good decision," he acknowledged. Raising a hand, he twirled his finger. "Turn around. I want to see your tight little ass."

Biting her lip to keep herself from talking, Rachel pivoted on the wood floor until she was facing the wall full of rows and rows of books. The room had fallen silent, and Rachel strained to hear any kind of sound, but there was nothing.

Suddenly, she felt a slither of fear slip into her mind. Closing her eyes, she reminded herself that this was not Ben. This was Cole, the man she loved and trusted to never hurt her. Telling herself to relax, she took several deep breaths. She almost flew out of her skin however, when a fingertip grazed down her back to the center bow of her panties where it held six ribbons together at the base of her spine.

"I have never seen such sexy lingerie in my fucking life," Cole said, his voice floating over her bare shoulder.

He must have been standing close, but Rachel didn't dare look or ask. Instead, she continued biting her lip while his finger traced the ribbons one at a time from the lace that barely cupped her ass cheeks to the pearl at the center of the bow.

After he outlined the final ribbon, the hot touch of his finger left her skin, and when his mouth moved by her ear, she felt moisture pool between her thighs.

"Move in front of the ladder, Rachel, and do not turn around until I tell you to."

With her heart pounding in her chest, Rachel moved to her left and stood in front of the large wooden ladder. It was attached to the top of the bookcase by a brass bar and secured at the base in a similar fashion. The only difference was the bottom had bulkier rollers.

Knowing she was unable to ask why, she found herself focusing on the books behind the rungs of the impressive ladder—Hemingway, Dickens, and, *huh*, Aristotle. *Classics.* Next to those, she saw thrillers written by James Patterson, Stephen King, and Stieg Larsson.

God, is there anything sexier than a man who reads?

"Spread your legs to the width of the ladder, and put your hands on the rung above your head."

Yes, Rachel decided, *there is something sexier.*

A bossy man that reads—that is sexier.

~

COLE PULLED his shirt out of his pants, removed it, and threw it on the desk behind him. He had to remind himself—and his impatient cock that was ready to sink inside her—that this was for Rachel.

What he was about to do was for her. It was about making her forget the terrible night she had just endured. It was also a fantastic opportunity to remind her of why she was in love with him, and one of the reasons was the way only *he* could make her feel.

As she parted her legs, Cole closed his eyes and said a prayer of gratitude for the sheer fucking pleasure he felt from her following his orders.

In the back of his mind, he knew that she would without question, but for some reason, now that they were married, he had a moment of concern that things would somehow change. *That* was certainly not the case, he was discovering, as Rachel raised her arms above her head and wrapped her fingers around the rung above her.

He'd never witnessed a more erotic scene in his life, and he'd looked and been in plenty of potential moments. There was something about her bare feet on the hardwood floors, the long creamy legs parted invitingly, the wicked lingerie that tantalized and teased, and the black symbols that marked her spine as they disappeared up and under her brightly highlighted hair.

Fuck yes. She was the most erotic picture he had ever seen, and she hadn't done anything other than stretch her arms above her head as she waited for him.

Stepping forward, Cole pushed her hair to the side and over her shoulder. As he leaned down to place his lips against the curve of her neck, he heard a swift intake of breath but no words. Brushing his lips along her soft, sweet skin, Cole couldn't help the little nibble he took of her ear.

"I'm going to take these," he whispered in her ear, raising a hand to the bow holding the ribbons together, "off now, and once they're gone, I want you to put your right foot up on the bottom rung of this ladder. Nod if you understand."

When he saw her head dip in acknowledgment, Cole felt his cock harden as he ran his tongue across his top teeth.

Don't speak. Don't speak, or he will stop, were the words repeating over and over in Rachel's mind as she faced the books with her hands above her head.

Swallowing back a moan that was threatening to break free, she tightened her hands around the wood and held on as she felt his dexterous fingers slip into the sides of her panties. Ever so slowly, Cole dragged the scrap of lace down her legs to her upper thighs. When he got there, she felt his warm breath on the back of her thigh.

"Close your legs for a moment."

Automatically, Rachel moved and shut her legs, so he could remove the panties the rest of the way. Once she stepped free of them she heard a clicking sound, like a lock beneath her, and then felt his fingers trail up her right leg from her ankle to her calf.

"There. Now that the ladder is locked, spread your legs again. Show me what I want to see."

Without any hesitation, Rachel moved her left leg back to where it was before at the edge of the left side of the ladder, and then as instructed, she raised her right foot to the bottom rung. The position bent her right leg and opened her up in the most intimate way.

Breathing hard, she tried to imagine what he was doing behind her, but when she did that, it just made her want to beg for him to touch her. Instead, she kept her eyes focused on what was in front of her—*Patterson, Hemingway, King.* That helped for the most part until she felt his fingers touch her left ankle. *Shit, what does that mean? That he's kneeling on the fucking floor?*

"You make a pretty fucking picture right now, Mrs. Madison."

Yes, yes, yes. His voice had definitely come from behind *and* beneath her.

"With your hands above your head, your hair so bright but still dark against your creamy skin." With a deep sigh, he blew a hot breath against her leg. "Your legs parted, and your perfect fucking ass."

She sucked her bottom lip into her mouth to keep her words to herself, but she almost lost the battle when she felt his lips against her left upper thigh. Gently, he pressed kiss after soft torturous kiss to her bare flesh, and when he nipped the curve of her ass cheek playfully, she felt the sweet sting of his teeth. It was just as it had been that night she had stood on the trunk in his room. *Wait. Our room.*

That was when she felt his hand slide under her right thigh toward her knee as he gently pushed her bent leg aside to spread her even farther apart. As his breath caressed the curve of her back, she realized he must have now been kneeling behind her.

"Hmm, this is getting you all hot and bothered, isn't it? I wonder if it is the challenge of keeping quiet, the fact that you are so vulnerable, or the thought of what I plan to do next that has you so fucking turned on."

As he whispered the final thought across her back, she felt his fingers slide up from her knee to her bent thigh, and then he dipped in between her legs to stroke her very sensitive flesh.

"Ahh, yes. So fucking wet," he muttered as he slid his fingers through her slick juices.

Rachel knew she was going to draw blood as she bit down hard on her bottom lip while Cole continued his sensual assault from below. His fingertips pushed inside her as his lips brushed her ass cheek again, and she couldn't help but thrust her hips back at him.

The deep chuckle that made its way to her ears did nothing to quell the desire he was provoking as he pulled his fingers from her before he pierced deeper inside. Squeezing her hands tightly around the rung above her, Rachel continued to roll her hips back onto Cole's hand as he kissed and bit her ass while he drove her insane with a good, hard fingering.

Rachel was convinced she was about to come from that alone, but then his fingers suddenly left her body and his mouth was gone. The sheer agony of losing his touch almost made Rachel scream. It was only the knowledge of what she *wouldn't* get that kept her lips firmly sealed.

"Remember, not one word. Now, turn around and put your hands back above your head."

The command was so guttural and intense that Rachel didn't even recognize it as Cole.

Breathing so hard she felt as though she had run a marathon, Rachel released her right hand and lowered her leg to the ground. As she turned, she shifted her eyes to where she knew he would be. When she finally saw him, she almost lost the will to do as she had been told. He was completely naked, kneeling at her feet, with his cock in his right fist.

Please, she sent up a quick prayer, *don't let me say a fucking word. I want him more than my next breath.*

As her eyes met his, she felt the full impact of his raging lust. His scorching gaze heated her as he worked his hard-on and waited.

Raising her hands back above her head, she gripped the rung, and became aware of the way it pushed her bra-covered breasts up even higher and closer together. She noticed Cole's eyes zoom in on them, which in turn made him fuck his hand a little bit faster.

"Put your right leg up on the bottom rung Rachel."

In doing so, the position now spread her wide open, so he could see everything. As his eyes swept from her face, down her body, to where her sex was glistening and no doubt causing her piercing to twinkle and shine, she felt her pussy clench from his visual caress.

"Look at you," he murmured as he rose on his knees for a closer inspection.

From the position she was in, Rachel could see the top of his blond head as he leaned in and placed his mouth on her lower abdomen between her navel piercing and the top of her pelvic mound. She sucked in a breath as he scraped his teeth against her flesh.

When he turned his face up to look her in the eye, Rachel knew that whatever he was about to do to her was going to blow her fucking mind.

~

STILL DOWN ON HIS KNEES, Cole released his cock, and reached out to press his palm flat against her raised thigh, holding her in place. "I'm going to put my tongue on you, and then I'm going to put it inside you. You are not going to say one damn thing if you want me to replace it with my cock. Understood?"

Licking his top lip, Cole waited for her response. Her beautiful breasts heaved with agitation from being confined in the last sexy piece of lace covering her, and as she closed her eyes and moved her head in the worldwide signal of yes, Cole leaned in and wrapped his lips around the top stud of her piercing. He heard a strangled moan get trapped in the back of her throat as her hips bucked forward toward him. Groaning around the silver ball, Cole stroked it with the tip of his tongue.

The taste of her flooded his senses, and his fingers dug into the soft skin of the thigh he was holding out of his way. Out of the corner of his eye, he could see her other leg, the one holding her up, shaking, and he felt his lips spread into a smile against her vertical piece of jewelry. Glancing up at her, Cole knew exactly what he wanted.

"Hold onto that rung tightly," he rasped against her flesh.

As her fingers tightened around the wooden rail, Cole gripped the leg propped up on the bottom step and placed it over his shoulder.

Her eyes popped opened and widened on him as she realized what he was about to do.

Giving her a wicked smile, he reached down to the foot planted firmly on the floor. Wrapping his fingers around her ankle, he gently urged it forward and up until he placed it over his other shoulder. Cupping her ass cheeks in his palms, he ran his tongue over his top and then bottom lip as he took in a deep breath, his nose now only inches from the wet heat of her.

"Remember, don't make a sound, Rachel, or your greedy little pussy will stay hungry and empty."

As her jaw clenched, her eyes burned down at him with a mixture of annoyance and overwhelming desire. Cole dipped his head and brought her hips up to him. As he buried his tongue deep inside her, his nose brushed against the bottom stud of her piercing. He pushed his tongue in and out, devouring her with every forward and backward motion.

He felt her feet cross over against his back as her thighs tightened around his head, and Cole couldn't help but run his finger down the crack of her ass, which made her swing her hips up even closer to his insatiable mouth.

His tongue licked from the bottom of her slit to the top. He sucked one of her swollen folds between his lips, and pulling his head back slightly, tugging it gently before releasing. He speared his tongue back inside her, and groaning against her needy body, Cole could feel his own climax building as she raced toward hers.

The fact that she was absolutely silent during this sensual feast was such a fucking turn-on that Cole was finding it difficult not to come like a horny teenager. The woman was a star pupil when it came to following orders.

Ready to finally reward her, Cole found his way back to her hood piercing, and he sucked and flicked her clit with his agile tongue. As she tilted her hips up higher, practically pushing her herself onto his tongue, Cole raised his eyes to hers and groaned against her hot flesh.

"Come, Mrs. Madison."

And just like that, her knees tightened, her ass cheeks flexed in his hands, and her eyes squeezed shut as she came silently all over his tongue.

~

I THINK I'M DEAD, was all Rachel could manage to think.

Her fingers remained around the ladder rung above her, and her legs relaxed over Cole's shoulders. He had destroyed her.

Abso-fucking-lutely destroyed me.

With his nimble tongue, strong hands, and filthy mouth, he had reduced her to a silent, greedy sex addict. He was still kneeling between her thighs, kissing and petting them, as he gently placed first her right and then her left foot back on the floor.

She was about to release her hold on the ladder when he stood—all six foot four inches of naked, tattooed, and pierced Cole—and wagged his finger back and forth.

"Not yet. Now, it's my turn," he informed.

He stepped up close to her, raising his hands to cover hers on the rung. Leaning in, he took her mouth and as she parted her lips and he pushed his tongue between her lips, Rachel couldn't help the high keening moan that finally left her throat.

He ground his hips up against hers, and as he moved his hips in time with his tongue, she felt his cock and piercing brush against her. Wrenching his mouth from hers, she cried out as he reached and gripped her chin, tilting up her face, so her eyes could meet his. As hazel met blue, the fire started to spark again deep inside her stomach before it spread slowly up to her breasts, heating her entire body.

"This time..." He paused, lowering his hand down her chest to the pearl clasp of her bra. Unsnapping it, he gave her an unholy grin as her breasts spilled free. "You can make as much noise as you fucking like."

Taking both his hands away from her, he gripped her hips and warned, "Just don't let go."

With that, he jerked her feet off the floor until her legs were wrapped around his hips, and he took a step back, stretching her body out and slightly away from the ladder. When he was at the right distance, he widened his stance, and without any more talk, he thrust his cock deep inside her body.

She screamed out in sheer ecstasy as his throbbing length finally pushed into her needy pussy and staked its claim. Rachel made sure to keep her eyes open, and for the moment, she focused on the tense muscles of Cole's arms as he held her hips in place, thrust after hard thrust.

His pierced nipples had hardened and were begging to be licked, bitten, or pinched, but that would have to happen some other time. Right now, she was too busy hanging on to a ladder—*a fucking ladder*—and getting pounded by her sexy-as-fuck husband.

Cole's eyes were focused on her naked breasts that were now moving with each forward punch of his hips, and she could tell he wanted to touch them and was pissed that he couldn't. He clenched his jaw in annoyance as his hips sped up with his race toward completion.

Tilting her hips at a certain angle, he dragged his thick cock out of her, causing his piercing to hit that secretive spot deep inside, and Rachel screamed so long and loud she was surprised the neighbors didn't call 911.

"Oh yeah, just like that, huh?" he asked as he did it over and over.

She panted as he pounded into her. "Fuck."

"Oh, we're fucking, wife. We are fucking *real* hard."

With that, his fingers tightened against her flesh as his hips rolled and pummeled into hers. As Cole tensed and let his head drop back, he groaned out her name as she felt his warmth flood her deep inside.

At that moment, Rachel knew she would never find a connection like this with anyone ever again. He had set her free, and now, she felt like she was finally home.

CHAPTER 24

"You and I need to talk."

Rachel lifted her eyes from the computer and turned to look down the hall of the small flower shop. She had known Mason wouldn't leave what had happened last night alone for long, but the fact that he was here at seven in the morning the next day showed her how much it had been on his mind.

"Well, I was ready to talk last night," she pointed out.

As her brother moved farther down the narrow hall toward her, Rachel straightened her spine, getting ready for a battle. Lately, it had seemed like she was arguing with him much more than usual, and right now, as he got closer, she felt as though the air in the shop was becoming tense.

"No, you weren't. You were there to shock us all and hope no one said anything."

"Believe what you like, Mase. I knew there was no way you would understand. I just figured—"

"Safety in numbers?" he interrupted as he moved to sit on one of the stools behind the counter.

His black hair was pushed back from his face, and now that he was sitting down, Rachel could look directly at him. His blue eyes were just like hers, but the laugh lines that were usually there when he smiled were missing right now. Instead, he had a frown, one that was becoming more permanent with every conversation they had recently.

"Maybe," she muttered, deciding to choose the easy option.

"Maybe?"

Yep, Mason isn't letting me get away with that.

"Come on, Rach. Did you really think I was going to be okay with what happened last night? What brother who cares about his sister would be?"

God, no one can guilt me as well as Mason.

"Why do you dislike Cole so much?" she asked, trying to divert his attention.

"I don't," he answered quickly before adding, "I don't know enough about him. It's not so much a matter of disliking him. It's more that I'm worried about you."

"You don't need to—"

"Don't tell me not to worry, okay?" Mason interjected with a deep sigh. "You're my little sister."

"Mase, I'm hardly little."

"You will *always* be my little sister, and I don't care if you're dating —or in this case, marrying—Josh, Cole, or a stranger. I will worry until I know you are happy."

Rachel leaned against the counter, and for a minute, she had to look away from his probing gaze. He was doing that thing where he managed to say everything right, and it was really annoying her that she found herself feeling bad for yelling at him last night.

He deserved it. Didn't he?

"You just haven't been the same since Mom passed away. I know I dealt with my—"

"Stupid phase?" Rachel replied sarcastically, looking back to him.

"I was going to say I know I dealt with my grief in a less than mature way, but I'm not sure you ever dealt with it."

Mason stood and took a step closer to her. When she crossed her arms in front of herself, he didn't even hesitate to wrap his arms around her.

"I just don't want Cole to be a convenient distraction from other feelings," he whispered into the empty shop.

Despite wanting to stay annoyed, Rachel felt a laugh escape her at those words. "You might be right about me not dealing with everything, but trust me, there is nothing convenient about Cole Madison."

~

MASON PULLED AWAY from Rachel and sat back down, giving her the space she seemed to need more and more of lately. Today though, she seemed different, calmer than usual. It was almost as if she was a relaxed version of herself, standing there in her leather pants and a bright pink shirt with black polka dots.

"Tell me," he prodded as he kept his eyes on her.

"Tell you? Tell you what?"

"Talk to me, Rach. We used to do that all the time, remember?"

"Yeah, when we were kids," she pointed out.

"And that has to change now, why? You seemed fine when Mom..." Immediately, he trailed off, recalling a conversation he'd recently had with Josh. Josh had told Mason that he thought something was up with Rachel as far back as the wedding, maybe even a little bit before that. When Josh had told him, Mason had felt like shit for not even noticing.

Well, Mom always said that love made you stupid and blind.

He just hadn't realized it would make him blind to the only other woman in his life that he loved with all his heart.

"It's okay. You can say it," Rachel urged, breaking through his thoughts. "You're right. I was fine when Mom was still alive...because *she* made it all okay, Mase. Having her here was like having an anchor to cling to. Losing Dad...god, I didn't think I'd ever be the same. He took all my secrets with him, and I had no one left to talk to about it."

"Secrets?" Mason questioned.

What the hell is she talking about? What secrets?

~

"SIT WITH ME," her father said as he sat down at her kitchen counter.

Pressing the ice pack she had handed him to his eye, he pinned her with the one that was still open. Rachel sat down beside him with her own makeshift ice pack, frozen peas, placed against her cheek.

"You are going to sit here with me until you are ready to talk," he told her in a voice that signaled he had all day.

Hesitantly, Rachel peered up into the face that made her feel safe, loved, and cherished. "What if I'm not ready yet?"

"Then, we sit here some more," he told her, proving that it was as simple as that.

Rachel closed her eyes and tried to ignore the insistent ringing in her ears. She wanted to finally unburden herself of this mess. The only problem was that she was so ashamed of how it had begun and how long it had occurred, so she was finding it hard to form the right words.

Opening her eyes, she looked at the man beside her and wondered how she had gotten so lucky. She had wonderful parents—two people who loved one another and who had raised their children in a home full of love.

But for Rachel, it was always her dad who was her pillar of strength. He was the one person she knew who could chase away everything that was bad. Whether it was consoling her in a strong embrace or dancing in the kitchen to a song from her childhood, her dad was the person who always made her feel safe.

As she sat beside him, she found that she didn't know how to tell him everything Ben had done to her, but she had to start somewhere, and he was waiting.

"He's been doing this for a while now," Rachel blurted out. She ceased talking to brave a glance at her dad.

When her eyes met the one that was uncovered, she knew he was having trouble containing his anger.

"Did Mason know what was going on?"

Quickly, Rachel shook her head, causing the ringing in her ears to get louder. "Oh god, no. Mase would've—"

"Mason would have killed him, so I suppose we're lucky that he didn't know. Although, considering how close you two are, *I'm surprised he didn't guess."*

Rachel could feel the tears escaping and rolling down her cheeks. She knew that she had done everything she could to hide this from her parents and her brother, the people she loved very much.

"I'm so ashamed of myself, Dad," she mumbled, unable to look at him anymore. "I'm ashamed of who I was with him."

"Hey, there'll be none of that. He *did this to you. You didn't do anything wrong."*

"I let him do it," Rachel choked out between sobs.

"Rachel?" her father said, lowering the ice pack from his swollen eye.

When she finally raised her head to look at him, the expression in his eyes was something she had never seen. He was pissed but not at her. She could sense the anger simmering beneath the surface, and it made her truly glad that Ben was nowhere in sight because, at that moment, she feared her father would have killed him.

"Listen to me, young lady. You have nothing to feel ashamed of. What he did to you was wrong. It was cruel and the lowest form of cowardice. A man should never make his partner feel anything other than loved, respected, and special. He should never get pleasure from making her cower in a corner or from making her hide from the people she loves." Reaching out his large palm, her father cupped her reddened cheek. "You don't ever need to feel ashamed because of this. Never. And don't settle for anything other than being loved the way you should be."

"Dad, please, please don't tell Mom or Mason. I just want to put it behind me and forget I was ever this stupid."

"You're not stupid," he said. "Maybe you were looking for something in Ben, something you thought he could give you. There's no harm in looking for what you need. In the end, it just turns out that he was not what you or anyone ever deserved. And, Rachel, if I ever see that little fucker near you again, I will kill him."

She didn't know why, but that dire threat made all her fears leave—at least for the moment anyway.

~

"HE JUST KNEW me better than anyone else," Rachel muttered.

"Well, you were always closest with him, just like I was with Mom. Funny that we gravitated to the opposite," Mason acknowledged with a fond smile.

"But so perfect, right? It makes sense really. We had two amazing parents. Mom felt like my final piece of Dad. With her here, we still got the stories, all of the remember-whens. When she passed, I felt lost. I felt like I had nothing left to hold on to."

"Rachel, that's not true. You always had me."

"Not at first. When Mom died, you disappeared, Mase. You were grieving and so angry. You didn't even see me, and I understood. That's why I didn't push."

"Well, maybe you fucking should have," he cursed.

Rachel could tell he was more pissed off at himself than at her.

"Maybe. But where would that have gotten me? You were in no frame of mind to listen."

"So, instead, you retreated? And don't say you haven't because everybody has noticed."

"Yes, I admit things changed, that I changed. I needed someone I could talk to, relate to. You had Lena, and then Josh came back to town. He, as usual, was his easygoing, fantastic self, and he tried to get me to open up, but even I knew that he was too wrapped up in Shelly. I wasn't going to be the friend that had all the issues—yet again."

Rachel decided that this next part of the conversation really needed to be done with some distance between them. Moving around Mason, she made her way over to a vase that held some colorful tulips, her mother's favorite.

"So, I decided to check out a place called Whipped," she finally made herself say, turning to gauge his reaction.

"Yes, I've recently been informed *all* about that club." Shaking his head, Mason frowned. "I just don't see it—you all decked out in leather. I mean, yeah, I see the loud, fun hair and the leather pants. But, Rachel, you're too sweet, too soft for that kind of place."

Rachel laughed, thinking about Cole's accusation that everything she had done in that club was fake, that it was all part of a uniform. It was ironic that the two men in her life that had yet to see eye-to-eye with each other both knew her so well.

"You're right, but I wanted to be in control of who I decided to let in. In there, I knew that I could."

"Is that what Charlie's attraction was? That he was so easygoing you could do whatever you wanted?"

"It was definitely part of it. You never seemed to have an issue with him," Rachel mused out loud.

"Because he was harmless."

"And Cole's not?"

"No, he's not. He has the ability to really hurt you. I can see it in the way you look to him, the way he seems to calm you just by sitting next to you. He reminds me of your first boyfriend, Ben."

"He's *nothing* like Ben," Rachel replied in a frosty tone.

She could tell Mason was instantly aware of his misstep. He just wasn't sure why.

"Okay," he drawled out slowly. "I'm sorry for the comparison. I know things ended badly with him."

"No. Things were terrible with him. He was...was...Cole is *nothing* like him," she reinforced.

"Hey, hey, I'm sorry. I didn't mean to bring him up. You never did tell us why you broke up with him."

Taking a deep breath, Rachel walked back to stop in front of her brother.

"Only Dad knew why."

"Well, you always were closest to him. Daddy's little girl," Mason tried for a lighter tone.

"Not about this, Mase. I never wanted him to know this, but I couldn't keep it a secret."

By the way Mason's jaw clenched and the hands that had been resting on the counter fisted, Rachel could tell that he sensed something bad was about to come out of her mouth.

"Rach, you're starting to really worry me. Talk to me, please?"

Rachel closed her eyes, blocking out Mason's curious but compassionate look. Compassion was not what she wanted right now, not when retelling this story.

"The reason that Ben and I broke up..." *Stop, swallow, breathe*. "Was because he used to do things to me."

"What kind of things?" Mason managed to say through gritted teeth.

Once again, Rachel had no words, so she sat in silence.

"What kind of things, Rachel?" Mason pressed, determined now to know everything.

With what little voice she could find, she whispered, "He used to hurt me."

The silence that filled the room after her confession was deafening.

Then, Mason was up. He stood tall, which was impressive even when he wasn't pissed, and that wasn't now.

"How? How did he hurt you?" he asked.

Rachel looked up into her brother's eyes that were narrowed and full of frustration. She knew this was what Cole had been referring to when he had said sometimes anger came from feeling useless.

"He would get jealous and possessive about stupid things, things that didn't even matter. He'd yell at me, push me around, hit me. The night we broke up, I was asking him to leave, and Dad came over. He saw Ben slap me."

"Jesus Christ, Rachel," Mason hissed, his fists clenching by his side.

The look on his face was murderous, so unlike any she had seen there before, and she felt ill for putting it there now.

"That wasn't the first time he had done it, but Dad made sure it was the last," she ended softly. She crossed her arms over her stomach as though it would help hold in all the emotions she was feeling.

"Where is he now?"

The question was filled with such menace, and it was so unexpected that Rachel found herself asking, "Why?"

"Because I want to kill the fucker."

She felt her eyes widen as she dropped her arms and stepped forward to her tense brother. Reaching out, she placed a palm over his chest. "You sounded just like Dad then. He was worried about what you would do if you knew. But, Mase, it's okay. Well, it is now."

Mason raised his hands and gently gripped her shoulders. "What does that mean—that it's okay now?"

She didn't expect to say it, but she found she couldn't stop herself. It was like the truth was all lining up and dying to come out. "It's okay now because of Cole. He makes it okay."

"I don't understand," Mason said, struggling with all this new information. "How does he make it okay? Did he kill him first? Because if he did, I need to shake that guy's hand, possibly even hug him."

For the first time in the last hour, Rachel found herself smiling.

"No, that's not it. Cole has never met Ben, which is lucky for Ben, I think. But for so long, I had nightmares about what he did to me. I was terrified to let anyone touch me. So, I made sure I dated easy-going guys, guys like Charlie, that let me control everything."

"I don't want to hear the rest of this, do I?" Mason asked with a hint of humor and an arched brow. "Because I sure as shit know that Cole is nothing like Charlie."

"No, he's not. He's the exact opposite. I couldn't control him any more than I could you. I know Cole comes off as serious and stuffy, but he's so much more than that. He's kind and honest. He's the one that wanted to tell all of you about us from the very beginning. Why do you think he came to the restaurant last week? And last night? That was all him."

Mason's lips twitched, and the usual easygoing smile that was so familiar started to come back. "Well, I believe that. He's a cocky bastard."

"Mase, he makes me feel safe. He chases all the nightmares away."

"And you really love him, don't you?"

"Yes, I really do."

Mason sighed and shook his head with a small chuckle. "Only you would fall in love and marry a man in less than two weeks."

"I think I might have started to love him the first night I met him. He told me that he was exactly what I needed, and I was convinced he was a lunatic, so I told him to get lost." Rachel laughed, remembering the intense and sexy stranger with the tequila in the club.

"That seems to run in our family—falling for a person who drives you insane. Isn't that what Dad always said? He was a wise man," Mason reflected.

"He married Mom, and she was a pretty amazing woman, so I think he knew what he was talking about."

"We had the best parents in the world. You know that, right?" Mason tapped under her chin.

"I know. I think they'd be pleased with us. Don't you?"

Mason's smile widened, and his eyes filled with mischief, just like they had when he was a boy. "Well, me definitely. What's not to love?"

Rachel found herself holding back tears as happiness swelled inside her. "Well, as much as I hate to admit it, I couldn't have asked for a better brother."

Mason opened his arms and hugged her. "Bring Cole around. I want to meet him."

"You don't need to worry about Cole. He loves me."

"I'm starting to see that, but I still want to know him because I love you, too."

Rachel leaned up as Mason lowered his head, and she pressed a kiss to his cheek.

"Best brother ever."

Mason chuckled. "You didn't think so last night."

"That's because you were a jerk last night."

Letting her go, Mason walked around her and made his way down the back hall. He stopped to pet Tulip, who was sitting up on the table in the back.

"See you at eight on Friday at my place. Okay, Mrs. Madison?"

Hearing her name on her brother's lips, Rachel's eyes widened.

Mason snickered. "See? Even you still think it's weird."

Rachel poked her tongue out at him. "We'll be there."

With that, Mason chuckled and left, leaving the small flower shop feeling much lighter than it had earlier this morning.

CHAPTER 25

The minute Cole set foot off the elevator, Logan stopped him.

"Well, if it isn't my absent partner back from his impromptu trip out of the city to see his ailing mother."

Cole rolled his eyes, not even sparing him a glance. Making his way down the hall to where Jane was seated behind her desk, Cole nodded and smiled as she held out several envelopes to him.

"These came for you this morning, Mr. Madison. All your other mail is in your inbox."

"Thank you, Jane. Did you have a nice weekend?" he asked, ignoring the fact that Logan was still hovering behind him with an annoying-as-shit smirk on his face.

"I had a lovely weekend, sir. And you?"

Jane was barely containing the grin she was holding back. She knew exactly what he had done this weekend since he had called to have her make sure several things were in place.

"My weekend was..." Cole paused as though thinking about it. Just to further irritate Logan, he said, "Interesting and eventful."

"Well, something must have happened besides the norm. Usually, you come back here pissier than when you left. Although, this time, you did leave after a date with that hot piece of—"

Before the words left Logan's mouth, Cole turned on him and pinned him with an icy glare. "Stop before you say something that will not only embarrass Jane but will also come back to bite you in the ass."

Logan raised a dark brow from behind his glasses and looked to Jane, who was now much more composed. "My apologies," he offered.

Cole turned and made his way to his office. Pushing open the door, he walked inside and hung his coat on the rack. Unbuttoning his jacket on his way toward his desk, he didn't bother looking behind him to where he knew Logan was standing.

"What, Logan?" Cole demanded as he placed his briefcase down on the floor.

As he sat down in his chair, he pulled the large stack of mail from his inbox and started to flick through it. He didn't bother looking up at the man who had now stopped in front of his desk.

"Want to tell me what happened this weekend?"

Cole leaned back in his chair and finally looked at Logan. Raising his hands, he let his fingertips come together at a point in front of his face. Feeling a grin tug at the corner of his mouth, he realized he was looking forward to shocking the hell out of Logan. Sitting silently, Cole began to twist the platinum band that was on his left hand.

"Come on, Cole. What's happened with Lydia?"

"Mom's fine. You should come and visit her sometime," he said, still playing with his latest accessory.

"I don't know that she would like that so much. Your mother wasn't my biggest fan," Logan pointed out as he turned and walked over to the couch that was pushed up against the wall.

Sitting forward, Cole rested his arms on the table. "Well, that's true. Can you blame her though? She found out pretty late in the game that her husband had another child."

Logan shrugged as he undid his jacket before sitting. "Didn't seem to bother you."

"Yes, it did. I hated you." Cole chuckled.

"At first, but my charm, intelligence—"

"And annoying habit of never, *ever* going away."

"Wore you down," Logan tacked on the end.

Cole frowned, remembering those first few meetings. "You made sure we roomed together at college. Although how you managed that, I will never know."

Logan gave Cole a look that was all too familiar. It was his victory smile, arrogant and cocky. It was almost the exact replica of Cole's.

"It was my amazing power of persuasion, which was another reason you agreed to become partners with me."

Cole narrowed his eyes on his half-brother.

Yes, Logan is right. It had been a huge shock when the section of his father's will regarding his college trust fund had been read on his eighteenth birthday. That had been the day that he and his mother had found out that his father, who had passed away before Cole had turned five, had fathered a second son—a son by the name of Logan Mitchell, who was a year younger than he was.

That day changed Cole's life forever. At first, he'd been certain it was in a bad way, but as he had gotten to know Logan, he'd found he actually liked him.

Even though Logan was currently annoying the shit out of him.

"Is there a reason you are still sitting on my couch?"

"Is there a reason you are avoiding my question?" Logan fired back, placing his right ankle on his left knee.

"No reason," Cole replied, once again twisting the ring on his finger. Sitting back in the chair, he looked Logan directly in the eye and announced, "I got married this weekend."

He had to give the guy credit. Logan's expression barely changed, except for the slight rise of his eyebrows over his glasses and the widening of his blue eyes.

"Excuse me? Did you just say you got married this weekend?" As Logan said that, his eyes finally dropped to the ring Cole was twisting around his finger. They locked on to it, and before Cole could say a word, Logan shot out of the couch and shouted, "You're not fucking joking, are you?"

Cole, serious as ever, shook his head and replied casually, "No, I'm not."

That seemed to ignite a second round of incredulity.

"Un-fucking-believable," Logan scoffed as he crossed the office. "A ring and everything, huh? I'm assuming it's hot cheetah pants from last week, right?"

Cole couldn't help but laugh at that description. He knew Rachel would get a kick out of being described that way. *She's definitely not a cheetah, but she's a tigress, for sure.* "Yes, a ring and everything, and her name is Rachel."

Logan pushed his hands into his suit pockets and rocked back on his heels, letting out a long whistle. "Oh boy."

"What?" Cole responded to the intentional provoking before he could help himself.

"You're so screwed."

Cole thought about that before replying thoughtfully, "Yes, that is one of the benefits— nightly. Hell, sometimes hourly. How are you doing in that department, Mitchell? Who's the flavor this month, Candace or Luke? I can't seem to remember or keep up."

"Fuck you, Madison. Neither. I'm currently flying solo."

"Or playing with yourself solo, right?"

"Laugh all you like. I'm not the person who just signed up for one partner for the rest of his life. Mind you, she's an extremely sexy partner."

Cole glared at him. "Do you mind? Don't you have enough to choose from, considering at nineteen you doubled your options?"

Logan walked back toward the door, laughing. "Don't get mad at me because you just narrowed yours down to *one*."

"I'm not mad at all. I'm the luckiest fucker in the world, and for all your talk about options, you admittedly have none right now."

Logan tsked him as he turned to open the door. "Why would I pick one when there are so many yet to try?"

"Get out. I have to catch up on some work."

Logan gave him a final look of what Cole could only call mock sympathy.

"Poor Rachel. You always were the all-work-and-no-play guy."

"And you were always the pain in the ass."

Logan gave a wink behind his glasses, and as he left the office, he replied, "Truer words have never been spoken but only if they behaved and asked nicely."

THE MORNING FLEW BY, and it was around four thirty when Cole heard a knock on his office door. With the phone to his ear, he covered the mouthpiece and called out for the visitor to come in. He was so busy concentrating on the person speaking at the other end that he didn't notice Rachel slip inside the door.

"Yes, I realize that, but like I told you this morning, there's nothing we can do until we hear back from their lawyer, Dan." Cole shook his head as he listened to Daniel Pearson. Once again, Daniel was underlining the reasons it was of the utmost importance that Cole hurry along his company's hearing. The problem was that it was currently out of Cole's hands, and nothing could be done but wait. *Ahh, patience. So little people have it.*

As Cole felt a headache starting to form, he remembered someone had knocked on his door. Looking up, he felt a sense of happiness and warmth rush in to replace his previous annoyance. There, standing with her back leaning against the door, was Rachel.

His eyes locked with hers as her brightly painted pink lips mouthed the word, *Hello*. Honestly, he could have stared at those lips for hours. Lucky for him, he now had the rest of his life to look, touch, and taste them.

Raising his hand, he crooked a finger at her, signaling for her to come to him. The look that came into her eyes as she started forward had Cole shifting in his chair. Everything about her called to him, and she knew just how to use it.

Her hair was out and falling over her shoulders, just as it had been this morning when she had left his—*no, our*—bed. The leather pants she had poured herself into now seemed glued to her legs, and the outrageous pink top she had matched it with...well, it suited her perfectly.

Yes, there are definitely perks to being married, Cole thought as she came to a stop opposite his desk, *like knowing she will be coming home to me every night.*

Raising his eyes to hers, he watched her place her small black purse on the table. She pressed her palms to her thighs, like she was finding it difficult to stand still. Leaning back in his leather chair, Cole noticed her eyes drop to his lap before she quickly averted them.

Ahh, so it seems everything about me is calling to her as well, and Cole loved it.

"I can definitely try to get a hold of them today. Maybe we could set up a meeting for tomorrow?"

Daniel reiterated that he would prefer to know this evening, and

Cole continued to pay attention...well, as much attention as he could with Rachel moving her hands to the laces of her leather pants.

Cole reached out and rapped the wooden desk twice with his knuckles. Instantly, she froze, and her eyes warmed as he motioned with two fingers for her to come around the desk. Slowly, she stepped back and pivoted to make her way around to where he was sitting. Swiveling in his seat, Cole spread his legs apart and gestured for her to step forward.

"Dan, listen to me. This morning, when I spoke to Michael, he was very clear that they had not yet made a decision. I know it's hard to be patient..." Cole raised a brow at Rachel, who had stepped forward between his legs. "But sometimes there's no other option."

Rachel smirked as he reached out and tugged at the bow tied in the center of her abdomen, low on her hips. As the tie came free, he dipped a finger into the top of the leather and slid it along the front, causing the crisscross laces to part.

"Dan, we have done everything we possibly can," Cole placated as he sat up straighter in his chair.

Glancing up at Rachel, he indicated with a nod of his head what he wanted from her. She knew straightaway because with one quick move, she raised her shirt, baring her unlaced ties and her navel ring.

"Uh-huh," Cole mumbled. He was now tracing the silver piercing and moving his finger over to the bottom of the tattoo on her ribs. He was about to sit back and finish up the conversation when he felt her hand thread through his hair.

She gripped it in a small fist and tilted up his head, so he was looking at her.

As Cole listened halfheartedly to the man on the other end of the line, he found himself staring up into the blazing blue eyes of Rachel, the tigress.

~

It's really such a shame his mouth is busy, Rachel thought as she gripped his dirty-blond hair in a loose fist. Somewhere deep inside her, she thrilled at the fact that he allowed her to tip his head back.

"I will be here first thing in the morning. No, I was out of town Friday and Monday," he explained to the apparently very needy client on the other end of the line. All the while, he kept his eyes focused on hers.

Rachel licked her lips slowly and brought her left hand up to her mouth. She licked the tip of her index finger, and Cole's gaze followed it as she dipped it inside her mouth. His eyes narrowed as she sucked a little more suggestively than she probably should.

See? I can tease, too, she thought, remembering back to his little game in the library last night.

"I can call them up in the morning, and if they haven't gotten an answer by then, we can definitely try to push them a little harder."

Speaking of harder, Rachel mused, glancing down between Cole's legs, *it's definitely hard alright*. As she looked back into his eyes, she moved the finger she was sucking down to her loosened pants.

He pulled against the grip she had of his hair to follow that hand down to the top of her pants. "Dan, how about you let me give them a call, and I will give them a heads-up about tomorrow?"

Rachel had a feeling that at this stage, the words coming out of Cole's mouth were complete lies. As his left hand grasped her hip to hold her in place and his thighs came together to keep her still, he sure as hell didn't seem to be about to make another business call.

Pushing her fingers inside the leather, she flattened her palm against her stomach and slid it down farther into the snug pants. As she did, she gripped his hair tightly, and he pulled against it. He glared up at her, not with anger but with burning heat and frustration.

"Okay, yes, that sounds good. Nine tomorrow morning. I'll wait to hear from you," he replied. This time, he seemed less controlled. He sounded strained, and his voice was taut. Finally, his right hand reached over and hung up the phone.

As soon as it was in its cradle, Rachel pulled his hair much tighter, tilting his head back. As his eyes blazed up at her, she leaned down with her hand still in her pants and licked from his cheek to his ear where she bit it playfully.

"Good afternoon, husband."

"Rachel," Cole growled as he tried to move his head.

She couldn't help the lust she felt, knowing she was keeping him in place with her tight grip. "Uh-uh," she warned. "Behave."

Dragging her tongue back across the stubble on his cheek, she flirted with the corner of his mouth. He parted his lips, and Rachel couldn't help but take a bite of his bottom one. Both of his hands gripped her hips as he tugged her in close. As she bent down, he strained up in the chair to get closer to her.

"What are you doing to me?" he finally whispered against her mouth.

Rachel finally released her grip in his hair and smoothed her hand down to cup his neck. With her other hand still wedged down her pants, she let out a small squeak as Cole stood and turned with her, crowding her against the desk with her back to the door.

"Did you lock the door?" he asked as he looked down between their bodies to where her hand was now trapped between them.

"I didn't know there was a lock," she admitted, thinking he would stop.

Instead, he gave her a shrug and a casual head tilt. "You better hope no one walks in then since you have your hand in a very compromising position."

Rachel couldn't help the small giggle that escaped her mouth as Cole leaned down and nuzzled her neck.

"And what about you?"

"What about me?" he countered. This time, it was his mouth by her ear. "You're blocking me from anyone's view. I could unzip my pants and have you give me a hand job, and Jane could walk in and be none the wiser."

"That sounds like such a good plan," she agreed. She turned her head, so they were staring at each other.

"But?"

Rachel shrugged as if she were indifferent, and then she moved her fingers against her own flesh. "But my hand's currently busy."

The look that came on to Cole's face told her she was about to get it—and good.

That was when, just as he had predicted, his office door swung open, but it wasn't Jane, who would leave as soon as Cole told her to. It was Logan, a man she had met once. And she knew he would not leave until he was damn well ready to.

Cole's head snapped up as he crowded in against Rachel, who still had her hand inside the leather he wanted out of the way. *Of course, fucking Logan has to walk in*, Cole thought as he glared at the man standing in his door, sizing up the situation.

Cole could only hope that he didn't catch on, or he knew there'd be no making Logan leave. Logan was perverse that way.

"Oh, look who's here. It's Mrs. Madison."

Cole felt Rachel stiffen as she looked over her shoulder to stare at Logan.

"I see you heard," she said, trying for light but coming off tense.

"And I see you're still a hot piece of—"

"Logan," Cole growled as he rubbed himself up against Rachel, who had turned back into him. "Are you here for a reason?"

"Well, of course. I didn't come all the way down to your office in the hopes of catching you with your pants down...well, not literally anyway." He paused.

If Cole had thought that was the end of it, he was sadly mistaken.

"Good to see that I found the hot cheetah with her hands down her pants instead. It makes this much more interesting for me, I must say."

When Cole felt Rachel shake against his body, he thought he would kill Logan if he had made her cry. He looked down at her, and as she tipped up her face, he was surprised to see laugh lines crinkling her eyes as she shook with silent laughter. Every day, she had managed to surprise him, and this, right here, was no different.

"Something amusing here?" Cole asked, staring down at her.

Closing her eyes tightly, she let out an even louder giggle. Just as he was about to push the issue, he heard Logan's voice chime in.

"Oh, Cole, don't you realize that you are the only stiff prick in here?"

Cole glared up at his brother and business partner and growled through gritted teeth. "Get out."

Rachel's laughter seemed to increase as she removed her hand and started to tie the strings of her pants. "It's okay, Cole." She pulled herself together and turned around to face the man she had met last week, Logan. "You know, you remind me a lot of Cole—arrogant and persistent. The only difference is that you mask it better."

"Hear that?" Logan scoffed to Cole. "She thinks I'm better than you."

"No, she essentially said you *lie* better than me," Cole pointed out.

Rachel looked back and forth between the two of them. "How long have you two worked with each other?"

"Too long as of three minutes ago," Cole responded quickly.

"Aww, it's so heartwarming to hear how much your own brother cares."

"Wait, what? You two are brothers?" Rachel asked as she looked at first Logan and then Cole.

Cole let his head fall back as he stared at the ceiling, searching for sanity. "God give me patience," he mumbled.

"Yes, shocking, isn't it? I'm the much better looking one," Logan said with a laugh as he walked forward and placed the file in his hand on Cole's desk.

"Sometime today or tomorrow, do you think you could take a break from your husbandly duties and use the desk for something it was designed for?"

Cole brought his head back up and pinned the man across from him with what he hoped was a look that would kill or at least certainly hurt. "Who told you she was here?" he finally asked.

"Marissa," Logan admitted and held up a finger. "In her defense, I asked her to alert me of strange women going into your office."

Cole shook his head and pointed at the door. "Leave. Now."

Logan turned to Rachel and gave her his usual killer smile accompanied by an easygoing wink. "I will talk to you later, Mrs. Madison."

As he exited the office, Rachel turned to face Cole with a shocked look on her face. "That's your brother?"

"Half-brother, and now, you get to claim him, too." Cole felt his lips twitch.

"Well, speaking of brothers, mine invited us to dinner on Friday night."

Cole pulled back and looked down at her skeptically.

"A friendly one," she added with a grin.

Cole hugged her in close. "Maybe we should bring Logan, you know, as a party trick."

Her laugh bubbled up and out of her, and Cole realized nothing could have ruined that moment for him as she nestled into his chest, like she felt just as home as he was.

CHAPTER 26

Tuesday evening had passed by in a blur almost as if she were living in some kind of dream—one she got to wake up from with a smile on her face instead of being jolted from in terror. Rachel still couldn't believe that she had found her peace with the one man she thought would cause chaos.

Making her way into Exquisite on Wednesday afternoon, Rachel took a moment to reflect on all that had happened over the last—*holy shit*—week. *Okay, maybe a little more than a week. Who knew that was even possible? How did Cole manage that?*

As she wandered down the back aisle toward the kitchen, she reached the entryway, and she was surprised to see Mason in there. He was showing around—

Cole? What the hell?

Stopping where she was, Rachel looked at the two men who were, for the first time, standing side-by-side. She watched apprehensively as they talked to one another, wondering if she would be called to testify if one murdered the other.

What is Cole doing here?

"Quite a sight, isn't it?"

Rachel spun around quickly to find Lena standing behind her with a smile stretched across her mouth. Narrowing her eyes, Rachel walked toward her sister-in-law and placed her hands on her hips.

"I suppose you had nothing to do with this?"

Lena shrugged and glanced past Rachel's shoulder. "I didn't call him if that's what you mean."

Rachel tapped her foot and crossed her arms as she pursed her lips.

Lena's green eyes twinkled as she raised her chin in the men's direction. "I think it's important that their first meeting—"

"Third," Rachel interjected.

"Okay. I think it's important that their *third* meeting be done before Friday. They need to know each other if they're both going to be in your life."

"And you decided to what? Nudge them together? Are you crazy? You don't nudge men like that."

"No, I asked Mason to give him a call, that's all."

Rachel cocked her head. "And he agreed? Just like that?"

Lena gave her a look that told Rachel *exactly* how she had persuaded Mason to call up Cole, and it had nothing to do with talking.

How weird, Rachel thought, looking back at her brother and husband. They were both so completely different, *yet they are both so vital to my happiness.*

Rachel moved to stand silently beside Lena to watch the men. She had so many good memories in that kitchen, and as Cole made his way around all the stainless steel in jeans and a casual black shirt, Rachel knew this was one more she could add to the pile.

No matter what she had told herself, the sight of the two most important people in her life actually getting along made her heart happy.

"You can say it now," Rachel whispered to the woman by her side.

"Say what?" Lena asked as she nudged her arm.

Rachel faced the doctor who was as much of her sister as Mason was her brother. "That I was wrong from the very beginning. That, from the first moment at Whipped, I was hiding."

Lena shook her head as she faced her. "I know a little something about hiding. I think we do it to try and keep ourselves safe. The only problem with that is we sometimes miss what's right in front of us." Lena paused for a moment, and then she chuckled. "Or, in your case, we see it, grab it, and marry it."

Rachel smirked and reached out to poke Lena in the arm. "I'll have you know that *he* asked *me*, not the other way around."

"Who asked what?" Mason's familiar voice filtered through the air.

Spinning back around, Rachel found herself face-to-face with her brother and Cole. She was about to make something up when Cole spoke up.

"I have no doubt that Rachel was just telling your wife that *I* was the one who asked her to marry me. To be honest, she was actually a tough sell. I had to pull out all my negotiating tactics."

Rachel's mouth opened and then shut. Once again, she found she had nothing to say.

"Really?" Mason asked as he turned to look at Cole. "You asked her? I have to say that I honestly thought it was the other way around."

"I told you what they would all think," Rachel finally managed to say.

Cole pushed his hands into his tight jeans, and with a wink, he acknowledged, "Yes, I seem to remember you saying something of the sort."

Rachel felt an unfamiliar blush rise up her neck and heat her cheeks at the memory of *that* particular discussion.

Beside her, Lena cleared her throat. "So, Cole, has Rachel cooked for you yet? On our first...well, really, our second date, Mason made me dinner and a peach pie."

Rachel let out a laugh and almost snorted as Mason glared at her.

"It's wrong on so many levels that you know about that," he informed her.

Lena barely stifled her own laugh as she batted her lashes innocently at her husband. "Girls talk."

"You three are not girls. You're women, and you don't find me and Josh standing around talking about—"

"Sex deals, secrets, and Josh's preference for blondes? Yes, I'm sure you and Josh *never* talk about that," Lena added, tongue-in-cheek.

"Actually, Joshua was very chatty when he first met Shelly."

Rachel's eyes widened as she grinned mischievously at Cole's statement. "Ooh, you have to tell us," she practically begged, bouncing on her toes.

"No, that wouldn't be right, especially since the poor man was so distracted I took all his money in a game of poker."

Rachel slapped her leg and hooted. "I love it. He's so getting it when I see him again. He was walking around in a daze the minute Man-Eater showed up."

"Man-Eater?" Cole inquired.

"Yeah, the perfect blonde with the annoying mouth. That would be Shelly Monroe."

"Also known as Man-Eater?" Cole caught on.

"Yep, the one and the same." Rachel beamed, delighted with this new piece of information. "Let's just say, she doesn't lack in confidence, and leave it at that."

Mason shook his head and began muttering something about the women in his life. That was when Lena took the opportunity to defend her absent friend and colleague.

"Shelly's great. She's loud and outrageous, and she tells it exactly like it is. Doesn't she, Mason?"

Cole looked at Mason, who was frowning, and then back to Rachel. "I'm missing something here, right?"

"Oh, Mason likes to forget, but these two lovebirds hated each other when they first met," Rachel pointed out.

Cole raised a brow. "Now, that sounds familiar."

Rachel's frown matched her brother's as she looked into amused hazel eyes. "I didn't hate you."

"Well, you certainly didn't like me. If I recall, you told me something like no, thank you. you aren't my type."

Mason finally let out a chuckle as he told Cole, "Don't feel too bad. The first time I met Lena, she asked me if I could read."

Rachel snorted, very unladylike at that. "Remember the first date you two had? Lena turned up in this horrible pantsuit..."

"Hey. It wasn't horrible. I still have that suit."

Rachel turned and pointedly ran her eyes down Lena's red pencil skirt and black blouse. "Yes, but you no longer wear it or dress like a nun."

"And what do you dress like? A wannabe rock star?" Lena fired back.

Rachel looked at her tight blue jeans, which had a rip across her right thigh and were frayed around the bottom where her black boots peeked out. "I like my jeans."

"So do I."

Cole's smooth voice reached across the space and pretty much stroked all her naughty places. As her eyes met his, Rachel found herself chewing on her bottom lip.

It wasn't until Mason cleared his throat that she blinked and focused on him.

"I told Cole he could watch you work your magic tonight. It's something everyone should experience at least once. Your desserts are out of this world."

As Mason's praise sank in, Rachel stepped forward and pressed a kiss to his cheek. She whispered, "Thank you for this."

He returned the move by quickly smacking his lips against her cheek. "You're welcome. I love you." When he pulled away, he stepped around her toward his wife.

Rachel looked at Cole, who was watching her with a mixture of love and affection.

Holding out her hand to him, she asked, "Ready to heat up the kitchen?"

With the look he gave her, she knew he was remembering the way they had heated up his only last week.

He took a step toward her and slid his palm over hers. "With you? Always."

~

COLE FOLLOWED Rachel through the kitchen and into her small office.

"So, have you ever spent an evening behind the scenes of a restaurant?" she asked, dropping her bag on the floor.

He watched as she removed her coat and threw it over her desk. She took down the bright purple chef's jacket hanging on a peg secured to the back of the door.

"Can't say that I have."

She gave him a quick smile and reached for a long black apron that had been hanging behind the jacket. Turning to him, she extended her arm. "Here, this is for you."

"An apron?"

"You don't have to look so appalled. It's not a skirt, you know."

She chuckled as he took the black material from her.

"I'm more appalled at the thought of what you want me to do once the apron is in place."

Cole wrapped the ties around his waist and found that they were long enough to come back around, so he secured it just under the button of his jeans. Once he tied it off, he looked up to see Rachel staring at him.

"Did I not do it right?"

She stepped toward him in her button-up jacket and reached out to the sides of his hips. Without a word, she rolled the top of the apron down over the ties and then smoothed her hands around to grip his denim-clad ass, pulling him in close.

Cole felt his entire body tense and his cock harden at the ease she obviously now felt in touching him.

She winked up at him. "As usual, you did it perfectly. I was just thinking that this is probably the first time I will ever be in danger of sexually harassing someone in the workplace."

"As opposed to sexually harassing them elsewhere?" Cole questioned, raising his palms to her shoulders.

Rachel slid her hands into his back pockets and continued squeezing his ass.

"Are you enjoying yourself?" he asked.

"I am actually."

Cole reached behind and removed her palms from his ass. Holding her hands in his, he informed her, "Your brother told me two things tonight."

"And what were they?"

"That I was welcome in his restaurant—"

"*Our* restaurant," she corrected.

"As long as I stayed out of the way and kept my hands off the pastry chef while she worked."

"Well, I hope you told him to get lost. You're my husband, and you can touch me whenever you like."

"And he's your brother, and he's just starting to warm up to me. I'm going to respect that," Cole told her, taking a step back.

The look of absolute annoyance on her face made her entirely too appealing for him to be within touching range.

"So, what?" she asked incredulously. "You're going to stand four feet away from me all night? I *knew* he was being way too nice. Jerk."

With a determined look on her face, she started to move toward him, and Cole took another step back. She stopped and threw her hands up in the air. Shaking her head, she made a move to pass him.

"This is ridiculous. I'm going to go and tell Mason he can shove—"

With catlike reflexes, Cole reached out and grabbed her arm, halting her on her way out the door. As she spun back on her toes, she almost slammed into him with the force of her momentum.

"Whoa. Slow down."

"You know, I'm surprised you're so relaxed about this."

Leaning down so they were on eye level, Cole informed her, "I'm not relaxed. Your damn hands gave me a hard-on, and now, I'm standing here, trying to calm it the hell down. But you, all feisty and pissed off, is not helping the issue."

"Then, why won't you let me go and—"

"Think of this as foreplay," he whispered, letting his warm breath float across her lips. "Four hours of close proximity without touch." Pressing his mouth to hers, he ended with, "Followed by seven hours of the hands-on approach."

He felt her lips part beneath his, inviting him deeper, but Cole was determined not to piss off Mason. No matter what Rachel said, her relationship with her brother was vital. That much was obvious, and there was no way he would do anything to jeopardize it.

Raising his head, Cole released her arm and gestured to the open door. "Lead the way."

"And you'll follow? Yeah, right. Since when do you follow anyone's orders?"

Cole walked with her to the door. "Since around forty minutes ago."

"And how does that feel?"

"I fucking hate it," Cole admitted honestly.

"You have such a filthy mouth," she pointed out, stopping in the doorway to the busy kitchen.

Cole made sure to press his entire front to her back while keeping his hands to himself as he acknowledged, "You're right. Maybe you can clean it for me with your tongue later."

When she looked back at him, she seemed to have regained her sense of humor because she dropped her eyes to his mouth and seductively licked her lower lip.

"Maybe. Ask me in four hours," she sassed and turned, walking out into her kitchen, leaving Cole to follow for the second time that night.

~

THREE AND A HALF hours into the dinner service, Rachel found herself once again being surprised by Cole. All evening, he had stood beside her, keeping his hands to himself, and he had followed directions, right down to, *Throw this in the trash, would you?*

She never would have dreamed of him being a part of this, even for one night. As he listened, comprehended, and then executed every little thing she told him, Rachel was not only buzzing from having him there, she was also extremely impressed.

The other kitchen staff had gone about their business in their usual way. Ryan had barked out the orders while the other chefs were cutting, cooking, and plating the meals. Wendy would come to the service window to let them know if they were on schedule or running behind, and the waitstaff all delivered the food to their hungry clientele in a timely fashion.

Yes, Rachel thought, *tonight ran exactly the way Exquisite should, and I'm finally enjoying it in a way I haven't for months.*

Looking over to where Cole was standing by the prep table, Rachel made her way to him with a special treat in mind. He had played by the rules all night and hadn't touched her once. Admittedly, it didn't surprise her, given his unwavering patience and the pride he took over his self-control. Still, as far as she was concerned, that kind of annoying dedication to his cause should not go without reward.

Wiping her hands on the apron tied around her waist, she stopped beside him, bumping her hip to his. "How's it going chef?"

He looked over to her and placed the towel in his hands down on the tabletop. "Interesting."

"Interesting good? Or interesting bad?" she pressed as she turned to rest her backside against the stainless steel.

"You're fascinating to watch. Actually, the entire process back here is fascinating. It's so loud and chaotic, but at the same time, it seems to run like a well-oiled machine."

Rachel found herself liking that description because it was exactly how she felt about the kitchen. "That seems about right. I love working in the midst of chaos."

His eyes took in her purple jacket and then moved up to the colorful hair she had pulled up and under her black cap. "Now that, I truly believe."

"Well, we're winding down for the night. The last orders have gone out, and I wanted to teach you something. Up for a lesson?"

His eyes narrowed on her. "What kind of lesson? Is it one I'll regret later?"

Rachel shook her head. "Nope, it's more a lesson of survival—for you anyway."

She loved the confusion that came over his face because it had never happened before. She spun around and reached for a stainless steel pot from one of the shelves under the table.

Pulling it out, she walked to the back stove and placed it on one of the front gas burners. She noticed Cole had followed her over to the stove, and he seemed to be waiting patiently. That was, until he opened his mouth.

"A lesson in survival? I hardly think I will have a gas-burning stove if I am stuck somewhere needing to survive."

Rachel rolled her eyes at his logic and sighed. "Oh, don't be so damn literal," she stated as she moved around him to the walk-in pantry.

She picked up all the ingredients she needed, and when she came back, she placed them beside the stove in front of him. She could see he was about to ask her another question when she asked, "Do you like apples?"

Cole paused halfway through a word that was about to come out of his mouth, and instead, he laughed. "Yes, why?"

"You'll see," she said in a singsong voice. She moved away from him again, but this time, she went into the fridge and returned with two Granny Smith apples. Placing them down near all the other items,

Rachel winked up at him. "Okay, we need a cup and a half of sugar. Over there." With her chin, she indicated to the large silver cylinder.

Cole picked up the cup she'd placed in front of him, and he measured the cup and a half she needed to perfection. She took the cup and dropped the contents into the pot. She turned back to him and pointed to the corn syrup. "I need a tablespoon of that."

Silently, he poured it out, and she stood aside to let him put it into the pot.

"Okay, now, cut the lemon in half and squeeze it in."

With a small paring knife, Cole did as she had asked and moved closer to her to squeeze the lemon juice into the pot. After that, she added in the little bit of water she needed and turned on the heat.

"What are we making?" he asked as he moved back out of her way.

Rachel began swirling the ingredients together with a flick of her wrist. "I told you, I'm teaching you how to survive...in the horrifying event that you don't have any of your little caramel squares around."

With her eyes on the mixture that was starting to bubble up, she felt him step closer.

"That's going to turn into caramel?" he asked, his voice full of excitement but tinged with skepticism.

Turning her head, Rachel grinned at him. She was pleased he was so excited. "Yep, all it needs now is cream."

Cole's eyes moved from the amber-colored concoction back to hers.

"Cream?"

He might as well have said, *Sex?* Because all Rachel wanted to scream was, *Yes, please. Now.* Instead, she nodded and gathered her brain cells, at least what little she had left.

"Yes, I need the cream. It's right over there."

He turned away to pick up the container, and then he handed it to her. As she took it from him, their fingers brushed, and she was close to saying, *Forget the damn caramel.* The only things that stopped her were the other staff members and the knowledge that when they did get home, she could enjoy him as loudly as she wanted to with no one listening.

"Step back," she instructed. "When I add it, it's going to bubble up and spit." Turning off the heat, Rachel added in the cream, and just as she had said, the mixture bubbled up to the top of the pot. Reaching over to the sticks of butter, she picked them up and put them in, all the while whisking the sweet syrup.

"Is it wrong that this is totally turning me on?" Cole's voice hummed through the air.

Rachel removed the pot from the burner and continued stirring as she waggled her brows at him with mischief in her eyes. "Not at all. Makes perfect sense, considering the last time you had caramel sauce was—"

"When I spread it all over your naked breasts?"

"Yes." Rachel sighed as she picked up the first apple.

"Are we nearly done here? I'm almost certain that the four hours are up."

Raising her eyes to the clock on the wall, Rachel regretfully informed him, "Actually, you still have another five minutes." She slipped her hand into her pocket and pulled out two little sticks.

"Caramel apples?" Cole questioned.

She jabbed the sticks into the top of the Granny Smiths. "Yes, do you like caramel apples?"

"Rachel, you could put caramel on broccoli, and I would eat it. I will say that I haven't had a caramel apple since I was a little boy. My mother used to make them."

As Rachel dipped the first apple into the sauce, she gave him a warm smile. She was happy to be the one to give him back such an obviously fond memory.

"My dad used to make them with me. He loved to cook."

She pulled the first apple free and placed it on a plate, and then when she reached for the second, she felt Cole's palm cup the back of her neck.

Looking up at him, she felt their connection deeper than ever before. It was a connection that had been forged almost overnight, and it was unlike any she could have hoped for.

"Thank you," he told her as he squeezed her neck gently.

"For?"

"Being exactly who you are. For being impulsive, strong, and mine. "

As he dropped his hand, Rachel took a deep breath and dipped the second apple into the mix. When she pulled it free, she placed it on the plate next to the other one. As Cole picked up the first one, she asked, "Can you please take me home now? The five minutes are up, and the foreplay is over."

She thought he'd never looked sexier as he lifted the apple to his lips. Licking the warm dripping caramel, Cole's eyes met hers right before his white teeth sank through the sweet layer to the crisp tart apple beneath, effectively turning her little game of seduction around on her.

Rachel watched him chew slowly on that piece of apple. Her insides flipped, and just breathing had her almost jumping out of her skin. Her panties brushed the piercing, which was currently sitting above her throbbing clit.

He swallowed, and in a voice she wanted by her ear, above her mouth, and sliding inside her, he told her, "I thought you'd never ask."

CHAPTER 27

I hate moving.

The following afternoon, Rachel stared at the boxes surrounding her in her small apartment. Luckily for her, Sarah had wanted some extra hours at Exquisite, and when Rachel had given them to her, Mason hadn't been around to say no.

She wanted to take the night off. She wanted to sit in her apartment by herself and really think over everything that had and was about to happen. The only problem was that every time she thought about what had happened, she thought of Cole, and that led her to thinking about last night and how his mouth had—

"Open up. We know you're in there."

Rachel's head snapped up, and her eyes latched on to her front door where the shouting and pounding were coming from.

"Don't try and act like you're not."

Oh jeez, save me now. Shelly Monroe was standing outside her door, making a ridiculous amount of noise.

Rachel quickly stood, stepped over the box holding all her DVDs, and jogged to the door.

Just as her palm hit the handle, she heard through the door, "Shelly, keep it down."

Thank. You. Lena.

With a twist of her hand, Rachel opened the door to find Shelly and Lena standing in front of her. Shelly was dressed in tight fashionable blue jeans and a turquoise sweater that molded to every bodacious curve she had. Her blonde hair was pulled up into a high ponytail, and her face was perfectly made up to make her look like some kind of model. *Playboy or runway*, Rachel couldn't quite decide. Lena, on the other hand, looked relaxed and casual but still gorgeous in jeans and a green cowl-neck sweater that brought out her eyes. She'd left all her brown curls out and curling over her shoulders.

"Is there a reason you're making so much damn noise outside my door?"

Lena shrugged and almost looked apologetic. Shelly held up two bottles of red wine and announced, "We are here to gossip and drink."

As she peered past her shoulder, Rachel almost groaned as Shelly's pink lips widened into a grin. "And apparently pack."

Lena shook her head as Shelly pushed in past Rachel.

"I tried to prevent the invasion," Lena told her. She stepped forward and hugged Rachel. "But you know Shelly."

Laughing, Rachel shut the door and turned around to follow Lena back into her small living room. Shelly had removed her shoes, and with her legs tucked under her, she had settled onto the couch in the corner. Shelly had placed the two bottles of wine over on the kitchen counter, and as Rachel noticed them, she wondered if it was bad to start drinking at five in the afternoon.

Lena took a seat on the loveseat against the wall and patted the spot beside her. Moving over to her sister-in-law, Rachel curled up in the corner of the couch and pinned Shelly with an undaunted look.

"Oh, just get it over with already," Rachel whined.

"You married him," Shelly shouted as though she could no longer contain herself. Then, she began to laugh like a lunatic. "I mean, I knew you'd cave and sleep with him. *Hello*? The guy is so goddamn sexy. But damn." Shelly shook her head as if she were truly flabbergasted. "Getting hitched. Holy. Shit."

Rachel arched her brow at the blonde with the mouth. It always surprised her that they were friends with the way they bickered and sniped at one another. Then again, that was what family did. *Right?*

"Well, at least I go after what I want, unlike some who take *forever* to decide."

That shut Shelly up quick. "Touché," she muttered.

"Would you two quit?" Lena asked as she glared over at Shelly.

"Okay, okay. I just can't believe it. And Mason and Josh? Ha. Talk about being shocked stupid. I still don't think Josh believes it."

Rachel couldn't help but laugh at that. She had definitely shocked the boys. That much was true. Josh, even more so, she figured, considering he knew Cole better than anyone else. Josh had understood how out of character this was for Cole.

"Mason is coming around," Lena admitted and winked in Rachel's direction. "Sometimes, you just know. Right, Rach?"

Rachel nodded in agreement. "As crazy as it seems, it definitely feels right."

"I'm sure it *feels* very right," Shelly teased.

"Do you ever think about anything other than sex?" Rachel asked as she looked pointedly at Shelly.

"Well, I try, but honestly, with all the testosterone we have around us, it's hard."

Lena snorted. "All the testosterone? There are approximately two men in our lives."

"Well, three now," Shelly interjected, looking at Rachel. "And let's face it. I wasn't the only one in the club that night, thinking that her guy was like testosterone on steroids. I swear we all just stood in awe."

When Rachel thought back to that night, she did remember the way Lena and Shelly had stood mute while her and Cole had sparred over a shot of tequila.

Lena tapped Rachel's foot as she smiled. "Well, in our defense, we were rather—"

"Drunk?" Shelly supplied.

Lena laughed as Rachel stood and made her way to the kitchen.

Pulling out a bottle opener, Rachel uncorked the first bottle of red and poured three glasses. For the rest of this conversation, she had a feeling that she would need liquor. Making her way back to the other women, she passed Lena a glass and then turned to Shelly. When she held it out to her, Shelly shook her head and grinned widely.

"I'm sorry, but for the next nine months, you two will have to drink all the red wine and cosmos for me."

The room fell silent, and Rachel found herself staring down at the Man-Eater, who had suddenly turned into a gooey ball of mush.

"You're pregnant?" Lena yelled as she bounced up from the chair and came to stand beside Rachel.

Shelly beamed up at them, nodding like a fool. "Yep. We found out last week."

"What?" Lena demanded. "Why didn't you say anything?"

Shelly looked at Rachel and chuckled. "Well, there were other things going on. Josh and I were going to tell you all on Monday, but—"

"Oh shit, Shelly. I feel terrible," Rachel muttered.

As Shelly stood, Lena moved forward and pulled her best friend into a tight hug. "I'm so very happy for you and Josh. I know you both want children so much."

Shelly hugged Lena back, thanking her, before she turned to look at Rachel.

"Don't feel bad. When we turned up on Monday night and Josh found out about you and Cole, I don't think he really wanted to bring this up right then. Not to mention, Mason was freaking the hell out. So, we just decided it was best to tell you guys on our own. Josh took Mase out for beers," she added with a wink.

Rachel stepped forward and hugged Shelly tightly. "I still hate that I ruined your moment. You and Josh mean so much to me."

"Oh, stop it. You didn't ruin it. You gave us one of the most interesting nights of our lives. Not to mention, we were all blown away. *You* mean a lot to all of us, Rachel, and you caught us all off-guard. No matter how much fun I poke at it, I'm happy if you're happy. Are you sure this is what you want?"

Rachel moved back and looked at Lena and Shelly before nodding and reassuring them both, "I know it's crazy, but I don't think normal applies to me. I love him. He's unlike anyone I've ever met, and honestly, he has shocked the hell out of me."

Shelly leaned down and lifted the glass of wine, handing it back to Rachel. "Well then, how about you two celebrate my amazing news? A baby out of wedlock. I love following the rules. My mother will probably die. Raise your glasses and congratulate all of us on our good taste in men. Damn. How did we get so lucky?"

Lena and Rachel laughed as they clinked their glasses.

"Because we are completely awesome of course," Rachel decided as she took a sip of her wine and saluted them all.

~

Two hours later, Lena and Rachel were on their second bottle of wine, and Shelly was pumping for information on Josh.

"So, come on, tell me," she coaxed as Rachel continued shaking her head. "I bet he was such a cute teenager, all of that floppy brown hair and big brown eyes."

Lena giggled as she brought the glass to her lips. "I bet they both were, Mason and Josh. How weird that you knew them back then."

"Well, one is my brother," Rachel reminded dryly. She didn't think it was weird at all. It was just part of her life, her history.

"Were they good boys? I bet they were always in trouble." Lena asked with a grin.

Rachel chuckled at that. "Oh, as teens, they were always in trouble. God, Mom and Dad were forever looking for creative ways to punish Mase. They were also good guys though."

Closing her eyes, Rachel leaned back in her chair. "Josh's family was just like ours, but you know that." Rachel opened one eye to look at a relaxed Shelly. "He has his brother and two great parents, and he was my brother's best friend. He also happened to be the boy I—"

"Wanted to maaarrryyy," Shelly sung like an idiot.

Rachel found herself giggling at that. "Yes, I guess I did. It's a good thing you came along and weaved your sex spell. It rendered him deaf, dumb, and blind to all those around you."

"Or you would have eloped with him instead?" Shelly quipped.

"Eww, no, you moron. Josh is like a brother to me now. After high school, he went to college with Mason, and my attention was diverted to a different type of man. A man I thought was good for me, but he wasn't."

Lena sat up and reached out to Rachel, squeezing her knee. As Rachel raised her eyes to her sister-in-law, she immediately knew that Lena knew about Ben. In the silent communication, Rachel felt the solid support from the newest member of her family.

"So, that's why you were such a pain in the ass when Josh and I—"

"I was protective, not a pain in the ass."

"Oh, come on, you were a bit of a bitch."

Rachel's eyes widened, and she looked to Lena for support.

Lena shrugged. "You kind of were, but it all makes sense now."

Rachel slumped back in her couch and blew out a long breath of air. "Well, it's just that I know what a good guy Josh is. I didn't want you to jerk him around, you know?"

Shelly's smile changed from smart-ass to sappy in the space of a minute. "I know exactly what you mean. Josh is a total sweetheart. Strong, caring, and god, he's so good in bed." She paused before asking, "Is that weird for you to hear?"

Rachel's laugh exploded into the room as she shook her head, "Ahh, no. I'd be more disappointed if you said he was terrible."

"Speaking of good in—" Lena started.

"Um, excuse me, you don't get to contribute. I do *not* want to hear about my brother in bed."

"But you just said Josh was like a brother," Lena protested with a wink to Shelly. The wine was finally catching up to her.

"Yeah, but he's *not* my brother. That's the difference. Plus, I've kissed him. Guess I was always curious if he was a rock star in bed."

Shelly licked her lips and sighed. "In bed, in his truck...oh, oh, and in the parking lot."

Rachel's eyes widened as she stared at the blonde doctor.

"What about Cole?" Shelly asked with a wink. "We're not related to him."

"What about him?"

"Bet *that* guy's a rock star." Lena giggled.

Rachel turned her eyes to her sister-in-law, feeling a smug smile pull at her lips. "Well, he has a real sweet tooth when it comes to caramel sauce."

The satisfaction Rachel got from the way their mouths dropped open was probably unhealthy in some way, but she relished the feeling just the same. She was about to mention the library and the ladder when there was a loud knock on the door.

Looking around the room, Rachel asked, "Expecting anyone, ladies?"

As they shook their heads, the knock came again.

Getting up and placing her glass on the table, Rachel jumped over Lena's legs, stumbling slightly and giggling as she righted herself. "Whoops."

As the girls' laughter filled the room behind her, she straightened her white shirt hanging off her shoulder, '80s style, and wiped her hands on her black stretchy leggings. Tipping her head back, she shook her hair out behind her, and then she reached out and opened the front door.

ALL DAY, Cole had been thinking about getting back to Rachel. It was like she had infected his brain, and now, she was all he could think about. Originally, they had discussed that she would spend the afternoon and evening at her apartment, packing up as much as she could, and he would come and help her with the rest on the weekend. They had agreed to meet tomorrow for lunch, but as far as Cole was concerned, tomorrow was too damn far away. He wanted her now.

So, there he was. He hadn't even bothered stopping at home to change. Instead, he had come straight from the office.

As the door opened and she came into view, he pounced. Stepping forward through the door, he reached out and slid his hands across her cheeks and into her hair as he backed her up into the small apartment hall.

Kicking the door shut, he kept his eyes on hers. As they widened, she went to open her mouth, but before a sound could slip free, Cole lowered his head and sealed her mouth shut with his own. Sliding his tongue deep between her lips, he turned and walked them back until she hit the wall. Dipping his knees, he pushed his body flush with hers until he was rubbing his cock up against that delicious warm spot between her thighs.

Running one hand down her neck, Cole moved the flimsy material of her shirt off her shoulder, continued sliding his hand down her arm, and then he wrapped his hand around her to cup her tight ass through those sexy black tights.

With his other hand in her hair, he gripped it tightly and tilted up her head to him as he raised his head from her lips to stare down into eyes that had clouded over with lust.

Fuck yes. Now, if I could just get these pants down, he thought as he dragged his palm over her ass, flirting with the elastic band around her waist.

Lowering his head, he placed his lips against her shoulder and bit gently before he swiped his tongue over it, and Rachel let out a loud moan.

"Well, as hot as this is, I think it's only fair to let you know that other people are in the house."

Cole's head came up at the teasing flirty tone, and he froze where he was. He had a hand in Rachel's hair, and his fingers inside the elastic at the back of her pants. He could feel Rachel's heartbeat thrumming against his chest as he looked down at his wife.

"Thanks for the heads-up," he mumbled as her eyes focused on him.

"I tried," she offered with a giggle.

"Not very hard."

Rachel arched out her hips and rubbed herself against him. "Oh, it's *very* hard."

Cole could now taste the wine on his own tongue from their thorough kiss. "And how much have you had to drink?"

"Enough to not care that they're standing here, watching you rub all over me."

He felt his lips twitch as he looked over his shoulder, still not moving away from Rachel. Right at this moment, she was the only thing hiding his massive hard-on.

"So nice to see you ladies again," he greeted Shelly and Lena, who were both now standing at the end of the small hallway.

The blonde had a grin across her face and looked like she was barely holding back laughter, and Lena had her brows raised and was biting her bottom lip.

"I'm sorry. I didn't realize Rachel was having company this evening."

The woman Cole knew as Joshua's fiancée, Shelly, winked at him and Rachel. "I'm sure she's wishing right now that she didn't have company either."

"Shut up, Shelly," Lena mumbled as she whacked her friend on the arm.

"What? After seeing *that*, don't tell me you aren't going to go home and jump Mason. I'm definitely going to find Josh. That was hot."

"Oh god." Rachel finally made a sound from where she was still pinned to the wall. It wasn't *oh god* as in she was feeling ultimate pleasure. It was more, *Oh god, make them stop*.

Cole found himself starting to laugh. When he felt that his body was somewhat back under control, he moved away from Rachel and asked the women, "So, what have you three been up to?"

"Not as much as you," Shelly pointed out, dropping her eyes to his pants with an inappropriate laugh.

Rachel finally snapped to. Stepping up next to him, she assured him, "Ignore her. We all do." Slipping her hand into his, she looked up and asked, "I thought we were going to just meet up tomorrow for lunch?"

"Seems like someone was impatient. It's quite sweet really," Shelly interjected.

"Does she ever shut up?" Cole asked good-naturedly. He looked first to Lena, who was shaking her head, and then to Rachel.

"No, this is pretty much it. Isn't it strange that someone as nice as Josh end—"

"Hey," Shelly complained. "I'll have you know that Josh totally understands and loves everything about me."

Rachel leaned into Cole. "Yeah, I'm sure he does. Maybe that's why he's always occupying your mouth when he's around. To shut you up."

Lena giggled at that, and Shelly glared at her. "What? It was funny."

Shelly moved back into the living room and picked up her purse and Lena's before she strutted back to the hallway and handed the purse to her friend. "Well, one thing I do know is we should get going."

Looking at the three of them, Cole grimaced. "I'm sorry. I didn't mean to interrupt."

Shelly laughed and Lena pushed her non to gently out of the door as she tried to assure him, "You didn't don't worry. Have a good night."

Shelly called back over her shoulder, "A really good night."

As the door slammed shut behind them, Cole turned to look down at Rachel.

She shrugged. "I didn't know you were coming."

Taking her hand in his, Cole tugged her toward the bedroom and snagged the open bottle of wine. Over his shoulder, he told her, "I'm not, *yet*."

And as she followed him with a wine-induced giggle, Cole shut the bedroom door, ready to have a nice long drink.

CHAPTER 28

As the bedroom door clicked shut, Rachel turned to see Cole minus his jacket. He was leaning up against the door, holding the opened bottle of wine down by his side.

Rachel let her eyes run over him, and as she brought them back up his suit pants to the tailored white shirt and bright red tie, she couldn't help the thrill that she got from knowing he was hers.

Keeping her eyes on his, she reached down and lifted her shirt up and over her head, flinging it off to the side. As she did so, Cole lifted his left hand and loosened his tie.

Without a word, Rachel pushed her fingers into the top of her leggings and stripped them down her legs. When they hit the floor, she looped them on her toe, and with a flirty wink, she kicked them toward him.

No words were needed as Cole removed the tie over his head and threw it on the floor. He then began to undo the buttons of his shirt from top to bottom as his eyes zeroed in on her lacy, white strapless bra and matching miniscule thong. When he reached the bottom of his shirt where it was tucked into his pants, he pulled the material free.

Rachel's entire body felt like it was about to overheat as he pushed away from the door and sauntered toward her with his shirt hanging open and the bottle of wine tapping against his thigh. When he got to her, she tipped back her head and raised her hands to touch. That was when he shook his head.

"No hands," he whispered as he leaned down to touch his mouth to hers.

"No hands?" Rachel asked, blinking up at him. "But I want to touch you."

He took a step back and raised the bottle to his lips. Keeping his eyes on hers, he took a swig of the red, and then he lowered the bottle back to his side. He leaned down to her, taking her mouth with his. As she parted her lips, she tasted the wine as it entered her mouth right before his tongue did. Moaning, she moved up onto her tiptoes to get closer, and she felt some of the liquid escape and slide down her chin and neck.

"Tonight, let's try something a little...different."

THE MOMENT the words left his mouth, Rachel's eyes glazed over, and he knew he had her.

No hands, it is.

Stepping back from her, Cole looked to the bed. She didn't need any other words. Immediately, she got up onto her bare mattress, turned to face him, and waited on her knees.

Lifting his hand, he crooked his finger, and she made her way to the edge. When she reached him, she moved her arms behind her, like she was going to remove her bra.

"No, leave it. I like your lace. It turns me on." He reached down to the button of his pants. "I must be perverted because the white makes you look so innocent."

Her eyes followed his hands as he unzipped.

Holding out the bottle to her, he asked, "Will you hang on to this for a moment?"

She held the bottle and took another sip as she kept her eyes on his hands.

Quickly, Cole removed his clothes until he was standing before her naked and fully erect. She lowered the bottle from her mouth and licked her shiny wet lips.

Holding out his hand, he was pleased when she passed the bottle back to him.

Taking it from her, Cole lowered his voice and invited, "Come here."

~

RACHEL KEPT FOCUSED on Cole as she scooted forward on the mattress. When she was close enough that she could feel the heat emanating from his body, she let her eyes wander. First, her eyes took in the tattoo on his pec, and then the piercings through his hard nipples, and last, she let her eyes fall to the engorged cock that was currently nudging her leg.

"Hands behind your back, Rachel."

Oh god. His voice was so fucking sexy that she felt it all the way inside her.

Moving her hands of her own free will, she placed them behind her back and waited for her next instruction.

"Lift your chin, and close your eyes."

As Rachel did as she was told, she was intensely aware of his body as he moved even closer to the bed. Swallowing slowly, she waited in the silence of the room, and the thrill she got from the wait was such an enormous turn-on that she could feel her core clench with anticipation.

"Would you agree that you no longer need this mattress?"

Rachel tried to comprehend what he was asking. She tried to keep up, but all her focus was centered on the throbbing between her thighs as she waited with her hands behind her and her head tilted back.

Completely open, completely vulnerable.

Again, he asked, "Do you agree that you no longer need this mattress since you will now be sleeping in my bed? Or should I say, *our* bed?"

A shiver raced up her spine at the repeated words, and Rachel parted her lips to tell him, "Yes."

"I can't tell you how glad I am to hear that." His voice was louder in her ear this time.

When cool liquid hit her collarbone, Rachel almost opened her eyes and reached out to grab him, but at the last second, she caught herself as the red wine slid between her breasts, over her pure white lingerie, into her navel, and dipped down over her pristine white panties. With her eyes shut, she didn't know what he was thinking as he looked at her, but she didn't have long to try and work it out.

The first thing she felt was the tip of his tongue as he licked along her collarbone to the dip at the base of her throat. She could feel the tickle of his hair under her chin. As he moved his head lower, his tongue tracing the path of wine down between her breasts, Rachel found it almost impossible not to touch him.

"Rachel?" Her name floated through the air. "Rachel?"

Opening her eyes, she looked down to where he was nibbling the top curve of her right breast that was still covered by the wine-stained bra.

"Yes?"

Holding the bottle to her, he asked, "Can you please hold this?"

Rachel reached out a trembling hand and took the bottle from him as he moved his hands behind her and unsnapped her bra. Throwing it on the bed, he stepped back to look at what he had just revealed.

"You look so fucking corrupted right now. Your hair is all wild and crazy. It looks like you've had my hands in it while I've been inside you for hours. Your breasts are a work of fucking art, but the best part, my dear wife," he told her as he licked his top lip, "is you holding a bottle of wine as you kneel there with your bare breasts in your innocent little panties." Stepping back to the bed, Cole asked, "Not so innocent though, are you, Rachel?"

"No," she breathed out on a needy sigh as he reached out for the bottle.

"Lie down in the middle of the bed. Put your hands up over your head, touching the headboard."

Rachel's heartbeat sped up as she moved to the center of the mattress. Lying down, she raised her hands above her head and squirmed a little at the moisture that had soaked through her panties to mix with the wetness from the wine between her thighs.

~

COLE'S COCK was hurting as he climbed up onto the bed. It currently hated him from denying it access in between Rachel's sweet, tight thighs. But tonight, he wanted to play, and for quite some time, he had been dying to do what he was about to.

With her arms stretched out above her head, her breasts were pushed up together, plumping them out to him like an offering. It was one he was about to take. Moving over on his knees to her side, he looked down at her as he straddled her waist.

"There's one rule tonight. No touching. Hands stay on the headboard. Got it?"

She nodded as her teeth clamped down on her bottom lip.

Raising the bottle, Cole tipped wine onto her stomach, and leaning down, he kept his eyes on hers as he licked it off. Moving to the piercing in her navel, he nibbled around and dipped his tongue into the small indentation before sitting back up.

Shifting up her body, Cole rose up on his knees right above her breasts and raised the bottle, spilling the wine down over his own body. As it spilled over his chest and stomach, it gathered and slid off his cock. He glanced down to see Rachel's eyes riveted to him, and her mouth was slightly parted as her breasts rose and fell with each deep breath she took.

"Definitely not innocent." He chuckled as he raised his arm and poured the wine over himself again, getting his cock nice and wet as it hovered above her.

As wine dripped down between her breasts, and into her cleavage she gasped as it trickled down to her neck before sliding behind her.

Raising the bottle to his mouth, Cole drank the final remnants of wine and let the bottle fall onto the bed as he moved over her to grip the headboard she was hanging on to. She looked up at him with lust-heavy eyes as he let a wicked smile curl his lips. Lowering himself down until his stiff cock was nestled between the two most beautiful breasts he had ever seen, Cole rocked his hips, thrusting his shaft up between them. A low moan left her mouth as her eyes watched his pierced cock pushing forward between her breasts.

The wine made her skin slick and allowed him to move back and forth with ease as he started to flex his hips. He hadn't been exactly sure how Rachel would react to this, so when her mouth opened on every thrust forward of his hips, he felt desire shoot through him all the way to his balls. His woman was so fucking turned on that he could feel her pushing her hips up into nothing as he continued working himself between her breasts.

"You're breasts are so fucking sexy. Round and soft, they feel amazing around my cock."

As the last word left his mouth, her eyes shut, and he felt her buck up hard behind him.

Fucking hell, did she just come with no other stimulation than me talking?

White-knuckling the headboard, Cole snapped his hips faster as he looked down into wide blue eyes that were cloudy from, *Yes, her own climax*. He knew what he wanted, and he didn't care that it was slightly barbaric, just like he didn't give a fuck that what he wanted was possessive as hell. As his climax spiraled down his spine and gathered in his tight balls, he let go of the headboard, scooted back, and gripped his cock in his hands.

As her breasts heaved, she continued to keep her hands in place as Cole started to pump his shaft with hard and fast strokes. As her eyes ran all over his sexed-up body—from his chest, to his cock, and finally, to the piercing that she seemed mesmerized by—it didn't take him long. Cole felt his climax hit him, and as he dropped his head back, he came all over her belly and breasts with a loud groan.

RACHEL COULD BARELY FORM a coherent word as Cole came, groaning her name.

Fuck. The possessive way he is now looking down at me—I want that look forever.

He swung his left leg over her and leaned down quickly to kiss her forehead. He got off the now wine-stained mattress and made his way into the bathroom. As he came back to her, he was wiping a cloth over himself.

When he stopped silently beside the bed, Rachel asked, "So, does this mean we will be going through a lot of mattresses?"

With a decadent grin, he ran his eyes over her where she was lying spent in her ruined panties. "Maybe I should buy stock in Sealy."

"Good thinking," she replied as he crawled back onto the bed and made his way over to her. "Because that, Mr. Madison, was fucking hot."

CHAPTER 29

On Friday night, Rachel waited beside Cole outside of Mason and Lena's condo. She couldn't help the quick glances she kept throwing his way as he stood there, staring at the door. It had been several minutes, and he still didn't seem like he was about to raise his hand and knock.

Turning to him, Rachel touched his shoulder. Cole looked down at her, and she found herself offering him a soft smile.

"You okay?" she asked.

He pushed his hands into his jeans. "Yes, I'm fine."

Rachel didn't buy it for a minute. "Funny, you don't seem fine."

"I suppose I'm nervous."

"Nervous, huh? *The* Cole Madison? Mr. Cool, Calm, and Collected is nervous?"

He ran the back of his index finger down the bright purple streak in her hair. "You're the only person who seems to see that side of me," he admitted. "Or maybe I should say, you're the only person who brings out that side of me."

Rachel placed her palms on his chest as she stood up on her tiptoes. "You have nothing to be nervous about. I love you, and my family will love you, too. They just need to get over the shock."

Bringing his hands up to cup her face, he laid his lips to hers. "I hope so."

"Cole," she said as she pulled her lips from his, "I know so. So, let's do this."

Just as he was about to knock on the door, the elevator dinged behind them, and Rachel turned to see Josh and Shelly getting off. As they started walking toward them, Josh had his arm firmly wrapped around Shelly's waist. She looked up at him, laughing at a comment he must have just made. As they continued forward, Josh turned his head, and when he saw them standing there, his smile pulled tight, but he nodded in their direction as they stopped in front of them.

"Madison," Josh greeted in a neutral tone.

Rachel stepped forward. "You and I need to talk. Now."

At the fierce tone in Rachel's voice, Josh's eyebrow moved up his head, and he took a step back. As she walked around him and down the hall, she heard Shelly say, "Hey, rock star, ready for round two?"

Rachel almost rounded on her to tell her to quit it when she heard Cole come back with, "Sure am. Bring it on Man-Eater."

As Shelly's brow winged up her laugh filled the hall, and Rachel kicked herself for thinking that he couldn't look after himself. Just because he was nervous didn't mean he wasn't still Cole.

Turning to where Josh had come to a stop at the end of the small hall, Rachel moved in front of him.

"Do you have something you want to say to me?" she asked.

She watched as he pushed his hands into his jeans pockets and looked over her shoulder. Rachel turned and watched as the door to the condo opened, and Lena came out to hug Shelly and then Cole.

Lena stood aside and invited them in. When Cole moved to let Shelly pass, his eyes connected with Rachel's, and he gave her a small smile and a wink.

As the door shut, Rachel rounded back on Josh. "Well?"

"Would you calm down? You're as prickly as a porcupine," he told her in that lazy, relaxed voice he always seemed to have.

"Well, between you and Mason, can you blame me?"

"Can we blame you?" Josh scoffed. "Yes, we can blame you. You went away for a weekend and came back married. Most people would be a little shocked, so why don't you get that?"

Rachel shut her mouth and turned away from him. *Damn him for using logic.* She pushed a frustrated hand through her hair, and as she was about to speak, she felt a hand grab her arm and turn her.

"We were worried, Rach. That's all. It has nothing to do with *who* you married." He paused and shrugged. "Well, not for me anyway. Mason might have thought differently, but I was worried about *you*."

Rachel brought her eyes up to his big brown ones. "Do I seem unhappy?"

That was when Josh's mouth broke into his usual easy-go-lucky smile that reached all the way to those eyes. "No. This is the happiest I've seen you in months. Honestly, since I moved back."

Rachel beamed at him as she stepped closer. "He makes me happy."

Josh reached out and wrapped his arms around her shoulders, pulling her in close. "I can see that," he told her as he hugged her tightly. "I can also see how happy you make him."

Pulling back from Josh, Rachel looked up at him with a smile. "Really?"

Josh laughed at that as he took her hand, and they walked back up the hall.

"Really. I don't think I've ever seen Cole this relaxed—*ever*. He's always been about work, always so serious and stressed."

Rachel nodded. It seemed accurate enough to her. Cole had been like that. It was only this last week when he had started to change. She liked to think she had a lot to do with that.

"He's got a lot going on with work and his mom."

Josh looped an arm over her shoulder as he knocked on the condo door. "Yeah, he told me about his mom this past weekend when he had to leave town. He forgot to mention he was marrying my best friend's little sister."

Rachel leaned her head on Josh's shoulder as she heard footsteps coming to the door.

"He's perfect for me. How weird is that?"

Josh squeezed her shoulder as he whispered, "It's about as weird as the Man-Eater being perfect for me."

Rachel let out a booming laugh as the door opened, and Mason stood staring at them with a smile in place. "Did you two kiss and make up?"

"They better not have been kissing," Shelly called out from inside the condo.

As she and Josh walked inside, Rachel's eyes moved around the room until she found Cole standing by the large window with Lena.

When he smiled at her, Rachel felt her insides warm.

"No kissing, Shelly. Keep your panties on." Josh chuckled.

Rachel moved away from him, and as she was halfway across the room, she heard Shelly point out, "Who said I'm wearing any?"

As the room broke out into laughter, Rachel knew that she was home.

~

COLE WATCHED Rachel move across her brother's condo toward him.

As she got closer, Lena, who was standing beside him, said softly, "You have someone special there. She and her brother have two of the biggest hearts. Please be careful with hers."

Cole looked down into the green eyes of the woman who was now a part of his family by marriage. He assured her, "I don't know how it happened, and I don't know why, but this—what she and I have—it's solid. You don't need to worry about her. I'd rather cut off my own arms than hurt a single purple hair on her head. I'll look after her."

Lena stepped up on her tiptoes and kissed his cheek. "Like I said once before, thank you."

"For?" Cole questioned as she started to move away.

"For bringing her back to us. She left for a while, and you brought her back. For that alone, Mason is grateful."

Cole looked back to Rachel, who was almost to them, and he mumbled, "Maybe she was looking for something."

Before she moved away, Lena took a sip from her wine glass, and then she softly told him, "Yeah, you."

She passed Rachel and gave her a hug and kiss before moving into the kitchen where her husband was standing at the oven.

"Hi," Rachel said as she stopped in front of him.

Cole reached out and encircled her waist, pulling her forward. "Hello. Everything okay?"

Her lips tipped up into a smile. "It is now."

"Joshua?" Cole questioned as he searched his friend out in the room.

Rachel placed her hand on his chest and patted it. "Josh is fine. He just wanted to—"

"Make sure you were okay?"

"Yes." Rachel chuckled. "These people need to quit worrying about me."

"These people love you," Cole pointed out as he tipped up her chin, so her eyes met his. "I love you."

She dropped her eyes from his and snuggled into his chest where she rubbed her cheek against his navy sweater. "I love you, too."

"You are lucky. There are four people in this room who all want you to be happy and who have *all* told me what a wonderful person you are."

"That person disappeared for a while," she mumbled as his arms tightened around her, "but you helped her find her way home."

"I'm glad. Because the girl who used to dance in the kitchen with her dad, the little sister who cried because of silly girls at school, and the teenage girl with the crush...that girl? *My* girl belongs in this room with these people."

Cole rested his lips down by her ear, remembering a story Mason had told him the other day, and he did something he had never done before. Quietly, he began to hum in her ear, and then he started to sing, "What can make me feel this way? *My girl.*"

RACHEL LOOKED up into the hazel eyes that now held her heart, and as Cole softly hummed a song that meant so much to her, Rachel was reminded of all the good memories that came along with it—her father, her mother, Mason and Josh.

She was lucky. She belonged to the people in this room, and now, Cole belonged with her. Loneliness had gone, and in its place was peace, happiness, and something even better—a sense of belonging.

EPILOGUE

Two years later

"Stop pacing. You will wear a hole in the floor."

"I can't help it. I'm nervous," Rachel replied. As she looked over to her husband, she shrugged. "I don't like hospitals."

Cole lifted his denim-clad leg and rested his ankle on his knee.

Ever since they had arrived, a little more than thirty minutes ago, she hadn't been able to sit still.

"Well, I'm not really fond of them either," he pointed out, tracking her steps with steady eyes.

Rachel moved to his side and took a seat. Reaching out, she took his hand in hers and rested her head on his shoulder.

How can she be so insensitive?

It was only a little more than six months since Cole's mother, Lydia, had passed away. While it had been peaceful, it was still such a difficult period to watch her slowly fade.

"I'm sorry. I wasn't thinking."

Cole reached down and squeezed her thigh as she snuggled up against him.

"You have nothing to be sorry about. Today is a good day, Rachel. Today, you become an aunt."

Rachel looked up at him as he leaned down and laid his lips against hers.

"And you become an uncle."

Cole lifted his mouth from hers and patted his palm over his chest. "Yes, I do, and I'm ready."

Rachel laughed, shaking her head. "Of course, you are armed with the celebratory cigars."

"Well, Joshua was freaking out about getting the crib complete before the baby got here, so it seemed like the right thing for me to do. Mason has been so stressed out these last couple of weeks. It's the least I can do." Cole paused and chuckled. "Maybe I should have bought him a bottle of scotch?"

Rachel slid farther down into the waiting room chair as she took Cole's hand. "He has been a little insane, hasn't he?"

"I don't think 'a little' covers it. Did you see the way his eyes were almost bugging out of his head when he wheeled Lena in here?"

Rachel let out a loud laugh, and when other people in the waiting room turned to look at her, she quickly covered her mouth. "The best part was when Lena told him if he didn't quit asking her how she was, she'd order him out of the room."

"Well, if anyone has Mason's number, it's Lena," Cole said.

Rachel smiled fondly. "He worships the ground she walks on, and he acts like a lovesick dope the rest of the time."

Cole's eyebrow winged up as he turned his head toward her. "Is that how you talk about me when I'm not around?"

Rachel giggled and bit her bottom lip.

Two years.

She had now been Mrs. Madison for a little more than two years, and she had loved every crazy, sexy, happy, and sad moment of it.

"Nope. I tell everyone you're obsessed with how sexy I am, and you have issues leaving the bed in the mornings because you are sooo in love with me."

Cole slid his palm over her thigh and down between her knees, enjoying the smooth leather under his palm. "That seems accurate enough. Although, I would like to point out that it was you who would not leave our bed this morning. You were the one trying to persuade me with dirty tactics to take the day off of work."

Leaning into him, Rachel reminded him on a sultry whisper, "You didn't seem to mind my dirty tactics when you told me to wrap my lips around your—"

"Has it happened yet? Did we miss it?"

Rachel looked up at the interruption and stood as Shelly practically ran down the corridor toward them. Following behind his wife was Josh with their eighteen-month-old daughter, Savannah.

"Nope, not yet," Rachel told her, moving past Shelly to reach the little girl in Josh's arms.

Savannah was adorable in every way. With her platinum blonde curls and big brown eyes, it was obvious which part of each parent she had inherited.

"Hello, angel," Rachel cooed as she reached out. She was happy to see Savannah give her a big, gappy smile as the toddler lunged toward her.

"Me go," she announced, her chubby little arms reaching out to Rachel.

Josh passed her over and tapped his daughter on the rump. Rachel took her favorite little girl in her arms as she winked at Josh.

"Pwetty," Savannah declared as she took a fistful of Rachel's blue hair.

Josh reached out and flicked a piece of Rachel's hair over her shoulder as he kissed his daughter's cheek. "Pretty, for sure."

Rachel leaned in and pressed sloppy kisses to Savannah's cheek. "You're the pretty one. Pretty, pretty, pretty."

Savannah started giggling and squirming in her arms.

Josh made his way over and sat down beside Shelly, who was now currently tapping her foot incessantly beside Cole.

"How are you so damn calm?" she demanded, turning to face him.

Cole shrugged and pointed out logically, "I'm not the one giving birth."

Rachel couldn't help the snort that escaped her as Shelly narrowed her eyes on Cole and shook her head.

"Typical male answer delivered in a typical lawyer tone."

Cole had become quite used to Shelly's mouth, and instead of taking offense, he nodded and pointed out, "One could say yours is a typical woman's reaction, but then one would be accused of being sexist."

As Josh chuckled, Shelly turned her head quickly to pin him with narrowed eyes. "And I suppose you agree with that?"

Josh leaned back in the seat and stretched his long denim-clad legs in front of himself. He crossed his work boots over and stretched his arm out behind his wife. “Hey, I didn’t say that, Georgia. As far as I’m concerned, you have every right to be nervous for Lena. You’ve been through this all before.”

“And got an angel in return,” Shelly replied as she lovingly looked toward her daughter.

“Kiss ass,” Rachel piped up.

Josh looked over at her and let his eyes move to his daughter before bringing them back to Rachel’s. “Uh, do you mind not cursing around my little girl? I would prefer she grow up a lady.”

Rachel glared over at the man who was as much her brother as the one currently waiting for his first born to be delivered. “I’m a lady.”

Shelly scoffed, “Out of the bedroom?”

“Well, definitely not in it,” Cole added, giving Rachel a wicked smirk.

Standing, he made his way over to where she was swaying back and forth with Savannah, who had rested her head down on Rachel’s shoulder.

“Really, Madison? Keep that to yourself, would you?” Josh complained. “She’s practically my little sister.”

Cole ignored his friend as he reached Rachel and the gorgeous little girl in her arms. Rachel looked up into his eyes, and as he raised a hand to run it over Savannah’s hair, he gave Rachel a smile so warm that she felt it all the way down to her toes.

“I like how you look right now,” Cole admitted.

Rachel raised a brow in silent question.

“With a baby in your arms, you look very—”

“Very?” she pressed, feeling her heart start to beat a little harder.

He was about to answer when the waiting room door flung open, and a weary-looking Mason walked toward where they all stood and waited patiently.

His black hair was all over the place, like he had been running his hands through it several hundred times, and his shirt was buttoned incorrectly.

When he finally stopped in front of them, Rachel stood frozen, waiting for whatever news he was about to deliver.

Surely, if it were bad and something had happened to Lena, he would be crying and be unable to come out here.

What the hell is wrong with me? This is giving birth, not open heart surgery.

Just as that thought crossed her mind, Mason's face finally broke into a smile so wide that it looked like it was going to fall right off his face.

Rachel felt Cole's arm come around her waist as Mason continued beaming at them.

"Well, spit it out, Mase," Shelly finally piped up.

"He's speechless. Leave the man alone," Josh joked as he hugged Shelly in close.

As Mason looked at them all, he nodded, and Rachel could see tears welling in his blue eyes.

"Lena and Catherine are both beautiful and perfect."

There was silence for a moment, and then—

"Hell yeah. Another girl in the group," Rachel hollered with a little wriggle, making Savannah sit up and pay attention.

Moving in close to her brother, Rachel leaned up and kissed the cheek he offered.

"I'm so very happy for you, Dad," she told him with a wink as she pulled away. "Full name?"

"Catherine Carly Langley."

Mason pulled Rachel and the baby in close and hugged them tightly as he kissed her on the head. He whispered, "I'm destined to be surrounded by women, and I'm so happy I can't even think right now."

When he let her go, Rachel took a step back and watched Josh step forward and offer his hand. Mason reached out, shook it, and pulled his best friend in for a hug.

"Pretty amazing feeling, huh?" Josh asked him.

As Mason let him go, he turned to Shelly and nodded. "Yep, have to say, you women are pretty damn incredible."

Shelly stepped forward and wrapped her arms around his neck, kissing his cheek. "You better believe it. It helps that we have wonderful men in our lives. We can't do it all on our own, you know."

Mason chuckled as he let her go, and Josh pulled his wife in for a hug and kiss.

"Thank God for that. Half the fun is in the doing."

As they all started to laugh, Mason turned to where Rachel was standing beside Cole.

Cole held out his hand to him in congratulations, and Mason took it in a strong shake before he tugged him in and hugged him, just as he had with Josh.

"Congratulations, Mason."

As Mason thumped him on the back, Rachel's heart warmed when she heard her brother reply, "Thanks, brother. I appreciate that."

As they parted, Mason pushed his hands into his jeans. "So, how about it? You want to come and say hi to the new woman in my life?"

Everyone answered, "Of course."

As Mason turned and started down the hall, Josh and Shelly followed behind, and Rachel turned to Cole as she hugged Savannah to her.

"I love you," she told him, once again finding it incredible that she had almost overlooked him.

"I love you, too," he replied. As he glanced at the child in her arms, his eyes took on a look of affection.

As they made their way down the hall and into Lena's hospital room, Rachel couldn't help but remember a moment years ago when Cole had told her that he was exactly what she needed. It was a relief to know that he had known what she couldn't see, and as she stood in the hospital room, being introduced to her brand-new niece, she knew that this was home.

There would never be a moment where she would ever feel alone again because the people in this room, each and every one of them, were her family, and she was the luckiest person in the world to be loved so very well and so very much.

As she handed Savannah back to Shelly, she gave her a quick kiss and whispered, "I have to go and meet another little angel, but I'll be back."

Shelly and Josh smiled at Rachel as she turned and walked around the bed to where Lena was sitting up with baby Catherine in her arms. Mason was on the bed beside them, and when Rachel reached him, she felt tears gathering in her eyes. Stopping beside her brother, she placed a hand on Mason's shoulder and looked over at the sweet pink bundle in Lena's arm.

"Do you want to hold her?" Lena asked, offering her to Rachel. "Aunt Rach."

Taking the swaddled baby into her arms, Rachel pulled her in close and looked down into the perfect little face, and somewhere deep inside her, she truly felt that her mother and father were in the room with them.

Turning to face the man standing in the corner of the room, Rachel rocked the baby as she moved toward him. She kept her eyes on the small bow lips and the black hair that was peeking out from under the pink hat.

When she reached Cole, she looked up at him with tears falling down her cheeks. "Isn't she perfect?"

Cole reached out and brushed a tear from her cheek as he looked down at the tiny baby in her arms. "Yes, she's absolutely perfect."

Rachel blinked watery eyes and whispered, "I want one."

Cole grinned and leaned down to kiss her quick. "Me, too." He lifted his head and reminded her softly, "But you can't keep that one."

With that soft reminder, the entire room began to laugh. Rachel pouted and turned to face Lena and her brother, who were sitting on the bed watching her.

"Well, I don't know about all of you, but I think it's time to pass on a family tradition."

Everyone stared at her as Rachel began to hum and then started to sing, "I've got sunshine, on a cloudy day—"

As everyone joined in, singing the ode to girls everywhere, Rachel felt the love in the room grow. That was the moment when she knew she would not have changed one thing on her journey to right now.

This was her life, this was her truth, and not one person could have ever convinced her how perfect it would all be.

THE EXQUISITE SERIES

Exquisite (Lena & Mason)
Entice (Shelly & Josh)
Edible (Rachel & Cole)

***

Spin-Off Series
(Featuring Cole's half-brother Logan Mitchell)

Try (The Temptation Series I)
Take (The Temptation Series II)
Trust (The Temptation Series III)

Four Years Later...

Tease (The Temptation Series IV)
Tate (The Temptation Series V)
Untitled (The Temptation Series VI)

ACKNOWLEDGMENTS

A huge thank you, of course, to my fantastic editor and, more importantly, friend, Jovana Shirley. This process is long and difficult, and it's often pulled off under timelines that require early and late hours, depending on how you look at it. I can't thank you enough for all the hours you spend helping me.

You truly are a genius, and your attention to detail and immaculately polished work reflect only a portion of your immense talent. I feel fortunate that I get to work with you.

And to my husband, thank you for being exactly who you are. I love you.

ABOUT THE AUTHOR

Ella Frank is the *USA Today* Bestselling author of the Temptation series, including Try, Take, and Trust and is the co-author of the fan-favorite contemporary romance, Sex Addict. Her Exquisite series has been praised as "scorching hot!" and "enticingly sexy!"

Some of her favorite authors include Tiffany Reisz, Kresley Cole, Riley Hart, J.R. Ward, Erika Wilde, Gena Showalter, and Carly Philips.

For more information

www.ellafrank.com

Made in United States
Cleveland, OH
11 April 2025

16004651R00199